Sunset

The epic saga of an American family

1917 - 2002

By Charles Gingold

Published by Hemingway publisher

Cover design by Hemingway Publisher

ISBN: Printed in the United States

DEDICATION

For almost 20 years, Superior Court Judge Phrasel Shelton and I had breakfast together. Every Tuesday at 9 AM, we would meet to discuss everything from religion to politics. The conversations could go on for hours. The Judge passed away in 2018, and to this day, I miss my dear friend.

MEMORIUM

In memory of my beloved son, Matt

"Grief is the price we pay for love"

THE SILENT GENERATION

Born in the 1930s, I am a member of a very special age group, the "Silent Generation," the smallest number of children born since the early 1900s who can remember the winds of war.

We are the last to remember ration books for everything.

We saved tin foil and poured fat into tin cans.

We remember milk being delivered to our house early in the morning.

We are the last to see gold stars in the front windows of those whose sons went to war.

We are the last generation to have spent our childhood without television.

We played outside.

We went to the movies on Saturday and watched two movies, cartoons, a newsreel, and a serial.

We often shared telephones, and computers were called calculators.

We had typewriters driven by pounding fingers, and the internet did not exist.

We experienced deep-rooted Depression, the Second World War, polio, the Korean War, and the Iron Curtain.

We are the only generation that can remember the Great War and a time when the world was secure.

We grew up at the best possible time when the world was getting better, not worse.

TABLE OF CONTENTS

CHAPTER 1

AND THEN THERE WERE TWO

In 1917, William Doyle and his brothers, Vincent (Vince) and Mark, were part of the American Expeditionary Force that was en route to support the French, British, and Russians, who had been fighting Germany and her allies since 1914. The three brothers enlisted immediately when the U.S. entered World War I. Neutrality ended when German U-boats sank American ships. The boys, like many young men, looked at the War as a great adventure and a moment in history that they were eager to be a part of. They were first-generation Americans, the sons of Irish immigrants who immigrated to America in 1889. The First Division disembarked at Saint-Nazaire, and soon the Doyle boys found themselves in the trenches that separated the two armies, locked in a horrible new form of devastating, mind-numbing warfare. The brothers were baptized by fire at St. Mihiel, which was the first major battle led by the U.S. Expeditionary Force. The attack caught the Germans in the process of retreating, leaving some artillery behind, and the American attack proved more successful than anticipated.

That was just the beginning, as more than a million American Doughboys were thrown into battle during the Meuse-Argonne offensive, which began in late September 1918. It proved to be the largest offensive in American military history. The region was of significant importance to the German army, and the campaign supported the entire Allied offensive, which would extend from

Verdun, France, through Belgium, and all the way to the English Channel. Vince, the elder Doyle brother, was wounded during the battle of St. Mihiel and suffered a severe chest injury that was more than enough to send him home to Boston. Vince, in every sense, was the leader of the trio who accepted and wholeheartedly recognized a deep father-like responsibility. In appearance, he did not look the part of a take-charge brother. He was shorter than his two siblings, with a thatch of black hair, a deep chest, and sturdy, muscular legs. His quiet, thoughtful demeanor had given the boys a sense of confidence and security, which was now shattered. William and Mark missed their older brother, but with a deep sense of loyalty, they continued and were part of the First Division in the bloody Meuse-Argonne offensive. During the 41-day battle, over 26,000 Doughboys lost their lives, and nearly 100,000 Americans were wounded. It was the deadliest campaign in U.S. military history, and the irony was that Mark would succumb to the Spanish Flu, which was rampant throughout the trench ranks. William was devastated, and the reality of facing the ongoing brutality alone was almost more than he could endure. The three Doyle boys had been traumatized by the ferocious and bloody act of warfare, and after two months into the Meuse-Argonne campaign, one brother was badly wounded and on his way home, and Mark had passed—a victim of the Spanish Flu.

Captain James Sinclair, commanding officer, was sympathetic to the loss of William's brother and offered him a transfer to safety in the rear. In the face of searing anguish and unrelenting sorrow, William Doyle, now a sergeant, decided to remain with his unit. As the youngest of the three brothers, William's willingness to stay the course was almost predictable. In reality, he was incredibly loyal and serious. Vince may have been the father confessor, but William was the kind of guy you would want to share a foxhole with. He was the tallest of the brothers and handsome with a rugged Irishman's look, with deep blue eyes, unruly curly black hair, and a square jaw. The Meuse–Argonne offensive continued right up until the Armistice in early November.

Sergeant Doyle and his squad continued to face the grinding, nightmarish wasteland that was the signature of trench warfare. Despite using wooden planks and sandbags to keep out the water, the men dealt with constant dampness, which in many cases led to a condition known as "trench foot." If left untreated, this condition could require amputation. Trenches became a garbage dump, filled with empty ammunition boxes, spent cartridges, soiled bandages, broken helmets, and torn uniforms. Trenches were also a place of deep despair. Sergeant Doyle's men experienced constant bombardment of artillery and rapid firing of machine guns. The territory between the opposing lines was a wasteland of broken tree stumps, mud, and tangled barbed wire, referred to as "no man's land." In battle, soldiers had to charge out of their trenches, cross no-man's land through a hail of bullets, shrapnel, and poison gas. Thankfully, William's men would rotate every six or seven days to safety in the rear. Doyle recognized that his men were demoralized as they were asked to traverse no man's land.

On one over-the-top charge, the sergeant lost three of his men, and one of his soldiers was lying severely injured approximately ten yards from the relative safety of the trench. Of all the men in his unit, Jim Walsh was the least capable of dealing with the demands and terror of this maddening form of combat. Jimmie was slight in stature and always had a look of fear in his eyes. Sergeant Doyle could not bear the cries of one of his men, and without hesitation, he alone breached the wall in an attempt to rescue Jimmie Walsh. As he reached the wounded man, gunfire from the German lines screamed past them, but undaunted, William dragged his man back to the trench, but not before one of the missiles tore into his left leg. He had saved his private, but his wounds would be so severe that he was evacuated to the rear.

At the hospital, it quickly became clear that he might lose his left leg. After two weeks of dedicated care, Doyle breathed a sigh of relief when he was told that his leg would be saved. The rest of his men, now on rotation, came to bid him a safe journey as he was scheduled to return home on the next hospital ship. William had a tough time dealing with any outward display of emotion. Upon learning of his extraordinary bravery in selflessly rescuing his wounded comrade, he was awarded the Silver Star, the Army's second-highest medal for valor. His wounds proved to be a significant obstacle to his return to Boston and civilian life.

A hero's welcome would be an understatement. For Sergeant William Doyle, the entire South Boston had come out to welcome him home. He was not only reunited with friends and family, but also with Vince, who, despite his own injuries, was there to embrace his little brother. William's mother had died of lung cancer when he was just ten years old. He never really knew a mother's sympathetic warmth and affection. The boys' father, Patrick, had difficulty showing any physical affection, but William "Billy" Doyle always knew that their father loved him. The emotional expressiveness often associated with being Irish was not part of Patrick Doyle's way of showing love. He was a complicated son of Ireland who knew pain, heartache, and a deep sense of loss stemming from the death of Mark and the devastation of losing his beloved wife, Mary.

CHAPTER 2

HOME AGAIN

Being home in South Boston was a shock to William's system, as his mind was still on the battlefield and the men with whom he had shared his life. The memories of his experiences in France, his unit, and all the mind-bending hopelessness of war continued to take their toll on his fragile sanity. It would be a while before William would return to a semblance of civilian reality. For now, he recognized that it would take all his acquired discipline to cope with a return to the life he had envisioned.

The Doyle family and all the incumbent affection were not what William needed. All the boisterous, well-meaning brood of family overwhelmed him. He had no idea how he was going to deal with a constant barrage of affection, let alone figure out what he was going to do with his life. The thought of driving a truck, which was the family business, had no appeal for William.

Over the years, Patrick had built a business delivering beer and soft drinks to South Boston and beyond. Over the past ten years, he had accumulated a significant family-owned operation that employed uncles, cousins, and some young women who were put to work in the office. There was a fleet of 20 trucks that bore the name "Doyle and Sons." In post-war Boston, there was reason to celebrate, and business was booming—especially with the delivery of beer to all the bars and taverns in South Boston. The senior Doyle had always planned for his three boys, after the War, to return and manage "Doyle and Sons." The thought never crossed Patrick's mind that he would lose a son in the "War to end all wars."

Both William and Vince were recuperating from their wounds, and only Vince would consider joining the family business. The idea of driving a delivery truck was not William's vision of life after the War. His immediate concern was telling his dad not to include him. He knew that Patrick would be crestfallen, but he wanted more than a life in Boston surrounded every day by family members who, by and large, had no thought of life beyond the confines of South Boston. William dreaded the required conversation he would have to have with his father. Not wanting to cross that bridge, which he knew would not end well, he decided, for the moment, to concentrate on healing and put off decisions that he knew would not sit well with the family.

William had once thought of moving to California, which had been sparked by his buddies in France. The way they described the state was nothing short of the illusory land of milk and honey. That aside, the idea of moving West was appealing. If not milk and honey, California would spell opportunity for a twenty-two-year-old decorated veteran. For now, frequenting the taverns and renewing long-standing friendships was a panacea. William was especially in need of female relationships, and more than anything, he needed to end his delayed celibacy. He had not been with a woman since before the war. To say that he was in need would be a vast understatement. With his good looks and maturity brought on by the War, William was an explosion in need of release. Women in Boston were war-weary and, for that matter, exhausted and relieved that the devastating Spanish Flu had been contained.

He had known many of the girls who frequented McGlade's tavern, and after almost two years, it was as if time had stood still. Among the girls, now women, was one of William's high school bed buddies. Annie Donovan had matured into a beautiful, red-haired woman who, like William, was more than ready for an encounter. After an interlude of drinking Boiler Makers, the partners of bygone days were renewing old familiar sexual appetites. Annie was always pretty, but today, the awakening of real womanhood turned her into the most desirable and enhanced sexual partner William could ask for. The lovemaking fueled by drinks seemed endless. They both stayed in Annie's apartment and, except for infrequent cigarette and sandwich breaks, took part in marathon lovemaking that stretched into days.

CHAPTER 3

OPPORTUNITY KNOCKS

William Doyle knew he could not put off the conversation with his father. He had talked to Jimmie Walsh in Los Angeles, the soldier William saved, traversing no man's land in France. Walsh, looking for a way to show gratitude to his sergeant, offered to put him up once he arrived in LA. Jimmie was home in Southern California, living west of Long Beach, where he was employed in his family's furniture-making and retail business. The door was wide open for William to come to grips with his father.

Patrick was unpredictably not totally surprised when his youngest son approached him and shared his plans. In the conversation, he halfheartedly tried to convince William to stay in Boston. He recognized that his son did not participate in any of the family talks about the future of "Doyle and Sons." There was a stark contrast in the positive way that Vince approached the family business and the silence and total lack of interest on the part of his brother. Patrick wished William well and told him that he sadly had plans to include all three brothers in the future of Doyle and Sons. At least Vince and his enthusiasm for the company would allow his father to substitute the "Sons" for the singular format. For William, his father's painful acceptance of his son's need to find a life beyond Boston was all he could hope for, and what of the impending threat of Prohibition? He had saved most of his army pay and bought a train ticket to Los Angeles.

Saying goodbye to the Doyle clan was tearful, but the most difficult parting was with Annie Donovan. For William, their time together had been based on a sexual coming together, but they both recognized there was more to their superficial lovemaking. The couple held each other for what seemed an eternity and promised to stay in touch.

Ultimately, the conversations over the family business were moot. Prohibition began in 1920, and the legislation had a dramatic impact on any business where alcohol was at the foundation of remaining viable. Soon after William left Boston, Patrick was forced to sell his crippled business at a significant loss. A cabal of Doyle family members determined that the delivery business could survive even in the face of Prohibition. John Doyle, Patrick's first cousin, had no aversion to dealing with Irish gangs who were among the creative liquor lawlessness that surfaced soon after Prohibition became the law of the land. The loss of the company was devastating to Patrick, but the thought of ignoring the law was not an acceptable compromise. The dream of "Doyle and Son" as a family business was put on the back burner at least for the present.

In the meantime, Patrick drew on his extensive experience as a railroad facilitator, responsible for monitoring daily operations. Finding employment was almost immediate. His skill was highly prized, and for Patrick, it meant earning a salary appreciably more than he had earned from his defunct business. The final sale of "Doyle and Son" lingered for a year after William left Boston. For William, the coast-to-coast train ride took an arduous three days, but it gave him a chance to think about what he might do once he reached California. Jimmie Walsh met his former sergeant at Union Station in Los Angeles. The largest West Coast city was more than he had been led to believe. Everywhere he looked, he resonated with growth.

Jimmie was not the frightened soldier in his unit that William remembered. He had put on weight, was well dressed and had a genuine look and air of success. He was driving the latest model Buick, which embellished the picture of wealth. Jimmie Walsh was anxious to please the man who had saved his life on the French battlefield. The drive to Long Beach was much longer than anticipated. In fact, California's fourth-largest city was a full thirty miles south of LA.

CHAPTER 4

LAURALIE

The drive along the coast with one beautiful vista after another confirmed all that he had read about the Golden West. They passed through one beach community after another with bright umbrellas, people in swimwear and the sparkling surf of the Pacific Ocean. Names like Santa Monica, Hermosa, Manhattan and Redondo beaches peppered the road to Long Beach. When they reached Jimmie's home in Palos Verdes, he realized it was just west of Long Beach. It was an area of large, palatial homes with extensive gardens, stables, and an aura of wealth that married estates to the sparkling Pacific. The Walsh family furniture business in Long Beach was not only successful but also highly lucrative. The Walsh home was consistently resplendent among the estates that made up Palos Verdes.

Jimmie's family greeted William in a way that was sincere and welcoming, recognizing that this was the man who had rescued their son on a far-off battlefield. Walsh's parents did nothing to flaunt their position of wealth. They were genuine upper-class entrepreneurs who enjoyed the trappings of wealth. In addition to the senior Walsh and Jimmie, there was a family member who had not been recognized in any of the conversations William had with Jimmie. Lauralie Walsh was the younger sister who, at 18, had totally embraced all the trappings and cultural characteristics of the flapper generation. The family had not disowned the girl, but her antics and alcohol abuse tried the patience of Walter and Barbara Walsh. Lauralie had registered at the University of Southern California and had her application approved only after her parents made a significant contribution to the university. She was currently on the edge of being expelled, not because of her intellect, but rather her excessive non-conforming behavior on campus. William was to meet Lauralie as he was unpacking for his open-ended stay at the Walshs.

The accommodations that the family offered were much more than William had anticipated. The apartment over the garage in the rear of the estate boasted a living area, a bedroom, a fully stocked kitchen, and a bath. Lauralie appeared in the doorway and took William's breath away. She may have been a problematic family member, but to William, she was an absolutely gorgeous young woman who seemed to float when she entered a room. Jimmie's younger sister was a knockout, and she knew it with an overwhelming sense and confidence that comes with the awareness of a beautiful woman. Her professionally applied makeup could not conceal the natural evidence of her lucent, unblemished skin. Lauralie's violet eyes, glorious raven-black hair, and stunning figure were sensual reminders of her power. The usually confident William Doyle was unable to articulate a response to this 18-year-old vixen.

William escorted the girl to the house to join the others for dinner. Wine was served to everyone but Lauralie, who embarrassed her parents when she nonchalantly retrieved a silver flask from her evening bag. William was amused and aware that their daughter was taunting them. William knew that Jimmie's sister could endanger his relationship with her parents if he spent any time in Lauralie's presence. He had to admit she was tempting and conceivably Walter and Barbara would approve, but the warning signs were flashing red.

William said goodnight after a sumptuous dinner that included more wine than he was accustomed to and retired to the guest rooms.

As he was climbing into bed, there was a knock at the door, which was essentially Lauralie's way of saying the red light had been lit. She had nothing on but a light robe, which she dropped as she entered the room. To William, seeing this spectacular girl/woman ushered in a vision of every movie love scene or chapter in Lolita. With light behind her, which accentuated every curve of her flawless, slim figure, he felt like he was acting out a movie script, and the extra glasses of wine merely enhanced the gauzy scene. Was he dreaming? Without a word, this 18-year-old siren was next to him, and any level of protocol was gone. How could he resist this dream sequence, which was unlike any encounter he had experienced with the ladies of Boston? Lauralie had total control of the lovemaking, which vaulted William into a version of sex that accelerated through the remaining night hours and early morning. Few words were spoken, but there was an awareness that tapped into an incredible mutual attraction, and neither of them had any choice. Lauralie had complicated William's life to the point that he recognized it could impact his plans dramatically. It was clear to him that she was of deep concern to the Walsh family, and here he is, tantalized by this beautiful 18-year-old who obviously loved to perform sexual acts creatively.

On the one hand, William felt deep gratitude to the Walsh family, who had welcomed him into their home, provided sustenance, lodging, transportation, and, in general, blanketed him with genuine warmth and kindness. It was the other hand that concerned him. William was convinced that the midnight visits were in the throes of an insatiable, lengthy launch. How could he resist the sensual capacity of this extraordinarily beautiful young woman? He was soon to realize that any intended resolve was not an option. For much of the week, Lauralie appeared in his room and controlled the sexual decision-making. She was totally in charge and irresistible. It was night after night of passionate lovemaking that was new and adventurous. How could this teenager have the capacity to introduce William to the kind of sensual experimentation that was far beyond anything he had realized, and how would it end? William was soon to find out. Evidently, one of the servants felt it was their responsibility to alert Walter and Barbara about the tryst. He was embarrassingly confronted, and while he was not asked to leave, he felt that he had no choice. The idea of staying on after what had transpired with William and their daughter was out of the question. Even under circumstances that would try any relationship, the Walshs made it clear that he was welcome to stay. William knew from the start that Lauralie spelled trouble, and he had decided to leave. Jimmie was not surprised by the turn of events and knew that his sister had the capacity to charm his friend without hesitation. He knew that William would be a likely target for the advances of his sensuous sister.

Jimmie recognized that William had no honorable choice and offered him the use of a car, along with some recommendations on what his best options were for renting an apartment in LA. William found comfortable lodging in Hollywood primarily because he was determined to try his hand at acting. After all, wasn't this strange community the capital of movie-making? Friends had told him he had the looks that could potentially open doors to the motion picture industry. He had not really considered it, but without any training or education, William had limited options. His lodging was in essence a small cottage in one of the U-shaped bungalow apartment complexes that were common in Hollywood. Most of the tenants were, in one way or another, nascent actors. They were all looking for that big career break that would land them a part in a major film. The physical structure of the cottage complex provided a way to interact with your neighbors and exchange experiences, as well as opportunities.

Next door to William was a "real pro" at navigating Hollywood with all its complexities. His stage name was, of all things, "Johnny Walker," and evidently, the name was consistent with his character. Johnny was a great source of the kind of fundamental knowledge that William required, if he could just stay downwind of the actor. He was rounding the corner to his fifties and had spent his adult life at the studios playing bit parts, stand-ins and the ubiquitous "extra." Throughout it all, Johnny Walker had been married three times and had fathered four children, whom he saw infrequently. He was one of those people you would put in the category of "unforgettable characters." William spent much of his initial time querying Walker on how the Studio process was structured and where to get started. The two men, one young and the other in the throes of middle age, became friends. They were strange bedfellows, but for whatever reason, they just plain found some friendly compatibility. Johnny proved to be a great source of knowledge that was basic to what William needed. The information was instrumental in his initial job search.

After a week of getting to know some of the Hollywood insights, William walked the four blocks from his new lodging to Paramount, where he learned that the studio was casting a new feature film that required several extras. Upon his arrival at the studio gates, he encountered a sea of hopeful new arrivals and experienced hands who knew how the game was played in selecting extra players. When the casting director and her assistant arrived at the gate, she announced that she would need extras in a variety of "types" suitable for the new feature film. To William's surprise and amazement, he was selected in the first round and was told to show up at the back lot of Paramount the following morning at eight. The flat fee for his initial role as an extra was $150 for the duration of the new production. When he returned to his Hollywood cottage, he was buoyant and shared his good fortune with Johnny Walker, who was visibly pleased for his new friend. Together that evening, they shared dinner at a local cafeteria. The fact that he had been selected in the first round gave cause for a celebration, even though William knew that being an extra was the lowest status in the production of a movie.

The next day, however, proved to be more than William had expected. As required, he showed up the next morning, anxious to be a part of the production of a motion picture. The ten extras were milling around the traditional Green Room coffee and donut table when the casting director came over to William and asked if he had appeared in any feature films. She then proceeded to share with him that he looked very much like Douglas Fairbanks. The fact is that on many occasions, friends and acquaintances had made the same comment about William's peculiar resemblance to Fairbanks, the star of many swashbuckling action and adventure movies. William was obviously flattered, and because he was not really aware of how other people saw him, he took this one step above an extra as a significant opportunity that could lead to a real career in pictures. The look-alike Fairbanks proved to be a liability in many ways. He was called only when the adventure star was in the throes of making a picture. He tried to supplement his meager pay by doing "stand-in" work for Ronald Coleman, another established Hollywood star.

Other issues initially obscured his potential in the movie industry: he looked so much like the swashbuckler that it disqualified him for independent opportunities. Second, the wounds he sustained in France also hindered his professional progress. No matter how hard he tried, William could not hide the fact that he limped when he walked. Each month since the War, he would drive to the Veterans hospital on Sepulveda to be examined for the serious wound that a German machine gun was responsible for. To enjoy any semblance of life in Hollywood, William was forced to take a job outside of the movie business. Just as Jimmie had helped him out in so many ways since they had returned from Europe, there were other vets he knew whom he had also served. Tony Fernandez was the medic who helped save his life on the battlefield in Argonne Woods. The two men were reacquainted when Jimmie brought the three veterans together at Jost's Bar in Santa Monica. During that reunion, Robert mentioned that he was working at The Hollywood Men's Store and earning a decent income with a base salary and commissions. The store could use a good-looking guy like William, especially because he was a Silver Star recipient. He was hired instantly by David Grossman, the owner of the men's store, who was indeed pleased and impressed to have a real hero employed at his store. Grossman was also very accommodating, allowing William to work in his off hours at Paramount. That proved to be the bulk of his time.

Working as a salesman had some significant advantages that he had not taken into consideration when he took the sales job. He met some industry professionals, earning more money in commissions based on his charm than from all the work as a stand-in and double work. His lifestyle had changed considerably. He continued to live at the Hollywood cottage primarily because he had established friendships and a genuine sense of belonging. Johnny Walker was that kind of personality and a surprising advisor who was unconditional in his friendship. William also recognized that the Los Angeles Basin was so spread out that it was nearly impossible to get around without a car. To that end, he found a beautiful, affordable used Stutz Bearcat convertible that fit his newfound style. This purchase also allowed him to return the "un-Hollywood" Model T that Jimmie and his parents had so generously loaned him. The car also seemed connected to the lovely Lauralie, who was almost constantly on William's mind. Returning the car was, at least partially, eliminating the urge to see her again.

In the few months in Hollywood, he had dated several ladies, and the little cottage proved to be an ample location to bed down some sexual partners. No one could compare to the lovely Lauralie until one day at the Hollywood Men's Store. William was working late one Friday night when she walked in. He had not been drawn to the kind of women who frequented the bars and restaurants, thinking only of stardom. If anything, he was not impressed with the superficial feminine creatures who seemed to populate Hollywoodland. This girl was, by all standards, very different and could easily compete with Lauralie's attributes, but with more class. She was stylishly dressed and carried herself with the confidence of a woman who needed no one or nothing. As she approached, he was dazzled by her dark features, including hazel-green eyes that could stare a hole through you, coal-black hair, and full, sensuous red lips. He was sure that he could complete the picture if she removed her coat. Thankfully, the months in LA had dissipated his fundamental lack of confidence, and even in the presence of beautiful women, William Doyle had achieved an aura of self-assurance. The young woman was in the store to buy a birthday tie for her father, and William was making sure that this was the one customer that he would move heaven and earth to serve. The other salesmen, including Tony Fernandez, had never seen William so territorial when a customer entered, but they could see the reason why. William did not believe in anything as trite as "love at first sight." It was an embellishment closely associated with Hollywood and all the ambiguities it implied. But when the lady looked up from the tie counter, their eyes met, and the coined phrase faced reality. The two potential lovers were smitten with each other, and it was clear that they shared a strong mutual attraction. Without hesitance, they exchanged names.

CHAPTER 5

RITA

When Rita Geller met William Doyle, they both felt incapacitated with small talk. Rita and William left the store and sat in the neighborhood diner, talking until morning, when customers began arriving for breakfast. Nothing seemed to matter… not even the fact that Rita Geller was Jewish. After their initial introduction, the couple just could not get enough of each other. For almost a week, they mutually vacated their daily commitments, obligations, and responsibilities in the haze of being together. Ultimately, they had to find out if sexual compatibility was part of their romantic liaison. Up until now, they knew without hesitation when the right moment would be. For now, William and Rita were content with the awe of their limitless attraction. They challenged their instincts with touch, visible fondness, gentle kisses and an awareness that did not question whether physical lovemaking would be anything less than an extension of their star-crossed attraction. After sharing every nuance of their lives and the pure wonderment of their meeting, they found themselves in William's cottage. The usual excitement that lovers experience in that initial first physical contact would be for them the natural, limitless affection they felt for each other. The lovemaking was an introduction to a level of compatibility that left Rita and William exhausted, yet satisfied, and naturally extended into the next day.

Ultimately, the couple returned to the recognition that the complexities of their union would require care and thoughtful consideration. The coming together of two people, one Jewish and the other Catholic, would need cautious sensitivity in dealing with two judgmental, sometimes volatile families. Rita Geller was 19 years old and currently a premedical student at the University of Southern California. She was extraordinarily bright, and in 1923, just one year after women had achieved voting rights, it was still unique for women to attend USC medical school. Her father, Herman Geller, was a highly successful real estate entrepreneur who owned some major properties in downtown Los Angeles. His only daughter was the focus of all of his attention. He was genuinely proud of Rita's maturity and beauty. Herman loved to brag about his daughter's accomplishments and was especially pleased with her intention to become a physician. There was a good reason why he doted on his only child, who filled some emotional gap that partially filled the void of a loveless marriage.

Sylvia Miller, on the surface, was fortunate to be Herman's wife. They met in high school in Pawtucket, Rhode Island, and because he was such a find, her middle-class salesman father encouraged the relationship. The beautiful Sylvia Miller totally entranced Herman. After all, she was the most popular, accomplished girl at Washington High. He was flattered that she responded positively to his overtures, and Sylvia was being continuously pushed by her parents to encourage this "Nice Jewish Boy." The Millers had limited means, and the idea that their daughter had the potential of ultimately taking the wealthy Herman Geller down the aisle was a Jewish parent's dream. Sylvia and Herman were married at the Sherman Oaks Beth Israel Temple in an Orthodox ceremony. For him, marrying the beautiful Sylvia was the most fortunate event of his life.

The downward slide in their loveless marriage began on their wedding night, and after twenty years, the relationship became an exercise in contempt. Rita was the only bright light in her otherwise miserable marriage. It was the one thing in her life that provided her with a reason to go on with life.

The entry of Rita into William's circle complicated his way of life, mostly in a positive way. He had never been genuinely in love, and after a month of spending every free moment with Rita, he was even crazier about her, acting like a schoolboy. She was unquestionably the girl he wanted to spend his life with, and that involved the issue of marrying outside of her religion. For William, the thought of meeting Rita's parents gave cause for concern. He had absolutely no interest in Catholicism or converting to another religion. Rita, on the other hand, followed Judaism not because she was religious, but rather to please her parents' deeply held religious views. The union with William, a Catholic, would be problematic, but the idea of losing William for any reason was more than she could contemplate. They both recognized that ultimately, they were going to have to meet with both families. For William, he shared with Rita the fact that his father would welcome Rita. Yes, the Doyles of Boston were Catholic, but with few exceptions, they were secular. However, her mother and father painted a different picture. They were steeped in Judaism, and Herman was the most rigid of the parents. Rita explained that her mother, once she accepted William, would be a non-issue. Factually, Sylvia Geller would take pleasure in doing anything that would be contrary to her husband's wishes.

After two months of skirting the necessity of meeting her parents, Rita finally convinced William that there was no way of avoiding the dreaded greeting with Herman. The Gellers were pleased that Rita was dating someone who obviously had stolen their daughter's heart. The couple never considered the possibility that William was not Jewish. Rita had carefully sidestepped providing his name, and her parents believed this was part of the intrigue. The occasion was set, and Rita and William were invited for dinner the following weekend. The ensuing few days were spent developing a game plan that hopefully would neutralize any potential drama. William's heart skipped a beat when they arrived at the Gellers' Bel Air estate. This was a community that catered to the truly wealthy elite, and "Billy" of Boston felt totally out of place. The moment they entered the home, a butler took his coat, and alarm bells were ringing. Rita carefully introduced William Doyle to her parents, and you could cut the silence with a meat cleaver. The strained, difficult conversation set a confusing tone throughout the evening. The only relatively comfortable conversation was initiated by Sylvia, who was obviously taking great pleasure in Herman's disdainful mood. Rita's father could not restrain himself from asking the dreaded question: "What are your intentions with my daughter?" William knew that with Herman's dour mood, the potential for an explosion was more than a possibility. He had very few options and considered them all before he responded. William unmistakably showed his ability to control his Irish temper and clearly let the family know that his love for their daughter was intense, profound, and genuine. Herman listened, but he did not hear. Rita's father was incapable of dealing with the possibility that his daughter could bring home anyone but a Jewish boy. There were tears in Rita's eyes as she tried to navigate this unfortunate turn of events. She knew that her father would not be pleased, but she hoped that he would see how much in love she was. Rita hoped that, for once, her father would be able to make an exception for his only child and think of someone other than himself. It was clear that

Herman Geller would not give his approval for any union between what he inwardly deemed his most precious possession, and this Irishman. Rita was tearful, crestfallen, and unable even to consider her future without William Doyle.

The evening that she had so much hope for turned into a disaster. Sylvia tried to neutralize the disappointment by appealing to Herman's love for his daughter and his desire to prioritize her happiness. The appeal fell on deaf ears, and William recognized that trying to please the Gellers was not in the cards. There was no chance of consoling Rita's rigid, uncompromising father, and the only thing that made sense was a quick, unplanned departure. If anything, the evening did have a silver lining. No matter how disconsolate her father was, it served to reinforce her unbending, genuine love for William. The young couple had their whole life ahead of them, and while it was incredibly painful for Rita to challenge her beloved father, she had made her decision.

CHAPTER 6

MANSFIELD

Rita and William were married at the Los Angeles Courthouse in a civil ceremony one month after the dismal confrontation with Herman Geller. The one witness was the inimitable Johnny Walker. Mr. and Mrs. Doyle were jubilant as they left the courthouse. All was right with the world. Two very beautiful people were deeply in love and never looked back. There was no honeymoon, no wedding party, and no parental approval, but there was a unique reception at the cottage. In addition to Johnny, it seemed as if the entire community of neighbors was in attendance. Margaret Chavez, a charming 29-year-old waitress and mother of two, prepared tamales, and Ted Leven, a local bartender, supplied drinks from Prohibition stock that the bar owner would not "miss." Ted was Johnny's primary supplier and, along the way, became friends with William. Perhaps the most surprising unanticipated guests were Jimmie and the Walshs, with the understandable absence of Lauralie. A celebratory crowd of friends and neighbors raised their glasses to a couple who had, over the months, endeared themselves to this diverse community of celebrants that included David Grossman and Robert Fernandez from the Hollywood Men's Store. David, who was genuinely appreciative of William's friendship and skill as a salesman, showed his affection by presenting the newlyweds with a check for $150, a lot of money in 1923. Patrick Doyle and Vince were apologetic about not being able to attend based on the fact that Patrick was in the throes of wrapping up the sale of his business. However, they did send Rita a lush bouquet of roses and a loving, warm note welcoming her to the joyous Doyle clan. Not a word came from the Geller family though.

In the years that followed, Rita and William ultimately determined that the cottage was too small and certainly not an appropriate address to raise a family. Rita announced her pregnancy in July 1924, and while some newlyweds would find the birth of a child problematic, for William and Rita, the announcement of a baby was a jubilant and welcome news. They both were anxious to have a child, and the timing seemed just right.

William was making a reasonable living through his work at Paramount, and in addition to his status as a double for Doug Fairbanks, he was getting callbacks for some bit parts that paid relatively well. William was also serving an expanding commission clientele at the Hollywood Men's Store, which was a significant contributor to the couple's income. Rita, too, was adding to their earning power. While she was saddened to not continue her education as a pre-med student at USC, she was justifiably thrilled with married life. Her love for William had no bounds. In lieu of school, Rita found employment at the Los Angeles County Hospital. She had completed her freshman year at college, which qualified her as a Nurses' Aid. Although it was a relief, it ended up being a short-term employment. Their first child was due in early 1925, and while it would complicate their earnings, William was doing well at the Studio, and the anticipation of a child was a perfectly welcome phase in the Doyles' young marriage.

The search for a new apartment was bittersweet for the couple. Over the months, they had established the warmth of friendship from the colony of cottages that served as an unconditional circle of friends.

Almost to a person, the renters who surrounded their home articulated the promise that they would visit the Doyles with regularity. In the final analysis, that pledge is, in most instances, a common response to loss. The search for the right apartment had the requisite need to include a nursery, which meant a two-bedroom home. Rita had enjoyed a life that included no concern about what something would cost. She had lived a worry-free life, and now, for the first time in her young marriage, she was dealing with budgetary restraints.

To Rita, all the challenges of setting up housekeeping were more than welcome… She felt like she was a genuine contributing partner in her marriage. Rita was fundamentally liberal in her views, and now she was being put to the test in the real world. In their initial search, admittedly, finding an affordable two-bedroom seemed next to impossible. Patience proved daunting after almost two weeks of trying to find the right place that they could afford. On a Saturday afternoon in mid-October, they ventured out feeling that any day now they would find the right home at the right price. Patience finally paid off in the form of Mrs. Robert Greeley, a middle-aged widow who had inherited a small apartment building on Mansfield just off Wilshire. Sarah Greeley fell under the spell of William and Rita's undeniable warmth and charm. This was a newlywed couple whom she sensed deserved a fresh start and a loving home for the child in waiting. Ironically, she had just accepted notice from the gentleman living in apartment 109. The stars were aligned, and the vacancy was a two-bedroom unit that would be available in two weeks. The Doyles were ecstatic and thanked Mrs. Greeley profusely. They would not see the apartment for almost three weeks, but their new landlady showed them her two-bedroom apartment, which was right across the hall. Instincts prevailed, and they were thrilled with their new accommodations. The layout could not have been better. The nursery was next to their bedroom. A jubilant William hugged their new neighbor, who blushed and was thrilled to be embraced by this handsome young actor. Life was good.

In early December 1924, Rita and William moved into their first home together at the Ethel Arms apartment, and, like everything in their lives together, it was brimming with surprises. Their friends from the cottages were given access to their apartment, and with the help of Mrs. Greeley, they decorated unit 109 and planned a surprise welcome when the Doyles took occupancy. With excited pleasure, they stocked the icebox with food, including Maria Chávez's now-famous tamales, hung a colorful welcome banner, and generously decorated the rooms with multicolored balloons. There was also a predictable supply of paper horns and confetti. Finally, what would a surprise party be without champagne? David Grossman, William's employer and unconditional friend, stepped up with the funding for half a dozen bottles of Prohibition bubbly. When the couple arrived, it was not only a complete surprise, but the warmth and affection they received was something they were very grateful for. Rita had never found herself in a situation that showed such joyous, genuine caring. Her life to that point had been so conservative and sheltered that rubbing elbows with "real people" was a revelation. The welcoming party was a resounding success. The surprises had no limits. Johnny Walker excused himself and emerged from what would be the newborn's nursery with a white wicker bassinet. Both William and Rita were overwhelmed by the generosity of their friends. Rita finally broke down, and the tears could not be held back. This genuine affection from their neighbors was utterly overwhelming.

Rita had a surprise of her own, which William had not anticipated. With Sylvia's help, Rita had secretly returned to her former home and retrieved items that were both functional and sentimental, which included an easel and an array of artists' tools. The new Mrs. Doyle had not mentioned that she was an accomplished sketch artist. Rita had been overly modest about her skill. Factually, she was truly a talented artist who had specialized, although not exclusively, in portraits. She was the kind of exceptional artist who did drawings purely for her own pleasure. Rita had confined her art to occasional sketches of a close family friend and, in every case, had been profusely complimented and encouraged to develop her talent and consider a studio. William was not easily impressed, but his new bride's talent was a huge surprise. For Rita, the unabashed compliments from her husband were the kind of motivation she needed to take her abilities more seriously. But, for now, all her attention and energy would be dedicated to providing a home for William and their new baby. She was in for her own form of surprise in what it takes to deal with the anxiety and complexity of building a secure home. The only thing missing in Rita's new life was the recognition and love from the father she adored, who had chosen to abandon his only child. Thankfully, Sylvia supported her daughter and, whenever there was an opportunity, took pleasure in sharing her enthusiasm and pride in being part of the young couple's lives. She also began to appreciate William and all the loyalty and character he represented, despite the fact that he wasn't Jewish. The potential was there for a future with her new son-in-law that could spell genuine affection. Due to their restrictive marriage agreements, Sylvia would find it difficult to provide financial assistance to the couple, who literally needed everything to set up housekeeping.

CHAPTER 7

MARK

On May 9, 1925, Mark Herman Doyle was born at the Los Angeles Community Hospital. Rita Doyle was one of those fortunate women who had no problem delivering her first child. She was in labor for approximately one hour. William was jubilant and was able to take Rita and their newborn home the next day. Naming Mark was relatively easy. In the Jewish faith, it is not appropriate to name a child after a living relative. Mark, William's brother, had passed away as a victim of the Spanish Flu Epidemic of 1918 while serving in the United States Army. The couple was unanimous in recognizing and honoring the deceased older Doyle brother. "Mark" may have been an easy choice, but the baby's middle name was a different conversation. Because of the way Rita's father had been dismissive of the couple, William was less than thrilled when Rita insisted on the name Herman after her stubborn father. William was amazed at his wife's willingness to name her child after a father who had shown no recognition of his daughter's marriage, let alone the birth of his first grandchild. Rita insisted on "Herman."

The threesome returned to their Mansfield apartment and were once again elated that their friends had seen fit to celebrate the birth in such a magnanimous way. Mark Herman Doyle was warmly welcomed with a huge, colorful banner stretched across the entrance to the Ethel Arms apartment building. The nursery had been fully furnished with gifts from friends, including a two-year supply of diapers from

William's dad and older brother. A wire from his family announced that they were not only planning to visit, but Patrick had also completed the sale of his company and secured a position with the Pacific Electric Railway Company, which provided daily railway service throughout Southern California. It was anticipated that Vince, who had a lengthy recovery from his War wounds, would find work with the new Railway. Sylvia Geller had also made a thoughtful contribution in the form of a high-end crib and bureau. She evidently had a secret source of funds which she could access independent of her recalcitrant husband. In the purest sense, the newlyweds were understandably thrilled with the warmth and affection from friends and family. Rita, William and the most recent member of their family, Mark Herman, could not have been more grateful for the elaborate generosity.

In the ensuing months, the young family experienced the reality of caring for a newborn. Sleepless nights, mixing and feeding formula, continually changing diapers and a myriad of parenting responsibilities ruled their sleep-deprived life. After two weeks of sharing childcare, William went back to work at Paramount, where he had the opportunity to announce the birth of his child with the predictable *"it's a Boy"* cigar. His timing couldn't have been better. Although it was a minor role, William was cast in the best role of his career. Not to be outdone, David Grossman at the Hollywood Men's Store saw fit to pay the Doyles' rent for the next two months. In the following years, Rita and William solidified family life and took great pleasure in the pure act of guiding and loving their baby boy. Mark was a precocious child who was at the center of every aspect of Rita and William's busy lives.

In the midst of devoting most of her life to the care and feeding of her son, Rita Doyle, with limitless energy, found time to sit down at her drawing table and reinstate her art with some exceptional sketches of friends and occupants of Ethel Arms. William admired his wife's talent and encouraged her unique style of sketching. Rita looked at her work as a shortcoming that, in essence, seemed to deny the skill of her art. People who appreciated her talent were highly complimentary, but even the high level of recognition did not erase her sense of not being an accomplished artist. Also, during this formative time, young Mark Doyle flourished and fed on being surrounded by a family and friends who adored him. As planned, Patrick and Vince had moved to Los Angeles and added to the cadre who doted on his only grandchild.

Patrick Doyle had significant funds from the sale of his business and would be looking for an opportunity to invest. The job with the Southern California railway proved to be everything that he could have hoped for. He was an accomplished, experienced railroad man who was welcomed and appreciated by management. Vince, on the other hand, was having a much more difficult time adjusting to the Southern California lifestyle. Patrick had rented an apartment off Wilshire just a mile or so from William and his family. Vince's inability to embrace this foreign way of life was probably due in large part to his problems finding work. Vince found no satisfaction in the relatively menial jobs for which he was qualified. The 1920s were a decade of consequential events that contributed to the success of the Doyle family, that is, until 1929.

The years of seemingly endless success of the American economy came to an end with the devastating Stock Market Crash. In October 1929, overinflated shares, growing bank loans, panic-selling, and a number of other contributing factors led to the worldwide economic disaster. No one was spared, one way or another, from being caught in the maelstrom. Overnight, the lives of most Americans were turned upside down. Layoffs and termination of employment were the order of the day. Soup lines and unemployment offices serviced long lines that included people from all walks of life. Suicides became common, and responsible people could not pay their monthly mortgage or rent. Even the ability to buy a bag of groceries became questionable. Businesses—large or small—were forced to liquidate their assets. The country was being tested to see whether Americans could rise above the financial disaster and ultimately return the country to some form of sanity.

The Doyles were not excluded from the nation's tragedy. William's work at Paramount was in flux. A year earlier, studios had to address the newfound excitement of making movies with sound. Al Jolson's movie, "The Jazz Singer," had been a huge success, and with it, the age of silent movies came to an end. William Doyle, to make ends meet, thought he could rely on David Grossman and his Hollywood Men's Store to offer an avenue of hope, but that wasn't to be. Men of wealth who were the foundation of William's commission clientele stopped buying custom suits, and even over-the-counter sales were in a downward spiral. David did not let William go, but without commission, there was very little money in serving as a retail salesman. Grossman kept the store open, but sales plummeted to an unsustainable level.

Admittedly, there were some silver linings in the otherwise difficult time. The arrival of Patrick in their lives proved to be a very welcome addition. Rita almost immediately struck up a very healthy and positive father/daughter-in-law relationship. While she was still dealing with her father's excommunication, Patrick provided her with a much-needed father figure to lean on. He was totally bonding with young Mark, and whenever Patrick could get the time off, he spent every waking moment with his grandson. William, too, was amazed at the almost immediate connection Patrick initiated with Mark. He had not seen this side of his father, and during the Depression, the Doyles, like so many American families, welcomed the material and emotional contributions that could be rendered by every member of their clan.

CHAPTER 8

VINCE

1934.

- **Inner city slums clearance began in New York and other major U.S. cities.**
- **John Dillinger dies after a shootout.**
- **Bonnie and Clyde were ambushed by the FBI.**
- **The Loch Ness monster was sighted for the first time.**
- **Charles Lindbergh's baby was kidnapped, and Bruno Hauptmann was arrested.**
- **Donald Duck made his first cartoon appearance**
- **Hitler declared himself Führer.**
- **Stalin began the Great Purge. Fascism, Nazism and Communism dominated the political landscape.**
- **Tom Doyle was born.**

Vince, unlike his father, spent very little time with the Doyle household. His ongoing difficulty finding employment proved to be an emotional impasse that quite naturally forged a feeling of inferiority. William recognized that his older brother was in crisis, and he felt helpless.

There was a surprising turn of events that created a solution to Doyle's financial concerns and, at the same time, introduced some friction between William and Rita. The idea of his wife contributing to their household was a blow to William's male ego. Rita was flattered that many of her artistic admirers continued to encourage her to put some of her sketches up for sale. It was by no means charitable, but that was how William interpreted these offers. There was no question that the sale of Rita's art would provide a legitimate avenue to deal with the family's financial shortcomings. The demand, once Rita opened the floodgates, was near phenomenal, primarily because there were so many art collectors who were able to remain viable during the calamitous Depression. Although William was having difficulty accepting the revenue, Rita's artwork was in demand and generating a real line of much-needed cash. The truth is that William, more than ever, realized that Rita's talent was proving to be a lifesaver for the Doyles.

As the Depression entered its fourth grinding year, the Doyles prepared to greet their second child. Their finances had improved to the point where they felt that the pregnancy provided the balance needed in their family. In 1934, Mark was 9 and proved to be highly intelligent, well-adjusted and extraordinarily blessed with good looks. Mark was ready for a sibling, and Rita and William were more than a little pleased when they were told that another son was on the way. Rita had set up a small studio in the corner of their living room and increased her sketching to meet the surprising demand. Her art had more than adequately proved to be a huge adjunct to William's income. Rather than require her subjects to sit for the portrait, Rita did her sketches from photographs that she controlled in terms of setup and lighting. The technique proved to be highly effective, and at the same time, she was able to control her schedule, especially as she approached her due date.

1934 was proving to be a happy and productive year for the Doyles. Rita's water broke while she was sketching a portrait of her beloved father-in-law, Patrick, which was taken as a positive sign for her delivery. William was on location in Utah for a Western starring Ward Bond outside of Ogden. William had a significant minor role in the picture, and word of the impending birth arrived via telegram. Fortunately, his portion of the shooting schedule was completed, leaving William free to travel home in time for the birth of his second child. Unfortunately, births arrive on their own schedule, and William's attempt to beat the stork wasn't to be. Thomas Patrick Doyle was born at 4 am on Thursday, August 3, 1934. Rita was rushed to the Hollywood hospital in Vince Doyle's Chevrolet. Mrs. William Doyle, true to form, gave birth 10 minutes after arriving in the delivery room. Rita was one of those women who naturally had a capacity for childbearing. Thomas Patrick was born with the same ease that had welcomed Mark Herman Doyle 9 years earlier.

The welcoming party was predictably already gathering at the Ethel Arms apartment to greet mother and child. Sylvia Geller was disappointed that she wasn't at the hospital, but Rita's rapid birth left no time for the family to attend the main event. Sylvia had organized the reception party, alerted their friends and, true to form, catered the party. Gifts from their old neighbors at the cottages filled the living room and arranged space for big brother Mark's bassinet and crib, which had been carefully stored. The Doyles had, over the years, maintained the friendships from their loving initial home.

William had left Utah with all the urgency of a father-to-be. Based on the years of loyalty to Paramount, the location crew and production executives chipped in to fly William back to Los Angeles, the most time-saving method.

He was shocked to find that Rita had already returned home with their newborn. He, too, was greeted by a celebratory group of friends and neighbors who had arrived on Friday, one day after Thomas Doyle made his entrance. Rita and William felt that while they both loved a large family, they agreed that Thomas would complete the family unit.

The only missing member of the family was Herman Geller. After all that had transpired, Rita was the forever optimist and felt that her father would ultimately concede. That wasn't to be… even with the advent of a second grandchild. Sylvia, on the other hand, had been a caring, consoling mother who had given up trying to convince her husband to join his daughter and accept their secular son-in-law finally. The absence of the Jewish grandfather wore heavily on Rita, who maintained a smiling exterior, but inside, she could not have been more disappointed. How could her father ignore the fact that she loved William, who was a wonderful father, and together they had presented him with two beautiful boys? The birth of Thomas Doyle was a summation of all the joy, with few exceptions, that Rita and William could ever hope for. William had steady employment, and his roles at Paramount seemed promising, and Rita had the ideal set of circumstances… Staying home with her boys and, at the same time, maintaining her burgeoning art trade.

It seemed as though the success of William and Rita Doyle was never-ending, and then… 1935 came along while the Depression ground on with no immediate end in sight. A huge portion of the American public was barely getting by in dealing with the crush of unemployment. Soup lines and human despair were the order of the day in many American homes. The Doyles were incredibly grateful that, up to this point, they had escaped the grinding throes of impending poverty.

Since Thomas' birth, Vince seemed to be reveling in the joy of his new nephew. His inability to cope with despair and a feeling of hopelessness seemed to be waning. He was 30, drinking, and the loss of weight was alarming, but not enough to trigger his family to intervene. Early in April, just one month after Thomas' birth, the phone rang. The police were on the line asking if William was the brother of Vince Doyle. His elder brother had committed suicide. The news seemed beyond belief, and the dark shadow of despair took control of William. He knew that his older brother was having a difficult time adjusting to LA and knew there were some danger signs… but suicide was beyond his comprehension. The crush and reality of Vince's depression had a demoralizing impact on the entire Doyle family and, surprisingly, the many people to whom he evidently had endeared himself. The impact of Vince's passing seemed to catch the family totally unaware of the extent of his desperation. At the Catholic funeral, some believed that a suicide burial should be denied. In his anguish, Patrick did all he could to hold back the anger he felt. The few faces that held that belief were quickly silenced. The fact that dark clouds appeared on the day of the funeral, and a subsequent, uncommon deluge of rain, seemed to further the uncompromising sadness of the day. The pall cast over the Doyles and their circle of friends was palpable, but like all things, dealing with life and living seemed to blunt the death of Vince… The world moves on.

The family stopped and thought about who they were and, in so doing, showed a sense of pride in the fact that they stayed together and endured. Mark, a full nine years older than Thomas, showed an extraordinary level of maturity and, even at this early stage of adjusting, proved to be protective of his little brother. Rita and William looked at their oldest son with awe and approval. They were aware of the fact that quite often an older child can be jealous of a newborn, whom he believes is an intruder. Such was not the case with Mark. The couple could not have been more pleased with their two sons… Mark was protective, and baby Thomas only produced tears when he was hungry.

CHAPTER 9

SAVE MY LEG!

The next few years, the crisis was centered on William's difficulty finding enough work to pay the bills and feed his family. In all actuality, Rita was holding the finances in check with her artwork. They both were aware of this discrepancy but chose to ignore this ego-shattering reality. The cruel Depression added another jolt to the Doyles. William was finding work in pictures that offered a premium for on-location shoots. The studio paid the player's expenses, allowing William to save most of his salary for his family. Between Rita's sketches and William's contributions, the Doyles were getting by until tragedy struck again… During a Western which was shot on location in South Dakota, William was to ride his horse and gallop out of town as he was being chased by the 'Posse.' A local cat ran directly in the horse's path, and the animal reared up and threw William to the ground as its hoof struck him in the leg… the leg that he almost lost in France. Through the web of pain and anguish, William found himself lying on an operating table in Pierre, SD, looking up at strange creatures with masks. Was he back in St. Mihiel? Once he returned to reality, he was near hysterical when he realized they were talking about his leg. Later, he was told that he literally screamed, "Don't take my leg!" as the anesthetic wore off. In truth, that possibility was part of the surgeons' conversation. They became aware of his War wounds and determined that taking his leg was what should be done, but as patriotic Americans, they thought better of it. The surgeons had enlisted all their skills and training to rebuild the leg as best they could. It would be attached to this Veteran, and that would be all. This Silver Star recipient, they thought, would never walk again.

The Studio took care of all expenses and flew him to LA, where it had been arranged for William to be transferred to the Hollywood Hospital. Rita picked up the phone and, for some unexplained reason, had a deep sense of foreboding. The Studio executive was calling to notify her that William was a patient at the Hollywood Hospital and, in halting terms, told her that her husband had been in an accident, which Rita was soon to learn was understated. Rita and Patrick entered William's private room only to learn that the doctors felt he might eventually lose his leg. After a month of recuperation and therapy, he was released from the hospital in a wheelchair.

On the ride back to Mansfield, Rita attempted to make conversation, but William was understandably in no mood. When they wheeled him into the apartment, 10-year-old Mark was there to greet them, not knowing what would be in store. The sight of his son overwhelmed him, and William burst into uncontrolled tears. The emotion finally rose to the surface and framed everything he was holding inside. For several weeks, Rita was by his side, reading to him, fixing his favorite meals, bathing his wounds, and doing everything she could think of to bring him back to her. After the second month, William told Rita that he would need her to help him learn to walk again. She was obviously pleased, and for the first time since the accident, there was a semblance of hope and determination. Friends and neighbors came to visit, and that added some solace, but William's real concern was employment. There were flowers and well-wishes from friends at the cottage, the men's store, and the studio's actors and crew. They were all sincerely concerned about William's injury. Some people supplied real surprises. One such arrival was David Grossman, owner of the

Hollywood Men's Store. William's employer was genuinely shaken but did his best to assure William that his job would be waiting for him when he "got well." In the meantime, he would maintain William's salary, which was helpful but really not more than a draw on his commissions. David was having a difficult time just keeping the store open during the Depression, so this level of caring was truly a gesture of pure kindness.

No matter how hard he tried to put on a positive face as well-wishers came and went, William could not shake the deep sense of depression that permeated his soul. Then one afternoon, when he was hitting an emotional downward slide, two people showed up who, to say the least, he was not expecting… the appearance of Jimmie Walsh and Lauralie. Jimmie could be anticipated, but his sister? William had not seen Lauralie for over 10 years, and his memories of her were easy to visualize. As they entered the apartment, it was clear to Rita that the beautiful young lady was something more than a casual friend of her husband. The once girl of eighteen was now what can only be described as stunning. Over the years, the nonconforming patina had dissipated, and Lauralie carried her beauty now with confidence. The brother and sister stayed for over an hour, and during that time, Rita was well aware of the glances between the two. She was not usually threatened by other women, but this was as close to jealousy as she would ever come. Both she and William had affairs in their lives, and admittedly, Lauralie could not in any way be put in the category of "casual." William was indeed in awe of the way that Lauralie had matured, and at the same time, concluded that being aroused by a beautiful woman from his past was not unusual, but it tempted his allegiance. Seeing her did have a positive effect. William was now motivated not because of Lauralie, but more by the awareness and pride that she engendered, which would move him to walk again.

Over the following months, with the help and encouragement of Rita, William became determined, despite what the VA doctors had said, to throw his crutches away and stand on his own. Each day, he became a little stronger and drove himself to exhaustion. Now that he was making progress, there was nothing that could deter him from his goal of achieving independence and walk. After months of self-prescribed therapy, days of falling and getting up again, there was never a sign of giving up. That was not an option. Finally, the efforts paid off, and William, in a moment of intense will and determination, stood up. That was all the encouragement that he needed, and from that day forward, with the help of Rita, William was on a mission. Eventually, he did walk with the aid of crutches provided by the Veterans Association. Then, after months of excruciating pain and sheer desire, William ultimately accomplished his goal of independence with minimal support of a cane.

Now he had to turn his attention to supporting his family. Thankfully, Paramount provided him with a small stipend, but the primary source of survival was Rita's skill as a truly talented artist and the demand for her unique, detailed sketches. With no more than a number two pencil, she could capture the elusive character of her subject. Rita's admirers encouraged her to apply her talent by expanding beyond what some considered the limitations of a pencil. As an artist, she recognized that learning to use color, whether it was watercolor, oil or pastels, would require an extended period of learning to master complex media. Rita was well aware that her style of art had limitations, but to her, the character of the subject was best represented by her original style, and that was through the use of a pencil. As Rita's reputation as a talented artist spread, her fees accelerated. William was aware of this fact and tried to shed the feeling of inadequacy. Nonetheless, he felt a fleeting capacity to provide for his family. In the months that followed, he tried working a few days a week at the Hollywood Men's Store, but while he appreciated David's largess, the Depression had left the men's clothing business especially hard hit. His appreciation for his wife's contribution to keeping the family afloat was clear, but he needed to feel that, after the debilitating injury, he was still relevant.

William now devoted his time and energy to doing everything he could think of to find gainful employment. His days as an actor were over, and the same thing could be said for his sales job. Just when he felt he had exhausted all contacts, Jimmie Walsh showed up at the apartment and offered William an enticing career opportunity. The Walsh Furniture company was expanding in the face of the Depression with a new approach to owning furniture. The process required some assembling of the product with a set of relatively easy directions and the incumbent savings. Sales in Southern California were significantly increasing, and the Walshs felt that now was the time to expand to Northern California with a facility in San Francisco. Jimmie clearly stated that the offer of employment was not an exercise in pity but rather a recognition of William's qualifications. In the conversation that ensued, both men became animated with genuine enthusiasm. Jimmie put his emphasis on William's proven leadership in the War, his successful sales experience and, quite frankly, his charm and personality. The job description, after William accepted the fact that this wasn't in any way charity, was well-suited for his skills and experience. He would be responsible for hiring and the overall management of personnel. The Walsh family came through and was offering a job with real growth opportunities. William asked his friend to give him a little time to discuss the move to San Francisco with Rita. That evening, without wasting any time, William and Rita stayed up late into the night to evaluate and envision life away from Los

Angeles. At 2 am, they retired with a deep sense of accomplishment. They both were aware that the position would be a huge step forward for William, and Rita would merely move her artistry to San Francisco. The next day, they began the process of moving to the City by the Bay.

CHAPTER 10

SAN FRANCISCO

W ord of Doyle's move to San Francisco spread rapidly, and Patrick especially was filled with mixed emotions. On the one hand, he was genuinely pleased William had landed an excellent job, and on the other, he knew that leaving would be painful. He had established a granular bond like no other with his grandsons Mark and Tommy… There was a possibility that the Rail Service he worked for, which served LA and San Francisco, would allow him to transfer north. Mrs. Greeley was in tears as the Doyles were like a new family for her, and the two boys were the grandsons she never had. Friends from the cottages, the men's store and close relations from William's tenure at Paramount were all highly pleased with this opportunity, but like Patrick, would miss a family that had been an important part of their lives. Close friends like Johnny Walker, David Grossman and Anthony Fernandez insisted that San Francisco was only a few hours away, and to hide their disappointment, they stated they would see the Doyles regularly. Sylvia was a special case who, over the past decade, attempted to make excuses for her uncompromising, stubborn husband. Herman had missed any relationship with his daughter, let alone two grandsons who didn't know he existed. The talented Rita was a loyal, loving mate for William and, to Sylvia's surprise, a doting natural mother. Sylvia and Herman could have learned a lot about parenting from their daughter and son-in-law.

On Wednesday morning in July 1937, the Doyle family packed everything they owned, which was very little, into the used 1935 Chevy that Patrick generously purchased for the trip north. It was the first real trip away from the only home the family had known. It was with mixed blessings that William, Rita, Mark, and Thomas said goodbye to 1287 Mansfield and proceeded to say hello to the beginning of their new adventure. The open road seemed cleansing to William, although he questioned his qualifications for the new job and the demands of a completely new style of living. The family arrived in the Bay Area just as rain began to fall. Jimmie Walsh had rented a temporary apartment in San Francisco, but the boys were understandably tired, so William decided to stay the night in Oakland. The Clinton Hotel across the Bay from the City had the only vacancy. The availability was a one-bedroom unit, but to accommodate the family's needs, the friendly night clerk delivered two cots and bedding for the boys. They had stopped at a diner in Gilroy to eat, and everyone was ready for a good night's sleep. The Doyles were happy, excited and exhausted after the 480-mile trip to unknown territory.

The sound of the intense rain served to lull them to sleep. The next morning, William ventured out for coffee, orange juice and donuts, which would, at the very least, quell unfed stomachs until they arrived at their temporary home in the City. The last leg of their great adventure was the approach to the Bay Bridge, revealing the Skyline of San Francisco. Unlike Los Angeles, where everything was spread out, this was a large American city with tall and tight skyscrapers that exuded a sense of energy and opportunity. The rain had given way to bright sunshine, which seemed to provide a positive sign of what the future held for the Doyles. San Francisco was unlike any place William, let alone his family, had ever seen and with that initial sighting, the boys squealed with excitement.

Following the map that Jimmie had provided was relatively easy to navigate. They crossed the Bay Bridge, which had just been completed in 1936, took the off-ramp to Van Ness Avenue, crossed bustling Market Street, turned right on Van Ness, and followed it north towards the Bay. They found their new temporary home, which would do until Rita and William had an opportunity to find a more permanent address. The Bayview apartment building, one block away from the Presidio, instantly felt welcoming with its formidable brick facade and wide entrance. Jimmie Walsh once again had seen to their needs. He had rented their new home with the first month paid until William got settled, filled the icebox with food and drink, and had the beds in the two bedrooms already made and ready for the Doyles' first night in San Francisco.

The facility for Walsh Furniture was situated in South San Francisco, which harbored a community of industry just south of the city. As always, Jimmie was already on site, anxious to show William around the new building and introduce him to the management staff. The people he met covered a wide range of demographics, from very young and relatively inexperienced maintenance staff to long-time professionals who were veterans of the Walsh family business. Jimmie showed him his new office, which was close to the factory floor. William was not prepared for the next introduction, which was completely unexpected. He met his secretary, who added to his sense of importance. Doris McNulty was a highly experienced assistant who had been with the company for 15 years in various secretarial roles. Doris was a slender, attractive woman of 45 with prematurely grey hair, bifocal glasses, blue eyes and a personality that William soon would learn to appreciate. The fact that she was of Irish heritage provided an instant bond. William spent the rest of the day and the following week in orientation, and as he became more familiar with the Walsh furniture business, the more convinced he was that he had made the right decision. The environment and working conditions of the building were progressive and mirrored the attitude of the staff. William could not have been more pleased with the entire operation.

That first evening, he drove to his new home in the city feeling elation and enthusiasm to get started. When he arrived home, Rita had already organized the apartment and ventured out with the boys to explore the Marina neighborhood. While Van Ness was a main artery, the adjoining streets were full of enterprise and commercial activity. Mark and Thomas were wide-eyed and thrilled with potential adventures. William greeted his family with new enthusiasm for what turned out to be a great introduction to the Doyles' new life. The family celebrated with dinner at the famous Fisherman's Wharf, merely blocks away. The Doyle family ate Dungeness crab at Tarantino's restaurant overlooking the Bay. San Francisco was proving to be everything and more than they could hope for. The year spent in the heart of San Francisco would be filled with wonderful memories.

For the boys, Mark at 13 and his little brother Thomas at 4, every day was an adventure. They literally had the run of the neighborhood, and at that time in America, the ribbon of fear did not hang over the heads of small children. The boys did not venture too far from home, nor was there a need to. In close proximity to their apartment, there were the Presidio, the Maritime Museum, Fisherman's Wharf, and the Van Ness pier. Each of these locations and many others nearby provided the stuff that little boys loved. In the meantime, until Mark was out of school for summer vacation, the full-blown adventures with Thomas would have to wait.

Sherman Grammar School was just three blocks from the apartment. Even though Rita and William knew that life on Van Ness was temporary, they felt that the security of their boys was essential, and that meant school for Mark, even if it might be less than a year. For now, little Tommy would have to stay home with his mother. That was not anything that he dreaded. In fact, Rita was full of surprises and lots of fun for the four-year-old. She was teaching him to draw, read and play games that Rita invented for her son. For Tommy, however, the two months of Mark's school seemed interminable. Mom was great, but the kid needed his brother for a true adventure.

Summer finally came, and the two boys reveled in their freedom. Rita bought them yellow slicker rain jackets and head covers, which would protect them in the fog that was so heavy that at times it felt like rain. The boys had seen other kids fishing off the pier at the end of Van Ness, and they quite naturally needed simple fishing gear, which consisted of tackle wound around a wooden pole, hooks and a weight. For bait, mom took them to The Bait Shop at 2nd and Bay Street, where worms cost pennies, or they would venture to Fisherman's Wharf, where the Italian fisherman would provide free chum bait for the asking. The brothers would trundle down to the pier, drop their line into the bay water with two baited hooks and a weight at the end. Like magic, San Francisco Bay was a fisherman's delight, and for the two young Doyle boys, catching Shiners was an exciting event. When they had had enough of a catch, they would put them on a line and head home, where Rita would help them prepare a breaded fried fish lunch. The fact was they generally didn't like fish, but somehow the fish they caught was delicious. The ritual was only interrupted if Rita had a client she was sketching. In a little over a month, she had developed a clientele in advance by posting in various free want ads and solid, complementary word of mouth. Rita was successfully transferring her portrait skills from LA to San Francisco.

One afternoon, as they were leaving the Bait Shop, the boys heard excited laughing that seemed to be coming from the Maritime Museum across the street. What they encountered was a total surprise. When the tide went out, the small beach on the side of the museum was exposed. Boys around Mark's age were standing on the beach waiting for the tide to recede. In their hands were long poles, which they used effectively. The outgoing tide exposed Sand Sharks in the shallow water, and this was a target for the local kids. What Mark and little Tommy saw next was both fascinating and exciting. The neighborhood boys ran to the shallow water and used long foot poles to hit the partially exposed sand sharks to stun them and grab them by the tails, dragging them to the dry portion of the landing. After showing the meek boys their wondrous heroism, the young warriors took the wriggling fish to their home in the Bay. The brothers were totally enthralled by what they had just witnessed. Was there an end to the adventures they would experience in the summer of 1938?

CHAPTER 11

26TH AVENUE

Rita Doyle, like her children, was finding their new home in San Francisco, a city full of unique adventures. While William was working long hours at the furniture factory, she was venturing out with her boys to explore both her neighborhood and all the beauty and wonder of this compelling City. With the combination of streetcars, cable cars and buses, it really wasn't necessary to travel and explore San Francisco with a family car. Unlike Los Angeles, the city by the bay offered a community that was, in essence, huddled at the tip of a peninsula and relatively easy to find your way around. One of their exploits was a trip to Golden Gate Park, which stretched from what has been labeled "The Pan Handle" all the way to the sea. The park was the largest man-made green space in America. There was a museum, an arboretum and an outdoor concert stage, but what Rita found most appealing was the calming Japanese tea garden. Mark and Tommy were not impressed with tea and meditation. She would have to return in the coming weeks without the boys, who required a more active destination.

On Sundays, William and Rita used his day off to begin the search for a more suburban home. The boys were disappointed with just the thought of moving away from Van Ness. There was so much to do, and neither of them could imagine any place as enjoyable and full of adventure. The Doyles were especially impressed with the two areas that flanked Golden Gate Park. The Sunset district was on one side, and the Richmond on the other. It was abundantly clear that no matter where you lived in the Bay Area, fog was always a significant weather prediction. Surprisingly, fog would roll in primarily in the summer. The saving grace was typically that by noon, the fog would burn off. In September of 1938, with Mark out of school, the search for a more substantial home became a priority. After devoting every day off for five consecutive weeks, the Doyles found a flat on 26th Avenue that met their needs. The San Francisco version of suburb was common even in the city proper, but beyond the city limits, flats were the rule. A flat primarily consisted of housing two families upstairs and downstairs, and many with a garage at street level.

The unit that the Doyles found had recently been redecorated and offered three bedrooms. Mark and Tommy would for the first time have their own room. At this stage of his life, Tommy didn't want privacy. It was more important that he continue with Mark as his roommate. His parents knew that Mark, on the other hand, was thrilled as he was about to enter his teen years, and privacy was a priority. Tommy's big brother was his idol and protector, but Rita knew that her youngest son had to show more independence and not rely exclusively on his big brother. It didn't require a lot of conversation, and the availability of a bottom unit was a positive factor in their offer. The rent on the flat was well within their means, and the landlord was pleased to welcome this attractive family. By mid-October, the Doyles moved into 1371, 26th Avenue. Also, for the first time in their marriage, William and Rita would need to purchase furniture for their home. For obvious reasons, William working for a furniture company was a huge advantage, and for the first time, Rita would be involved with selecting and decorating a real home. The seasonal holidays with Thanksgiving and Christmas just around the corner would make the Fall of 1938 a very memorable New Year.

There was one thing the Doyles did not take into consideration, and that was the less-than-friendly couple in the upstairs unit. The Snows were middle-aged, childless and for the sake of a better word, crotchety. The less-than-compatible union began almost from the day that the Doyles moved into their new Home. William was pleased with the flat, and the move was smooth and uneventful until he attempted to introduce himself to the Snows. He climbed the short set of stairs, rang the doorbell, and the rest is unfortunate history. Robert Snow answered the door, and the first thing he said was, "Yeah, what do you want?" William was taken aback and responded that they were the new family that had just moved into the apartment below them, and wanted to introduce themselves. The response was an instant, accumulating turn-off. "Just keep your kids out of my portion of the yard." It should be mentioned that the traditional San Francisco flat had a long, narrow yard that was shared by the two-family occupants. Since the Snows had lived there for a couple of years, they had claimed the back half of the yard where they had constructed a chicken house for eggs. William had no trouble with this and would have told Mr. Snow that the birds were okay with him, but the so-called attempt at neighborliness was, in a word, disastrous. With that last comment, William had his fill of the Snows. They had succeeded in establishing a non-relation status between the two tenants.

William wondered how the Snows would react when they heard Mark playing the piano. From the time he was five, Mark had shown genuine musical talent, and not until they moved into the Sunset was there enough space for Mark to learn to play the piano. He had been taking lessons, and his skill was undeniable. Now that they were convinced that he had a natural talent and that William's salary would allow it, they purchased a small upright piano. In addition, Rita, almost from the time they moved in, was planning how she would organize their part of the yard. Not prone to anger, she was incensed that the people upstairs were so obviously unfriendly. But true to form, Rita did not allow this one negative aspect of a seamless move to destroy her positive attitude. She had laid out a thoughtful design for flower beds and a small lawn that would encompass the Doyles' section of the back yard. She grudgingly included a path to allow the Snows' access to their damned chickens!

It did not take long for Mark and Tommy to realize that the people upstairs were not friendly. A day after the move, they encountered the Snows, who showed no recognition when the boys greeted them. In later years, they expressed displeasure at their "gorilla war" against the grumpy Snows. Without going into all of the techniques that the Doyle brothers employed, there was one especially mischievous antic. Both families shared the garage and independent storage areas. The entrance consisted of a door with openings on either side with wide-spaced slats. There is no question that Mark and little Tommy were generally well-behaved, but they were also boys and full of mischief. When they were sure that the Snows were gone for the day, they would open their flies and proceed to urinate through the open slats on the upstairs family storage. That was just one example of a war without end. Thankfully, Rita and Will were unaware of the boys' version of War, and it is better left unsaid. They never got caught. Were the Snows really oblivious?

The commute to South San Francisco was a little longer than William had hoped for, but the tradeoff for 26th Avenue was well worth the drive, and for Rita, the announcement of her new address for potential clients had already preceded the move. The Doyle family was comfortably ensconced in their first substantial home with furniture that had been a gift from Jimmie Walsh. As always, there was a huge hole in Rita's heart in the continued absence of a father she loved but who had never shown any acceptance of William or the family. Almost instantly, Mark and Tommy struck up relationships with kids in the neighborhood who were more than pleased to add to their numbers.

The "new kids'" presence in adjacent blocks was like a telegraph, and they accepted both Doyles in their respective age groups. Approaching 13, Mark found connections with the MacDonald brothers, 14 and 4 years and the Netos, 14 and… 13 years old. The latter was [ugh] a girl. Both of their families were merely down the block from the brother's new home. In subsequent weeks, Mark and Tommy would explore the neighborhood, which, to their mounting pleasure, offered more in terms of exploration than they ever could anticipate. Childhood in the avenues of San Francisco was richly suited for kids to navigate with very little rulemaking or interference from their parents. Unlike generations in the future, these two young men were free to explore and travel to distant blocks within a mile of 26th Avenue.

Mark and his new instant friend, Keith MacDonald, were off on an excursion into Golden Gate Park, which was just a little over a block away. On this first day, they traveled north (walking) to Mother Grove and Stole Lake. The latter was especially interesting. Young people, boys and girls, were either alone or with their dads, navigating sailboats all around the lake by remote control. Mark had never seen anything as awesome. The two new friends vowed that they would save enough to one day buy a boat like this. Maybe they would chip in together? Mark had a better idea… What if he played the piano for money? They both nodded with approval, knowing that it never would happen.

The "vacant lot" was one of the shared empty spaces that served as "headquarters" for each neighbor gang (a label not used in negative modern terms). What took place in those empty lots was comprehensive and variable. On the one hand, there was the ever-changing community fort that quite easily could convert to a quasi-baseball field. A formidable stick and tennis ball would serve as equipment. Instead of a pitch, the "batter" would throw the ball in the air and swat it as it came down. Some of the older kids, like Mark, became very effective at hitting the tennis ball significant distances. Distances that could include all the way to adjoining house windows, and the "hitter" was instantly admonished in very angry terms by the homeowners. Playing "war" in the lot was eternally a game of choice, as well as how grand and sizable the fort could be. Neighbor kids would search far and wide for materials to build fortresses, and that would include extraneous pieces of flotsam found at nearby home construction sites. The elaborate forts were forever under construction. The caves and tunnels dug by an earlier generation were later embellished with walls and defenses that were built above the ground. It was literally deemed a work in progress.

The kids on 26th Avenue between Irving and Judah and beyond shared in their capacity and ingenuity to play outside and not require store-bought toys. It included neighbors with folding chairs in front of their flats, observing and commenting on the goings-on. Whether it was "Kick the Can," which on any night in the summer was played at twilight and beyond when the streetlights came on. Or the building and roar of homemade "coasters." These handmade transports were unquestionably the height of creativity. The materials to build a "race car" came again from the ubiquitous debris found at building sites. There were a number of unique, thoughtful designs, but they all relied on scavenging material. Typically, this kind of construction would be in the domain of the older teens on the block, but Mark was literally begging to help with one scooter that was under construction by Tim Miller, one of the older teens on the block. He had sawed a piece of two by four to size that would serve as the base of his scooter. On the underside of the base, he was attaching a pair of worn-out skates that he found in an ash can in the park and attached a wooden orange crate on the front of the 2x4, placed a wooden handle on top of the crate and attached a piece of scavenged wood to place his foot on. When the scooter was completed, Tim made the successful first run, and because Mark helped gather "the supplies," he was next up. He crashed the vehicle halfway down the street, joyfully unharmed, and couldn't wait for his next turn. That was an example of a young boy's life in the Sunset.

Girls in the 1930s also had their territory in their forms of creative, toyless games. "Hopscotch", "Jacks," and a version of "Kick the Can" were among the favorites. It can be said that boys were always willing to participate. While it was not a game, most kids made it a practice of climbing into the back of the ice truck when the delivery man was doing his weekly servicing, which consisted of shouldering a very large block of ice up to the house if the "ice sign" was displayed in the window. Kids would grab chunks of ice to suck on, especially in the summer. There was one other practice which may sound repulsive, and that is "chewing tar." When the street repair service was in the neighborhood, one of the ingredients was hot tar. When it cooled, it had the consistency of gum! Pieces of chewing tar were always left at the site. It did not taste like gum.

CHAPTER 12

BASEBALL

Mark was building a new circle of friends on 26th Avenue and was finding his little brother's attention sometimes inhibiting. Tommy was also finding less of a need to rely on Mark for every activity. Nothing could break the bond between the brothers, but there was no question that the new neighborhood was significantly different than the kid population surrounding their Van Ness apartment. Mark was also finding less of a need to constrain his young guardian sibling. It was time for Tommy to exercise his independence. The new address offered far more positive activities suited for his age group. Tommy found almost instantly that he could stand on his own while not breaking the strong connection with the big brother that he unquestionably cherished. It was an opportunity for Tommy to spread his wings and build his own relationships, and at the same time, give Mark the latitude to establish his own circle of friends and activities.

Mark loved baseball and became an instant fan of the Triple-A San Francisco ball club, the Seals. They were not the Majors but engendered real allegiance and popularity with most of the people on the western side of the Bay. The fans on the other side had their own Triple-A team—the Oakland Oaks. The Pacific Coast League was just one step away from the Majors, and quite often, players from the local team would be "called up" to the Majors, which proved to be a great source of pride. The Pacific Coast League played solid and good quality baseball with teams up and down the coast. In addition to the

Bay Area teams, the league included the Los Angeles Angels, Seattle Rainiers, Portland Beavers, Sacramento Solons, Hollywood Stars and San Diego Padres.

The local San Francisco team had a splendid playing field aptly titled Seals Stadium, and Mark was continually begging his father to take him to a live game. There was one potential setback, which was emblematic of the city by the bay. On any given night, Seal Stadium could become shrouded in fog, which had a dramatic effect on both the players and the fans. Interestingly, very few games were canceled. Fog was just a reality that fans recognized as part and parcel of their role as loyal fans, as they shivered from the damp blanket that surrounded the ballpark.

There was an attraction that was the highlight of the summer games. Major league teams would come to San Francisco for exhibition games, giving fans an opportunity to see some of their favorite big-league players and, at the same time, see how their home team could compete with America's best. Pacific coast teams were labeled "farm clubs," which were sponsored by Major League counterparts. For the Seals, it was the New York Giants in the National League and the Yankees in the American League. Just recently, the Yankees "called up" the Seals' best hitter, Joe DiMaggio, because of his ability to hit home runs for the Seals.

William was constrained at his job, which demanded almost every waking moment of his time. He often found himself at his desk even on Sundays. Rita understood the demands of his management job at Walsh Furniture, but the boys had a difficult time dealing with the very limited availability of their industrious dad. William recognized that his fatherly absence was unhealthy for his relationships with

Mark and Tommy. To some degree, the boys, with their own circle of friends, compensated for William's absence by exploring the attractions surrounding their new home. One of those "attractions" that beckoned to both boys was Playland at the beach. The amusement park was located in the Richmond district at the western edge of San Francisco. Initially, Mark explained to his little brother that, for now, he wanted to check it out himself before Tommy was included. It was a good decision, especially when Jim Neto and Keith McDonald told Mark that the only way they could get to Playland and the Sutro Baths was to hitchhike on Lincoln Way, which would take them a few blocks from the amusement park. Sutro Baths?… Mark was soon to find out.

The three boys walked the two blocks to Lincoln Way, the main thoroughfare on the Sunset side of the park and used the recognized signal for hitchhiking. Hold up your thumb in the direction you are heading and hope for the best. This form of getting around the neighborhoods was the transportation preferred by young boys, and most important, it did not require any expense. Cars passed the trio, and after ten minutes of signaling, a man in a late-model Ford sedan stopped for them. The driver was a young man in his early twenties who laughed when they said they were headed for the beach. He said that when he was their age, he used the same technique. He let them out two blocks from their destination. Mark, for now, was feeling pleased with himself after his first "hitch" ride. He didn't let Jim and Keith know that this was his maiden voyage. When they arrived at the expansive amusement park, Mark, once more, was taken aback by what he saw. It was 10 acres of challenging, fright-invoking rides and games, unlike anything he had ever seen.

Then it struck him… Without any money, how were they going to take advantage of Playland? Finally, Keith laughed and let the new kid know that they had no intention of going on any of the rides. They had a mission that did not include the park. The "mission" was to collect as many deposit bottles of soft drinks as they could until they had accumulated enough change to purchase tickets for the Sutro Baths, which had been at this location since 1894. It was a massive glass enclosure consisting of seven swimming pools at different temperatures. There was one really large pool that included diving boards, slides and a high dive platform. An hour after they arrived at Playland, they had accumulated enough deposit change to purchase tickets at the bath for all three. The tickets included the rental of a pair of wool swimming trunks and a towel for the whole day. Mark was totally shocked when he saw the extent of the Sutro Baths. The three friends reveled in a day of swimming, diving, and riding all the attractions in one of the world's largest indoor swimming pools. As they finally headed home, the boys were happy, laughing and reveling in a day of pleasure and play that didn't cost anyone a dime.

Hitchhiking home, Mark realized that he was now a genuine member of the neighborhood teen community. In his mind, he knew that the Sunset district, with all of its travel treasures, far exceeded the Bay Street adventures, and he was just getting started. He had reservations about sharing this day with his parents. When he did finally tell his mom and dad, Rita and William were proud of his ingenuity, skill, and willingness to try new things. The following weekend, William did indeed take a day off to spend family recreation time with Rita and the boys. Taking a cue from Mark's trip to Sutro Baths, and after a little research, he found a genuine San Francisco attraction that would provide a perfect opportunity for all of the Doyles to do something really recreational… a day at the San Francisco Zoo, which was adjacent to the Fleishhacker Pool, one of the largest outdoor saltwater pools in the world. Both attractions were a mere block from Ocean Beach.

After seeing all the exotic animals at the zoo and munching popcorn, the family adjourned to the giant outdoor swimming pool. There was so much to see and do in the Bay Area, and the Fleishhacker pool was near the top of the to-do list. Once again, for Mark, they would all rent swimsuits and towels. This would also be the first occasion that an uncomfortable Mark and Tommy would see their parents in swimwear. When William and Rita emerged from the bathhouse, the boys became satisfied that they had nothing to be concerned about. If there was any reason to feel embarrassment, that was laid to rest. Mom and Dad, still in their twenties and thirties, were blessed with positive genes that provided both with well-proportioned figures. Rita could still compete in any beauty contest with her youthful, sleek figure, considering she had given birth to two healthy boys. As far as William was concerned, the potential anxiety was over the awareness that his left leg, brutalized in the War, and reinjured 10 years ago, would be difficult for a five-year-old to digest. William's leg, which occasionally required the use of a cane when his limp became a problem with balance, was surprisingly regenerated. There were scars from countless surgeries, but through sheer tenacity, he had willed himself to walk again. The giant pool was an opportunity for William to teach his sons how to swim. The brothers were also fascinated to see Sammy Lee, an Olympic diving champion, who had won a gold medal for platform diving in the 1932 Olympics.

The move to San Francisco was proving to be the right decision for William and Rita Doyle. As the year came to a close and they welcomed in 1939, they had nothing but positive future plans and aspirations. Rita Doyle missed her friends and family in LA, and she could really narrow that down to her mother and, more than anything, the need and desire to finally resolve the long silence and unwillingness of her father to accept her family. She could never bring herself to let William know how much the separation hurt. Her mother, on the other hand, had totally embraced her son-in-law, and she did everything she could to convince her unreasonable husband that his absence from their daughter's life would only create more of a chasm as time went on. In the meantime, Sylvia vowed that she would do everything in her power to solidify her bond with the entire Doyle family. Her relationship, in the face of some family dysfunction, had only strengthened her relationship with Rita. Even in the face of Herman's disapproval, she made regular trips from LA to San Francisco and, with every extended visit, grew more appreciative of William and her lovable, demonstrative grandchildren.

The thing that kept Rita from dwelling on her father's absence was the acceptance of her talent by the Bay Area art community. She also began to recognize that her pencil sketches were indeed limiting, and to that end, Rita made the decision to expand her willingness to explore the incorporation of additional media at least. She had always appreciated watercolor, which she now felt could address what she believed to be her shortcomings. Oil and acrylics tended to intimidate her, but watercolor, on the other hand, she had at least dabbled in as a viable way to modify—and, to some degree, transform her style. Three evenings a week, she attended classes on watercolor techniques and ultimately settled on an amalgam of ink with watercolor as a form of multimedia. Rita also determined that her narrow focus on pencil portraits was beginning to feel less appealing. In addition to the application of color, she also saw the need to expand her subject matter as a new resident of San Francisco. Rita had fallen in love with the style and diversity of the city by the bay. Everything from the cloaking fog of the city to the Powell Street cable cars to Telegraph Hill and the Golden Gate Bridge offered an endless array of potential subject matter that would not exclude her magic with portrait art. She planned to combine the city and its people in her new art form.

As time went on, she remained concerned over whether she was devoting enough time to William and her two boys. However, it was clear that she and every member of the Doyle family were engaged in exploring the diverse, welcoming new community that was the Bay Area. William's job at Walsh was all-consuming and left little time for his sons. Mark and little Tommy spent time with new friends and getting comfortable with all the City had to offer young people. It did not require all the past adoration that a mother quite naturally provided. Maybe an appreciative rhythm and a way of life were beginning to emerge, and they all were experiencing a different view.

CHAPTER 13

THE AFFAIR

As 1938 proceeded to fade, William was more engaged with his work at Walsh Furniture Inc. than he could ever have imagined. His efforts to establish a relationship with the diverse personnel were beginning to pay off. As Vice President of Human Resources, he spent extended periods commuting between the San Francisco Bay Area and the expansive communities that made up Southern California. William's style and methods of managing proved to be exactly what the Walshes, especially Jimmie, had hoped for. William was patient, demanding, and honest with personnel. He had developed a positive and respectful community of workers who appreciated their new boss, who was responsible for improving the morale and work environment.

He was spending more time at the flagship facility in Long Beach, mainly because they had been relatively ignored under the auspices of previous personnel management. With patience and energy, William began to turn around the very real concerns of the SoCal staff. Jimmie Walsh had been absolutely correct in his evaluation of William both as a friend and now a manager in the family's expanding business. In the face of the Depression, when factories were fighting to stay afloat, and others were closing their doors, Walsh Furniture Inc. was surging with its progressive technique and policies in doing business. The high morale of the working staff, both white-collar and blue-collar, was directly attributable to William Doyle's honest management methods. Just as William had led his men on the battlefields of France, his reasonable fairness engendered loyalty among the people who genuinely appreciated his style of leadership. William was fast becoming a recognizable fair-haired boy at Walsh. His future had no limits unless he did something that challenged his position. The potential for something began to emerge when Lauralie returned to California. As the Christmas season of 1938 arrived, the company decided to throw its first Holiday party for all of its workers. Perhaps next year the families could participate, but this year, Jimmie was using Christmas to gauge future events. The party was held a week before the holiday. There was also one exception to the "staff only" rule: Jimmie Walsh's younger sister would attend. Lauralie had been engaged to an airline pilot shortly after William and Rita were married. After almost nine years, she decided that her husband's continuous absence from their relationship and the fact that he was cheating were reasons enough to call a halt to the marriage. The company party with all the gala trappings should have been nothing more than an opportunity to mix with his personnel and exchange humorous gifts, but it turned out to be far more than he anticipated.

Seeing Lauralie again was like nothing he could envision. When they were reintroduced to each other, it was clear that this night would usher in a period of unbridled sex. William was doing something that made him feel both dirty and disloyal. His marriage, unlike Lauralie's, was a bond that he thought would never break. The idea of a one-night stand with an old girlfriend could be justified as harmless, but William knew that it was more than just that. The truth is, he mused, a man could love two women. In clearheaded moments, he recognized that Lauralie was a dazzling carnal partner whom he really didn't know. With Rita, he exercised total sexual and intellectual compatibility and genuine love. He continued to justify his infidelity, knowing that he was ultimately risking the love and fidelity of a woman whom he knew was loyal to him only. It was the holiday season, and William did what, up until this point, was out of the question; he lied to his wife and carried on an insatiable sexual affair that he knew would eventually have to end if he wanted to save his marriage.

His excuse explaining his absence to Rita was relatively easy to lie about. He was traveling more to the company offices in Southern California. Lauralie had moved back to LA, stayed with her parents in Palos Verdes for two months, and eventually purchased an apartment in Santa Monica. Early in 1939, William and Lauralie were having lunch at The Dome on Sunset Blvd. William's intention in this conversation was to tell his paramour that it was time to end the affair. He was concerned that his wife was beginning to question the amount of time he was spending in Southern California. Lauralie knew that this eventuality would come to pass, but to her, the relationship with William was more than just a sexual relationship. She had fallen in love with him. She knew that William was having reservations about their secretive sexual rendezvous, and it was clear to her that she was not replacing Rita. William had not stopped loving his wife, and that was apparent from the start of the affair. Initially, Lauralie had no intention of carrying their relationship beyond the amorous excitement of sexual compatibility, but she was aware that affairs of the heart were beyond conscience.

William and Lauralie were deep in conversation when William looked up to see Sylvia Geller heading for their table. He did not panic, but he was aware that friends or family members might see them together. He was prepared. William stood up to greet his mother-in-law and warmly embrace her. Without pause, he introduced Lauralie, noting that she was a member of his staff. Small talk ensued, and after the usual farewells, Sylvia returned to her table, where she was having lunch with a girlfriend. Without any signs of panic, William and Lauralie continued with their meal, and as they were leaving, they stopped by Sylvia's table with the requisite "nice meeting you." In truth, as they departed, William was convinced that even though they had kept their composure, Sylvia had no part of it. William had a grinding in his stomach that presaged a potential confrontation with Rita.

Lauralie suggested that, for now, they should take a reprieve from seeing each other. More than anything, she did not want to be perceived as "the other woman." The thought of not seeing Lauralie was painful, but they both agreed that the Sylvia meeting could conceivably prove to be problematic. The New Year did portend the possibility that Sylvia could share the fact that she casually ran into William and a stunning staff member at The Dome, but she was not someone who would gossip. The thought that she could prove to be instrumental as a threat to her daughter's marriage was inconceivable.

Both Rita and her mother were dealing with some chilling news from family members in Germany. In November of 1938, they were certainly aware of harsh antisemitic acts being perpetrated by the Nazi Reich, but the latest news was far more ominous. Hitler and his thugs were now moving to a far more alarming series of anti-Jewish pogroms. The "Night of Broken Glass" was the first act of real violence against the Jews. The Gellers had close relatives living in Germany, and many were considering leaving the only home they had ever known. Herman was among many American Jews who felt the need to act against this frightening turn of violence. Anti-Semitism had always been a part of American life, but of late it had surfaced at an alarming rate, influenced by events in Germany. Henry Ford and Charles Lindbergh were whipping up new levels of hate with their America-First anti-Jewish and anti-war propaganda. On the radio, Father Coughlin was authoring his own version of evil and hate. Anti-Semitism was reaching a frightening zenith in America. Also, it was clear that the Reich had no intention of leniency as they were building a formidable war machine. Sylvia felt that what was happening in Western Europe was far more profound than what she perceived at the Dome in LA, and for now, she made the determination to internalize her suspicion.

CHAPTER 14

WALSH INC.

In his fourteenth year, Mark was more than a little excited about entering high school. He was not an especially good student and settled with B's and C's. His parents were displeased with his lack of academic enthusiasm, but they had no intention of doling out any form of discipline. Rita was a firm believer in education and felt that Mark was far from reaching his potential. He had four years to improve his grades, which would qualify him for the best colleges. Mark was highly enthusiastic about sports, placing more emphasis on baseball than algebra. He entered Lincoln High and tried out for the freshman-sophomore baseball team. Coach Lacy was instantly impressed with Mark's talent. He had never had a player in their early teens with so much skill. Lacy was frustrated about where to play Mark. He was a talented pitcher with a fastball that was better than varsity pitchers, and as far as hitting was concerned, Mark had no peers. Frank Collins, the varsity coach, asked Lacy if he would allow this baseball prodigy to play for the varsity team. Lacy agreed to compromise and would release Mark after his freshman year. In essence, Mark knew that his education was an important component in his future, but he found everything, except history, uninspiring. He was a good son and would do almost anything to please his parents, but they had never attended any of his games. Throughout his high school career, the coaching staff would argue over how they would employ Mark's unrivaled athletic talent. Lacy and Collins were thoughtful coaches who, in addition to leading Lincoln sports teams, were also credentialed members of the teaching staff.

There was no end to Mark's talent and capability. Through his formative years, he had maintained his interest in music and tended toward the kind of progressive jazz that was happening in San Francisco. The piano that his parents purchased proved to be the right investment. Mark had a perfect ear, and his playing just came to him naturally. The Snows did not agree and had lodged several complaints over the years.

Tommy Doyle was the polar opposite of his brother. At 5 years old, unlike his brother, Tommy was not the least bit interested in sports. He was quiet, unassuming, and, even though his age did not warrant any real conclusions on his interests, he was reading anything dealing with science and technology, specifically how things work. If a toy Tommy received for Christmas could be taken apart, he would— predictably—do so, and then put it back together. Rita was finding it difficult to gauge what he would find challenging. He was, as always, incredibly close to his big brother, but the days of needing Mark as a protector had passed. Tommy was a sturdy first grader who let everyone know that he could stand on his own. With almost ten years separating the brothers, they had both reached an age where dependency was not at the foundation of their relationship—love was. There is a skill that should be mentioned when defining Tommy's interests. It was no surprise that he inherited a talent for art. He would sit for hours watching his mother painting and sketching her subject. He did not ask Rita for her help in recognizing his interest. He just watched, and it totally confused Rita. In looking through his schoolwork, recognition began to emerge. Tommy sketched classmates in the margins of his papers. Like her mom in so many ways, Rita decided to let her son determine when and if he wanted to ask for her help. His sketches were incredibly skilled for a 5-year-old.

1939 gave Americans some sense of marginal relief from the Depression. President Roosevelt had initiated a series of national programs that were helping put people back to work. With the repeal of Prohibition, it seemed that the nation was on a positive path. For the Doyle family, their status was, if anything, showing upward mobility. The Walshes were highly pleased with their son's judgment in hiring William Doyle. Their initial impression was that Jimmie was just rewarding a war buddy. Those reservations were sharply curtailed once William grew into a significant role as a Human Resources Manager. He was abundantly skilled at managing and was clearly a key member of the management team of Walsh Furniture Inc., with a bright future as the company expanded.

There was one aspect of William's personal life that concerned Walter and Barbara Walsh: the fact that William and their daughter, Lauralie, were having an affair. They both felt that William and Lauralie were two consenting adults, and while they had strong reservations, they were loath to interfere. William had so much to lose, but the Walshes were well aware that this was an affair that he had started almost ten years earlier. If an opportunity did come to pass, Walter would express his profound concern to reinforce the fact that the couple had no future and could jeopardize their status. William was well aware of the danger that his affair had created for both of them. If the clandestine meetings with Lauralie were to continue, they both would be highly aware of the hazards. It was also a possibility that, after seeing them at lunch, Sylvia could at any moment blow the whistle. He had no idea that the elder Walshes knew of the ongoing tryst. William's primary concern was how Rita would react if Sylvia shared her suspicions. He was dealing with a combination of longing and guilt. His selfish actions were now at a point where he could totally destroy his marriage, and he could conceivably lose his family. Both William and Lauralie knew that, painful as it would be, they had to end the affair. Lauralie was not what would be termed a homewrecker. It was always clear that William was deeply in love with his wife, and that reality motivated Lauralie to give up the man whom she finally, in her heart, knew she loved. The alarm that Sylvia engendered was more than anything the voice of finality whispering that the affair was over. There were just too many blinking red lights. Rita did have some questions about William's behavior. Lately, the amount of time that he was spending at the Southern California office was somewhat disconcerting, but not enough of a concern to confront her husband.

As 1939 moved into Spring, with all that was happening in Europe, she was hearing from many of her relatives that the Nazis were perpetrating a series of appalling actions against all the Jews. The German liner Saint Louis sailed from Hamburg to Havana, Cuba, with over 900 Jewish passengers seeking sanctuary based on Nazi persecution. Cuba did not allow the Saint Louis landing papers and turned the ship away. Saint Louis sailed north to the United States and Canada to seek refuge, but was not permitted to dock. The ship was forced to return to Europe, and the passengers were ultimately victims of Hitler's murderous policies for the extermination of Jews. Two cousins and their parents, close relatives of Rita, were on board the doomed ship. She never experienced such a feeling of being so completely helpless. Hitler and the SS finally invaded Poland and methodically began to round up Jews. Their fate at the time was not known, and once again Rita and her family lamented ominous news of their treatment. All of Europe and most of the world were becoming aware of the Nazis' brutal policy of conquering all of their neighbors.

Attempts at seeking a negotiated peace were ignored as Hitler invaded France and Belgium. Two weeks later, most of Western Europe surrendered. America continued to maintain a policy of neutrality in the face of the gathering storm. England remained the final bastion and stood alone against the rampaging German Blitzkrieg. Roosevelt attempted to avoid any direct U.S. participation by providing England with weapons negotiated by a program called "Lend-Lease."

The Walshs were invited to Washington to meet with the Roosevelt's Office of Price Administration to discuss a possible contract with their company. This diversion allowed a proper cooling-off period for William's affair with Lauralie. He was invited to join the team of company managers that flew to Washington in early 1940. Even Jimmie Walsh and his parents could not help but be surprised at the magnitude of what the U.S. Government had in mind. This was the initial step in the negotiation, but it was a detailed plan that would require all the planning and organizing that Walsh Furniture Inc. could muster. While the U.S. had not entered the War in Europe, the President was convinced that ultimately, the U.S. would declare its intentions. America was building an arsenal that would require the engagement and power of the U.S. corporations and manufacturing. Walsh was asked to come up with a detailed plan and estimated cost of manufacturing and installing the furniture in the wardrooms and quarters for officers in the West Coast Sixth Fleet. This would be a monumental monetary task, but after the initial meetings, the Walsh managers agreed that this contract would be a challenge, but at the same time, organizationally feasible.

The Walshes became much more aware of William's contribution to the success of the company. In a relatively short period, he had totally reorganized the structure of hiring, promotion, and salaries. In general, after observing William's skill at leading people, the workers at Walsh Furniture Inc. appreciated his positive approach in dealing with the entire workforce. Now more than ever, he would be called on to handle the demands of staffing for the formidable challenge that Walsh had landed with the Federal government.

The company would start with 200 new employees who would be integrated with the current staff of craftsmen, designers, accountants and general workers. William recognized that he had minimized the hiring, but he believed that you could always hire more people as the need arose. At this early stage of increasing personnel, the important thing was to hire qualified professionals who would help him grow the company. He also had ideas that, in some quarters of management, were resented.

A good example of William's judgment and creative style was his suggestion to Jimmie and his parents that they consider modifying the company name. If Walsh Furniture Inc. was going to be competing with the big boys, it would require a new level of sophistication. The current company banner was "clunky," and William had done some research and found that simplifying the name would position the company for the future. Key management supported a multi-poster presentation that would be favorable for the new moniker. Walter and Barbara approved of William personally, but they were less than enthusiastic about changing the name that Walter's parents had built over 50 years ago. William was well prepared for the presentation that would, on the surface, not be well received by the majority of managers. Except for William, Jimmie and a couple of designers, no one had seen the idea that William was proposing. His confidence in the presentation was apparent as the management staff of Walsh Furniture Inc. filed into the room. An easel was set up on the dais next to William, and that was the extent of what he had to present. Everyone in the boardroom was less than impressed, except for Jimmie and a couple of designers. With an air of confidence, William led the pessimists through a series of sales charts and graphs that pointed to why a name change was logical and necessary. All this led to the final card when the lights in the room faded, and the curtain glided open, revealing William's intentions. The bold idea was attractively bathed in a spotlight, and supportive music played dramatically as the screen revealed: 'Walsh Inc.' William contended that the new logo positioned the company for the future without being pigeonholed with the word "furniture." There was a hush in the boardroom, followed by whistling and resounding applause. Walter was standing with an appreciative look on his face. The room of leaders could not be more responsive and pleased. The "Walsh" name was intact, and it became clear that William's only intention was to modify it for the future.

As the men dispersed, Walter and Barbara asked William and Jimmie to stay. What followed was not anticipated but steered William in a direction that would ensure his future with the company. Walter stood up and offered kudos to William and Jimmie, who together had brought his company into the 20th century. The patriarch took them back to the start on a battlefield in France, where loyalty and instincts bound the men for life. William was incredulous and wondered why Walter had called them together. He did not have to wait long… Barbara spoke and almost reduced William to giggling. Walsh was promoting him to a new position as Vice President of Personnel and Marketing with a monthly salary of $5,000. Just a little over a year ago, he wasn't sure he could pay the rent. William excused himself with "Wait till Rita hears this!" When he arrived home, he had champagne and flowers in hand. Rita understandably was thrilled and, at the same time, proud of what her husband had accomplished. A jubilant couple spent that evening drinking champagne, eating potato chips and making love. To the Doyles, this was the best day of their lives together. $5000 a month was more than enough to afford their first taste of homeownership. Timing could not be better. Halloween was two weeks away, followed by Thanksgiving and Christmas. They talked and toasted to the incredible turn of events.

As 1940 was approaching, Rita and William had much to be thankful for and so much to look forward to. A real celebration was called for, and before the night was over, they began making a list. Rita would send an invitation to her family, aware that she would exclude her father, as longing turned into anger. Patrick, David Grossman, Tony Fernandez, Sylvia, Jimmie, Mrs. Sarah Greeley, and Johnny Walker would be at the top of the list. For a moment, William's mind turned to Lauralie. The next morning, Mark and, to some degree, Tommy were included in the good news, followed by, *"Can I have a bike?"* At almost fifteen, Mark did not totally understand what had transpired, but it was beginning to set in. He was mature for his age, and no one should be surprised at his next query, *"Are we going to move?"*

William was somewhat taken aback, and he genuinely did not know how to respond. He knew that soon, he and Rita would have to discuss a potential move commensurate with a VP who earned $5,000 a month. Because of the many discussions between Rita and William that the boys overheard, maybe it was time to discuss it as a family to eliminate a sense of insecurity on the part of Mark and, to a lesser extent, Tommy. The conversation was intense, but it was clear that the two boys were not having any of it. Mark was playing baseball and football as a freshman on the varsity team at Lincoln High, and

Tommy was in kindergarten at Lawton Grammar School just a few blocks from their home. They were understandably upset at the prospect of moving in the middle of the school year. Rita and William were somewhat surprised at the instant reaction of their sons, but it was a legitimate argument. Rita expressed that she was not getting the time she needed to deal with her customer base. William found the conversation to be entirely different than what he had anticipated and was totally entertained by the passion that his sons felt about 26th Avenue. They both loved "their block" and the thought of moving now was unthinkable. The senior Doyles had a subsequent conversation, which took all the negative concerns to heart and settled on the reality of waiting until the following year… 1941. In the meantime, they would start looking at homes that would be satisfactory for all family members. They both felt that the San Francisco Peninsula was the most attractive and yet close to work. San Mateo and Burlingame fit their needs and, in truth, would be more convenient than the Sunset, and they both offered a wide range of home values and excellent schools. They were almost pastoral towns with main streets that mirrored suburban America. Next was the "Can I have a bike?" conversation with Mark. Rita made the point that kids in the Sunset didn't ride bicycles for any number of reasons, so when the reality was put to Mark, he would understand and consider staying on 26th Avenue a good trade-off. More than anything, he wanted to be one of the very few kids who owned bikes. Mark's popularity was important to him.

CHAPTER 15

THE BEATING

October also ushered in the most exciting time of year for the brothers; Halloween was just around the corner. The Sunset, with flats close together, was ideal for "trick or treat," and in those days, the "trick" was purposeful. Mark and 6-year-old Thomas each dressed up as hobos and carried a bag at the end of a stick for the treats. With her creative skills, Rita reveled in putting together a down-and-out look for her boys. Hoboes were part of the Depression hallmarks that America could not shed fast enough. Halloween was one of those pseudo-holidays that called for a real get-together of all the kids in the neighborhood. The "crew" that represented their block consisted of the Doyles, Jimmie Neto, Keith McDonald and Donnie Stark. Young girls, for reasons unknown, were not part of the yearly horde. As the evening progressed, the kids from the adjoining blocks would share which flats were the most generous with treats. For Mark and Tommy, that night was one of the most exciting they had ever experienced. Going from house to house with two families in each flat was, in most cases, a bonanza of goodies. The most popular seemed to be saltwater taffy, candy apples, and black licorice whips, but the mischief was what most of the older boys enjoyed the most.

Nothing done was destructive, but it definitely was in the trick category. There was a five-story apartment on the corner of 26th and Irving. It seemed to have the most appeal for trickery, primarily because the neighborhood kids had no idea who lived there. The marauding legion stuck pins in the entry buttons, and the buzzers went off in all the units. It created a worthwhile frenzy. Next, the group consisting of representatives from adjacent blocks ran down Irving Street, waxing all the car windows as they headed for Mari's Beauty Salon. They knew it would be open on a Friday night, and Keith had the idea of stacking milk crates blocking the front door exit. It looked like the optimum trick, but no one realized that there was a rear exit— but it didn't matter. Instead of havoc, the escape route in the rear echoed with laughter as the ladies exited Mari's. The Doyle boys' first Halloween in the Sunset was a resounding success. Mark had been the best big brother and included Tommy in all the evening's activities.

Early in November, William and Rita threw a get-together for their closest friends to celebrate William's promotion. There were some surprises, both good and, to say the least, painful. The party was a celebratory success, with Patrick arriving with Sarah Greeley, the landlord at the Ethel Arms Apartments. Now that was one of the many highlights of the evening. Sylvia once again took on the responsibility of determining the menu that was predictably catered. Herman Geller, as always, was absent. With Prohibition in the rear-view mirror, champagne and hard liquor flowed as a disparate group of friends convened to wish the Doyles much success and prosperity. In addition to Patrick's pleasant surprise, Jimmie Walsh was there with his latest date, and the couple looked very seriously taken with each other. At 40, it was time for their dear friend and employer to take a wife. Johnny Walker, David Grossman, Tony Fernandez, Doris McNulty, his secretary and their spouses were in attendance, along with established friends from the Men's Store as well as couples from Mansfield. The fact that Mark was skilled on the piano, as always, added entertainment to the evening. He played by ear, and if he wasn't reading music, he would improvise.

As the party wound down, Jimmie Walsh asked to have a moment with William, and there was a need for the two to convene in the next room. Jimmie was almost apologetic about having to break the news to William that Lauralie was in the hospital after suffering a beating at the hands of her current boyfriend. Because Walsh was aware of the romantic connection between his sister and William, he felt he was taking a chance in notifying his friend, especially considering the nature of the evening. She was badly bruised with contusions on her face and arms, and other injuries that included three broken ribs. No one could predict it, but William glazed over and felt faint. It was his response that relieved Jimmie of any doubt about including him sometime that night. Lauralie had just been admitted to the LA County Hospital early last evening. After the initial shock, William felt an unfamiliar sense of anger, yet he also felt a deeply rooted caring for a woman who occupied an unfathomable place in his heart. He wanted to know who her attacker was. Jimmie felt there was time for vengeance in the future, but for now, Lauralie needed support.

Later that night, William shared the news with Rita, who reacted with genuine concern. She had met Lauralie on several occasions in recent years, and her instincts told her not to dwell on possibilities. She remembered a moment two years ago when she had experienced what could only be described as jealousy. A foreign emotion she had never before experienced, which gave her cause to wonder. Rita's concern was magnified when William announced the next morning that he was flying to Los Angeles to deal with some personnel issues. She could not let him leave without asking if he was going to the hospital to see Lauralie. He was hesitant to respond, but did add that if time allowed, he would stop to see her. Alarm bells were going off. William knew how the trip to LA might look, but he could not lie to her, especially since he had announced her condition last evening. William searched his soul to help him decide to be at Lauralie's side. His wife was suspicious, but for now, he would deal with her concern later. When he arrived at the hospital, he was notified that Lauralie was only allowing visits from direct family members.

William asked the nurse on duty to tell her that he had arrived from San Francisco. William was instantly granted a positive response and held his breath as he entered her room. Lauralie had been badly beaten with bruises and contusions all over her body, but that did not stop her from feeling sheer joy at seeing William. She burst into tears the instant she saw him. Even with all the superficial injuries, William could still see the beauty of his paramour. William stayed long enough to assure her that he would be there for her as she recuperated from her serious injuries. An hour later, he talked to her doctor, who shared that the healing process, considering the seriousness of some of the wounds, could take at least a week.

During the subsequent days, William shared the visitations with Walter and Barbara Walsh, as well as Jimmie Walsh. There were moments of discomfort, but the concern over Lauralie preempted all personal feelings. William left the hospital with the recognition that he needed to call Rita to inform her that he would require a week or more to deal with a problem at his LA office. There was silence at the other end of the call. That pause without words clearly surfaced the feeling that Rita was more than a little suspicious. To her, the fact that Lauralie was hospitalized and there was family taking care of her needs, she was having difficulty understanding why William was in close attendance. She absolutely hated being put in this position, but her female instincts could not be held at bay much longer. During the following week, he spent as much time as was allowed by Lauralie's side. Over and over again, she insisted that William's absence from home would create a problem with Rita's marriage security. He knew she was right and ultimately took it to heart and flew back to San Francisco with a promise that he would see her as soon as he could legitimately return. During his return, he could not help but think about the man who beat her. For now, he would have to quell his anger. His priority had to be convincing Rita that Lauralie was a family member whom he owed so much, which is why, outside of the immediate family, he was the only close friend allowed in the hospital room. Good luck.

William returned home late that evening, and Rita was asleep. He was thankful because the last thing he wanted that night was a confrontation with Rita. The next morning, Rita followed her routine of taking care of the boys and fixing their lunches. She was less than enthusiastic about the meal that the school offered. Mark and Tommy greeted their dad on the way out the door. It was anything but a "normal" morning at the Doyles. Other than a smile and the requisite kiss, nothing was said. Throughout the return trip, William was literally rehearsing how he would defend himself, but Rita had a different idea.

As they sat for coffee, she had words that did not involve any response from her husband. In emphatic, clear terms, Rita started to speak. She opened her comments with a sentiment-inducing reality, saying she loved William with all her heart, and through the almost ten years of their marriage, her feelings towards him had not changed. William started to speak, but Rita put her hand on his mouth. She was taking command over the first real crisis in their time together. Rita continued; she was not sure that William and Lauralie were in the throes of an affair, but her instincts told her so. She went on… The one thing she would not do is play the poor little wife's role or position herself as a victim. She was much too proud for that. She continued… If William was in love, she would be heartbroken and give him his independence. She had no thought of reducing herself to highly charged emotions… Rita was owed the truth, and ultimately, if she was wrong, she would profusely apologize. Continuing… She was not going to put herself in a competition with another woman. What she knew of Lauralie was purely platonic, and she would admit that Lauralie was a beautiful woman. If William can deal with the potential of choosing between two admittedly attractive women, let her know now. She added… My guess is the relationship was going on long before they were married, but if he continued with the affair, that is where Rita would draw the line. She would divorce him.

To say that William's wife's comments totally took him aback would be an understatement, coupled with shock. While Rita was speaking, he strangely felt a sense of admiration for the way she dealt with the sensitivities of the moment. Foremost, his response was fear of losing the woman he truly loved and wanted to spend his life with. There was an interminable silence until William spoke. Yes, the relationship with Lauralie Walsh dated well before he had asked Rita to marry him, and there was no question that her instincts were generally correct. He added that to him, Lauralie was a broken woman who had been traumatized by the terrible beating. He cared very much for her, but he had no question about his intentions. He loved Rita with all his heart and would not do anything that would put at risk the one thing in his life that he had absolutely no doubt about. When he realized how emphatic and brave Rita was, the reality of what transpired brought him to the edge of tears. Rita came over to her husband and gave him the kind of kiss that said, *"I think we are going to survive this."* If he ever needed reinforcement of the way he felt about Rita, the last hour would bear witness. William had to put Lauralie in the legitimate category of "a friend." Time will tell.

That Christmas, the Doyle family of San Francisco celebrated what was probably the most joyous Christmas William could ever remember. His family was happy to be staying in the Sunset for at least another year. He had been promoted to a new job as Vice President of Walsh Inc. His salary was more than he ever could have dreamed. His boys were healthy and a source of deep pride. He had salvaged what might have been the end of his marriage, and most important, William revealed how much he genuinely wanted the beautiful Rita to forgive him. Christmas was a unique, almost foreign holiday that was beginning to feel more comfortable. Jews did not celebrate Christmas, and if she had her way, they would not. Rita had learned that the highest of all Christian holidays could be modified enough to make it palatable for a "nice Jewish girl." The tree was decorated with ornaments that did not in any way suggest anything but religious neutrality. While William's Christmas as a young man was Catholic orthodox, out of respect for Rita, a church service was not part of their Holiday.

A Bar Mitzvah for the boys, conversely, was out of the question. The day was gala in other ways; the elder Doyle, with Sarah Greeley on his arm, announced that they were engaged. At 71 years old, Patrick was overjoyed to have a second chance to share his life with Sarah, who was already a favorite of Rita's. The Grossmans, while also feeling a little out of place on Christmas, took comfort in the Jewish ally that Rita represented. Finally, Jimmie Walsh was in attendance and, would you believe it, with the same girl on his arm. His good friend let him know that Lauralie was out of the hospital and recuperating at their parents' home. Using good judgment, William thought follow-up questions about her health were better left unsaid.

CHAPTER 16

TRAUMA

As 1941 rolled into focus, the world seemed to erupt with Germany's Hitler invading many of its neighbors. After telling the West that he had no intentions of additional aggression, Poland was invaded, and soon all of Western Europe was occupied. Rita was preoccupied with the news after she had attempted to make contact with her family members in Germany and Holland. While information was scarce, there were ominous signs of Jewish genocide. She attended several meetings of Jewish unity in Hollywood, Beverly Hills, and Santa Monica, but the news that could be gleaned from a few reliable sources was all tragically disconcerting.

Sadly, Rita felt the disaster that the Jews of Europe were dealing with was close to home. Tommy had been looking for a brush in his mother's art supplies to paint a model airplane he was working on. In his search, he found a couple of publications along with several devastating pictures of the Nazi's unimaginable treatment of European Jews. Articles painted torturous visuals of Jewish families being stuffed into railcars and murdered if they didn't obey. The horrific pictures were more than Tommy could begin to comprehend. He was hesitant to tell his mom what he had seen, but he hoped to understand what was happening to those people. In truth, he should not have rummaged through Rita's things, but that was not enough to dissuade him.

With the evidence in hand, a very innocent Tommy asked his mother what they meant. Realizing what he had uncovered, she haltingly took her son into the living room, sat him down, and attempted to explain the pictures in a way that a 7-year-old would understand. It was a binary choice that offered no feasible options, and Rita was left with telling her son what was transpiring in Europe to her people. She never could have anticipated the possibility of her children seeing this documentation, but now she had to tell Tommy more than she ever intended about her Judaism. Seeing the quizzical look on his face made her realize that going too far would risk traumatizing her youngest impressionable son. The choice created a dilemma that Rita knew she had to avoid. She soft pedaled the publications, saying the people in those pictures were actors in a movie. Tommy was not satisfied and asked, *"What movie?"* Rita abruptly ended the conversation and began to wonder if this tragic series of events would ever end.

With the Emergency Shipbuilding Plan underway, San Francisco was the largest repair facility on the West Coast. Both Mare Island and Hunters Point were in the process of building warships as well as merchant ships to aid Great Britain. In addition to the Bay Area, Long Beach and Puget Sound were busy with shipbuilding and repairs. There were many other facilities beyond this core group that Walsh Inc. also contracted with. It was clear to the Walsh team that while the U.S. had not entered the war in Europe, the U.S. government was rapidly building both merchant and warships in shipyards on both coasts. Roosevelt was surely anticipating that we would be drawn into World War II, and through Lend-Lease, we were already building a fleet of Kaiser Merchant ships bound for England.

William and his team of designers and skilled project managers went to work instantly to get started with a demand that was going to test the skill and capability of Walsh Inc. The work was all-consuming as William traveled up and down the coast from Long Beach to Puget Sound. Encouragingly, it was anticipated that San Francisco would have the most extensive shipbuilding on the West coast, with Bethlehem and U.S. Steel almost adjacent to Walsh Inc. in industrial South San Francisco. The Naval yard in Long Beach was also in demand and convenient for Walsh's offices and factories in close proximity. Thankfully, other furniture builders on the East Coast would be responsible for their respective areas.

William needed to find time to spend with his family, especially considering how close he came to losing Rita. He would, at some time in the near future, find himself in a room with Lauralie, but with the stakes so high, there was no returning to what might have been. Mark and Tommy missed their dad, but Rita had explained that his new responsibility at Walsh Inc. was highly demanding. Hopefully, in the very near future, he could spend more time with his family. The boys seemed to understand. Thankfully, they both had enough going on in their young lives that they presumably could deal with the limitations of not seeing their dad for now. Mark, at 15, was doing well at Lincoln High and had developed a circle of friends that included some very attractive young girls. Mark's priority, however, was baseball. The coaches at Lincoln all recommended that they should manage Mark's athletic talent slowly. He was unquestionably capable enough to play for Varsity, but for his first year, he would pitch for the Freshman/Sophomore squad. The love of sports was one of the activities that kept his mind away from seeing his father less often. He knew that his grades were directly linked to his ability to participate in team sports.

That was not an issue for Mark. He was a quick learner and a favorite of almost all of his teachers, with the exception of Mrs. Hadley, who taught World History. One occasion when she was discussing the history of the Middle East, she made a comment that Mark took issue with. Mrs. Hadley explained that, historically, the Jews were responsible for the death of Christ. Mark raised his hand, and when his teacher called on him, he cautiously referred to his textbook and pointed out that the Romans killed Christ. Mrs. Hadley said that was incorrect and pointed to the Bible. Mark knew he would be in trouble if he responded, but he felt his teacher was blatantly wrong, and that is how he responded. She told him to sit down, and with that, Mark left the room. What followed was a two-week suspension requested by Mrs. Hadley. As the news spread, Mark's friends gathered in front of the school and could not believe what had transpired. They wanted to demonstrate, but Mark talked them out of it, saying it was not the end of the world. That evening over dinner, Mark explained what had happened at school and that he had been suspended for two weeks. Fortuitously, it was a night when William was home with his family. Upon hearing the story, both Rita and William were incensed. Mark was an excellent student who did not deserve to be suspended. The next day, still angry, Mark's dad decided to deal with the injustice proactively. Unbeknownst to Mark, he had made an appointment with the school principal, who had said he wasn't available until the next day. William showed up anyway and demanded to see Mr. Heller. William walked right into his office and asked if the principal condoned what had transpired in Mrs. Hadley's class. Heller said he knew that Mark had been suspended due to his blatant disrespect for Mrs. Hadley. William was fuming and told the principal in no uncertain terms that he wanted Mark back in school, but not in Mrs. Hadley's class. The principal was visibly shaken by William's commanding presence and adhered to the demands. Mark attended class the next day and was assigned to the senior class on World History. When word got out that Mark was reinstated, they were in awe of what Mr. Doyle had done. To no one's surprise, he was lauded, and Mark was more popular than ever.

CHAPTER 17

INTERNMENT CAMPS

1941

- **President Roosevelt announced plans to build 300 merchant ships at a cost of $300 million.**
- **The Senate passes the Lend-Lease Law, providing for the U.S. to supply military equipment to the Allies.**
- **Massive German armies launched Operation Barbarossa and invaded the Soviet Union.**
- **The first Allied convoy to Russia takes place as Churchill promises Stalin that a convoy will sail to Russia every 10 days.**
- **U.S. Declared War on Germany and Japan**

Mark Doyle, as a Sophomore at Lincoln High School, was going to play baseball for the varsity. At 16, Mark was to pitch and play outfield when he wasn't on the mound. As a member of the Freshman/Sophomore team in his first year, Mark pitched all 6 games and won all of them, including a no-hitter against Lowell High School in the Richmond district. There is no question that Mark was probably the finest athlete that Lincoln High had ever produced. Some in his direct contact were even more impressed with his burgeoning skill at the piano. Over the years, Mark's talent was impressive and revered by the family, but for now, athletics was his priority. The piano was a natural extension.

Tommy Doyle was in the first grade at Lawton Grammar School and was struggling to keep up. It became apparent that he probably should have been held back. His teachers felt that since he had celebrated his birthday in August, starting school in September may have been premature. Rita and William both felt that holding him back could cause unanticipated damage to Tommy's self-esteem, especially with the awareness that his classmates would be moving on without him.

William Doyle spent the months hiring 200 new employees to be assigned to the huge government contract awarded to Walsh Inc. With the volume of work anticipated, this was going to be merely the first phase of hiring.

As reports continued to surface out of Western Europe, Rita was devastated when she learned that her aunt and her uncle Geller had been arrested in Dresden, and along with her cousin, were sent to a camp named Auschwitz. She had no information about their fate after they were in the custody of the Nazis.

While all the headlines in 1941 were dealing with the War in Europe and the Japanese invasion of China, the American people were, by and large, opposed to the United States entering World War II. Isolationists under an "America First" banner sought to influence American public opinion, led by aviator Charles Lindbergh and radio priest Father Charles Coughlin, who, along with Henry Ford, were patently antisemitic. Meanwhile, for most of the U.S., it was life as usual. Rita's up-close concerns, along with many American Jews, was attempting to sound the alarm. With the exception of Rita, the Doyle family was relatively neutral about the events unfolding on the European continent.

The Sunday, December 7th's attack by Japan shocked the nation. President Roosevelt convened Congress and, to no one's surprise, declared War on Germany and Japan. William knew from his meetings with the government and his contract conversations on behalf of Walsh Inc. that the U.S. ultimately would enter the War. America's relationship with Japan had been tense for the past year over criticism of their invasion of China and other Far East countries, and America's unwillingness to supply the Japanese forces with fuel. The devastation of the U.S. naval fleet in Pearl Harbor and the 2400 American lives lost was a bitter blow.

The world for the Doyle family, like so many others, would never be the same. At 41, William knew that with his terrible injuries suffered in World War I, he would not be enlisting, but with two sons, his mind turned towards their potential fate. Mark was just 16, but if the War continued, he would be engaged and that aside, he knew his son would enlist. That would have to wait a year or two until he graduated from high school. Mark was enrolled in the ROTC, the Reserved Officers' Training Corps, which he joined when he was a freshman. If he improved his grades, he would at least enter the Navy as an officer. Every member of the Doyle family would be involved in the War effort. William, as had been anticipated, was traveling up and down the West coast, moving from one project to the next. The fact that the largest shipbuilding facility was in the Bay Area at least allowed William to spend a considerable amount of time at home in San Francisco.

Walsh Inc. was not only designing wardrooms for officers on U.S. Naval vessels, but was also engaged in totally appointing those quarters and dining areas. Jimmie Walsh did alert William to the fact that he had hired Lauralie to work at the company's design facility in

Long Beach. He also made it clear that his sister was very capable and had convinced Jimmie that she was clean and had gone for almost a year without any relapses. A month later, William visited the Southern California facility and made it a point to stop by Lauralie's office. He took a deep breath and asked her assistant to tell her he was here.

Since the finality of their relationship, William had not seen Lauralie in two years. When they greeted, his thoughts of their time together were poignantly relived. At 38, she looked fresh and rejuvenated, which was a long way from the last time he had seen her in the hospital. She looked wonderful and, in the time apart, she had turned her life around. They hugged and lingered for what seemed a warm eternity. Whatever the flame was that brought them together had not totally expired, and they both knew it. After exchanging pleasantries, they laughed over the little amount of time it took for yesterday's lovers to feel comfortable. Time does have a way of forgetting and healing. Lauralie emphasized that, in essence, she was working in his department and at the same time, she had the advantage of being the daughter of the company's owner. They both had a good laugh, and William was thinking about asking her to dinner, but on second thought, he knew it would be a mistake.

Tommy was almost as industrious as his father and was looking for opportunities where he could contribute to the War effort. Still, he was confused about some of the actions being taken by the Federal Government. A classmate of his was Japanese, and Tommy knew that the Japanese had attacked us at Pearl Harbor, but Roy Takashita was an American. The U.S. was also waging war against Germany and Italy, so why weren't Americans from those countries put in concentration camps? Tommy was asking these questions because of what he had seen on a trip down the peninsula and driving by the

Tanforan racetrack in San Bruno. What Tommy saw was an expanse of tight living quarters surrounded by an electric fence and U.S. Army soldiers standing armed guard in towers around the internment camp. Tommy asked his father about the camp, and William responded with comments that merely reinforced the judgment made by Washington. That still did not answer his questions, and maybe as a 7-year-old, he just wasn't old enough to understand.

As they drove by the camp, he saw mothers hanging clothes on the line, little girls playing Hopscotch, and teams of young men engaged in playing basketball. Tommy remained confused. William was genuinely uncomfortable responding to his youngest son's questions. On the one hand, he was pleased that Tommy questioned the government and was sensitive to the plight of those American/Japanese. If William answered Tommy with the true reason why California citizens of Japanese heritage were imprisoned, he would, in clear terms, see the injustice. If Tommy knew that his friend was considered a potential enemy of the people, he could easily be disenchanted with their unfair treatment. In truth, these Americans were forced to leave their homes and farms and everything they had worked for over the generations. Even more appalling, the government paid families 10 cents on the dollar for their property. The hypocrisy became even more galling when the U.S. accepted American/Japanese young men to fight in Europe. The "Gung Ho" division fought with unrivaled heroism in the major battles they volunteered for throughout the European campaign. If Tommy knew the truth, it would totally demoralize him.

There was one activity that Tommy found truly satisfying, and that was shining shoes. He had saved his earnings selling the Call Bulletin and San Francisco Examiner on the Island that ran down 19th Avenue.

Not even 8 years old, Tommy had lied about his age and took the job selling these papers every Sunday. He wore a coin changer on his belt and had absolutely no problems making change. Tommy saved enough money to buy a shoeshine kit that was inside a box that he could throw over his shoulder. His parents knew about selling papers and felt that the enterprise for an 8-year-old would serve to teach him independence and how to earn a dollar. The plan for shining shoes was something that Tommy did not feel the need to ask for permission. There was a good chance that they might disapprove. He didn't like subterfuge, but for now, he wanted to keep this project secret.

Every day during the summer of 1942, Tommy would hop on the "cowcatcher" on the rear of the "B" streetcar along with other young people who liked a free ride. Tommy had his shine kit slung over his shoulder and was unquestionably the youngest kid riding what could be called a "fender." He would ride down Judah Street for at least a mile, endure the darkness of the Sunset Tunnel and ride the streetcar until they were downtown. At Van Ness and Market Street, Tommy knew that he would be chased off and run two blocks to catch the next streetcar, which took him all the way down Market to Third Avenue, where he hopped off and crossed the street to his destination… The Pepsi Cola Center. This is where servicemen from the varied military facilities in the Bay Area took advantage of the huge recreation center. Tommy would arrive early, usually around ten, to claim his spot on the Center's steps. Being the youngest had great advantages when hawking for customers. He would charge the affable servicemen 25 cents a shine, and in most cases, the tip would be more than he charged. He did a really good job and, in no time, became one of the favorites. Tommy would shine shoes for these high-tipping soldiers and sailors until around 4 o'clock, when he would use the same technique on the B streetcar to get home. This was Tommy's schedule for the entire month of July and most of August.

Coincidentally, Rita was also working at the center where she gave art lessons and free sketches on a first-come basis. In addition to her approachable, mature beauty, her attraction was also a reminder of home for these young men… many still in their teens. After a week at the Center, one afternoon as she was leaving, she was totally shocked to see her eight-year-old son shining shoes for the servicemen! Conversely, Tommy was just as surprised to see his mother, who proved to be more than a little reasonable. Rita's first emotion was that he should not be there, but admittedly, she admired her son's entrepreneurial spirit. She did not raise her voice. The men surrounding them made complementary comments about how industrious Tommy was and how proud she should be that her kid was so ambitious. Rita felt the same way, but before she made a judgment, Tommy's father should have a vote. For the first time, he would be a paying customer as he climbed onto the B Streetcar home.

Rita had been skeptical about whether or not servicemen and women would embrace her idea of sketching their likeness and providing drawing lessons. She was genuinely surprised when the servicemen surrounded her easel and expressed overwhelming enthusiasm for sharing her sketching expertise. This was her way of contributing, and for the past two weeks, she enthusiastically committed to 3 hours each day at the Pepsi Center. Like many women approaching middle age, Rita had the impression that, as the mother of two boys and her age, these young men would certainly not consider her appearance. It never occurred to her that these boys in their late teens and twenties found her to be incredibly attractive. The flirting initially could easily be brushed off as typical of young men away from home, but on occasion, she began to see that officers, generally older, did not attempt to hide their appreciation. She was flattered and never considered the possibility that one of these men would appeal to her.

Frank Simmons, a Lieutenant Commander from Saint Louis, found Rita to be very attractive and began flirting with her harmlessly. Rita thought it strange and somewhat disconcerting that she felt attracted to this handsome young man. At first, it seemed like a game of nuance would be inappropriate for her to respond to, but then he asked her to lunch. Rita was taken aback, but admittedly was flattered and hesitantly dismissed Commander Simmons' advances. Not one to easily give up, after several attempts and charming insistence, she agreed to have a one-time lunch. This invite was totally harmless… right? Aqua, one of the premier San Francisco restaurants, was less than a block away from the Pepsi Center, where they would meet upon arrival. Frank had ordered a glass of chardonnay and invited Rita to join him. This Naval Officer was not lacking in charm, and his sophistication and good looks could not be ignored. Hesitant at first, she agreed that one glass of wine would be harmless. Two hours later, as the staff of Aqua was setting up for the dinner clientele, Rita and Frank Simmons left the restaurant after what turned out to be a thoroughly enjoyable repast. He had not only entertained her with stories of his childhood in the suburbs of Saint Louis, but Rita inwardly felt disappointed that the seemingly platonic lunch was over. As they parted, Commander Simmons commented that he was shipping out in a few days and asked if he could see her again. All of the danger signs were now at play. It was one thing to have lunch and another thing to accept an invitation that could be more than a tete-a-tete. The temptation was real, but Rita knew that their first meeting had to be the end of anything that might be.

Her mind flashed back to William's affair with Lauralie, and she recognized now how easily two people could find themselves in an uncompromising relationship. She ultimately knew that she had gone far beyond the way she would deal with a sexual encounter if William had not entered into an affair with Lauralie. Rita finally realized that she had not emotionally dealt with her husband's infidelity. Part of what was hidden in her subconscious was the awareness that anger and pain remained very close to the surface, and her temptation "to get even" was very real, although she was not willing to accept her motivation. For whatever reason, seeing her youngest son at the Pepsi Center reinforced a sense that both Tommy and William had not been honest with her. What of Tommy's behavior in not asking her permission or feeling the need to lie? Had she fallen short in her parental responsibility? Rita's mind was racing with thoughts that in the past would not have been a consideration. The way her son had kept his plan to shine shoes at the Pepsi Center a secret. On the one hand, his confident entrepreneurship was admirable, along with the audacity of an 8-year-old to fund and organize his business plan. Should she share her feelings with William? How would she come down on grounding Tommy's premature entry into the world of business? The truth is, if she had known about his plans, would she have scotched the whole idea of her child hitching a ride on a streetcar? The answer is yes, she would never approve or agree to anything that could put her child in danger. So, if it comes down to it, Tommy recognized how his mom would predictably respond. To him, the money-making adventure was exciting and confidence-building.

Later that evening, the entire Doyle family sat down after dinner to discuss Tommy's impropriety. One thing was clear: William did not want to quash his son's ambitious plan, and Mark agreed with him even though it meant disagreeing with his mom. In the forties and fifties, parents at large did not embrace all-consuming protection and allowed their children much more latitude. Rita could not, in her right mind, condone the action of her youngest son. Since there were only two weeks before school would start again, she made a mother's emphatic decision to say no. The family might have to deal with Tommy's indiscretion next year, but for now, the Mama Bear has spoken. Now that there was a judgment, Tommy had to deal with a two-week reprieve. He wanted to do something, anything, to support the War effort. With that in mind, he asked his parents if he could borrow the money to buy a wagon. He planned to collect tinfoil, rubber, and paper, all of which definitely contributed. During those two weeks and beyond, Tommy would enlist the help of neighborhood kids and scour the area to find anything that the U.S. needed to continue the War. William and Rita proudly glanced at each other and offered their approval to buy that red wagon.

Initially, news on the progress of the War was disheartening. Hitler had invaded Russia after their success in conquering most of Europe, and the Japanese had been victorious in almost all of Southeast Asia, including the American protectorate of the Philippines. Thousands of U.S. servicemen and women fought valiantly, but when they ran out of supplies, they were forced to surrender. After nothing but gloom and doom, the Army Air Force, under the command of General Jimmie Doolittle, launched an ambitious plan to bomb Tokyo early in 1942. They accomplished this morale-building attack by using B-24 bombers to fly off the deck of the aircraft carrier Enterprise. The American people, for the first time since Pearl Harbor, were jubilant. Rita and William were hoping that their oldest son, Mark, now 16, would not have to join the military. His athletic prowess dominated the conversation in the Doyle household and in many ways served to take their minds off the potential of his coming of age in 1943.

Mark was considering joining the Navy and lying about his age, but he knew that 16 was just too young to enlist. He also knew that his ROTC training would require him to attend officer training after he graduated, and he just plain could not wait and wanted to enlist as a Seaman. Several of his 17-year-old senior friends had lied about their age and were successfully accepted into the Army. In 1942, most of Major League Baseball had their players either drafted or enlisted in the military. As a star high school baseball player, Mark was contacted by the San Francisco Seals in the Pacific Coast League and the New York Giants and Boston Red Sox. He was flattered, but he had clear intentions to enlist when he turned 17.

There was one person who had a distinct influence over Mark. Jill Neman was also 16 and was head over heels in love with Mark. The relationship was distinctly more than the typical "puppy love." She was not only the prettiest girl at Lincoln High, but Jill felt her looks could be too much of a distraction. She was an excellent student with a genuine scientific bent, and if the world was still at War when she graduated high school, she would enlist in the Waves, the female service wing of the U.S. Navy. Jill had something else about her that was unique in Mark's eyes. Her father, Charles Neman, was a scientist who had already been in contact with the Army to help develop new weapons to fight the Axis. He was Jewish, and his religion and his secular attitude were similar to Rita, Mark's mother. Both teens had a Jewish parent, and they would have a good laugh when they joked that, put together, they would have a "Whole Jew." While both Mark and Jill could laugh at some things, they were both proud of their Jewish heritage and genuinely concerned about the Jewish population that was being arrested and sent to hideous labor camps in the European continent. Each of them had extended family in Germany and France. They feared the worst with a sense of frustrating helplessness. Jill, like Mark's family, knew that he was anxious to join the Navy. She was also realistic enough to know that Mark was like so many young men approaching military age who wanted to join the War effort.

To the pleasure of both Mark and Jill, their parents had met at a recent PTA meeting. They lived very close on 32nd Avenue, and Jill had a younger little sister whom they laughingly were saving for Tommy! The future had not been ordained, but for now, both the Doyles and the Nemans were satisfied and supportive of their teens' liaison. The Nemans did have one concern about whether the teens had a future together. Mark was a star athlete who conceivably could have a future in professional sports, but without a plan that superseded sports, they were inwardly concerned about their daughter's future. Mark was highly intelligent, but sports distracted him from academics. Intelligence was one thing, but outside of sports, what were his interests? There was always the piano, which everyone seemed to take for granted, but someday could prove to be a valuable talent. William had discussed the possibility of Mark getting a college degree with an emphasis on business and potentially joining Walsh Inc. Mark seemed interested, but it was just too early in his young life, with the nation at war, to make any decision about his future.

In July of next year, Mark would be 18, the same month he would graduate from Lincoln High. His near future could be decided in the next eight months. He had considered enlisting when he turned 17 in his junior year, but realistically, he knew he would be sorry if he did not graduate. Thankfully, he would not have to lie about his age or have to ask for his parents' permission. Mark's Senior year at Lincoln High was everything "the most likely to succeed" Mark Doyle could envision. He succeeded in being named "all-city" team in Baseball.

In addition, Mark and Jill were named King and Queen for the Senior Prom. To most students, this kind of social recognition would be all that a teenager could aspire to, but all that Mark could think of was enlisting. The Senior accolades were a source of pride for both Mark and Jill, but they had already heard from friends who had succeeded in joining the armed forces when they turned 17. One of those very young warriors was an African/American kid named Victor Allen. Vic was Lincoln's star halfback on the varsity football squad, and somewhat to do with their Quarterback/Halfback compatibility. Mark and Vic were genuine friends. San Francisco had a very small Black community, and like most American cities, the African/American families in the 1940s were almost invisible to most white people. Vic Allen's family had lived in the Bay Area for the last fifty years, and Vic was one of the young black people of the future who conceivably could provide the leadership necessary to integrate fully. Mark did spend time with Vic, but in the final analysis, they had very little in common beyond the playing field. Maybe this war will usher in some equality.

In January of 1943, Mark learned that Victor Allen had been killed in action at Guadalcanal. He was a Navy corpsman who died attempting to attend to a badly wounded Marine. In June of that year, Mark Doyle enlisted in the United States Navy.

With Mark enlisting and heading for boot camp in San Diego, Rita was feeling relatively alone. Tommy was the last immediate family member still at home on 26th Avenue and William traveling up and down the West Coast. She needed something other than her dwindling artwork to keep her mind occupied. The Pepsi Center had too many conflicting issues for her to deal with. An 8-year-old Tommy running around the City without any meaningful supervision, and the potential of meeting Commander Frank Simmons face to face was far more than anything she wanted to deal with. The Snows living above them were creating a significant series of irritants that were challenging any positive movement as neighbors. The most blatant was their attempt to expand their portion of the narrow backyard. Expansion meant more chickens in the back half of the yard. Mr. Snow began to clear the area that was lawfully specified as the Doyle half of the territory. The enmity of the two families was ongoing, but this invasion was crossing a red line. With that in mind, Rita recognized that it was time for a confrontation, which she deplored, but under the circumstances was essential. Gathering her pride, she marched up the steps to the Snows' portions of the Flat. Mr. Snow answered the bell and, as always, totally ignored any semblance of greeting unless "what do you want?" was his form of recognition. His surliness was all that Rita needed to respond. Her anger came boiling up, compounded with two years of conflict, as she let the Snows know that she was not going to accept their invasion of her portion of the yard. As she began to express her dissatisfaction with the Snows' actions, she became well aware that he was not able to respond to her attack, which only served to support her argument. As she retreated from the Snow's doorway, she did so with an air of some newfound pride in having finally successfully confronted the "neighbors."

Rita had been thinking about whether she wanted to deal with the desert, which encompassed the Doyles' portion of the narrow yard. She concluded that there was a trend of various families on 26th Avenue who had converted their yard into "Victory Gardens." Once Rita made up her mind about any project, she addressed it with predictable zeal. She had grown some flowers, let alone a garden of vegetables, in the past. After reading everything she could get her hands on that served as instructions. Rita began to clear her territory and prepare the ground for planting. Next, she went to a nursery located on 19th Avenue and selected seeds for lettuce, radishes, carrots and green onions. Rita Doyle had outlined what she envisioned and began to prepare her Victory Garden for planting. She started this project to thumb her nose at the "scrooges" upstairs, essentially, but to her surprise and pleasure, she was genuinely enjoying the whole process. Before planting, she had read that the soil in her yard was of poor quality and infused with sand, being so close to the Pacific Ocean. Unlike her neighbors, she determined that if she wanted a truly productive garden, it would require a layer of topsoil. It turned out to be a lot more than just planting the seeds. She purchased a hose for regular watering and gloves, a gardener's apron and the tools she would need to dig and rake the yard. The more she applied instructions, the more she realized how much she could grow and benefit from a well-planned garden. As an example of her burgeoning skill, Rita constructed a pathway up the center of the yard, which would allow the Snows access to their portion. After a full day of prepping and planting, Rita viewed her efforts with distinct satisfaction.

Three weeks later, the product of her labors began to bear fruit. As the garden matured, she gathered the high-quality vegetables, which, due to careful planning, turned out to be a bumper crop. The Doyles would enjoy the first results of Rita's Victory Garden. When William returned from his recent inspection of Walsh Inc.'s work in progress, he could not believe how Rita had literally transformed the yard into a professional garden of high-quality vegetables. There was no end to Rita's ability to plan and execute any project with zeal. William was in awe, and Rita was beaming. To top off her pride, she ran into Mr. Snow, who was obviously tipping his hat to her accomplishment in turning their yard into a chicken vegetable paradise!

Not to be left out of an effort to support a wartime effort, William seized on the notice that residents were needed as Air Raid Wardens to provide drills in their neighborhood. He was awarded a helmet, whistle, and armband, which identified him as the person who would respond to enemy attacks. He would go door to door, citing residents who had not turned off lights during a drill. In addition to drills, streetlights facing the ocean were painted black, and the city would have to adhere to the practice of regular drills. This level of preparation was not without some incursions of Japanese submarines lurking very close to the San Francisco shoreline. Another wartime expression was the banners in the windows of families who had a direct member in the military. Typically, the star in the center was blue and would change to gold if the serviceman was killed in action. On their block of 26th Avenue, there were three families with men in the service. In certain instances, if a military vehicle were to drive up and park in front of those homes, it could only mean one thing. The family was being notified of a war-related death. It happened once in 1943 as the McDonald family was notified that their son Patrick, big brother to Keith, a U.S. Marine, had been killed in action on Tarawa. The whole block between Irving and Judah felt the loss as the star in the McDonald's window changed from blue to gold. Patrick was not a stranger to the block's residents, most of whom knew Patrick McDonald. He was 19 years old.

With Mark in the process of completing boot camp in San Diego, the passing of Patrick had a close-to-home impact that sent a shudder through the Doyle family. Once he graduated from initial training, Mark would be granted leave for one week, followed by instructions on where he would be assigned duty. Mark had specially requested sea duty, which he was guaranteed. His return for that short week entailed spending some valuable time with his family, but understandably, the bulk of his leave would be spent with Jill Neman. Rita and William were impressed with Mark's appearance after boot camp. He was solid, lean and sporting a healthy tan. Mark had never looked better. Mark and Jill discussed getting engaged before he shipped out, but after serious consideration, decided to hold off, especially with Jill scheduled to report for training with the Waves. While he was on leave, he received orders to report to the Officer of the Day on board the heavy cruiser USS Indianapolis. The USS Indianapolis was the ship that carried the President on three cruises. In 1943, it became the flagship of the Fifth Fleet under Vice Admiral Raymond Spruance. Mark was pleased with his assignment aboard the Indianapolis. The ship had a huge array of armament, including nine 8-inch guns and even more 40 mm anti-aircraft batteries.

After boot camp, Mark began studying to become a Gunner's Mate. As soon as he became eligible in six months, he would take the test for Petty Officer Third Class Gunner's Mate. For now, he was determined to be the best seaman in the United States Navy. As he began his enlistment starting with the lowest level, Mark was repeatedly asked, with his aptitude score, why he didn't apply for officers' training school. While many American boys drafted or enlisted would have the opportunity to play baseball for their entire tour, they would jump at it. Playing baseball was not what Mark signed up for. He wanted to be part of the War, and above all, that meant seeing action. Like many of America's young men, Mark felt that combat would be exciting and honorable. They all would soon find out there is nothing glamorous about War.

In 1943, the Battle of Stalingrad marked the War's outcome as a tipping point in favor of the Allies. The battle that handed Germany its first decisive defeat was one of the longest, biggest and deadliest battles of the war that ended with 2 million casualties. In the Pacific, the U.S. launched a surprise attack on Guadalcanal, taking control of the airport, forcing the Japanese to retreat. With hand-to-hand jungle combat six months later, the Japanese suffered the final defeat with 31,000 casualties, and the U.S. lost 7,100 soldiers. After the battle of New Guinea and patrolling the Aleutians, the USS Indianapolis returned to the U.S. for refitting at Mare Island. Mark reported for duty while the ship was in dry dock. From San Francisco, the flagship moved on for the bombardment of Tarawa in the Gilbert Islands. Mark saw his first action as the Indianapolis shelled enemy strong points while valiant landing parties struggled against fanatical Japanese defenders in an extremely bloody and costly battle.

Throughout 1943 and 1944, the ship provided bombardments for the battles at Saipan and Peleliu. As a gunner on a 40 mm anti-aircraft gun, Mark received credit for shooting down 3 Japanese Zeros and a Dive bomber. The gun captain, Benjamin Bernstein, was from the Lower East Side of New York. His role was to direct, maintain, and determine the targets for Mark. The First-Class Gunner's Mate Eric had recently been promoted based on his skill and leadership. The two loaders on the battery were both very young Seamen. Bobby Johnson was from New Orleans, and Jim Tobias hailed from Birmingham. Both young sailors were 18 and loved being part of an Indianapolis gun crew. After working together for a little over a year, the entire team had established a form of rhythm where each man worked in concert with the unit. There was a source of pride that none of the men talked about because it was so much a part of their clearly defined responsibilities. They were good and they knew it.

As 1944 emerged, it was clear that the tide of war was turning, and the Japanese were initiating a form of warfare that was little more than suicide. The Kamikaze pilots would fly their aircraft with only one mission. They would use their Zero as a weapon as they dove into U.S. ships with devastating effect when they got through the American batteries. This method of attack was relatively new, and the 40mm anti-aircraft guns were the first line of defense. At the battle of Tarawa, Mark's crew was being tested as the pace of Kamikaze attacks had reached a zenith. The battle arena was an awesome picture of the suicide pilots being shot down, but all too often, they would get through the defenses. Several of the ships from the Fifth Fleet had been hit, and at least two of the vessels were sinking and exploding. After escaping with no direct Kamikaze attacks, it was not the case at Okinawa. The Indianapolis was hit twice, resulting in severe midship damage and the loss of 18 crew members and more than a dozen wounded.

As the firefighters fought the calamitous destruction, it became clear that the Indianapolis had suffered damage that would take her out of the line. She was ordered to Hunters Point in San Francisco for major repairs. Mark's battery had performed brilliantly, downing 6 enemy aircraft. In the melee, Bobby Johnson was severely wounded with an injury that would end his days as a loader on a 40mm aircraft weapon. The ship's captain recognized Mark's performance as Gunner, and he was promoted to Second Class Gunner's Mate. Arriving in San Francisco, Mark was anxious to see his family, but once again, his priority was Jill Neman. But before he used any of his three days' pass, he checked in with Bobby Johnson.

The unit Gun Loader was sequestered in a private hospital room at Oak Knoll Navy Hospital in Oakland. Bobby's condition was critical, but today, at the very least, he was showing some improvement. The Seaman from New Orleans was pleased to see Mark, and he was anxious to rejoin the unit, but both men knew this was not to be. Bobby's left arm had been amputated, and he boasted that he could be the first one-armed loader on a 40. His parents and 14-year-old sister were on the way to the hospital. Mark was in awe of Bobby's spirit and wondered if, dealing with the same circumstances, he could be as brave as Johnson. Upon leaving Oak Knoll, Mark made it a point to talk to Bobby's doctor to determine his status and whether he would survive. As Mark was leaving the hospital, he encountered Ben Bernstein and shared his meeting with Bobby. Mark and Ben decided to go for a drink after Bernstein visited Bobby. They met at a lounge in Oakland and shared their notes on Johnson's condition.

Ben was clearly shaken about the possibility that their shipmate might not survive. To Mark, Ben was showing a side that, heretofore, had remained hidden. The men left the bar two hours later, and Mark had established more than a superficial understanding of the Gun Captain, Ben Bernstein. Mark was more than a little curious when his shipmate shared some whispered gossip about the priority repairs to the Indianapolis. Evidently, their next assignment was so secretive that, unlike past orders, it had remained under wraps.

William and Rita were thrilled to see their son and again referenced the fact that his ship had returned to San Francisco for a second time in three months. As always, they were both contributing to the war effort. William was traveling up and down the West Coast from Bremerton to San Diego, helping refit both injured warships and newly launched warships to the U.S. fleet. Rita had applied her artistic skill that turned the flat's backyard from desert to a beautiful, blooming garden. The remainder of her time was dedicated to the morale of servicemen and women. Her sketching skill proved to be a favorite at the Pepsi Center as she had replaced her precise, detailed drawings with caricatures of the men. This technique allowed Rita to complete mass-produced drawings literally. To his parents, Mark had gone from tender teenager to a seasoned member of the United States Navy. Sharing a dinner at least allowed parents and sailors an opportunity to reaffirm their love and pride. A three-day pass evaporated rapidly. The remaining two days were spent with Jill, who was thrilled and surprised to see Mark, who showed up in his white dress uniform. He had matured, and the man she loved was never more handsome. Jill had joined the Waves and received her first assignment as a clerical assistant at Pendleton Marine base in Southern California. Mark found it difficult to say goodbye for a third time, but as the War continued to explode, even a short amount of time was cherished.

When he returned to Hunters Point, he was amazed at how the expedited repair process had transformed the Indianapolis back into fighting condition. As they headed out to sea, the entire crew was more than a little curious about the rumored secret status of their next assignment that remained the hushed topic of conversation. In record time, the Indianapolis reached Hawaii and took on some heavenly guarded cargo. During the next leg of their assignment, the Officers and crew were told they were on an extremely important mission, and once they were authorized, the ship captain would share that knowledge with his men. Their destination was a small island in the Marianas named Tinian. After the still-secret cargo was delivered, they departed on a quick turnaround and were back at sea. The USS Indianapolis was heading for the Leyte Gulf. The crew was jubilant, knowing that whatever they delivered was important and veiled in secrecy.

CHAPTER 18

USS INDIANAPOLIS

At midnight on July 30, 1945, a Japanese submarine fired three torpedoes that created havoc on the USS Indianapolis. The starboard midsection of the Cruiser was targeted with two torpedoes and one directly on the bow. The USS Indianapolis would sink in just 12 minutes. Of the approximately 1,200 crew members, 900 sailors were thrown into the ocean. What transpired after the initial "abandon ship" was one of the most horrendous events in U.S. Naval history. Three hundred men were trapped inside, and of the 900 men who were thrown into the water, many would die from drowning, shark attacks, and dehydration.

Mark Doyle found himself in the water, hanging on to a piece of debris and surrounded by sheer bedlam. He saw young sailors in tears from wounds that they incurred and just plain fear. Surveying the dystopian scene, there were a handful of life rafts, and caught in the endless field of debris were orange life vests. Were there any officers who had been thrown from the ship and could organize and provide a semblance of order? If not, someone was needed to assume leadership. Until an officer stepped forward, Mark would fill the vacuum. He yelled to introduce himself to the survivors nearest him and asked if there were any officers available to organize. A weak voice spoke up and said he was heading toward Mark. He asked Mark to keep talking so that he could more easily find him in the frightened maze.

Ensign Robert Swan had just graduated from the Naval Academy, and the Indianapolis was his first assignment. Robert and Mark finally met while all hell was breaking loose around them. They determined that the first thing they needed to do was to get some idea of how many life jackets were available, what to do about the danger of sharks, attempt to treat the wounded, and, most important, the availability of fresh water. Ensign Swan was somewhat helpful, but Mark recognized that the Ensign was deferring to him. Achieving any of this agenda would be next to impossible, but Mark felt they had to, at the very least, try. Mark and a small number of sailors began to tie life jackets together. In the bedlam, only a few actual rafts were available, and they were all fully occupied. No fresh water seemed to be available, or there was hoarding. Hopefully, they would be rescued the next day, but for now, they just had to get through the night. Mark, Robert, and a few men attempted to take inventory, but it was next to impossible with close to 900 survivors in the water.

The screams of wounded men punctuated the night along with the fear of attacking sharks. At dawn, the situation was just getting worse. When would their rescuers arrive? As the first day expired with no sign of help, Mark and Robert were at a loss for what to do. Day one turned into four days and five nights. Mark and other men organized to form a series of human rings to serve as a deterrent to the attacking sharks. Men without fresh water were choosing to drink salt water, and the poisoning took very little time. Dehydration in combination with shark attacks continued through the helpless days. Insanity and screams of pure pain punctuated the days and nights. Where was help? It was clear that the sharks were feeding on the growing population of corpses. Hopefully, this would keep them away from what remained of the living. As days passed, more and more sailors were driven to insanity by drinking salt water and dehydration. On two occasions, Mark attempted to divert the sharks by diving and literally attacking them with his Swedish knife, which he kept in his pocket at all times. The blood in the water is what attracted the feeding sharks. By the fourth day, it was clear that the survivors had significantly lost their ranks, and the remainder of the men were in various stages of attempting to survive in the savage water. Hope of being rescued was fading.

Late on day four, a Naval aircraft flew over the site, and the crew could not believe what they witnessed. It was just luck that they happened to see the tragedy below. Ultimately, the Navy responded and rescued the 321 sailors who were still in various stages of life. Once the few men who were in shape enough to provide information on what had transpired, shock set in. For reasons that were beyond any understanding or comprehension, the position of the Indianapolis escaped any attention and remained a frightening mystery. The ship was halfway from Guam and its destination, which was the island of Leyte, 600 miles away. The secrecy of their mission prior to Guam may have been a contributing factor, but the question remained… How could a heavy cruiser with all of its armor sink in such a short period of time?

After reality began to set in, the survivors realized, in addition to the nightmarish experience, that an atomic bomb had been dropped on Hiroshima. The Indianapolis had carried the nation's supply of plutonium and components for the first A Bomb. The sequence of events of failure remained unanswered, and with it, sheer anger on the part of the 321 surviving men. The physical and mental conditions ranged from broken bones to wounds that were the result of the Japanese attack. Mark did not realize that his left leg had been badly maimed, but thankfully, he had been spared by the army of sharks.

Many of the sailors commented on the heroism of Mark Doyle and, to a lesser degree, Ensign Robert Swan. After a week in the Guam hospital and endless interrogations and visits from some of his brother sailors, Mark was flown back to San Francisco and the Oak Knoll Naval Hospital. Like his dad's wound in the First World War, Mark too was facing the risk of losing his left leg. While the end of the War with Japan was over, the plight of the USS Indianapolis was almost shunned by the press and ended up below the fold in many newspapers. To Mark's family, just knowing he had survived the terror of the Indianapolis was the only story. They had experienced the horror of not knowing if Mark was dead or a member of the relatively few survivors. William was notified when he received a phone call from the Navy that Mark was indeed alive and would be destined for the Naval hospital in the Bay Area. The entire Doyle family was jubilant and thankful. Once Mark's condition was stabilized, they could accept direct family members to see him. With an avalanche of tears, the Doyles were beyond themselves with joy and pure relief.

The day after the second A-bomb was dropped on Nagasaki, the Japanese surrendered unconditionally, and the Doyles were allowed to see Mark at Oak Knoll. William, Rita, Tommy, and Patrick arrived at the Hospital, and before they visited Mark were warned about his appearance. He was seriously sunburned, had lost significant weight, and finally, his left leg was still a question mark. It was a good thing that the doctor warned them about Mark's condition because without it, they might have reacted with some alarm, which is not what Mark needed. The emotion of the Doyles, like so many war-weary American families, was a deep sense of gratitude that their father, mother, son or daughter was coming home. The reunion of Mark's family was joyous, tearful and a moment in time that just could not be duplicated. Yes, Mark looked gaunt and emotionally spent, but he was home, and in reality, that is all they could ask for.

As they left the hospital, William and Rita were ushered into the Chief Physician's office, where they were told that Mark could very well lose his left leg. If that were the eventuality, Mark's mother and father should be emotionally prepared. No one had to warn William. This sequence was all too familiar. Jill Neman was somewhat disappointed when she was excluded from the first visit to Oak Knoll, but she did understand. She was concerned about his appearance, but the Doyles had alerted her to exercise caution when they were reunited. Even with the warning, Mark's condition was a shock to Jill, but she knew that it was just a matter of time before he would return to his old self… with or without his left leg. In the ensuing days and weeks, a stream of friends and family trekked to Oak Knoll Hospital to express their concern and affection. The Walsh family arrived en masse, including Walter, Barbara, Jimmie and Lauralie.

Over the years, the Walshes were minimally like family. William deserved a lot of credit for the practices he introduced as VP of Marketing, including the hiring of some exceptional employees. They were also there when William and Lauralie were dealing with a romance that had no future. Walter, responding to Mark's diminished condition, parted with "come see me when you have gained your strength." For the first time since he had returned home, Mark thought about his future. Even if his leg was saved, his dream of becoming a big-league baseball player was just not in his future. Walter Walsh had struck a nerve that Mark would ultimately have to deal with, but for now, he needed to get well by fighting to save his leg.

CHAPTER 19

MISS BERRY

Tommy Doyle, at 10 years old, was finding it difficult to deal with his big brother's appearance. Even though the Doyle family had been warned about their hero's condition, it nevertheless shocked Tommy to his young core. While Mark was in the Navy, Tommy worried and experienced genuine anxiety every time Mark was brought into the conversation. When he was ushered into his brother's hospital room, he found it difficult to maintain his untrained composure. Tears welled up, but control prevailed, knowing that he had to measure his emotions for Mark's sake. He was immensely proud of his heroic big brother. When Mark joined the Navy almost two years ago, Tommy was just 7 years old and was surprisingly doing poorly in school. His performance in class could be attributed to the emotional stress of his brother being in harm's way. Ultimately, it was recognized that he probably was not ready to enter kindergarten. With his birthday in August and starting school less than a month later, he was just not emotionally ready, but in 1945, this proven concern had not been recognized. "Red Flag" children became a significant factor on when 5-year-olds should enter the school system. Fortunately, as Tommy entered the fourth grade, his parents discussed holding him back one grade. Rita and William determined that not allowing their son to join his current classmates could be compounding one issue with another. They did decide that spending more time on their youngest son's schoolwork would be beneficial. It seems that it really was not necessary.

Enter Miss Berry. Elizabeth Berry was Tommy's fourth-grade teacher, and the timing was impeccable. The 22-year-old teacher had just graduated from San Jose State Teachers' College, a school dedicated almost exclusively to training and graduating Californian classroom teachers. She was almost instantly drawn to 10-year-old Thomas Doyle. She had evaluated all of the students in her fourth-grade class. The young Doyle's circumstances and performance in school raised a genuine concern. As a very young member of her class, she recognized signs of immaturity with the impact of his brother in the service, and she had to add that Tommy had an appealing personality. Her method in terms of helping Tommy with school would probably be questionable in today's learning practices. His limitations, in her estimation, could be corrected with personal attention that would extend beyond the classroom.

In early April of 1945, Miss Berry invited Tommy to join her at her apartment for personal tutorial schooling. The 10-year-old had a real crush on this pretty schoolteacher and responded to her invite instantly after she called the Doyles and discussed her intentions. Unusual, yes, but they believed that personal attention could not hurt and may be worth the effort. Tommy took the Lincoln Way bus to Haight Street just north of the Golden Gate Park panhandle. In total, there were four Saturdays of tutorial schooling. Last Saturday, Elizabeth Berry decided to take Tommy on a picnic on the lawn of the beautiful Palace of Fine Arts, just two blocks from her apartment. She had been pleased with her instincts about her young student's potential, and hopefully, the special sessions would put Tommy on a better course in learning. It was a beautiful spring day in San Francisco, and Tommy was thoroughly enjoying the days with the beautiful Miss Berry... and then the bubble burst. As they were enjoying the chicken and potato salad lunch, they were joined by

Elizabeth's Navy boyfriend. Tommy was crestfallen, but almost instantly saw the Gunners' Mates connection with his big brother in the Navy. Ted Grimes was instantly interested as Tommy told him about Mark's deployments on board the USS Indianapolis. He was now willing to accept this interloper and share Miss Berry with him.

There is no question that the personal tutorials were effective. Tommy's scholastic abilities improved significantly over the subsequent two and a half months, providing a solid platform for young Tommy's promotion to the fifth grade. There were additional signs that pointed to his newfound confidence. The local theater on Irving was probably number one on the list of activities for the local Sunset youth. The Irving theater across from Jefferson grammar school on 19th Avenue featured a Saturday matinee that included a double feature, a cartoon, a serial (Zorro was featured), a newsreel and once a month, a local talent show. Young people would be selected from the day's audience and perform in front of their peers. In the past, Tommy would never have considered getting up on stage and losing some inhibitions. The performers took the stage one by one and usually sang a song. Thomas Doyle was last on the program and sang "General Washington, a general brave was he…" The winner was selected based on applause as a hand was held over their head. To his surprise, Tommy was the winner and was awarded a full case of 7UP!

Tommy's parents had still another surprise in store for their youngest son. The family was well aware of his lack of interest in sports. Perhaps living in the shadow of his older brother's awesome athleticism was the reason; however, they soon found that Tommy just wasn't interested in team sports. He did like to enter into individual events, and at the top of his list was, of all things… boxing!

Unbeknownst to his parents, Tommy had become a regular at the San Francisco Boys Club in the Haight/Asbury district, where he played chess and trained for boxing matches. The winner in each weight category would be awarded two weeks at the Club's Camp Marwadele, north of San Francisco in Lake County. Tommy made it to the finals in the 100 lb. weight and the boxing night was highly appreciated by the parents of the local athletes. Rita and William received an invitation in the mail that Tommy Doyle was one of the featured events… more surprises! Their son had not even mentioned that he was training for a boxing match. On San Francisco Boys Club boxing night, all the parents convened in the audience and waited for the night's "card."

Just before his match with a young black kid named "Fury", Tommy was notified that his older brother was on leave from the hospital so he could attend his brother's premier boxing match. If the little brother needed any additional motivation, Mark filled the bill. Tommy's first appearance in the ring was a resounding success. The referee called the fight in the first round as the "26th Avenue Mauler" had totally outboxed his erstwhile opponent, the hapless Buddy Dewbury. Mark had not seen this side of his little brother, but it was consistent with his need to separate himself from the pack. On the surface, Tommy seemed to gravitate towards anything that was the opposite of his performance at the Boys Club Gym. Tommy's reward for winning his weight class was a two-week fully paid trip to Camp Marwadele. For him, this would be his first trip away from home and ostensibly alone without any family members in tow.

Situated in Northern California, the Camp was everything Tommy hoped it would be. The campsite included ten 8-person units, a nearby latrine and outside shower, a large screened-in dining area, housing for the many crafts Camp Marwadele offered and an inviting swimming hole. There were also several outdoor evening campsites, and a narrow river with a dry dock for a host of colorful canoes. The young boys that Tommy was introduced to came from almost all the San Francisco neighborhoods. The next step in navigating the process was the assignment of cabins, which consisted of a wooden frame and roof with canvas siding. Each cabin was assigned an older boy who served as a counselor. In essence, the counselor had the responsibility for guiding his young charges through all the camp had to offer and making sure that his boys were exercising safety standards and general awareness of some obvious, potentially dangerous challenges. The five campers in Tommy's assigned cabin included boys in various age groups from 8 to 12 years old, and almost all had competed and won their city-wide boxing championships. Tommy immediately struck up a friendship with the only other 10-year-old with a bunk next to the one he was assigned. Charlie Benedict was also from the Sunset district of San Francisco, but his home was located at the westernmost reaches of the neighborhood. Charlie was a head shorter than most but made up for his perceived shortcoming by being an absolute terror in the boxing ring in the 80 lb. weight class. Throughout the entire two weeks, Tommy and Charlie were inseparable. They seemed to like doing the same things and, at the same time, exercised their own style of participation.

The first dinner at the large dining hall served all 80 young outdoorsmen. The makeup of the population was wide and varied. There were three Chinese kids and, to a lot of surprise, four African Americans. The black kids were not expected to be mixing with whites in 1946 America. The meal that was served that night was almost predictable—hot dogs, potato salad, and a drink that was laughable, referred to as "bug Juice." In truth, it was no more than the familiar Kool Aid, but there was an endless supply, and the boys loved it with every meal from that moment on. That first night, there was a lone voice in the adjacent cabin singing "Milkman keep dos bottles quiet." His loud screeching was off-key and totally irritating. The smallest of the three black kids continued to sing for three straight nights, but to add to his irritation, he just would not shower. Some of the older boys in the young "singers" cabin had had enough of Donnie Jefferson's loud nightly serenade and the odor he emanated. One of the three black kids grabbed Donnie and proceeded to give him a good scrubbing while he screamed during the entire event. When they finished the bath, they made him promise that he would bathe and quiet down "dos milk bottles." From that evening on, Donnie Jefferson refrained from singing off-key and took regular showers.

For the first week, Tommy and Charlie were among the first at the swimming hole and tried to be the first to "break the ice." Adjacent to the swimming hole was a series of steps that had been carved out on the hill. Depending on your willingness to jump or dive in from one of the top steps was perceived as an act of valor. The nights in Lake County could get cold enough to freeze a thin layer of ice on the water. Brave campers would queue up to see who would jump in and break the ice, allowing for unencumbered days of swimming. Tommy was reveling in everything Camp Marwadele had to offer, including participating in making gifts for his parents. For his mom, he took a tin pie plate, painted it, added personal embellishments and let it dry. For William, he made a pipe stand out of a nearby piece of hardwood. Never mind the fact that his dad did not smoke a pipe. It was indeed the thought. In the evening, the young boys and their counselors would sit around a large fire, and the older camp workers would tell scary stories with frightening endings that proved to be immensely effective on the younger kids.

Near the end of the second week, Tommy and Charlie decided to play "Mumblety Peg", a popular knife game, and they found the perfect place to play on a nearby wooden train trestle. When they stood up to leave, Tommy lost his balance and fell into the dry riverbed at least 20 feet beneath the trestle. Tommy had seriously broken his right wrist, and Charlie ran for help. They proceeded to take him to the camp infirmary, and since there was no facility for repairing a compound fracture, they put his wound in a sling. Poor Tommy was in real pain, but the duo had to wait for the train that plied a route from Willits to Fort Bragg, the nearest hospital on the coast. The local train was known as "The Skunk." Tommy's wrist was indeed badly broken, so the Fort Bragg physician on duty set his arm and proceeded to apply a firm cast. With that, the Camp-trained nurse called Rita and William to inform them of what had transpired. It was two hundred miles north of the City, but Tommy's parents made the trip in record time. When they arrived, their son was in good spirits as they completed the round trip to San Francisco. Tommy had said goodbye to Charlie Benedict when he left Camp Marwadele with a promise to see each other soon.

When the Doyles returned home, Tommy complained that his wrist continued to cause pain. William noted that it was all part of the healing process. When two weeks later he continued to experience significant pains in his casted right wrist, Rita decided to take him to the University of San Francisco Hospital in the City. The doctor there examined Tommy's wrist after temporarily taking the cast off and x-raying his injury. The image showed that his wrist had not been set properly and would need to be rebroken! The last thing Tommy Doyle remembered as they provided the anesthetic was his castless right wrist being placed in a vise with the intention of rebreaking it! When he came to, his arm was in a new cast, and after three weeks, his wrist would heal properly. Tommy's schoolmates took turns applying their names to the formidable white cast.

Mark's attendance at the fight was his first day out of the hospital, and dealing with a wheelchair brought into focus the reality of what could be in his future. In truth, his leg continued to be a major question mark with Navy doctors, and the pain that he was experiencing at Tommy's fight did nothing to encourage the outcome that he hoped for… Saving his left leg. Mark felt a deep sense of foreboding, which was going to be realized when he returned to Oak Knoll. Three days after his return, Mark was confronted with the dreaded worst outcome. The staff of surgeons asked to meet with him, and the resolution was precisely what he was anticipating. All too often, Naval surgeons found themselves dealing not only with physical treatment but also with sensitivity in responding to the emotional needs of American sailors returned from the war with mangled limbs. Mark Doyle had been subjected to countless surgeries, and while there had been moments of encouragement, in the final analysis, doctors could not save his leg. It was not a matter of choice. Not amputating his limb would have dire consequences. The entire hospital staff was aware of Mark's condition, and it was colored by the fact that Mark Doyle was a Bay Area star athlete before the war. Losing his leg was Mark's worst possible dream. Sensing the difficulty of delivering the terrible news, in his predictable style, he attempted to put the trio of surgeons at ease. He knew he had run out of time and had to face the reality of the moment with sheer resolve. The news had to be shared with his family, and strangely, Mark was dreading that moment even though he was the subject. Oak Knoll was unfortunately familiar with this painful messaging. No matter how many times they had to take this role, it was never less tragically difficult. Weeks later, William, Rita, and Tommy, who insisted on coming even though his parents tried to discourage his presence, knew from the tenor of their phone call that the doctors would be delivering the news that they all dreaded. The family was shocked to hear the words, but sadly, on the other hand, they knew what was coming.

They were somewhat surprised that Jill wasn't present, but it was conceivable that she knew. Mark had called Jill, and she was among the last people to hold out hope for a different resolution. While she had been among the few family members and close friends who were entirely supportive of Mark's plight, Rita came away with a different view of how Jill might respond to the reality of Mark losing his leg. She would hope that she was wrong, but her instincts told her that Jill would not be at her son's side. Rita was also sure that Mark, if she was right, would put on an understandable face, when in all actuality, he would be devastated. What Jill had said through all of this travail was that nothing mattered, and they would face whatever the future offered together. At 18, Jill was not capable of the heroics required. Several days later, Rita would see her female instincts come to fruition and in a short conversation with her son, he agreed that it was futile, and Jill would not be sharing a life with him.

CHAPTER 20

THE SHELTONS

Mark was recovering from his surgery when he received a phone call from President Truman, who informed him that he had been awarded the Congressional Medal of Honor. Many of the Indianapolis survivors had come forward to express their stories about Mark's heroism throughout the four endless days of terror. Mark was almost incapable of responding. The recognition was totally unexpected, which was the kind of response that was typical of most recipients of the nation's highest award for bravery. For a moment, Mark forgot about the loss of his left leg and haltingly expressed his appreciation to the President. The President's Aide came on the phone. He congratulated and informed Mark that he, alongside his immediate family, would be formally invited to the Oval Room of the White House to accept the Medal of Honor. The San Francisco and Bay Area press had already been notified. Mark would not be released from the Naval hospital for another month. His trip to Washington would have to be scheduled at least a month in advance.

Once the dramatic news of Mark's heroism was released, the hospital, family friends, and the public at large offered sincere congratulations to the hometown Navy warrior. In subsequent days, Oak Knoll experienced a flood of interviews. The reporters didn't just request engaging Mark, but were also asking for participation on the part of patients and staff. The phone next to Mark's bed was relentlessly ringing with good wishes from anyone who had experienced even a passing moment in Mark's life. Ultimately, the hospital had to screen the volume of requests and phone calls. Mark had become an epitome of the selfless warrior who was totally overwhelmed by all the attention.

Sara

The nurse assigned to Mark's ward was a volunteer named Sara Shelton. She was the kind young woman whose patients were vying for her attention. Sara was not only a capable nurse, but she also had a great sense of humor and a personality that had a way of making every veteran feel special. She was 19 with the prospect of attending medical school and ultimately becoming a General Practice physician. The War had temporarily interrupted her personal goals, but Sara felt helping these badly wounded servicemen was, for now, her calling. There was one other thing that contributed to her popularity… Sara was absolutely beautiful, and half black or not, she was every man's dream girl. The only outlier in the ward was Mark, who was coming off his disappointing breakup with Jill. Sara was well aware of the tribulations that Mark was going through… the loss of his leg and a girlfriend who had proved to be anything but the woman who would stand by his side. The young nurse possessed a level of intelligence and instincts that told her that this young sailor needed time to navigate a series of disappointments. He had just returned from the surgery that removed his left leg. Sara was also aware of the respect that Mark engendered from his shipmates. Not even the highest honor that a serviceman could be awarded could compensate for the loss of a limb… especially an athlete who had hoped his skill would translate into a career. Her limited attention to his needs became curious and somewhat revealing to Mark's state of mind. Reconciling his very recent disappointing breakup with Jill was still sadly a very raw wound.

After almost a month of his recuperation, Mark gathered his confidence. In a jovial manner, he asked Sara why he didn't warrant equal attention. She responded that he was not very capable of judging a woman's mysterious ways. That comment took him back, as it was not what he might have anticipated at all. Mark was evidently on his way through the healing process because, for the first time in weeks, he began to notice Sara and understand why she was the favorite of the entire ward. She was a gorgeous woman and not the kind of girl he thought he would be attracted to.

It was 1946, and the nation and its people were not yet willing to offer a level of equality to African/Americans citizens. He had fought beside black sailors during the many attacks that the USS Indianapolis suffered. He never really asked why black men seemed to be restricted to paltry jobs in the ship's galley and mostly in service to officers. Battle stations on board the ship were the one exception when black shipmates achieved some level of equality. One minute they were servicing the ship's officers in their wardrooms and the next firing or loading a 40mm anti-aircraft gun. It caused Mark to reflect on the few Negroes he had known in his life. He recalled the conversations that he had with his dad when he asked why the Japanese were in internment camps during the War, and what about Vic Allen, the half black teammate on the Lincoln High football team. Where did he live? What was his life after a game? Strange how all of those limited racial comments were brought into focus

As he got to know Sara, he began taking pleasure that he could laugh and feel he was getting "equal time" with the ward's dream girl. Any remaining thoughts about his breakup with Jill, strangely enough, began to fade. He found himself attracted to this sensuous nurse and attempted to have a better understanding of his ambivalent feelings about a black woman. Sara Shelton lived in Burlingame, a bedroom community adjacent to San Mateo. Her father, James Shelton, was a Superior Court judge for San Mateo County. The family had been accepted in an upscale residential neighborhood in Burlingame.

Judge Shelton

Sara's father was raised by his grandfather, Abraham, in the 9th Ward of New Orleans. He was born as a result of his mother being raped by a white man. His mother was just 13 at the time of his birth. Melinda Carver was much too young to raise a child, and this limited maturity was reason enough to ask her parents to raise the child. By the time James turned 14, the concerned grandfather began to see some dangerous signs in their Parish that could threaten their "uppity" kin. He told his beloved grandchild that he should leave Louisiana because "he was of lynching age." James moved to California in 1891. While the Golden State had its own racial issues, through his tenacity, he worked in various jobs in the northern part of the state. Ultimately, he found the best opportunities for a black man in San Francisco. He enrolled in St. Ignatius High School, graduated, and was accepted at the accredited University of San Francisco. He applied to Creighton Law School in Nebraska and was accepted as the only negro to matriculate at Creighton. Upon graduation, he returned to California and the San Francisco Bay Area. James spent 4 years as an attorney for the NAACP, where he met Coralyn, and eventually set up private practice in San Mateo.

In the liberal San Mateo County, James was elected Superior Court Judge after a successful ten years as an attorney in the County. Coralyn Shelton was white, and marrying a black man, even in California, was fraught with painful memories. Her parents, who lived in Georgia, disowned her. It did not matter to them that James was a highly esteemed Superior Court Judge. Coralyn gave birth to her pride and joy, Sara Ann, who followed her father by attending Burlingame High School and completing her undergraduate degree at USF. When the War began, rather than entering medical school, she enrolled in nurse training and was accepted at the Oak Knoll Naval Hospital.

Mark's stay at the hospital encompassed several months of rehabilitation, including being fitted for a prosthetic limb. In addition to her work as a nurse, Sara was a valued member of the therapeutic team. Once Mark had recuperated from multiple wounds and regained his strength, he would be in for months of strenuous physical training to get used to an artificial limb. Sara made sure that she would be assigned to Mark Doyle. The process had been explained to him, as well as to his family members who would be important in terms of encouragement and support. Once Mark had reconciled with his breakup with Jill, he was bound and determined to get back to standing on two legs, even if one was artificial. Sara was highly influential in helping Mark achieve his goal. The therapy program was arduous and consisted of days of falling and getting up again. Sara Shelton was instrumental in exercising patience and encouragement. Sara would laugh at Mark in a mischievous form of banter that kept him enthused and convinced that he would walk again.

The more time they spent together, the more they both recognized that the relationship was far more than basic nurse/patient. Mark began to question his emotions. Sara was everything he desired in a woman, but the fact that she was half black continued to influence and confuse his feelings. Like so many Americans, he was tainted with generations of white conditioning. With one exception, Sara's race was blind to the Ward. Bobby Doby hailed from Mobile, Alabama, and didn't see fit even to attempt to change his polluted feelings about "them niggers." Bobby was 19 years old and absolutely believed that Negros should "know their place." In his young life, he had been told that they were inferior and didn't warrant any discussion of equality. His father and several of his circle were active members of the Klan and refused to countenance any consideration of black acceptance. Lynchings and other violent acts were a part of their hateful thinking. California's Black community was relatively small and, on the surface, not really visible, but the amount of antagonism was far more subtle and constrained. Many of the patients had experienced fighting alongside blacks and were not the least bit comfortable with Bobby's extreme racial views. Doby had been severely wounded at Iwo Jima and had lost both legs in one of the most ferocious battles in the Pacific campaign. The wounded sailors in the ward were initially willing, because of Bobby's condition, to give him a long leash to express his hateful views, but as they became warmly affectionate towards Sara, they did not have a lot of tolerance or patience seeing her hurt in their presence. Bobby's attitude towards Blacks had not changed, but for the sake of maintaining some level of acceptance, his tone changed.

As the months passed, Mark was not only responding positively to his therapy but was definitely getting closer to standing without support. His progress had a lot to do with his determined, disciplined athletic training. Mark was also serving as an inspiration to other amputees who were engaged in the same demanding process. It was a wonder to see these terribly impaired sailors show a surprising sense of humor and acceptance that seemed totally inconsistent with their loss of limbs.

CHAPTER 21

RACIAL THERAPY

Throughout the process, Mark became more and more interested in the woman who was directly responsible for the positive environment of their therapy. Sara was patient, enthusiastic, professional, and physically one of the most beautiful women, black or white, he had ever worked with. That was his dilemma. Could he dare have a relationship with this extraordinary black woman? In his heart, he was ready to say to the naysayers, "to hell with them," but what would Sara say about it? Mark knew that any social engagement would be difficult, even in so-called liberal California. It was 1946, and this form of social progress was on the back burner. The same thought process was part of what Sara was experiencing. She had a very strong attraction towards Mark. He was charming, handsome, intelligent, and yes, lovable. Could she dare have a relationship with him beyond the training room? Based on real-life experience, she had grave hesitation about carrying the flirting and mutual attraction to the next phase. She shared her feelings with her parents, and to her surprise, they suggested inviting Mark for dinner. He accepted enthusiastically, primarily because it gave him some clear awareness that Sara shared his feelings. It also meant that he had to put even more emphasis on his mission of learning to walk again. Wisely, Sara indeed asked him to dinner, aware that the invitation served as additional motivation.

One month to the day, Petty Officer Mark Doyle took his first unsupported step, which was greeted with envy and applause. Two months later, Mark was taking several deeply encouraging steps and the confidence to say to Sara he was ready for "their first date." Mark had many visits with family and friends, but in all cases, leaving the hospital in a wheelchair. On a subsequent Saturday night, Mark prepared for a first date with Sara that involved dinner with her parents. He had asked his dad to help him select a new suit as well as a shirt and tie. As he dressed, Mark realized that this would be a special evening, both from the standpoint of his physical progress as well as the first time in his life having dinner with a Negro family. Sara arrived at the portico of the hospital to pick Mark up and was impressed with the way he looked in civilian garb.

The Shelton home was situated in an upper-middle-class neighborhood in Burlingame. The beautiful tree-lined street complemented a feeling of warmth and a sense of stability. That feeling extended into the home, where Mark was introduced to the Judge and his family. The pot roast dinner was exceptional, and Coralyn was obviously pleased that her meal received high marks from their guest. After dinner, Judge Shelton invited Mark for a drink in his den. As he handed a brandy to Mark, he asked about Mark's experiences in the Navy. As was his habit, Mark responded in short terms with limited embellishment. It was clear that he was uncomfortable talking about exploits during the War. The Judge had checked Mark's record and was impressed with the fact that he was a Medal of Honor recipient. Mark began to wonder what the tone of their conversation was leading to.

As the judge went on, he began recounting his experience as a Second Lieutenant in the U.S. Army during the First World War. As an officer in the army, his conversation directly dealt with the exclusion of black soldiers in the military. During the First World War, in fact, Negro soldiers were not even allowed to fight at the front. Rather than take the option of demeaning service roles, black soldiers were warmly welcomed by the French military and fought heroically. They quickly dispelled the American impression that black soldiers were inferior, and wearing French uniforms, they fought valiantly in many fierce battles throughout the War. The Judge went on to say that almost 400,000 served in the Great War, and only 200,000 were sent to Europe. More than half were deployed and assigned to labor battalions. Mark surmised what was coming next, and he accurately anticipated where the Judge was leaning. Black soldiers returned from the War and found the same socioeconomics and racial violence that they experienced before the War. Despite their performance and sacrifices overseas, Blacks struggled to find decent jobs and instead endured racial prejudice, especially while wearing the uniform. Mark injected his experiences with African American sailors and his memories of black young men as members of his anti-aircraft gun mount. It was not a "me too" expression but rather a subtle way of introducing his knowledge of Black contributions on board ship, where they unfortunately engaged in dual roles. On the one hand, serving the officers in the wardrooms and on the other performing with valor during battle stations.

This initial talk provided a platform for the next phase of their conversation. Judge Shelton segued smoothly into comments about the current status of black Americans. Mark nodded in recognition and directly asked the judge, as an equal, where the conversation was headed. Shelton's response was predictable, especially after outlining the prejudicial treatment of American black soldiers during the First War. "Okay, I will be direct with you, Mark, and please understand what I am about to say has absolutely nothing to do with my very respectful and positive impression of you as a man and a soldier. I have the impression that you and my daughter are in the initial phases of a romantic relationship. You will be impressed to know that Sara has never invited any young man to join her family until tonight. You obviously are joined in mutual admiration that, if allowed to bloom, would probably break your hearts. I am almost 60 years old, and while intolerance and unreasonable prejudice have influenced my thinking, I don't want either of you to have to deal with a society that all too often dwells in mindless hate for mixed-race couples. I really don't know, beyond my initial impression, how serious you and Sara are, but I beg you to consider the repercussions if you intend to allow the relationship to grow. Frankly, it is painful for me to have this conversation, Mark, but Sara is a very special girl, and I just do not want my beautiful daughter to have her heart broken. Hopefully, you will, at the very least, recognize that my concerns are influenced by a demoralizing series of experiences throughout my life that literally brought me to tonight. Whatever you and Sara decide, just know you will have our blessings, but tainted with deep concern about your future together." Mark was taken aback and didn't feel that any response on his part would be called for. He merely responded that he understood the Judge's concern and made it clear that he would never do anything that would hurt Sara.

They retired to join the family. Soon after, Mark expressed his thank you to Mrs. Shelton for her hospitality and an excellent dinner, shook the Judge's hand with a warm thank you, and said goodnight. He was left with a nagging feeling and curiosity about why the Judge did not draw more definitive comparisons charting his life with a white woman. Coralyn's story would have been insightful. On the drive back to the hospital, Mark and Sara were strangely silent. It wasn't until they arrived that Sara asked Mark what her father had said because the whole mood of the dinner party changed. Mark was thoughtful and begged off any revisit of his conversation with the Judge. Sara nodded in understanding, and with that, Mark leaned over and kissed Sara with a level of intensity that surprised him. She looked at him with desire and returned his kiss with even more intensity. The alarm bells were going off, and if either had any question about expanding their romance, the third kiss was definitive! Even though Mark and Sara were in the early stages of a problem-ridden romance, they both knew what they felt for each other, despite the fact that society, for all intents and purposes, had laws in many states that made mixed marriages against the law. Mark was also aware that he had to relate to Sara what transpired in the private conversation he had with Judge Shelton.

With that in mind, where could they meet? Neither Mark nor Sara had their own home. Mark was due to leave Oak Knoll in two weeks after he had completed his therapy and anticipated spending time with William and Rita until he could determine his next steps. For Sara, at 19, the thought of moving out of her parents' home in Burlingame was not a priority until she met Mark. For most couples, this was not a dilemma, but with Mark and Sara, they needed to share a level of potentially painful realities. Seeing Sara every day in her role as a physical therapist was an emotional quagmire for the couple. They tried to create some normalcy in their relationship, but even a touch brought their inability to hide their feelings to a point where most of Mark's veteran peers were quick to recognize.

Robert Gibson was one of the patients at Oak Knoll who was dealing with the loss of both legs in the battle for Okinawa, which was the last major conflict before the Bomb was dropped on Hiroshima. Gibson was from Seattle, Washington and of all the patients, had struck up a friendship with Mark Doyle. Sergeant Gibson was an African

American who was also scheduled to leave the hospital within the month. Mark approached the Sergeant and told him that he had some personal issues that he would like to discuss. The two seriously wounded veterans decided to get together on the south lawn of Oak Knoll. Gibson knew from the tone of Mark's request to meet that it would be a very serious conversation. Admittedly, he was curious, and once Mark began to share his dilemma, the magnitude was one of those issues that in most circles was taboo. Initially, Robert made the point that all the members of the Unit would be incredibly envious of Mark's success at dating Sara Shelton. The attempt at humor did not sit well with Mark. His feelings were raw and uncompromising when it came to his search for answers. He shared with Robert his conversation with Judge Shelton and how his words literally were all he could think about, and the reason why he needed to talk to someone who could be objective. What seemed interminable, Gibson paused before he responded. Then he began to haltingly explain to Mark why the subject of black/white romances was considered more than a little problematic.

He explained that racial segregation was virulently practiced in much of American society. He went on to say that while California and other West Coast states were less de facto than the South, nevertheless, Jim Crow and established age-old customs were very much a reality. Mark listened carefully, and his response was dishearteningly defeatist. Was there any hope for two people in love to stand above the attitudes that angrily disapproved of their union? Again, Robert hesitated to gauge his friendship before he responded that he could not, in all good conscience, encourage an affectionate mixed-race relationship. Gibson could understand why the couple needed answers, but as a committee of one, he believed that he spoke for most of the African/American community even in California. Mark called his mother and explained in short terms the need to find a place where they could meet, and at the same time, hopefully, depend on Rita and William to provide a counterpoint of view. The Doyles, while still living in the Sunset, were actively spending weekends looking for their new home on the Peninsula, very close to the Sheltons' neighborhood.

While Sara was discouraged at the turn of events after Mark shared her father's comments, she realized that the couple quite naturally needed their mature guidance. Rita greeted her eldest son and his beautiful friend at her home on 26th Avenue. After thirty minutes of small talk, William arrived, niceties were exchanged, and they sat down for dinner. Rita and William determined that they would keep it light during dinner and save the serious conversation. Tommy had been in his room studying, and when called, joined the dinner party. He did not anticipate being in the company of such a knockout girlfriend. With some anxiety, Sara had agreed to dinner with the Doyles and thought to herself it was almost like "equal time." Dinner was thoroughly enjoyable, and Mark's family was all that she could ask for in terms of genial warmth. Any pretext of nerves dissipated rapidly as the evening progressed. This was the first time Sara had been invited to a white home. She was especially enthralled with Mark's younger brother. Thomas Doyle at 11 seemed far beyond his age when he entered adult conversation and was without pretense, at ease with this beautiful black young woman. Tommy was as entertaining as he was handsome, and Sara loved his sense of humor and genuinely comfortable manner. He also knew when to excuse himself with the pretext that he had homework.

When dinner was over, Mark opened the conversation with what Sara and he had experienced, including her father's concern about mixed relations in 1946 and the subsequent advice from Sergeant Robert Gibson. Sara added, unbeknownst to Mark, that she too sought advice and, to no one's surprise, was as disheartened as Mark. Rita and William obviously devoted considerable time exploring their emotions on the issue of mixed relations, and at the same time were honest enough to admit that they had unrealized biases. Add to that, they could not ignore the fact that in many States in America, mixed-race marriages were against the law. They explained this to Sara and added that they felt unqualified to give any advice on a subject that continued to be highly polarized. It came as no one's surprise that, like Judge Shelton, they felt that their life together would present more problems than any couple should have to deal with. Rita hugged Sara as they were leaving and hoped that they would carefully evaluate the potential future of a life together. The couple was beginning to question, after some really sound advice from clear-minded family members as well as friends, whether they could emotionally continue with a hopeless love affair and, at the same time, ignore all of the negative views they would have encountered. The fact that they had not slept together was the height of irony.

Painful as it was, Sara and Mark, without any further discussion, mutually broke off their unrealized love. At the same time, Mark called an end to his therapy, whether prescribed or not. The idea of seeing Sara after all they had been through was far more than he wanted to deal with. He had no plans for a future without Sara and, as agreed, would move in with his parents temporarily until he was comfortable with his artificial limb. The only thing that could conceivably take his mind off his breakup was the upcoming trip to Washington to accept the nation's highest military recognition, the Congressional Medal of Honor. The government allowed direct family members to attend the ceremony in the President's Oval

Office. In addition to Rita and William, his younger brother Tommy was included, and so were Patrick and Doris Doyle. Mark couldn't help but think what it would have been like if he could have had Sara by his side. The trip East was an opportunity for Patrick and William to return to Boston. For Mark and Tommy, it would be a chance not only to see where their dad was raised but also an opportunity to finally meet the family that they knew only by photographs. For some in the party, flying was also a first, and Tommy was especially thrilled with the prospect.

Mark suggested that the trip to Boston with a direct United flight should be the initial destination, followed by a train from Boston to Washington, DC. Rita Geller Doyle had additional travel plans, and the amount of baggage should have been a sign that she would share with the family once they arrived in Washington. Since the War ended in 1945, Rita had been even more intent on finding family, or even more, the likelihood that many close relatives had been murdered in the Holocaust. She had methodically been searching for any sources, especially in Germany and Poland, that could conceivably provide a resource that would help her realize her mission. Since the War, many agencies had begun gathering information on the status of survivors of the death camps. The plan included her mother, Sylvia Geller, as Rita's travel mate. There was a reason why Rita did not tell her husband about her plan. They had discussed the incredible revelation that the concentration camps existed in large numbers everywhere from Romania to Poland. The idea that six million Jews had died in the Holocaust, and unquestionably included close relatives, was too much to comprehend or ignore. She knew that William would do everything he could to convince his wife not to make the trip. The idea that she would put herself through what was sure to be a journey of sadness was something he wanted Rita to be spared from. In his heart, William knew that his wife had made up her mind to make the trip, and it had nothing to do with luggage. He was resigned to what Rita was determined to do, and after due consideration, knew that once Rita made up her mind, there was no turning back. At least her mother would be traveling with her and would share some of the anguish and sorrow they were sure to encounter.

CHAPTER 22

MEDAL OF HONOR

The Doyle family arrived at Logan Airport in Boston, which gave them time to check in at the Copley Hotel and prepare for the party that the Boston Doyles had planned for them. "Southie" is a primarily Irish neighborhood in South Boston that is home to the Doyle families. When the West Coast members of the clan arrived, they were met with an excited welcome that instantly embraced the perceived long-lost family, after the introductions that included uncles and aunts, boy and girl cousins, as well as close friends who couldn't wait to hear about life in the "Old West." While Doris (Greeley), Patrick's new wife, was not from South Boston, the fact that she was Irish was all they needed to welcome her to the Doyle clan. As the only non-Irish family member, the beautiful Jewish Rita, who initially felt out of place, was wrapped in the warmth and almost instant acceptance by William's family, which made her feel totally at ease. Mark tried to join in on the revelry, but the pain from the breakup with Sara occupied his lonely heart, and he had to try at least to put on a happy face. William, on the other hand, found it very difficult to release himself from the inviting hug of his Boston paramour, Annie Donavon. Annie's dad was a childhood friend of Patrick and had hoped that William and Annie would marry, but he knew long ago that was not going to happen.

William, like his oldest son, was preoccupied with Rita's plan to find members of her family in the unresolved lists of the victims of the most horrendous mass murders in recent memory. He wished that he could have convinced Rita that she was letting herself in for some painful, sorrowful days that she could carry with her for months, if not years. In the sea off the Leyte Gulf, when the USS Indianapolis was torpedoed and left 900 sailors to see their numbers decimated by hungry, unrelenting sharks, William carried visions of those four nightmarish days almost every day of his life. He had hoped he could intervene, but there was nothing he could add that he had not already voiced with Rita. After three days of lovable Irish family cheer, in California, Doyles bid goodbye to their "Southie" relatives with promises to "never let as much time go by" before the next reunion. Patrick and Doris, however, were not willing to say goodbye and decided that they really needed to extend their stay in Boston. It was more than a token of Patrick's Irish pride and the fact that he missed his eastern family members more than he realized. The thought of missing his grandson's Presidential Medal of Honor Award presentation was thoroughly discussed with Mark, who gave his grandfather his comforting approval.

The depleted Doyle family arrived at Washington National Airport, which they were pleased to find was very close to the Capitol. Once they had checked into the historic Willard Hotel, which was literally across the street from the White House, William, Rita, and their two boys had an early dinner and went to bed to be rested for the next day's ceremony. Mark's mind was not ready for sleep. After two hours, he dressed and went down to the hotel bar and asked if he could play the piano. The bartender gave him a green light, and what followed was a latent talent that he could always turn to and would invariably thrill the available audience. By last call at one, the bar patrons had multiplied when they heard Mark play, and as he waved to the late goers, they applauded with enthusiasm, and the manager offered him a job. The piano was something that he naturally took for granted.

At 2 in the morning, his thoughts were not solely dwelling on the coming day's honor. It was a combination of unresolved concerns that included whether he and Sara were doing the right thing by allowing circumstances to dictate their future. He was also facing the reality of a world without uniforms and prosthetic legs. What was his future? The Walshes had made it clear that they would like him to join their company, but is that what he wanted? He had always believed that his future would unquestionably be tied to professional baseball, but that was not to be. It was past 2 am and the bar was closing. Ultimately, with no resolutions and his mind tempered with four scotches and sodas, Mark returned to his room and was able to navigate three hours of sleep.

The early July morning brought the reality that Mark Doyle, Second Class Gunner's Mate, was going to receive the highest award the nation could bestow, and he would not be 21 for two more weeks. He was sleep-deprived and dealing with a mind-numbing hangover. He joined his well-rested family in the dining room for breakfast, and as expected, his discerning mother gave him a look of resignation that probably dealt with the dissipated way he looked. She could see through the well-scrubbed body, shaved face, and carefully combed hair. At least he had learned to apply a "four in hand" and didn't need his doting mother. The limo was not necessary as the White House was less than a block away. The family was ushered into the White House and led into the Oval Office by a Marine guard, who was obviously impressed with Petty Officer Mark Doyle.

Inside the room, which they all thought was much larger, was an array of Naval and Marine Officers, including Captain of the USS Indianapolis Charles McVay, members of the Cabinet, and members of the Press, including a camera which would document the event for posterity. The four members of the family were ushered into the seating area, and Mark sat at the seat of honor. President Truman was announced and the whole room respectably rose. After a short comment by the President, he asked the Naval Aid to read the commendation, which in accurate terms described the heroism of Petty Officer Mark Doyle and closed with the fact that Mark had lost his left leg. As the ensign read the document, several members of the people in attendance were reduced to guarded tears. Up until this day, Mark had not had his actions on those gruesome four days summarized, and it hit his inebriated brain like he was experiencing it for the first time. The President added some ad-libbed, highly complementary remarks and proceeded to clasp the Medal of Honor around Mark's neck. The room broke into genuinely appreciative applause, and the cameras rolled. The Press attempted to interview Mark, but he begged off after a few words. The story needed more of a human touch, and the reporters found William, Rita and Tommy a legitimate resource. The astute press did their homework and commented on the fact that William had been honored in the Argonne in the First World War with the Silver Star. The Washington Post reported that evening that heroism ran in the Doyle family. It was a memorable event, and while everyone had some rough idea about what Mark had done in the Leyte Gulf, it wasn't until this moment that they heard his heroism verbalized. Rita hugged her oldest son, and through her tears, she realized he was only 19 years old when he proved to have incredible, heroic maturity far beyond his tender years. Tommy Doyle was also affected by the content of the honorary ceremony, and while he had always appreciated his much older brother, this day engendered the 11-year-old with new respect.

The next day, William and his two sons said goodbye to their wife and mother with some understanding of why she felt the strong need to subject herself to agonizing research only to find an end result of devastating loss. Sylvia Geller arrived in Washington the following day with a minimum amount of luggage. Rita was at the National Airport when her mother arrived. It was an incredibly long flight, and after over 10 hours in the air, they were exhausted when they arrived in Warsaw. After a good night's rest, they visited the Jewish Ghetto, which during the War was populated with almost half a million Jews. Nine people lived in each room, with meager food rationing. Ultimately, they were sent to concentration camps and went to their deaths in Nazi killing centers.

In 1943, about 700 young Jews rose and fought the SS for almost 28 days. With only pistols, they were able to inflict real punishment on the Germans and return to their underground bunkers. In the end, the Nazi's succeeded in razing the Ghetto by burning it down block after block. Most of the Jewish fighters committed suicide rather than surrender to the SS. Rita and Sylvia toured what remained of the Ghetto and recited prayers in the small Synagogue still standing. The two Jewish women spent the next weeks researching through available records the fate of family members who remained in Warsaw until it was too late. Nazis kept fastidious records with name, date of birth, and eventual travel notations for every Jew in Warsaw. The surviving 42,000 members of the uprising were sent to the Treblinka death camp. The fact that some had survived the horrendous extermination camp offered hope for finding some family members. This is where they started their journey. They took a train to Treblinka, which was located just 3 miles north of Warsaw, where over half of the 20,000 prisoners were murdered after a revolt, and only 200 people escaped. Soon after, in 1943, Treblinka was closed. The 10,000 survivors offered the best hope of finding relatives. When they arrived at the information center in Treblinka, they were offered access to ledgers with carefully documented entries, which were a starting point for Rita and Sylvia. Sadly, they found the identities of 6 members of their direct family, as well as recognizable, more distant relatives, who were murdered. Treblinka offered no hope for family survivors, but this death camp was merely the first stop in their mission to research all of the Polish forced labor camps.

Treblinka was second only to Auschwitz, which was the largest extermination camp in all of Europe. Approximately 1.5 million Jews were led to their death at Auschwitz, which was the nexus for 45 smaller camps in the area. Rita and her mother were intent on visiting all of the death camps in Poland, which is where their family primarily resided. Auschwitz was closely associated with the Holocaust. They arrived at this sprawling camp, which consisted of two primary camps: Birkenau was the extermination camp where mostly women and children were gassed, and Auschwitz was used as a slave labor camp where men were assigned. Auschwitz-Birkenau became the emblematic synonym for the "final solution." After weeks of investigation, which encompassed almost all the slave labor camps, Rita and Sylvia faced the depressing reality that none of their family members had survived the Nazi's methodical campaign to exterminate all of the Jewish communities in Poland and beyond.

In their final stop in Krakow, they found one cousin who may have survived. David Zucker, the son of Rita's aunt who was listed as alive and living in nearby Krakow. With this potential of one sole family survivor, they were rejuvenated with hope. After an attempt to find David in the phone directory, they found the address for one David Zucker who lived on Grodzka Street in Krakow. With a sense of elation, Rita and her mother found the street and the apartment number in a beautiful section of the city. With trepidation, the women knocked on the door and were greeted by a curious young man. He had a limited vocabulary of English, but after very little time, it was clear that this was indeed her aunt Anna's son. The reunion made up for the weeks of disappointing searches, and now it was all worthwhile. David had survived Treblinka and was one of the 200 inmates who had escaped the death camp and found their way to Great Britain. He had not only survived but, after Germany was defeated, he returned to Krakow and found that his high school sweetheart had survived the camps. They were married two months later and 9 months later were blessed with a son. David's wife, Kasia, was a delightful young woman who spoke better English than David and exuberantly welcomed Rita and Sylvia to their home. David, Kasia and their two-year-old son, Emil, were a beautiful family who brought Rita to tears and an evening of dinner and conversation that confirmed that he was indeed the only surviving member of Rita's Polish relatives.

The following day, the two women bid David and his family goodbye with promises to visit his American family in the near future. When they returned home to San Francisco, Rita and Sylvia were greeted by William, Mark, Tommy and, of all people, Herman Geller. Rita had not seen her father in almost 20 years, and it was a shock to her system. Sylvia was visibly surprised to see her husband finally willing to enter the Doyle family circle. She thought it was unconscionable that Herman had wasted all that time, but the quote "better late than never" was probably appropriate. Over the years, while Sylvia had shared many prideful, poignant moments with Rita, William, Mark and Tommy, Herman showed no desire until now to embrace his daughter's family. After her experience in Poland, after her final success in her search for family survivors of the Holocaust, it was unerringly appropriate that Herman would choose today to ask forgiveness. Rita had sent a telegram to her father stating that she had found his sister's son in Krakow. For what they could ascertain, David Zucker was the sole survivor.

After the extraordinary introductions, Herman Geller admitted that the telegraph message was instrumental in divesting old wounds and the realization that he had indeed missed out on all the milestones of his grandchildren's lives. Breaking down in tears, Herman asked to be forgiven and hoped that he could, at this late date, seek membership in the exceptional Doyle family. Through all the discomfort, Herman presented a picture of a man who was genuinely sorry for his unrelenting, stubborn behavior over almost twenty years. The reunion, primarily from his daughter, seemed to have a "we will see" reception. After all the vacant years, Rita had finally recognized that it served no good purpose to try repeatedly to attempt reconciliation with her father. After the birth of Tommy, she had developed a resentful attitude that colored her rejection of her father, but now, with some hesitation, she agreed to embrace her children's grandfather. After all the disappointments and ultimately some success in Poland, one clear reality came into focus. Even with Mark's injuries and William's hurtful dalliance, Rita felt very thankful for her life and all its blessings. The disaster of the Holocaust, more than anything, made her grateful for her life with William and her two wonderful sons. Her feelings coalesced when she tightly hugged her loving family with a new level of appreciation.

Her thoughts raced back to the conversation she and William had with Mark, dealing with Sara's race and the perceived, although real, social encumbrances. Mark was in love and was finding it difficult to face life without Sara Shelton. It had been three months since Mark and Sara had mutually, painfully agreed to end their intentions to be in a relationship as a couple. During this interim, Mark had learned that Sara was dating a young attorney who offered some level of much-needed continuity in her life. Mark was crestfallen and was experiencing all the signs of emotional distress. He was having difficulty sleeping, and he had lost a significant amount of weight. Rita was abundantly aware of her eldest son's heartache, and a few days after her return from Europe, she decided to revisit her initial advice to Mark and Sara. She had a conversation with William, and together they recognized that Mark should follow his feelings and not let Sara, the woman he loved, get away… If it wasn't too late. The next day, they shared their revised feelings with Mark, who was aware that Sara was dating a young attorney. Rita emphatically told her son to fight for the girl, and if she turns you down, the relationship probably was never meant to be.

Mark had asked Sharon Miller, a wartime friend, out to dinner and saw no reason to cancel the dinner. Even with his parents' advice, he needed time to digest what they had shared. The reservations were made at the Tonga Room in the Fairmont Hotel. As they were being seated, Mark was dumbstruck. The table next to his sat Sara and her date, the attorney. As astounding as it could be, the two lovers selected the same San Francisco restaurant with adjacent tables. Their eyes met, and the interrupted feelings between Sara and Mark were being tested. Mark and his date signaled to the maître d' that they were leaving. Sharon was astute in recognizing that Mark and the girl at the Fairmont had a history. She was going to beg off the date, but Mark insisted on dinner at another restaurant. Over drinks, he felt it necessary to explain what had transpired at the Tonga Room. Sharon Miller proved to be a sympathetic ear and, under the circumstances, served to reinforce the advice from his mother. Seeing Sara had been so traumatic that it took time for Mark to recuperate. After three martinis and a steak dinner that Mark didn't touch, he took a sympathetic Sharon home.

The next morning, after a sleepless night, Mark picked up the phone at 5:00 am, and a somewhat perturbed Judge Shelton answered the phone. Mark apologized and asked to speak to Sara. After a short hello, Mark didn't wait for a response. He instantly said how painful it was for him to see her with another man, how his life without her was miserable, that he wasn't sleeping, he didn't give a damn about the color of her skin, and finally that… he loved her! There was a lengthy pause, and a tearful voice responded… I love you. Mark was absolutely elated and said he would pick her up at Oak Knoll that evening. By the end of the day, he was a nervous wreck, and, in all honesty, he had never even come close to what he was feeling. He loved Sara Shelton, and she loved him. The world was spinning. The meeting on the steps of the hospital was almost impossible to articulate. Mark and Sara had found each other, and that is all that mattered. They drove over the Bay Bridge and, without any consent necessary, checked into the Mark Hopkins Hotel on Nob Hill in San Francisco. The minute they were in the room, they came together with a promise of what was to come. This would be the first time, strangely, that they had sex, and it was everything they had hoped for. It was also the first time Mark had sex since his leg was amputated. That aside, the two lovers could not get enough of each other. If Mark ever wondered about their first encounter, the night (and day) at the Mark Hotel, it was immediately laid to rest. The marathon finally abated at

2 am the next day when they both realized they had not eaten since lunch the previous day. They ordered room service consisting of two club sandwiches and satisfied one of their cravings. The few words that were spoken merely reinforced their love for each other, and Sara called Oak Knoll to say she would not be in that day. The lovemaking continued through the day, and they again realized they were ravenous and ordered a Caesar salad and a steak at six in the morning! Towards the end of the second day, Mark asked Sara to marry him, and the response was predictable.

It was no surprise that Mark's notoriety as a Medal of Honor recipient was recognized by two hotel staff members, and they delivered a bottle of vintage Champagne and a beautiful bouquet, along with complimentary Eggs Benedict breakfast. There was no question… the stars were aligned. When they finally emerged from their room the following morning, the hotel sent up shaving gear for Mark and makeup for Sara. When they stepped from the elevator, the staff lined up to applaud the handsome couple, and when Mark attempted to pay, he was notified that the hotel too was complimentary. It just doesn't get any better. They drove to Burlingame, where Mark kissed his wife-to-be and drove to the Sunset, where his family was anxiously waiting for his arrival. William had stayed home from work long enough to find out the status of Mark and Sara. When he broke the news that he had asked Sara to marry him, there was some initial concern, but that soon ended with joy and jubilation. The fact that their son had the courage to deal with the intolerance that they knew was going to happen was all that they could hope for. Mark's whole demeanor had changed. Even without real sleep for two nights, he was a man in love, and the Doyle family was so pleased to see what real happiness looked like. There was a lot to digest, but for now, all was right with Sara and Mark… but how about Sara's family? Judge

Shelton had been emphatic and painted a very painful future if they determined that they needed to be together. Sara felt her father would maintain his initial warning to the couple, but in time, he would welcome her choice. To that end, Sara called her parents, and even if they still had an experience-based negative view, she loved Mark, and they were willing to face whatever the future had in store for them.

When they arrived in Burlingame, the Sheltons had a distinct feeling that it involved Sara and… Mark. Over the past few months, they tried to deal with an inconsolable Sara, and when she agreed to date a black attorney, they could not be more pleased, but that evidently proved to be nothing more than an impossible stopgap. The fact that Sara had asked to speak with her parents added to the strange 5 am phone call from Mark; the Sheltons knew what they were in store for. Rather than fret over what they anticipated, her mom and dad were resigned to what they knew was coming. If, after all the voices who warned Sara and Mark about the realities of what they would encounter, they remained loyal to each other despite what the world had in store for them. In truth, both James and Coralyn Shelton admired Mark and all that he had accomplished in his short life. For a young man not yet 21 years old, he had survived a monumental, fateful experience when the USS Indianapolis was sunk. His bravery was unquestioned, and who he was as a person could not have been a better choice for Sara. If only he was black.

When the couple arrived and stated their intentions, the Sheltons were unpredictably welcoming, and Sara and Mark were more than a little incredulous. Evidently, the idea of keeping them apart was a lost cause, and they admitted that they had some dark concerns, but nothing was going to keep this star-crossed couple apart. The fact that neither Mark nor Sara had their own apartment, and they were living at home with their parents, proved to be more than a little problematic. Sara had her nursing position to return to at Oak Knoll Hospital in the East Bay, but Mark had no plan in terms of gainful employment. Two priorities drove their planning. First, they absolutely needed to find an apartment and second was a wedding plan, which both sets of parents were insisting on. Stolen moments in hotel rooms felt uncomfortable, but the saving grace was the intensity of their romance. Regardless, the only way they could gain their independence was a home of their own, and to that end, Mark needed to get a job.

The way the couple was able to solve this priority was a story in itself. Mark had always enjoyed Jazz, and San Francisco in the late forties was increasingly popular with some of the best musicians in the country. The Fillmore District, North Beach, The Forbidden City, and Oakland were just a few of the clubs that dotted the City. One evening, Mark and his friend Robert Gibson, both Jazz and Blues fans, spent an evening at Blackhawk, probably the most popular location for BeBop in the San Francisco Tenderloin. Musicians like Miles Davis, Oscar Peterson, and Charlie Parker frequented the Blackhawk. The nightclub was, to say the least, shabby and not the least bit inviting, but the acoustics were so good that the Blackhawk was able to attract the best. For Mark, piano players like Red Garland and Art Tatum were of special interest, but on that evening, Count Basie was the headliner and was mulling over canceling his appearance because his piano player, Oscar Peterson, was ill. Robert stood up and volunteered Mark as a replacement. Everyone in the room laughed and told Gibson to sit down, while Mark was so embarrassed he felt like climbing under the table.

The Count found the outburst amusing and, in the face of catcalls, invited Mark to join him on the bandstand. Mark was genuinely upset with Robert, but he found himself in a position where he could either leave or sit in with one of the best jazz bands in the world. He did the latter with a show of curiosity that urged him to find out if he could contribute. Basie welcomed Mark, noting that this interruption would at least provide some comic relief for the disappointed aficionados in the audience. The Count asked Mark if he was familiar with "Take the A Train," which was a jazz standard, and Mark felt that he might at least have a chance of not totally embarrassing himself. With that, the incomparable Count Basie began to play, and what happened next is still talked about in the San Francisco jazz community. To the shock of the attendees at the legendary Blackhawk Jazz club, Mark began to play with the support of the musical score, which he periodically referred to. He closed his eyes and found himself encouraged to be able to join some of the top musicians in a jazz standard. Being surrounded by this quality of musical skill, Mark was playing at a level that superseded any of his casual past performances. When the Basie Band finished "Take the A Train," the audience showed their appreciation with a standing ovation. The fact that this "off the street" amateur could, without any rehearsal, just sit down and play jazz piano with the Count Basie Band was received with appreciative disbelief. Still on stage, Mark begged off any additional participation. He was obviously shocked and pleased with what he had just experienced.

To the sound of applause, the owner of the Blackhawk, Bruno Banducci, ushered Mark into his office and offered him a chance to play intermissions at the scheduled performances. He could not believe his good fortune, and when Banducci offered $300 a week, Mark immediately accepted. The next day, he drove to Oak Knoll

Hospital to tell Sara in person what had transpired. He had initially felt he could not wait to call her, but on second thought, felt he was emotionally too high to do the news the justice it deserved. Sara greeted him with the same smile each time they reunited. He just hoped that she would not have any concerns about spending his evenings at a nightclub. They sat on the veranda swing on the Sheltons' front porch, and Mark broke the news. He would be employed at the Blackhawk at least three days a week, and no matter how much time was involved, the $300 would remain constant. Mark had learned that trying to read Sara wasn't easy. Her face had not changed expression until it glowed, and that was what he was waiting for. She smiled widely and threw her arms around Mark, emphasizing her total approval of his news.

In the conversation that would follow, the two became elated when the reality of Mark's new job and her weekly salary would be more than enough to rent a downtown apartment in the City. With almost $500 a week, they could afford groceries and, in time, a car of their own. No more having to rely on their parents' vehicle. Sara had to share the news with her mother, who happened to be outside. Coralyn joined the couple on the porch, and they stepped all over each other and laughed as they shared the news. She was pleased, but like all parents in similar circumstances, she had reservations. A nightclub was not exactly the kind of place she would like to envision her son-in-law employed. As they talked, Mark became aware of the fact that Coralyn and her daughter looked very much alike. He should have paid more attention, but now, with some of the most critical concerns in their union being resolved, he could take the time to really see the Shelton women. Coralyn was, at forty-five, the picture of a beautiful, contented woman who had experienced some of the racial dangers that she knew her daughter would endure. All of the intolerance and bigotry would be front and center, and like her and the Judge, they would learn to accept this hateful side of a segment of the American public. Sara had been granted much of her mother's beauty, and in that moment, Mark realized that the blending of races is what gave her that head-turning, soulful beauty. Through all he had experienced, the horror of the Indianapolis sinking, losing his leg, breaking up with Jill and finding Sara was finally coming to fruition. Mark knew that his job at the Blackhawk would not fulfill his aspirations in life, but for now, it allowed them to take a deep breath and start to enjoy some of the pleasures in life.

That evening, they greeted Judge Shelton when he arrived home, and like Coralyn, he was pleased except for the fact that, as a young man in San Francisco, he too was part of a different era of jazz. The Judge was a trumpet-playing teenager who liked to think of himself as a disciple of Louis Armstrong, who was a regular in the early days of ever-evolving American jazz. The two men had not known each other long enough to share commonalities. The "I did too" followed in rapid succession. Judge Shelton had a gift he realized on a guitar, which was the only instrument he could get his hands on as a kid in New Orleans. In another life at Creighton College, he supplemented his meager income from waiting tables to performing on the street with his beat-up guitar. It was at that moment that Mark asked the Sheltons if they all could join him at the Blackhawk that evening. He knew that Dave Brubeck would be on stage that night, and the idea that he would be performing intermissions was somewhat unnerving. They all agreed, and with that assurance, Mark Doyle announced that he would turn 21 the next day. Up until now, he had been underage, and under the same circumstances, Sara at 19 was questionable. Mark assured her that Bruno Banducci, the owner of the Blackhawk, would make an exception… but no drinks!

CHAPTER 23

JAZZ

San Francisco in the late forties had been through much of what was happening to the jazz scene throughout the country. After the war, musicians began to tire of the big bands that required them to play the same arranged notes night after night. This began the move to a new form called "Cool Jazz." Great performers like Charlie Parker, John Coltrane, and Louis Armstrong were instrumental in developing this new sound, which allowed these talented musicians to create independent sounds unrestricted by written sheets of music. As a boy, Mark had listened to the likes of the great Thelonious Monk and Art Tatum, and that is where his creative, unscripted talent was born. Mark had called Bruno Banducci and asked him if he could reserve a table that night that would be close to the bandstand. When the Sheltons arrived, they were ushered into the dreary, smoke-filled room and seated one row back from the stage. Dave Brubeck and his quartet entered and played a series of rehearsed forms of melodies performed by his group as they improvised, much with their unfettered freedom that had been developed initially with black American musicians. It was clear that Judge Shelton was ignoring the dark, musty atmosphere and enjoying some really great improvised Jazz. The Brubeck Quartet finished their first set and retired for intermission, where most of the attendees ordered another round of drinks. Through the din of noise and the clinking of glasses, Mark sat down and began to play a version of Harlem Nocturne. He was alone with one targeted spotlight, creating a mood that complemented

Mark's talent. The Club became almost completely quiet as the room recognized that this was no average piano player. It was obvious that with eyes closed, similar to Erol Gardener, he was lost in his music, and the audience showed its appreciation. When Brubeck returned to the stage, he made a point of complimenting Mark and added that "the kid could threaten my job!"

On the ride back, the Judge let Mark off at his parents' home on 26th Avenue, where the newly crowned professional musician kissed his girl goodnight as he thought to himself what a wonderful evening this was. Mark and Sara spent the next weekend apartment hunting with an eye towards finding a location that would satisfy Sara's commute from Oak Knoll in the East Bay and Mark's job in the City. Ultimately, they found a charming two-bedroom apartment on Telegraph Hill. Over the next few weeks, the couple spent almost every free moment together feathering their new nest. The Walsh family was again instrumental in gifting Mark and Sara with foundational furniture, including a full bedroom suite, a sofa and two comfortable chairs for the living room. As a housewarming, both families contributed, with the Doyles delivering many of the kitchen utensils that included a set of stylish dinnerware. The Sheltons added comprehensive bedding and bathroom ensembles. The gift that truly was jaw-dropping was from the Walshes. In addition to furniture, they had a Steinway upright piano delivered! When Mark felt he needed to practice, he invariably found himself either staying at the club after closing hours or during the day. The idea and convenience of having his own piano was the kind of thing that he felt would be a consideration down the road when he felt it was economically feasible. Sara sat down and wrote a heartfelt thank-you letter to the Walshs, whose generosity was beyond anything they had received. In her mind, she knew that William must be a tremendous asset to the family business. Something she would never include in any correspondence. "Never look a gift horse…"

Both sets of parents had some reservations about the unmarried couple moving in together, but under the circumstances, living with their parents was more than a little problematic. Once the young people moved into their first home together, the next priority without question should be marriage plans! In 1947, living together without the seal of marriage was considered highly inappropriate by stable family units. Sara and Mark could hardly believe their good fortune. In a timeframe of less than a month, they shared their love for each other, vowed to marry, found a delightful apartment, almost completely furnished their nest and brought their parents together. Speaking of their parents, Sara felt that it was time for them to meet and what better time than this? A housewarming would be difficult based on the limited size of the apartment, and invariably, they were concerned about "who wasn't invited." Moms and Dads would be a much better option for a large housewarming. The risks of this invitation were probably opening the door to more warnings dealing with what the couple should anticipate based on race. Mark and Sara had felt somewhat relieved that they had not yet experienced any racial slurs in public. The reality of their mixed relationship was sure to be an issue in the coming days, but they were two bright young people who had no illusions. Hopefully, they would have the capacity to deal with what was sure to come.

Rita and William Doyle, Judge James, and Coralyn Shelton arrived for dinner within ten minutes of each other. Both parents warmly greeted each other, and their offspring looked at each other and smiled. The evening was off to a good start. Mark and Sara had spent the day preparing for the main event. Mark was pouring drinks, and here was another surprise… they all ordered Martinis, two vodka and two gin. In addition, Mark had selected a Pinot Noir that would go with Sara's Coq au Vin. Sara did not usually spend much time in the kitchen, even though she enjoyed preparing exotic dishes when she could dedicate the time. If there ever was a special moment for her to exercise her nascent skill, this was it. From the drinks and Hors d'oeuvres to the Caesar salads and Coq au Vin, Sara and Mark were immensely proud of their effort. Dessert was an excellent vanilla ice cream.

The conversation throughout the evening followed predictable lines. Coralyn and Rita connected instantly, and William and James were deep in conversation on the status of the economy. Mark and Sara periodically joined in the conversation, but more than anything, they stepped back to watch a true melding of personalities. Mark had an opportunity to show off his new piano and announced that he was open to requests. Having a professional piano man at the party was an added gift to the frosting on the cake of a spectacular evening. The couple finally disbanded at 1 am as the parents hugged each other and said their goodbyes. The evening was more than a passing success to a point where Judge Shelton and William would meet for breakfast every Tuesday morning except when there were unbreakable commitments.

At the Coffee Cup on Third Avenue in San Mateo, they became Tuesday regulars and this exclusive club of two had no interest in allowing "outsiders." Beginning when the coffee shop opened at 8, the two men of disparate backgrounds discussed everything from current events to history to religion for a minimum of two hours. Fast friends would be an understatement. It was in this environment that they chose to discuss race rather than preach to their children objectively. Both men believed that it was so sensitive that the only way for Sara and Mark to deal with the imposing, painful moments they would suffer was to let them experience it, and when required, they would step into the breach.

One of those moments was not far off. Mark and Sara had decided that an elaborate, expensive wedding was not to their liking, and both let it be known that they preferred an intimate, small ceremony. After an extended search, they settled on The Log Cabin at the Presidio. It was built in 1937, not far from the western shore of the campus, close to the Golden Gate Bridge. It was exactly the kind of intimacy they were looking for that could be available for an outdoor wedding. If the unpredictable San Francisco weather prevailed, they could move inside the historic, charming Log Cabin. The cabin interior was reminiscent of a grand country lodge with an oversized fireplace and chandeliers, and huge scenic windows with a view of the City.

Sara and Mark had spent a Saturday trying to determine where they wanted to get married. In the process, they decided to stop at a small Fisherman's Wharf restaurant and waited to be seated in the crowded eatery. An older man who served as a greeter said, "Sorry, mister, we don't serve niggers here." They knew it was just a matter of time before they would have to deal with blatant bigotry. People in the small restaurant were all gaping at a scene that you don't see very often in Bay City. What happened next was unexpected. Two couples got up from their tables and canceled their orders. They all walked out together to the chagrin of the elderly manager. The parties who let their feelings be known were from New York and Boston. The three couples laughed and decided to have lunch together at Scoma's, which they believed was "safe."

As they were escorted to their table, one of the men shared that he had been in the Navy, and San Francisco was his favorite port. He had been a Second Lieutenant on board a Destroyer which saw action in Okinawa and Iwo Jima, as well as other smaller island combat. In 1947, the war was still fresh in their memory, and young men who had served in the military were in no small way… brothers. The conversation came around to Mark, and while he didn't like talking about Indianapolis, he volunteered that he, too, had been in the Navy. The lieutenant was not willing to leave it at that and followed with, "Did you experience sea duty?" Mark Doyle was left with one choice. He responded with "Yes, a gunner's mate on the USS Indianapolis." The table became eerily silent. The story of the gallant faithful ship was still fresh in the minds of most servicemen. The middle-aged man from Boston chimed in with, "Did you know the sailor who received the Medal of Honor?" Mark hesitated just long enough for Sara to respond, "Yes, he was that sailor." The entire table was shocked and obviously impressed. The remaining time consisted of questions for Mark about the terror he experienced. The out-of-towners finished their meal and toasted Mark and Sara with congratulations on their upcoming nuptials and promised to stay in touch.

What started with a hateful remark from an obviously bigoted restaurant greeter ended with four people who walked out to support the couple after the race baiting remark. Sara and Mark were angry about the sequence, but the saving grace of four people who were willing to stand up for the couple offered some hope. At the same time, the experience was a wake-up call that supported the alerts from their parents. As the wedding date was rapidly approaching, Sara and Mark began to make out a list of family and close friends who would be invited to both the ceremony and the reception. After a series of additions and eliminations, they came to the conclusion that drawing a line on friends would inevitably cause some hurt feelings. Immediate families, it would be… with one exception. They just could not exclude the Walshs. The consideration had nothing to do with the gifts that included a piano, but everything to do with a long history with the family, who had generously expressed their support and friendship over the past thirty years. The invite would include Walter and Barbara Walsh and their two offspring, Jimmie and Lauralie.

Lauralie remained an enigma in both families. Two years ago, she checked out of the hospital after the horrible beating she took from her then-boyfriend. She had remained secretive based on the fact that she was being stalked by the same threatening ex-boyfriend. No one knew where she was, and that is understandable after what she had been through. The law could not be of any help unless she was attacked again. Lauralie did have one contact whom she swore to secrecy. Jimmie did let her know that Mark was engaged and that a date for the wedding had been set for early June. Perhaps she would come out of hiding based on her affection for the entire Doyle family. In truth, she had moved to the Bay Area and settled in Sausalito, a quiet, charming community in the North Bay. Adding to her careful need for privacy, she had purchased a houseboat in the harbor. It was a community of houseboats tied up adjacent to three piers on the edge of Sausalito proper. Over the past few years, she had established friendships with many of the houseboat owners whom she could depend on in case the threat reemerged.

One person who resided in a boat two units away was privy to her need for anonymity. Stewart Lawson was an ex-Marine from Virginia and was well aware of the threat that Lauralie was running away from. He had lived in Sausalito since he was discharged from the Marine

Corps. Stewart had been part of the ferocious island-hopping campaign in the Pacific, and in the battle of Guadalcanal, he had been wounded by shrapnel in one leg. After two months of recuperation, he chose to rejoin his unit when MacArthur returned to the Philippines in October 1944. Lawson was one of the Marines who fought in the Battle of Leyte Gulf. He was part of the regiment that freed the prisoners at the Palawan POW camp, where 13,000 American servicemen were murdered. After Bataan fell, American and Philippine soldiers, in addition to civilians and their families, were subject to cruel hardship throughout their years of captivity. The notorious "Bataan death march" included the massacre of thousands of combatants. Captain Lawson was in the vanguard of the American units that freed those prisoners. He was the kind of person Lauralie needed in her life as a friend and protector.

For the first time in many months, she felt relatively safe from her pursuer. Lauralie had long ago shed her spontaneous devil-may-care posture and instead chose a life of relative simplicity. She had adopted a Golden Retriever she named "Wilma," who she adored and was her constant companion. Lauralie had always been interested in food preparation and decided to open a small specialty restaurant in the highly competitive community of Sausalito. "Omelets Etc.," which opened three months earlier, had been an instant success from the start. Lauralie's idea was to offer three egg omelets as the base purchase, and the customer would select the filling from a wide choice of options… everything from mushrooms to seafood. The local periodical called Omelets Etc. "is uniquely refreshing and a brand-new treatment of the ubiquitous egg." Every morning, you could see Lauralie and her dog, Wilma, walking the three blocks to her restaurant. She felt respected and welcomed by the entire community of Sausalito. Her brother's news about Mark's ensuing marriage presented a dilemma that entailed leaving the safety and confines of Sausalito and venturing into the City, which was just the other side of the Golden Gate Bridge. She decided to accept once she enlisted Stewart Lawson to be her "date." With the wedding three weeks away, she had time to not only accept the invitation but also to shop for a gift and actually find time to get her hair done and put makeup on. Lauralie felt she had let herself go, but in the opinion of the people who knew her, she remained a mysterious woman of true beauty even without cosmetics.

Sara and Mark attempted to keep their upcoming nuptials simple and uncomplicated. The more elaborate planning took over, especially when the soon-to-be mothers-in-law got involved. Rita and Coralyn were actively insistent on helping Sara with the "simple but tasteful" wedding plans. The bride-to-be was feeling the pressure that she had hoped to avoid, but with the three families, which included the Walshs, she could see no escape. The saying that she constantly referenced in her mind was "the road to hell was paved with good intentions." If she ever thought she could maintain any level of authorship, just add the grandparents. Sylvia Geller, Doris Doyle, and the yet-to-meet parents of the Judge and Coralyn. In addition to the Presidio site, there was one other decision that bore no argument, which was that Judge Shelton would conduct the ceremony. Secretively but not realistically, Sara and Mark were considering a Justice of the Peace.

CHAPTER 24

PINCH HITTER

When the wedding day arrived, all parties were excited and genuinely thrilled that Mark and Sara had found each other. The wedding party convened at the outdoor setting, which featured an exquisitely manicured lawn overlooking a spectacular view of the City by the Bay on an unpredictable sunny day. The families of the Doyles, the Sheltons, and the Walshs were all in attendance. The "simple, uncomplicated" nuptials joining Sara and Mark were anything but simple. The beautiful and unique setting for the wedding was accompanied by soft jazz played by a quartet of some of the finest musicians in America, courtesy of Bruno Banducci of the Blackhawk. San Francisco's reputation for "June Gloom" totally spared the wedding party with a spectacular sunny, clear day. With jazz in the background, Mark waited for his bride to appear, and he wasn't disappointed. Sara came down the aisle with her father, who would also conduct the ceremony. Sara was one of those women who shunned makeup and applied very little, but on this day, she went all out and had a makeup artist apply her skill. The result was breathtaking for Mark. He had never seen his bride looking almost ethereal. She was a beautiful woman, but on her wedding day, she pulled off all the techniques of glamor. The entire event was a perfect success in every way, and hopefully, it was a sign of what their life together would portend. While the celebration continued, the new couple bid their guests goodbye as they headed for their Honeymoon in nearby Monterey.

There was one moment that no one could have predicted. Lauralie Walsh was in attendance, and since her family had not heard from her since she left the hospital, it was a welcome surprise. She had completely recovered from the brutal beating and, at 40, was a picture of full-blown mature beauty. Her appearance was welcome by everyone who knew her, but for the guests who didn't, she was seen as a dazzling mystery woman. To William, seeing Lauralie was colored with a sense of relief. She came over to him, and the one-time lovers hugged for what seemed an eternity. Rita observed her husband's greeting to Lauralie, but through the years, she had developed genuine sympathy for her husband's one-time wounded paramour. She knew that Lauralie had a special place in William's heart and, at the same time, respected his marriage. Rita hugged Lauralie.

Mark and Sara had planned to spend a week in the art community centered in Carmel by the Sea. The central coast of California was spectacular, and every turn along Route 1 offered a new, amazing vista. They had reservations at one of the most charming inns in Carmel. The newlyweds parked and were going to register at the front desk. When the young attendant saw Sara, a blush came over her face. There was no policy warning at Wayfarers Inn simply because they never found it necessary. Once again, the reality of being turned away because of Sara's color was more than they wanted to deal with. Mark's anger came boiling up, but Sara stepped in and attempted to soothe her husband. The receptionist was genuinely embarrassed and suggested that the owner of the inn should intervene. The fact that there was no visible policy and Doyle's reservations came into play as the owner of the popular inn arrived. Mark was nearly consumed with anger, but what followed was the unexpected. The middle-aged woman, who was half of the management/owner of the inn, expressed her apologies for not honoring the reservations. She went on to say that the inferred policy was inconsistent with the current hotel's practices, and she not only welcomed the newly minted Doyles but also upgraded their stay to a large suite overlooking the Pacific. All was forgiven, even though the couple once again found themselves in a compromising position.

The stay in Carmel made for a thoroughly enjoyable week at the Wayfarer Inn, and there were no more "incidents," but Mark and Sara were beginning to understand that until the nation became color-blind and practiced real equality, they unfortunately would be facing more hateful intolerance. The truth is, both families had warned them. With the unpleasantness behind them, Mark and Sara spent a lazy week lovemaking, wandering the charming streets of Carmel, having lunch at hidden bistros, visiting the countless high-end art galleries, and just plain radiating their love.

Upon returning to San Francisco and their newly furnished and decorated Telegraph Hill apartment, the Doyles reentered their day-to-day lives and incumbent responsibilities, in addition to their marriage vows. Both Mark and Sara had strong ambitions about what they wanted to do with their lives. Neither was satisfied with the status quo. They were, for the moment, content with the gratifying way of living they had enjoyed, but Sara wanted to go back to school to fulfill her ambition of being an Orthopedic surgeon. With the earnings that Mark was being paid at the club, in addition to help from her parents, she would have the means to realize her dream. She had already been accepted to the prestigious Stanford Medical School, and she merely needed to be reinstated after her work with veterans at Oak Knoll Naval Hospital was completed. She was pleased to find out that her wartime engagement with wounded sailors would count for units in her application. Stanford was in Palo Alto, about twenty miles from their San Francisco apartment, and that would merely involve a daily train ride down the peninsula. After the application to return to medical school was accepted, Sara would begin classes in September. In essence, with her time at Oak Knoll and her unfinished first year at Stanford, she would receive full credit, and in only three additional years, she would qualify for a residency. Sara was clearly on the right path.

But what of Mark's unrealized future? Playing jazz piano at the Blackhawk was gratifying, and his pay was more than enough to get Sara through medical school, but he just felt that the life of a musician was not exactly what he had envisioned. His goal to participate in professional baseball seemed like a distant, unrealized dream. There certainly was no place for a one-legged major leaguer. Despite the unlikelihood of playing ball again, with his daytime open, he spent a lot of time at the Lincoln High School diamond. It seemed there were always enough pickup players in the neighborhood to play ball. Mark had almost completely regained his strength. In fact, he had transformed from being a promising teen athlete to a stronger grown man of 22. Sara helped him fine-tune his prosthetic leg, and with adjustments, he found that he could perform almost normally as a first baseman. It was a position that required a limited amount of movement, except in moving to his right to cover the slot between first and second. His pickup teammates were cheering him on and offered enthusiastic support befitting a Medal of Honor winner (something they found out about in the SF Chronicle).

Mark's performance at the plate was another story. After weeks of practice in the batting cage, he wanted to try his questionable returning skill at the plate. Mark was hitting the ball harder and longer than he did in his younger days as a teenage prodigy in high school. The artificial leg did present shortcomings, but Mark felt that in time, he could become quicker and more agile. Most of the ball players who participated in these practices were retired Triple-A players and an array of minor leaguers. In the mix was a 60-year-old who had pitched two seasons with the Pittsburgh Pirates. He proved to be exactly what Mark needed to get his hitting eye back. Jess Farmer still could throw an 80-mile-an-hour fastball, which would be a change-up in the majors, but Jess could be a great partner, and they became fast friends. During one particularly near professional pickup game, one of the minor leaguers mentioned to Mark that the San Francisco Seals would be holding walk-on tryouts for two days next month.

Mark would probably ignore the possibility, but so many of his player buddies were encouraging him to try out. They argued that his hitting ability was more than just average, insisting that he was unquestionably the best hitter on the Lincoln diamond. His defensive play at first was passable, but in truth, he had a long way to go before he could qualify as a real first baseman. Ultimately, Mark relented after so many players were offering genuine enthusiasm. Maybe they knew something he didn't. What did he have to lose? "Nothing ventured, nothing gained." Mark discussed what had transpired on the field and was truly interested in what Sara had to say. She took the view that stranger things had happened, and why not, at the very least, test yourself.

The weeks before the tryouts, Mark was zealous about his training program. If he was going to participate in the tryouts, he was at least going to do his best. Lefty O'Doul, the head coach for the San Francisco Seals, had recently played for the Philadelphia Phillies. He had been a relief pitcher, and after developing a sore arm, he was forced to give up pitching. He became a hard-hitting outfielder for the New York Giants and won two batting titles, where he became a World Series champion. Lefty's career closely rivaled Mark's amateur playing. He had been a pitcher with a strong arm, but had chosen to play outfield, which allowed him to hit in every game. He was a power hitter who could hit anything that was thrown at him, from a fastball to a curve to a slider. As a handicapped veteran, he could still stand at the plate and hit. When Mark turned up for the tryouts at the beautiful Seals Stadium, Lefty had looked at his application and the fact that he lost a leg in the War. He was sympathetic but felt that Mark was just kidding himself. He did feel that, at the very least, he should talk to him. After one of the pitching coaches alerted Lefty to the fact that Mark was a Congressional Medal of Honor recipient, it would make the conversation that much more difficult. Mark was changing in the locker room when O'Doul decided to have that conversation, after other players had cleared the area. Lefty haltingly stated that he had genuine respect for Mark's attempt to try out but felt that because of his loss of a limb, he just wasn't being realistic, and he didn't want the ex-sailor to embarrass himself. Mark listened and said he understood, but asked for one turn at bat, and he would be satisfied. It was questionable that he would hit major league pitching, but couldn't he please try?

The Coach relented, and as the day wore on, with a series of talented, primarily amateur and minor leaguers, comporting themselves well in the batter's cage. Both Dom and Vince DiMaggio came up to Mark as he was waiting to bat. They shook his hand and wished him luck. The New York Yankees had recently called up big brother Joe. After more sympathetic pats on the back from one player after another, Mark stepped into the batting box. The pitcher, who was also concerned about not embarrassing Mark, threw a slow pitch over the plate, and Doyle hit it over the left field wall. There was a pause, and Tom Grimes, the pitching coach, went out to the mound and told the practice pitcher to give no quarter. Lefty nervously laughed after the initial pitch and decided to end the misery immediately. The hitting pitcher, while not a starter, did have a variety of pitches in his pocket. He wound up and threw a fastball with accelerated speed. Mark was waiting for it and stepped into the pitch and again found the left field wall. The entire coaching staff was now out of the dugout, and Mark's Lincoln High buddies were cheering loudly. This time, Lefty went out to the mound and told the hitting pitcher to muster his best curveball. Another windup, and the ball sharply curved inside to the left-handed hitter. This time, Mark hit a solid screamer into center field. Again, jubilation from the peanut gallery and complete awe from the coaching staff and players who were out of the dugout and watching what they thought was a rare moment. The pitcher was more than a little chagrined and decided to put all he had into his best 85-mile-an-hour fastball. The first pitch was a "duster" and nearly hit Mark to let him know that he meant business. Another windup, and Young Mark Doyle nearly tore the skin off the ball as it sailed over the 450 ft Center field wall. More cheers, and this time, the entire team and coaching staff were clapping their approval.

Sitting in the dugout watching the surprising performance was Lefty Gomez, who was slated to join the Yankees as their new starting pitcher. O'Doul went over to his best pitcher and asked him to throw the kid out with his fastball. Gomez was hesitant because he admired the heroic sailor's courage, but he agreed that it was time to see what Mark was all about. He walked over to the cage first and let Mark know that he admired him, but added that he was not going to show the amputee any mercy. The first pitch was high and inside, and Mark took a "ball." Next, Lefty Gomez threw his fastball and Mark lined it down the first base line… more enthusiastic cheers and the Major League bound Gomez yelled his approval and decided to teach the kid a lesson with a screaming fastball that Mark swung at and missed… one strike! With confidence, the great pitcher threw another high inside fastball that Mark was waiting for, and he met the ball with a solid whack as it sailed again over the center field wall. Gomez was scratching his head in disbelief as the players ran out to the mound, showing their appreciation of what they had witnessed. Mark had no idea that this day would end like this, and he was beyond elated.

Ultimately, he came face-to-face with Coach O'Doul, who told him he "did well," which was not consistent with the wild approval of everyone on the field that day. The Coach asked Mark if he could move as a base runner after hitting, and what position he thought he could play. Mark responded with honesty and said he could run, but he needed a lot more training to even get within an acceptable base running speed. He added that he was training to play first, and he was learning to cover for the second baseman to his right. These were questions and a conversation he needed to have. O'Doul left the locker room after asking Mark to wait as he went to the field entrance to meet with Gomez. Point blank, the coach asked his pitcher if he had let up at all in the pitches that he threw. The answer was an unqualified no; he had thrown some of his best stuff at the kid. Lefty O'Doul knew what he wanted to do. He sat down on the locker room bench next to Mark and said he would like him to come back the next day to resume his batting practice. He added that a day's grace would be stressful for Mark, but he had to see if he could handle it. He had an idea if he found that the kid was the real deal, but for now, he needed more performance truth. Mark agreed and thanked the coach for giving him a chance.

Coach O'Doul was thinking about signing Mark as a pinch hitter who could be called upon when there were men on base and the next man up needed to be replaced with a pinch hitter. By asking Mark to come back tomorrow, he was purposely adding stress to see how Mark could handle it. This was one way, although not definitive, to find out just how much anxiety the young man could handle. Mark left the stadium anxious to tell Sara what had transpired. The day had been almost dreamlike, and he had to pinch himself to prove it was indeed real. He returned home with a bottle of champagne that the players had given him, and when Sara arrived, he was almost jumping out of his skin to tell her about the unreal day he had. She screamed with joy and threw her arms around her returning hero. No one could have predicted this day.

Lefty Gomez was on the mound again for the second day of Mark's trial. This time, the whole Seals team was on the field after they heard what had transpired the previous day. Mark knew that Coach O'Doul would not invite him back if he didn't think he had talent. As Mark warmed up with the batting pitcher, he again was hitting the ball consistently over the left field wall of the stadium. It was impressive, but today Lefty Gomez was going to see if the kid could handle the best of his pitching repertoire. Immediately, everyone knew that the second day for Mark was not a repeat after he took two consecutive strikes. Gomez threw his breaking ball, and Mark swung and missed. The crowd at this point responded with disappointment… Mark was a one-day wonder. With a look of determination, Mark stepped up to the plate for "round two." Lefty Gomez doffed his hat as a warning and threw his signature fastball. Mark expected the fastball and stepped into the pitch, and the ball flew over the center field wall! Lefty was shocked, and the team lining the dugout was incredulous. It was tie-breaking time at bat. This time, Mark hit a curveball screaming down the first base line in fair territory. Through another series of pitches, Mark continued to show that he could hit the best. He did strike out once, but with the realization that most of the time he was hitting the ball with growing confidence.

Coach O'Doul had his answer, and the more he thought about it, the more he realized that Mark would be a huge plus for the team once the public learned that the Seals had signed a genuine American hero with one leg! Mark was invited to meet with Lefty O'Doul in the manager's office. Lefty began the conversation with genuine appreciation for what Mark had accomplished in the past two days… there was a lengthy pause, and his next words fell with disbelief. The San Francisco Seals wanted to sign Mark for an initial one-year contract. The Coach went on to say that he wasn't concerned about his convincing hitting but rather his ability to run to first base. Lefty added that if Mark reached first, he could insert a pinch runner. Doyle had not thought of that option, and he responded with a sigh of relief. Mark could hardly believe that he was going to sign with one of the best teams in the Triple-A Pacific Coast League. The meeting came down to assurances from Mark that he would do his best to improve his short-range running skills. His new teammates cheered when he entered the locker room and greeted the 22-year-old amputee with wonder and appreciation. Mark tried to put together what had transpired in just two days and could hardly believe what had just happened. He was going to become the Seals' number one pinch hitter, who had to learn to run to first base! That evening, the Doyles celebrated the incredible turn of events with a night of lovemaking and drinking the bottle of champagne he received from the team in "round one." Mark Doyle had accomplished the improbable. He would return to the Stadium in two days to sign a one-year contract with the San Francisco Seals. It would pay him $2,000 a week! Mark and Sara Doyle could hardly believe their good fortune. With that income, the couple could easily afford Sara's medical school expenses and even allow them to purchase a new car.

There was a significant issue that would require Mark's immediate attention. He had been working at the Blackhawk for almost 4 months under the auspices and good graces of Bruno Banducci, the nightclub owner. Mark could not commit to any modified schedule based on the travel requirements of the Seals. He had no choice but to meet with Bruno and explain what had transpired, and at the same time, thank him and offer his notice. He had loved his evenings playing intermission piano and certainly appreciated the kindness and reception of the Blackhawk jazz clientele.

CHAPTER 25

SAN MATEO

Both families were shocked by the turn of events. Sara's parents had no idea that Mark was an athlete. To learn that the San Francisco Seals had signed him to play baseball with one leg was more than they could comprehend. Mark Doyle was a young man full of surprises. First as a talented piano player employed by the best jazz club in the City and now as a professional baseball player! In fact, almost everyone who knew Mark before the War was aware of his aspirations to play professional baseball, but with one leg? No one could have predicted this turn of events, and without exception, he was thrilled with his success. The San Francisco papers, including the Chronicle, Call Bulletin, and Examiner, treated the story with front-page headlines. All three dailies went back in the archives, citing his potential as an extraordinary high school player, his heroic service in the War, the amputation of his left leg, piano playing at the Blackhawk, and now signing with the San Francisco Seals. This is the kind of touchy, warm feeling that Lefty O'Doul had hoped for. The Bay Area newspapers and Radio stations clamored for access at Mark's signing of his one-year contract with the Triple-A Seals. The only thing better would be a signing by the Majors.

Any concern that Mark had about having to quit his job at the Blackhawk quickly evaporated when Mark was greeted by warm applause when he stepped up on the stage for his last performance. Bruno and the people who worked at the Club were full of good wishes, and Banducci made it be known that if it didn't work out, he was always welcome to return to the Blackhawk. Mark and Sara's startling news was not the only major news in the Doyle family. William and Rita had been spending almost every weekend since the end of the War looking for a move to the peninsula. With the help of the Sheltons, they had settled on buying in one of two communities… San Mateo or Burlingame, where The Judge and his family resided. The beautiful homes in these communities were expensive, but with all that the Doyles saved during the War as a successful Vice President with Walsh Inc., they could afford almost every home on the listings. They finally settled on a charming three-bedroom Spanish stucco home with a front flagstone patio, two full bathrooms, a spectacular beamed ceiling living room and parquet floors throughout. The home backed up to Crystal Springs Road with a woods behind their expansive rear patio and lawn punctuated with beautiful mature trees. After their offer was accepted, Rita and William were jubilant, but while they were pleased, the thought of moving away from 26th Avenue would be painful for the entire Doyle family… Rita's Victory Garden, Mark's engagement to Sara, Tommy's adventures in Golden Gate Park, and William's mounting success were all milestones they would always associate with the 26th Avenue flat.

There was no doubt that moving away from friends and memorable events spanning the War years and family successes and painful failures would be traumatic, but it was time to purchase a family home that would serve as a base for whatever the future may hold. In September 1947, a moving van pulled in front of the Doyles' shared flat. As the workers emptied room by room, it became apparent to the entire family that they were experiencing the end of an era, and it was time to move on. Friends of Rita, William, Mark and Tommy were there to wish their neighbors a heartfelt successful move to San

Mateo. Many promised they would visit the Doyles, and it really was not that far away. In reality, they knew that today would most likely be the last time they would see their popular neighbors. The exception may be Mark, who had recently married and moved to Telegraph Hill. For Tommy, who was now 13, establishing new friends and exploring an unfamiliar neighborhood was both a little frightening and, at the same time, exciting. 26th Avenue was just 15 miles away, but it seemed like the other side of the world. He would miss his big brother, who was for the first time living in a close though different city, but the move also meant Tommy's first room of his own. He was concerned about the fact that suburban homes were much larger than the typical San Francisco flat. An expansive lawn in the front and rear of their new home was nice, but to Tommy, it meant that friends would be much farther away. He did look forward to attending Borel Junior High School, which served seventh and eighth-grade students exclusively, and that meant no little kids!

Also, his parents promised the move would mean it was time for his very own bike, but unlike many of the kids in the new affluent neighborhood, he would be required to buy his own bike with his Pepsi Center savings. He was getting his first serious lesson in responsibility and saving, and Tommy surprisingly did not resent his parents' decision. Throughout their young lives, Rita and William had made a point of not spoiling their boys and teaching them the value of a dollar and earning their own money. With that in mind, William took his son shopping at the bike shop on B Street in San Mateo. Tommy was somewhat disappointed at the unanticipated high price that would be required to purchase a new Schwinn bike. His dad asked the salesman if they had any used bikes that were less expensive. The young salesman showed Tommy and his father a choice of several used bikes. A 'Roamer' brand, which Tommy had never heard of, was probably the best value. He asked if he could try it out and quickly learned that riding a bike required some training. William stepped in and committed to taking the role of teacher and agreed that the 'Roamer' was a good value with very little wear. Tommy was thrilled to have finally purchased his overdue bicycle and, with his dad's help, rapidly learned to ride after a series of missteps. Being responsible for the purchase of his first bike was initially resented, but after due consideration, he realized the value of independence, even if it required most of the money he had saved, shining shoes. Tommy's next goal was to replace the money spent on his bike, and to that end, he rode his new purchase to the office of the San Mateo Times. He asked if the route that encompassed his new home on Cornell and the surrounding streets was available. While he was initially disappointed, the Times attendant offered the adjoining route in Parrot Park. Tommy signed up after he was told the rules and learned the responsibility of delivering the daily San Mateo Times.

Having been conditioned to understand what it meant to earn your own money, this after-school job was the right fit for the youngest Doyle. The process consisted of a delivery of the day's papers at the corner of Cornell Street and Alameda, taking them home, folding them to fit into the double-sided bag, which fit over the rear bike fender, checking off the delivery addresses, and finally throwing them as close to the front doors on his route as possible. It wasn't long before Tommy found where kids his age lived in the adjacent blocks. Directly across the street was 13-year-old Bradley Clark, whom Tommy quickly labeled as 'stuck up,' initially unapproachable, and unwilling to respond to his overtures of friendship. Over one block was another, soon-to-be classmate at Borel. Arthur (Art) Gillies was the polar opposite of Bradley Clark. He was in every way pleased to have a new friend, and it took very little time to offer his friendship.

On the same street, two doors down from Art, was a 12-year-old girl named Patsy Kramer who also would be joining the boys in September at Borel. Patsy, like her friend Art, was quick to welcome Tommy to the neighborhood primarily because of Tommy's good looks.

All in all, Tom Doyle was easily acclimating to his new environment. He would find in the coming weeks of attendance at Borel, a schoolyard full of potential friends. September came, and for Tommy, it could not come too soon. He had made some friends in the Baywood neighborhood, but it just wasn't the same.

On the 26th, the block between Irving and Judah and the adjacent streets were teeming with kids. He tried to imagine the Borel kids playing "kick the can" with families sitting near the curb to watch the bedlam of pure joy. Here, it was so conservative and cautious. There were no vacant lots, no stickball, no homemade coasters and no clod fights! However, at Borel Junior High, he was meeting kids who didn't know what the word "snooty" meant. It was an amalgam of young teens from all economic backgrounds that made the school just right for Tommy's wide-open offer of friendship. The schoolyard for recess was large and perfect for everything from baseball to the new game of "touch football" to a basketball court. With seventh and eighth grades only, there was little concern about whether you could join in on the school's activities. Tommy quickly learned that while most of what he was observing at Borel was welcoming, some kid creatures were labeled as "Bullies." A group of approximately 4 eighth graders took it upon themselves to determine who would participate in the organized activities.

On 26th Avenue, Tommy had learned what being a bully was all about. Billy Schultiest was a kid in the neighborhood who was picked on regularly because he was a "Kraut," meaning the family was of German heritage. Tommy always felt bad for him, even when he had the opportunity to stand up for him. On one occasion, Billy was being attacked in a 25th Avenue vacant lot as five or six neighborhood kids pelted him with clods, which were weeds that had dirt and rocks attached as you pulled them from the ground. Tommy knew what "clod fights" were, and he had many when it was one-on-one. To observe five against one seemed unfair, even if Billy was a 'stinking Kraut.' Billy gave as much as he received, and Tommy could see him cornered in the lot, throwing clods while crying in despair. Tommy never forgot that incident and felt bad knowing that he could have stopped the fight. What he was seeing at Borel was, in its way, another bunch of bullies picking on other mostly smaller peers.

For the first few days at school, Tommy was just getting to know the feel of his new school and, in most cases, really enjoyed what he was experiencing. There were plenty of kids from all backgrounds that he started to make friends with, a school yard, which wasn't all concrete, and teachers who seemed to really be engaged in their role and were willing to take time with every student, regardless of circumstances. In his second week, young Doyle was feeling comfortable with his new environment, except for the gang of bullies who took the view that they controlled the school yard. Jimmie Schmidt was attempting to participate in a game of baseball, but the bullies thought otherwise and pushed and shoved him until he started to cry. His tears just made the mean boys more intense, and then they started calling a much smaller Jimmie "a dirty Jew" and started kicking him as he lay on the ground. Tommy instantly conjured his feelings about not helping Billy Schultiest. He walked over to the three bullies and told them to

"Knock it off!" Tommy was the new kid who no one knew anything about, so the attackers just kept on pummeling the smaller kid. With a now-or-never move, Tom stepped in front of the bullies and once again repeated, "Knock it off." With that, the leader of the trio pushed Tommy and knocked him down. That is all our young hero needed. He got up, punched his attacker as he landed on him, and began to follow up his first punch.

This incident was a good thing for the kids in the yard to see, primarily because the bully began to cry, and his authority for the first time was questioned by the new kid. Tommy's image took a major step up, and before long, all that had transpired was the talk of Borel. He was surprised when the lunch recess was over and he was asked by Mr. Ekhart, his home room teacher, to report to him. When he sat down with the teacher, he was asked what started the fight, and in clear terms, Tommy explained what happened. Mr. Ekhart was not having any of it and chose to take him to the principal, who would mete out the punishment for "beating up another student." Tommy was incredulous, but with nothing more than a repeat of what really transpired, he was sent home and expelled for two weeks. Rita, who was home that afternoon, was more than a little surprised to see Tommy home at that time of day, before school had let out. Her son explained what had happened in the school yard, including the "dirty Jew" remark by the bully. Rita was incensed and told Tommy that he had every right to do what he did, and added that his dad would have more to say about the school's actions.

For the second time, Tommy told his version of what had happened, and after a series of questions, William showed discernible anger. He told his son that if he had not left anything out, he was right in doing what he did and should be proud of himself for sticking up for the victim. The next day, even though he had been put on expulsion, William and Tommy showed up at Donald Heller's Principal's Office. The secretary told him he would have to wait, and after almost half an hour, William told his son to wait as he barged into the principal's office, as his anger was mounting. The first thing that he noted was that Heller was not meeting with anyone and had purposely kept William waiting. The anger was now bubbling! He confronted the frightened principal and asked why his son was expelled, outlined what had transpired in the school yard and asked if the bully too had been expelled. The cowering head of the school tried to sidestep the question and attempted to condone what had gone on. William grabbed him by his lapel, almost dragging him across his desk and threatened to meet with the school board and go as high up as needed to right this ridiculous wrong. In addition, he angrily stated that Tommy had significant Jewish blood and that the epithet was a line in the sand! Donald Heller had been traumatized and promised that Tommy could return to school the next day, and added that he did not get the full story. Satisfied, William and his son left the school and returned home. It didn't take long before the students at Borel circulated one version of what transpired after another. In just two weeks at junior high, the Doyle family had turned the staid suburban school almost upside down and not in a bad way. Tommy was perceived as a schoolyard hero before his father arrived, but now, he was larger than life. The next day, Tommy Doyle did return to school, where Mr. Ekhart haltingly apologized to him and stated that he, too, did not fully understand what had gone on in the schoolyard. From that day on, there were no incidents of bullying at Borel, and Tommy unequivocally was seen as a true leader and savior. He did not brag about the turn of events but chose rather to say nothing and just let the whole sequence of events be laid to rest.

CHAPTER 26

THE SEALS

For the next few years, the Doyle family adjusted to suburban life in San Mateo and, except for a few negative adjustments, found life on the Peninsula all that they had hoped for. To no one's surprise, life on 26th Avenue was still cherished as a wonderful memory, but, for all intents and purposes, was relegated to the past. After graduating from Borel, Tommy would be attending San Mateo High School, and at 14, he was among the biggest kids in his class. His reputation, drawn from other kids at Borel, had preceded him, and almost immediately, he was seen as a leader. Tommy thrived in the larger size and number of opportunities he found in the high school environment. San Mateo High School embraced almost 2,000 students from Freshman through Senior grades, and the school was highly diverse considering that it was physically situated in the wealthy Baywood and Hillsborough districts.

Tommy soon found out that the Peninsula was carved into what would later be termed the "haves and have-nots." The line of separation was East of El Camino Real, commonly referred to as the community's main thoroughfare. Commonly referred to as the other side of the tracks. Regardless of where you were from, the school drew no distinctions and at least attempted to make the high school experience fair and equal for all students, regardless of their economic status. This equality was most observable in the many sports and activities that San Mateo had to offer. The school football team was one of the best in the state of California, due in large part to the Black and Filipino players on the squad. The same color blindness applied to many of the school's activities, but primarily to team sports such as football, baseball and basketball.

Following his brother's steps, Tommy tried out for freshman baseball and was immediately seen as their new left-handed pitcher, the position held by Mark at Lincoln High in San Francisco before he lost his leg in the War. Tommy could not hit the way that Mark did, but that didn't matter. His big brother had made him proud as a member of the San Francisco Seals baseball team. Like Mark, the coaches already were trying to determine how fast to move him along. As a freshman, he could throw a ball faster than any member of the varsity. For now, it was decided to let Tommy mature a little more, and if he did well, especially improving his control, he could join the varsity when he turned a sophomore.

Tommy was now doing much better with his grades, thanks in large part to tutoring from his first love… his fifth-grade teacher, Miss Berry. He liked all of his freshman teachers with the exception of Mrs. Hawkins, his history teacher, but five out of six wasn't bad. History was one of his favorite classes, but once again, Tommy Doyle found himself in a teacher's crosshairs. Mrs. Hawkins taught Ancient History and the Roman Empire. Not one to let important things pass, when she said that Jews crucified Jesus, Tommy raised his hand and said that was not what the history book said. (Those darn Jews again) The Romans were guilty of crucifying Christ.

The teacher and student began to argue, and ultimately Tommy was sent to his counselor to be reprimanded. Once again, he found he had to explain himself and was told it was inappropriate to argue with a teacher. The counselor, based on her knowledge of ancient history, said that he was right; however, that did not justify an argument with his history teacher. At the tender age of just turning 14, Tommy didn't understand and let the counselor know that if he was right, was it appropriate for Hawkins to continue to teach a lie? The counselor smiled and relented. This was a truly admirable young man, but the best she could do under the circumstances was to transfer Tommy to another history class.

High school also opened the door to the one social avenue that he had all but ignored, and that was coalescing with girls. The age of adolescence was upon him, and he was seriously in a state of recognizing the difference between a boy and a girl. He was seriously experiencing what it was like to feel the stirrings of a young man. There were many very pretty girls in the large Freshman class, but there was one girl whom the rest of her gender envied, and that was Joan Desmond. She was blonde and blue-eyed and the stereotypical "All-American Girl." The truth was, Joan didn't feel the way she looked to other classmates—as "untouchable." She was warm, friendly and anxious to please, but she couldn't understand why boys, especially, were not responsive. Boys in general, maybe, but not to Thomas Doyle. He found Miss Desmond to be the answer to his surging masculine desires. Joan Desmond was one of those young ladies who intimidated boys, who believed that she was just too pretty and above their social status. For that reason, except for Tommy, the boys in general felt unsuited to date someone that attractive.

The first dance of the year in the school gym had been announced. As ninth graders, it would be their first coed experience since they left middle school. To no one's surprise, Tommy asked the unattainable Joan Desmond to the dance. What the boys didn't know was that girls had some of the same feelings that they were experiencing. Thomas Doyle was the male version of Joan, and only someone with Joan's looks had a right to date the best-looking boy in class. Ultimately, members of the Freshman class of San Mateo High paired off and were thrilled to be going to their first real dance. Rita and William Doyle marked Tommy's first date as a true milestone. He had never talked about 'girls,' but it was just a matter of time and asking his mother for help in dealing with his first major event. Boys were told to wear a tie (a coat wasn't necessary), and girls must wear a dress. Tommy was fortunate because, in his capacity to plan for Tommy's future, Mark had left almost all of his high school clothes behind. Again, with his mother's help, he picked out a tie, sport coat and slacks that fit him perfectly.

The whole idea of a formal date was exciting, and Tommy welcomed this moment of graduating to a higher level of boyhood. After selecting a corsage for Joan, William and his son drove to the Desmond home, which was a mere two blocks away. It had been arranged that the Doyles would pick up the kids and deliver them to the dance, and the Desmonds would then pick them up at midnight. Tommy was not ready that evening for the sight of the prettiest girl in class, but there she was in all of her young female splendor as she opened the door. Joan Desmond lived up to her reputation as 'untouchable.' Her blonde hair was pinned up, and Mom had agreed to just enough makeup. Tommy almost said "wow," but his good sense told him not to be overly impressed, even when he was. William met Joan for the first time and, to himself, agreed that his youngest son had good taste. Joan and Tommy arrived at the dance and, without trying, made a grand entrance. They were truly a very attractive young duo. Thankfully, Rita had spent some time teaching her son how to dance, and while he was a terrific athlete, he was surprisingly awkward on the dance floor, but that was due to the fact that his mom was teaching him. But still, the lessons served him well, and Joan was impressed and proud to be Tommy Doyle's date. The successful evening ended, and from then on, Tommy and Joan were seen as a couple.

While Tommy was on his first date, Mark made every effort to see his little brother before his first dance and date in high school. Unfortunately, the Seals were playing an away game against the Seattle Rainiers. Mark had been making a name for himself as a pinch-hitter for the Seals. For each of his first five times at bat, he had hit two doubles and two homers! He had avoided being thrown out on only one occasion, that once was primarily because his prosthesis leg kept him from running fast enough. That was always a problem for Mark, compounded by the fact that a substitute runner had to be called to take his place on the bases. It was troubling, but he was genuinely thrilled with the way he had been received by both his team members and the fans. The press, which can be snarky, knew a good story when they saw it, and the idea that a Medal of Honor amputee was playing baseball, let alone for his hometown team, made for great press. The fact that he was living up to the hype made the story that much more appealing. After just 20 times at bat, Mark had shown that he could still play the game even with some shortcomings. The Major Leaguers were also aware of Mark's success at the plate. As a farm team of the Yankees, the Triple-A Seals were a solid contributor to the New York lineup, and Mark's success as a hitter garnered close attention, including the fact that his appearance alone had accounted for a significant increase in attendance.

Mark's visibility was enhanced when the team schedule called for some exhibition games with Major League teams, starting with a short series with the Cleveland Indians, who were coming to town with Satchel Paige, the legendary black pitcher from the Negro League. Approaching sixty, Satchel joined the Indians more for show to at least recognize the Negro League for all of the great black players that never saw the infield of a Major League Park. Jackie Robinson of the Brooklyn Dodgers was the first black player to participate in the Majors, and he was currently experiencing a lot of fan abuse. There were several other black players in the Negro League who warranted a shot in the Majors, but for now, Robinson had to bear the brunt of acceptance. Paige, with his famous 'hesitation' pitch, was fun to watch, but the great Satchel Paige had seen his day. It was rumored that, in addition to Robinson of the Dodgers, Cleveland was looking at the Negro League star Larry Doby. The owner of the Cleveland team was a born showman named Bill Veeck. Like Mark, he had lost a leg in the war and was anxious to see the Seals' one-legged batting sensation. Mark was well aware of Veeck's history, but that aside, playing on the same field as Satchel Paige was in itself an honor.

With two away in the bottom of the ninth and Cleveland leading 5 to 2 with 3 men on, Lefty called for his pinch-hitter. Like a game of chess, Lou Boudreau called for a time-out and decided to change pitchers. It wasn't just any pitcher; it was conceivably the best pitcher in baseball. Bob Feller, better known as "Bullet Bob," was typically a starting pitcher for the Indians, but on this occasion, he wanted to see if Mark had earned his advanced billing as a great pinch-hitter. Mark stepped up to the plate and waited for Feller's first pitch. It was a fastball that had the velocity of no pitch he had ever seen—strike one. Mark dug in with his good right foot, waiting for the next pitch that he was sure would be a fastball, which he swung on and missed… Strike two, Rapid Robert wound up again, and this time it was a changeup that was outside and away from the plate. Two and one. On the next pitch, Mark was looking for another fastball, although most hitters would probably guess it would be a curve. Feller just had to show this upstart kid what a real fastball looked like. This time, Mark had guessed right as Bob Feller delivered a sizzling ball that was sure to be a strike, but not this time. Mark swung and lifted the ball over the center field wall, and limped to first base and ultimately, with a homer, limped around all the bases as Bullet Bob shook his head in bewilderment. The crowd roared their approval. There was no question that Mark Doyle was a tremendous asset to the San Francisco Seals, and it was just a matter of time before the league-leading Yankees would call him up.

In truth, both Mark and Sara dreaded the day that he would get the call that he knew was coming. There was no doubt that the move would require a significant lifestyle change and a huge boost in salary. The thought of turning it down would be inconceivable, but it was the subject of deep consideration. Playing in the Pacific Coast League was relatively easy when it came to travelling with all the League cities on the West Coast. Mark was traveling, but with the Seals, it was controllable, and they were not separated for long stretches, but if they moved east to New York, travel would require many days on the road. Major League teams were as far west as Chicago, and there was conversation about expanding both leagues, and if that transpired, both San Francisco and Los Angeles would be adding to the travel dilemma. Mark and Sara both wanted children, and the travel issue could put their newlywed relationship in jeopardy. The thought that they were actually considering not taking the job of a lifetime made them both giggle with nervous laughter, but not because it wasn't a reality. Mark added that a pinch-hitter role in the Majors could have a limited life, especially if the cream of the pitching community in the league found that he may have a weakness. They ended the conversation in the air, but they knew that discussing what this great opportunity on the surface would entail and whether they had the audacity to say no. Sara closed with the obvious and the predictable 'Let's sleep on it.'

Rather than let the dilemma simmer, Mark felt he could talk to his manager, Lefty O'Doul and spread his cards on the table. Lefty listened intently, and after a long pause, he responded. He confirmed that the Yankees calling Mark up was a distinct possibility and certainly worthy of the couple's head scratching, but would they actually say no to the best team in baseball? Lefty also let it be known that if they did decide to turn down the New York Yankees, Mark would always be welcome as a member of the Seals. When he returned to Telegraph Hill, Sara was ready to continue the conversation, adding something they had not considered. She still had at least three years remaining in medical school, and even though the Pacific Coast League required some travel, it was manageable. Travel in the Major League became the point in round two of the conversation. She would be in California working for her medical degree, and Mark would be traveling regularly to teams halfway across the country and adding the real possibility of expansions.

They were stymied over a clear picture of what their life would look like. Sara could not and would not transfer to a medical school on the East Coast, and moving would totally upend the wonderful life they were now living. This time, they closed with an understanding that if the offer did come, they would have to reluctantly say no. (Can you imagine?) It was indeed a good thing that Mark and Sara had discussed all avenues of what a move would entail when an offer to join the New York Yankee came through. It was also important that Mark had brought Lefty into the discussion, so he would not be surprised if his star pinch hitter said no. Casey Stengel, the Yankee Manager, could not believe what he was hearing… A minor league player had actually said no to an opportunity to join the best team in baseball! It was a very short conversation between the two managers, but Lefty did explain Doyle's position and asked Stengel to understand that this was not an easy decision for Mark and Sara, who had discussed the possibility at length even before an offer was made.

What followed can only be described as total confusion and an inability for the press to understand what had transpired. The New York Times and the San Francisco Chronicle, alongside almost all the other dailies, covered the story, devoting long columns to Mark Doyle's decision to say no to the New York Yankees. There was anger on the East Coast, but in the West, fans cheered and admired Mark's decision to stay put with the Seals. The City of San Francisco feted Mark and Sara for their gutsy decision to stay home, and there was even a suggestion that the City hold a parade for them!

CHAPTER 27

ROBBERY

Staying with the Seals and the city of San Francisco was absolutely the right decision. However, a beautiful Bay Area evening after a winning game at home with the San Diego Padres… tragedy struck. Mark stopped at a neighborhood grocery store to pick up some items for Sara. He completed his list and guided his cart to checkout. As he approached the counter, he heard, "Hand over your cash, do it, do it. No funny business." Mark slowly moved forward to a position where he could see the robbery. He saw a very young man with a pistol pointed at the store owner and repeating, "Just do it. Do it!!" Mark moved slowly toward the back of the robber. Just as he was going to reach for the pistol and disarm the young thief, the kid turned around and faced Mark, who was approximately two feet away. Mark lunged forward and grabbed for the pistol. The two wrestled on the floor of the market, while the grocer called the police, the gun discharged, Mark was hit, and at the same time grabbed the weapon and had enough strength to hand the gun to the grocer, who held the robber at bay as a police patrol car pulled up. The officers disarmed the grocer as he was haltingly explaining what had transpired. The police sergeant had enough information to call for an ambulance and swiftly arrest the robber.

Mark was unconscious and bleeding profusely as the attendant applied a tourniquet and the ambulance sped toward Saint Francis Memorial. When they arrived at the emergency entrance, a team of physicians and nurses put him on a gurney and rushed Mark to surgery, where the doctors worked to save his life. The bullet had entered his body and breached a main artery. The team stopped the bleeding and delivered a transfusion. Doing all that was humanly possible, after four hours in surgery, they moved him to an intensive care unit. Mark had not regained consciousness, and his vital signs, even with all the transfusions, were remaining dangerously low. Sara was alerted by the hospital that Mark had been seriously injured. When she arrived, she was ushered into a private waiting room where a physician was there to provide information on Mark's status.

In tears, she called the family, and in less than an hour, they arrived in time to learn his condition was dire, and for now, no one was allowed into the ICU. Mark was hanging on by a thread. The two families were beside themselves with the anguish of knowing that Mark was in a very serious condition. They waited for hours and were given regular reports on his status, and even an ounce of hopeful information was not in the offing. At seven in the morning, the Chief Surgeon entered the room and urged the family to sit.

Mark Doyle passed away at approximately 6:20 am. The physician went on with details, but the family of Doyles and Sheltons heard nothing as they attempted to digest the shocking news. Sara Doyle was in a state of disbelief as she fainted upon hearing the news. When she regained consciousness, she was inconsolable and insisted on seeing her husband. As William Doyle braced her, they entered the ICU. The sight of her beloved husband was more than she could bear, and in total despair, she dropped to her knees. The next hours were a haze as the families gathered at the nearby Telegraph Hill apartment. Hours later, through the tears, William Doyle gathered enough strength to insist that they decide on the next steps and ultimately engaged in a conversation deciding painful, agonizing steps and approvals that must be addressed.

Paramount in William's and Rita's minds was how to break the news to Tommy. The brothers were extremely close, and even the idea of breaking the mournful news to Tommy was painful. Days later, the decision was made to cremate Mark as he wished. As soon as possible, family and close friends were invited to attend a ceremony that would allow all the attendees an opportunity to voice their personal moments. Mark did not want religion to be a part of his passing, even though he knew that certain family members would find disfavor with the exclusion of religious prayers, but he was so emphatic in his will, his wishes would be adhered to.

Everyone from family to friends, which would encompass the Seals baseball team, crew members on the USS Indianapolis, Lincoln High School teammates and friends, and the entire Walsh family, attended. As he had requested, his ashes were released by Sara and his remains were scattered into the Pacific Ocean, where Mark had saved so many lives when the Indianapolis was sinking. On the day of the "service," people who knew and loved Mark, as well as a huge crowd, gathered to pay tribute at Sigmund Stern Grove in the Parkside District in San Francisco. The friends and family who wanted to offer a remembrance were on the stage and consisted of almost 50 people who were selected by William and Rita Doyle, who would share their remembrance of Mark, including shipmates, friends, athletes and relatives.

Included in the audience of over 600 was a huge constituency of Navy Veterans who were shipmates on the Indianapolis, Minor and Major League Baseball players and many friends from 26th Avenue. Ben

Bernstein, the First-Class Gunner's Mate from the Indianapolis, was selected to introduce all of the people who had shared memorable times with Mark Doyle. One by one, many of the 50 friends on stage came up to the microphone to talk about their favorite, lasting moments. First to speak was Jill Neman, Mark's high school sweetheart, who talked fondly about Mark and the kind of athlete, gentleman and leader that he was. Next came Coach Dan Lacy from Lincoln High School, who shared moments when Mark was the number one pitcher for the team, always performed as a leader, and never let his outstanding skill and status go to his head. Then, Keith MacDonald, Mark's best friend at Lawton Grammar School, extolled Mark for his adventurous spirit and the wonderful times they had together in Golden Gate Park, Playland and Sutro Baths. He was followed by Robert Swan, now a Naval Commander, who gave Mark all of the credit he deserved for saving so many shipmates when the Indianapolis was sunk. Swan was in the water with Mark.

Then, Bruno Banducci, owner of the Blackhawk, had a difficult time expressing his emotions about Mark's character and talent as an extraordinarily self-taught musician. Robert Gibson, also a Navy veteran at Oak Knoll hospital, spoke of Mark's courage when his leg was amputated and his desire to make Sara his wife in the face of racial challenges. Lefty Gomez, now a pitcher for the Yankees, told the story about Mark's tenacity and the fact that he threw his best pitches at Mark and could not believe that this young one-legged kid could indeed respond by hitting a ball over the center field wall at Seals Stadium. Charlie Benedict, Mark's old friend from their days together at Camp Marwedel, broke into tears remembering the times they both boxed at the San Francisco Boys Club and the day that Mark broke his arm. He and Mark had been planning a fishing trip in Lake County.

Mark Doyle touched so many people's lives, and the size of the audience represented emotions that spanned from smiles of appreciation to tears of sadness. His was a life well lived in a meager twenty-three years. His death was so premature that the way he died was archetypal. People in attendance to show their love, respect, and sorrow included members of the United States Congress, Medal of Honor recipients, and Captain Charles McVey, Captain of the Indianapolis. Mark's immediate family, including William, Rita, Judge Shelton, Coralyn Shelton, Patrick and Doris Doyle, were present, but Sara and Tommy were so inconsolable that attending the memorial became more than they could emotionally deal with. Sara had planned to tell Mark on that fateful evening that she was pregnant with twins.

Less than a week after spreading her husband's ashes, she returned to Medical School at Stanford. Staying engaged was the only way she could deal with her immense sorrow. Sara was due to graduate in one year, and in 1949, she would start her scheduled internship at UCSF hospital. Many friends and family had a difficult time trying to understand Sara's desire to go back to school almost immediately after Mark's death. Those who knew Sara well understood the magnitude of her pain and could almost predict that the only way she could survive her husband's passing was to stay busy; otherwise, she would fall apart. The trip down the Peninsula each day to Palo Alto and being alone in the Telegraph Hill apartment only added to her despair. She asked her mother, Coralyn Shelton, to stay with her in the hope that it would be a saving grace. When both sides of the family learned, soon after Mark's passing, that she was pregnant with twins, it, at the very least, gave cause for light where there was only darkness.

Tommy was another member of the Doyle family who could not cope with the loss of his heroic big brother. He would not eat or sleep for days and reached a point where William and Rita understandably were concerned about the emotional well-being of their youngest son. Tommy had idolized his older brother and placed him on a larger-than-life pedestal. Because William was away so often during his early years, Mark filled the breach and became Tommy's primary teacher and mentor. Tommy Doyle was in such a state of shock that just coping with day-to-day was more than he could deal with. Rita had difficulty pleading with him to leave his room, and he implicitly refused to attend school. As time passed, Tommy regained his composure and gradually rejoined his family and schoolmates, but there was always a look of untenable sorrow on his face and manner.

While Tommy had an immense love for his parents, in subsequent months, he spent a significant amount of time with the Sheltons. The loyalty he felt had nothing to do with any level of preference but rather a safe haven to deal with his sorrow. In the following months, Tommy doted on Sara and took every opportunity to be there during the final stages of her pregnancy. The twins would be his profound connection that, through blood, were an extension of Mark. At the tender age of 13, Tommy expressed concern about the fact that Sara was attending class at Medical School and spending endless hours studying. Sara was abundantly aware of Tommy's sensitivity and explained to him that she was doing her best to get her rest and, at the same time, making sure that her diet was meeting all requirements. He was somewhat mollified, but at the same time asked to be available to take her to appointments with her gynecologist.

In August of 1948, Sara's water broke at night, and thankfully Tommy was there having dinner at her apartment. He rushed her to UCSF

Medical Center. Having just turned 14, Tommy was just in the process of learning to drive and really wasn't qualified to, but this, in Tommy's eyes, was an emergency. Sara understood his concern and tenderness, but in truth, as a medical student, she knew there frankly was no reason to be alarmed. Sara was experiencing all of the recognized steps in the birth process. She valued his presence, and his first role would be to call both families and alert them to Sara's status.

In the following hour, the San Mateo Doyles had arrived at the hospital, followed by the Shelton family. If there was ever a moment that could add even more to the existing strong bond between the two families, Sara's pregnancy served that purpose. The excitement in the waiting room was palpable, but it didn't take long before the attending physician entered the waiting room and announced that the birth had gone perfectly, and the mother and twins were doing well. What followed was a jubilant expression of happiness by two loving families who were sharing a moment they had all looked forward to… meeting Sara and Mark's two children. While Sara had the final word on naming the twins, there was one name that they all felt would have already been decided. The 5 lb. 10 oz. boy would be named Mark. The grandparents were allowed to see Sara, and for the first time since Mark's passing, she was smiling.

It was now 1 in the morning, and everyone agreed that a night's rest was called for, and at the same time, it was decided that the best place for Sara and her newborns to recuperate would be the Telegraph Hill apartment. The following day, with a full five hours of sleep, Sara was even more ecstatic as she embraced her son and daughter. Since the birth process went so well, the hospital agreed to release the trio after only one day. That morning, the prideful grandparents were on hand to deliver her to her San Francisco home. They had determined that they would rotate the care and needs of Sara and the twins. The first day, after flipping a coin, Judge Shelton and his wife would be the first on watch. All agreed that it was the right choice based on the special relationship between mother and daughter. Stanford Medical School had granted Sara maternity leave that would extend through six months. The families agreed that it would be enough time to make arrangements for childcare, and with this family, there would not be any concern about devoting time to the twins.

Without saying it, the two families realized that this birth would provide some welcome relief from the relentless sadness of Mark's passing eight months earlier. It didn't take long before family members commented on the resemblance that the boy had to Mark. Under the circumstances, this exercise could be legitimately expressed. In the days that followed, Sara regained her strength and doted on her two delightful children, who were so different not only because of gender but also because their temperament was so different. Yes, the name issue had been resolved, but there really was no comment to be made. Sara had decided their names before the birth of Mark and Olivia. The latter was the name of her maternal great-grandmother, who was born into slavery. Sara was never the kind of woman who would deny her heritage and attempt to 'pass.' She was proud of her African blood and the wonderful blend that Mark and Olivia represented. Mark was loving and relatively easy to please, while Olivia knew what she wanted and had her way of demanding attention.

The one thing they had in common was their genetic appearance. Mark and Olivia were both beautiful children with just enough of each race to provide a unique, almost exotic look. They also, at four months, began to show resemblances that clearly favored their father, but it wasn't just the junior Mark—Olivia obviously looked, in no uncertain terms, very much like the departed Mark, and nothing could make Sara and probably the entire family more pleased. Her baby, Mark, seemed to ignore all genetic tables. He was blond with dark skin and blue eyes that seemed to thumb his nose at what would be expected. At this early stage, Sara was genuinely concerned about spoiling her two young charges.

Over the next few months, Sara adjusted to a formula of care that would carry her through the six months of leave and after. Sara's bonding with her children was intense, and she could not conceive of leaving them in the care of anyone else, but she knew that she had to complete her studies at Stanford and what better hands than the two sets of loving grandparents? Between the four affectionate grandparents, there was no limit in terms of the love and tenderness they provided. Somehow, you could not ignore other younger members of the clan. Tommy was an absolute given who would spend all day playing with the twins, but what was not expected was the attention little Mark and Olivia would receive from both their young aunt and uncle. They had concocted their own form of baby talk that was a joy to behold, but in reality, difficult to listen to. Sara often mused on how Mark would have enjoyed the family dynamics that emerged from their beautiful twins. She was beginning to feel more and more comfortable with the thought of being able to leave her children in the hands of both loving families when, in two months, she would return to Palo Alto to complete her Medical School training.

CHAPTER 28

SAXOPHONE

1950

- **Strategic surprise landing at Inchon**
- **The Battle of Chosin Reservoir**
- **North Korea crosses the 38th parallel and attacks South Korea.**
- **The United Nations send troops to support South Korea.**
- **General Douglas MacArthur is named Commander of all United Nations forces.**
- **China enters the war and crosses the Yalu River.**
- **UN troops are pushed back to the 38th parallel.**
- **President Truman relieves MacArthur of command.**

With summer ending, Tommy would return to San Mateo High. In the first two years of high school, he concentrated on his education. The only thing outside his curriculum was to take up playing the saxophone. He also had to admit to himself that while he had loved his older brother, in many ways, he needed to compete with his giant accomplishments. My god, Mark was a natural athlete who was an accomplished musician and had won the nation's highest military award—The Congressional Medal of Honor. The best that Tommy could do was, at the very least, take up a musical instrument. The fact is, he was a big fan of such great jazz men as Charlie Parker, John Coltrane, and Coleman Hawkins, so he decided to learn to play the Sax. He knew his parents' view that if you wanted something bad enough, you could figure out a way to buy it. He had saved the money that he made with his San Mateo Times paper route, but he wanted to keep that money in the bank, earning interest. Tommy decided to purchase his used saxophone on time and make payments every month. He ultimately found just what he was looking for at Becker Music Store in Redwood City. The instrument that suited him was a 1913 silver Busher Alto Sax. The salesman at the music store told him how to pick a reed, which was an important component of all reed instruments. Tommy did not have the money to take lessons, so he decided to use a fingering chart to learn to play and, at the same time, read sheet music. He would make a payment of $1.30 every month until his loan was paid off in a year.

The house on Cornell was almost perfect for practicing with a soundproof space in the basement. The audacious Tommy Doyle, in the next months, spent endless hours teaching himself how to play his saxophone. With a fingering chart and an explanation of reading sheet music, Tommy literally taught himself! While it would take time to become proficient with the horn, Tommy found he had genuine musical aptitude for the Sax. Halfway through the year, he was close to mastering his ancient musical instrument. After achieving his goal of proficiency on the Alto Sax, he had two options for moving forward with his new skill. One was to try out for the school marching band, but he was no fan of March music, and the idea of marching and wearing a uniform at football halftime was repellent to him. The other opportunity would be trying out for the school dance band. There would be one opening in the saxophone section of the band, and as he finished his second year of high school, he knew he wasn't ready yet.

The summer of 1949 would require all his desire and patience to spend his time refining his burgeoning talent as an accomplished musician. When the new year of school reconvened, Tommy had one priority over and above his studies… trying out for the one opening on the school dance band. With only months of self-taught playing, being selected was indeed a reach, but no one would say that Tommy Doyle wasn't audacious. On the day of tryouts, the head of the Music Department set the rules and what would be expected. Each of the musicians trying out would be required to sit in with the band and play from sheet music. The selection for each of the five contenders would be different, and Tommy drew a jazz classic entitled "Eager Beaver."

As the four other musicians played with the confidence garnered after years of training, right or wrong, Tommy remained confident and was pleased with the fact that he wasn't given dance music but a jazz standard. Robert Guy, leader of the band as well as the school's Music Department, asked Tommy when it was his time to audition, about his musical background and how long he had played and who his teacher was. The other contestants could not help but smirk when Tommy responded. Even Robert Guy was more than a little unimpressed with Tommy's learning process, which was totally self-taught. Tommy was seated as the other members of the band began to play "Eager Beaver." He didn't miss a beat and played like a seasoned member of the saxophone section. It didn't take long for Robert Guy to select the newest member of the San Mateo High School dance band.

The leader was absolutely blown away by Tommy's well-earned audition. There was, in truth, no real competition. Tommy was by far the superior choice. Guy was incredulous and quick to announce that Tommy would be his selection to fill the open slot in the Sax session.

The seasoned members of the band broke into applause not only for Robert Guy's choice but also Tommy's amazing history with less than a year of learning without a teacher!

Throughout the school year, the band played for dance parties up and down the Peninsula. On occasion, he would sit in with some of the professional bands in the Bay Area. The "Big Band" sound was in, and there was plenty of work. The fact that Tommy was just turning 16 years old should have been of concern to band leaders, but the fact that his auditions were sophisticated and he didn't tell the truth about his age, preempted any reservations about his participation. Age should have been a concern, but even more significant was the way that many of the professional musicians offered Reefers, which was a parlance for marijuana, during intermissions. Tommy liked the fact that the drug gave him a lift to perform and a loss of inhibitions when he was called on to stand and riff, which was a solo. He found himself increasingly reliant on Reefers. The big band musicians provided him with a limited source and ultimately directed him to a contact for a dependable supply of the drug. As his habit escalated, he found that the money he was making as a stand-in musician was being lost and threatening to impact his ability to pay for his growing addiction. The unanticipated result tended to increase Tommy's dependence. His drug dealer saw an opportunity to move Tommy to a more effective drug that was far more dangerous and habit-forming… cocaine. Tommy did get to a point where cocaine was not only feeding his dependence, but also putting him in debt for several thousand dollars. It became a vicious cycle with no end in sight as his debt spiraled out of control.

After one of Tommy's "gigs," he was approached by an 'enforcer' demanding that he pay his debt to the dealer. Without the means to pay, Tommy asked to be given more time. It became so demanding that he would go to any means to beg, borrow or steal at any opportunity. His habit became so serious that family members began to show real concern about Tommy's negative change in behavior. His failings were manifest in the unaccountable slide in his schoolwork and the recognition of his teachers that something was terribly wrong. With nowhere else to turn in a moment of deep anguish, he confessed to his father the extent of his addiction and that he was in arrears with his drug dealer and was facing the promised threat of physical mayhem.

William listened closely and found his son's behavior disheartening, but as a minor incapable of making mature choices, William did, to some degree, understand. He was angry and disappointed, but accepted the fact that he was partially responsible for the sad turn of events. By insisting that Tommy pay for anything important to him, he may have created a chasm between himself and his son. There was only one way to resolve this painful choice. If he went to the police, he knew that Tommy would be charged along with the dealer, and he had an agonizing decision to make. He would pay his son's scurrilous debt, which essentially would be his only option if he wanted to keep his son from a conviction. A three-thousand-dollar payoff, while reprehensible, would be his son's way out and a promise from Tommy that he would take his addiction to a therapist and deal with getting off the drugs. William found that when his son went to pay off his source, he was told that "he owed interest" and, unless he wanted more trouble, the only resort was to adhere to the demand, and instead of paying three thousand dollars, he now owed four thousand. It was insidious, but a small price to pay to get his son back.

Tommy was forced to decline all offers from the area's dance bands based on his father's compassionate wishes. He appreciated his dad's support in helping to kick the habit of his brutal addiction to cocaine, but without ignoring his parents, he once again sought out Sara, who was his closest connection to the memory of his beloved brother. Reconnecting with the twins served to help him through his recovery, although he experienced many painful weeks of coming down from his habit. He still played his saxophone for personal pleasure and the hope that he could someday reenter the music world and maintain a level of sobriety which even now was a work in progress. He followed the strict process to kick the habit, which was absolute and highly restrictive. Each week, he was required to perform a urine test, report to his advisor, and attend a monthly Alcoholics Anonymous session, which now included drug addicts. This was a small price to pay in Tommy's effort to regain his place in society.

In 1951, a year before graduation, Tommy Doyle had finally gained full sobriety from his battle with cocaine, and when the Korean War began, Tommy saw an opportunity to redeem himself. When he turned 17, he lied about his age and joined the United States Army and began basic training at Fort Jackson near Columbia in South Carolina. Tommy's enlistment came as a shock to the Doyle and Shelton families. No one could contact Tommy while he was in basic training. To add to their concern, William learned that he had volunteered for the Rangers, which was an elite Special Forces unit of the army and would require additional training after basic. Tommy evidently had the skill to qualify with both his intelligence and physical requirements. This was no surprise, but the fact that he was just seventeen and had probably lied about his age. In the meantime, while Tommy was going through a brutal training period at Fort Sill, Oklahoma, William was able to find out more about the unique qualities that were required to complete the program. Rangers, in their training, among other assignments, conducted secret missions and were among the most elite of the military services. William learned that the current Ranger training program would be completed by October 1951.

With the war raging in Korea, it was a pretty sure bet that Tommy would be shipping out. William's mind turned to the fact that now Doyles will have fought in all wars in the twentieth century—William in WW1, Mark in WW2 and now Tom Doyle in the Korean War. The elder Doyle was about to learn that his son would be on leave for two weeks prior to his assignment as a U.S. Ranger. The loss of Mark just four years earlier was on everyone's minds. Tommy's volunteering for the army and the danger of qualifying for the elite Rangers were the reasons for concern. Now that the family was reconciled to Tommy's decision to join the military, they knew that he probably would be assigned to serve in Korea. With his training completed, Tommy returned home before his assignment. He was scheduled to fly into Travis Air Force Base, just North of San Francisco.

William and Rita were there to greet him as he stepped off the base. A family get-together was planned at the spacious Doyle home in San Mateo. Sara and her parents, Judge Shelton and Coralyn, along with the twins Olivia and Mark and finally, grandparents Patrick and Doris Doyle would all be attending. The sight of Tommy, after three months of intense training, was a joyous moment that brought tears to Rita and Sara. He looked much older in his uniform, and you could see the level of physical fitness that he had achieved in Ranger training. He definitely did not look like a little boy anymore. The way he appeared and his entrée into adulthood gave Tommy a bearing that projected maturity and confidence. In the drive back to San Mateo, the family was literally finding it difficult to get answers with everyone talking at the same time! The initial anxiety brought on by Tommy's enlistment turned to pride when they saw what the army had done for him. It also became clear that the military records of both William and Mark were apparent to enlistment personnel based on their Silver Star and Medal of Honor recipients. Tommy came from good stock.

Olivia and Mark junior were now three years old and were absolutely thrilled to see their favorite uncle, who had doted on them from the moment of their birth. They climbed all over Tommy, and their joy was palpable. He responded with the love and affection that was returned by his brother Mark's legacy. In the two weeks of leave, his priority was to spend as much time as possible with the twins.

CHAPTER 29

THE RANGERS

The party for welcoming Tommy home was a joyous event attended by all the people that he was close to. In addition to his immediate family, William had seen fit to invite the Walsh family, including Lauralie and Jimmie. Barbara Walsh had passed away two years ago, but Walter, now in his early eighties, looked spry as ever. Tommy's Aunt Laura had always been one of his favorites, and the proximity of living in Sausalito made it possible during his childhood to see her with some regularity. Her life on a houseboat and her successful restaurant, Omelets, Etc., had truly mellowed the once 'wild one' of the Walsh family. Now in her late forties, she had never married, but her exotic looks were still intact. Lauralie Walsh was now a beautiful, mature and successful career woman. Jimmie had finally settled down and married Karen Lansky, a Real Estate broker in LA, who had time to join Jimmie in raising their three girls. He met his broker wife when he was looking to buy a home in swanky Bel Air. Seeing the Walshs, who had always been like family, was an added bonus to a welcome home for Tommy. Through the years, the families had melded into people who genuinely loved each other and did everything they could to maintain their connection. William and Judge Shelton were still having breakfast at the Coffee Cup in San Mateo every Tuesday morning. Tommy's two weeks of leave seemed to evaporate all too soon for the family. After another tearful farewell, William drove him back to Travis.

Tommy had received his orders and would fly out of the air base and report to his Ranger unit in South Korea. He arrived in Seoul and reported to his commanding officer just north of the capital. As a young recruit from California, he took his share of kidding, but that was par for the course when it came to welcoming a new member of the unit; ('California is a place for Queers and Hotrods, and I don't see a tailpipe coming out of your ass!') The eight men that made up the Army Rangers were all young and most of them were about Tommy's age except for their leader. Top Sergeant Daniel Salerno was from the Bronx and had been an enlisted man in the army during the WW2 where he served his first stint as a Ranger. He had been awarded the Silver Star for gallantry during the Omaha beach landing and was now a hardened 12-year Ranger veteran. The rest of the unit hailed from North Dakota to New Orleans to Arizona, and there was one thing they had in common… the desire to serve their country.

After 10 days of getting to know each other, the mostly new Rangers would receive their first assignment. Tommy liked all of the men, but there was one soldier with whom he had most in common. John Sheer was from Moss Beach on the central coast of California. Like Tommy, he was a musician who played trumpet in a band and loved Jazz. His parents, like Tommy's, were mixed, with a Catholic mother and a Jewish father. As another Californian, the two took a lot of friendly abuse from their mates. Tommy genuinely liked the team he had been assigned to. They had all been through the tough Ranger training, and four of the men had combat experience. The remainder, like Tommy, were relatively recent graduates.

After the initial get-to-know-each-other, Sergeant Salerno called a meeting to say that they had received their first mission. There were two American airmen who had been shot down over North Korea and were signaling for help in enemy territory. They were near the coast and in the middle of an area of known North Korean soldiers. Salerno pointed to an initial dilemma about how they would enact the rescue. One consideration was an airdrop, and the other was a landing on the coast. Ultimately, the approach from the sea seemed most efficient. They would board a Destroyer Escort, which would put the Rangers on rafts almost one mile from the beach to avoid detection. This would entail rowing the two rafts to the shore and homing in on the signal from the downed pilot and his gunner. The captain of the Destroyer joined the Rangers to say that he would get them as close to the beach as possible, but pointed out that the water was choppy and rowing that distance would be difficult. He would then provide his coordinates once the Rangers returned from their rescue.

This is one time that intense Ranger training would come into play. The men checked their weapons, donned black wetsuits and launched their rafts. Thankfully, the night was very dark and overcast, which would help provide the element of cover. The rafts with four men in each would reconnoiter at an agreed-upon location on the beach. The choppy sea became much more problematic in that the rafts encountered heavy surf off the beach, which they were ultimately able to navigate. Once the landing was accomplished, the two teams joined together, carried the rafts to a secure location off the beach and moved inland. As intel reported, the area was mountainous once you traveled several tics off the beach. The unit initiated a signal with the airmen and immediately received a recognition that included the coordinates for their location. The two airmen were about one mile from their landing, and hopefully, the moonless night would provide the cover of darkness. As they moved forward, their radio picked up signs of the enemy in the area that seemed to be almost on top of the airmen's location.

Moving carefully through the densely wooded area, they maintained a stealth presence with the awareness that they had indeed crossed enemy lines. Three hours after their landing, the Rangers reached the pilot and his crew member. The Gunner had been badly injured when his parachute made a rough landing. His left shoulder had been dislocated, and he was bleeding from a wound in his right leg as well as other injuries. The pilot had applied a tourniquet, which at least would stop the bleeding and prepare him for the last leg of the rescue. Just as they were leaving the jump area, the Rangers encountered a unit of the KPA ground force. Two of the team were carrying the wounded airman, and once the firefight started, they put him down and joined their comrades in the fight. They knew they must move forward, or more of the enemy troops would hear the gunfire and stop their progress to the beach.

Salerno made the decision that five of his men would carry the injured man, help the less seriously wounded pilot and prepare the rafts for the rescue once he, Doyle and Sheer were clear of the firefight. In the next hour, the three Rangers were able to terminate four of the attacking five KPA, but in the process, Salerno was badly wounded as the remaining North Koreans escaped. With two wounded men, Tommy and Sheer each carried Salerno and the airmen through their escape route. The fight had taken an hour of valuable time as they feared being followed. Tommy, who was carrying the sergeant whose wounds were more severe, told John to move on with the pilot as he helped resuscitate Salerno, who continued to bleed from a chest wound. Sheer agreed and promised to hold the rafts. After applying a bandage and tapping it to the sergeant's chest, Tommy moved on after hearing enemy troops closing in. Carrying Salerno on his back, he traveled the last leg of the trip to the beach. Thankfully, one of the two rafts with John Sheer, as promised, was waiting.

The two friends and their wounded charges were barely underway in their raft when they heard gunfire from the beach. The almost total darkness and dark clothing probably saved their lives as bullets ricocheted around them. When they finally reached the Destroyer, the exhausted Rangers were greeted by other members of the team who jumped into the water to help their comrades and the wounded men to board the ship. Once they were clear, a sailor noticed that Tommy's right leg was bleeding. Evidently, in the intensity of the fight, he didn't feel the wound. Once he was helped to the ship's small infirmary, the corpsman dressed his leg as best he could, and he was reunited with his unit. Salerno was still alive; however, the Airman Gunner didn't make it due to his severe wounds.

The pilot went over to Tommy, lit him a cigarette and thanked him. The last thing he remembered was a hug from John Sheer as he fell asleep. When he woke up, they were near their port of embarkation and were preparing to leave the ship. As the Destroyer tied up, an ambulance party was waiting to rush the wounded men to a hospital in the rear. Sergeant Salerno would survive, but his chest wound was severe. Tommy's putting pressure on the bleeding, applying that bandage, and physically carrying him saved his life. Tommy's leg needed attention with an injury that included a partially broken femur that would eventually heal. All Tommy could think of was that after one mission, he was probably going to be discharged! He was wrong about that. The entire team and the two airmen were airlifted to their base at Travis, in California.

The Rangers' families had all been notified of the incident and the condition of their loved one. No sooner had the men been treated when families were allowed to visit, and the first two coincidently were Tommy's, followed by John Sheer's wife and parents. In all, from the time that he landed in Korea to being evacuated to California, it was a total of three weeks! If Tommy wanted action and adventure, he got it in spades. Later that week, the surviving Rangers arranged to visit Dan Salerno once he was treated for his injuries. The sergeant was all smiles and asked for a recap of the last leg of the rescue. He looked at Tommy and uttered, "You are one strong son-of-a-bitch!" They had performed quite a mission, and although they lost one man, the rescue was deemed successful. Tommy was told he would be given leave from Travis after he had made enough progress in healing from his leg wound. Sergeant Salerno, with his serious chest injury, would take much longer to recuperate. John Sheer, after just a week, was returning home to Moss Beach, where he would spend two weeks with his wife and children before returning to duty. All three of the rescue team were notified by the War Department that they had been recommended for commendations. Tommy and John were to receive the Silver Star, and the wounded Dan Salerno a Bronze Star. The surviving pilot they had rescued evidently told the top brass of the Rangers' heroism. There would be no celebration, no parade and in truth very little recognition because that was the understated Ranger way.

To Tommy, the important thing was that he had once again brought honor to the Doyle name with another Silver Star to complement his grandfather's commendation in WW1. Tommy was promoted to Corporal and released from the hospital on crutches. His family had visited almost every day and were obviously pleased that he had been recommended for the second-highest award for bravery in the army, but there was one alarming hitch. When noting that Tommy was a candidate for the Silver Star, the upper echelon of the Army, for the first time, paid real attention to Tommy's enlistment papers and therein was a problem that needed to be addressed. First, he had lied about his age. In 1951, he was barely 17 years old. They did note that Tommy's indiscretion was common and could be overlooked, but it was the second disturbing response that just could not be overlooked. Tommy had responded "no" when asked, "Are you now or have you ever used or been addicted to drugs?" This was indeed serious. The Army was rightfully opening a line of questioning about 1951 that was becoming a significant issue. Drug use among young people through the Fifties was rapidly accelerating, and the Army needed to address a policy that would make drug use among its ranks dishonorable and subject to discharge.

Tommy's recommendation for the Silver Star was held up in light of a hearing and investigation. Tommy was genuinely alarmed, and any plans he had for the future would have to be postponed. He was scheduled to complete his enlistment in less than a year, and now he was in danger of being dishonorably discharged. He was notified that a hearing on the matter would be scheduled in two months. He was informed that he would be the subject of a Summary Court-Martial, which was the least serious of the three possibilities. He would not be represented, and there would be a single commissioned officer who could levy punishment of no more than 30-day confinement, along with forfeiture of a portion of his pay.

Tommy had no excuse to keep this dire situation to himself because it would just be a matter of time before others would find out. The first person he alerted was his father, whom he could always turn to, specifically on grave matters. William was surprised… not that he wasn't knowledgeable about Tommy's past drug use, but rather that the military was being so severe about an issue he thought had been resolved. He did realize after second thoughts that drug use per se was not the issue. The issue was that he lied about it. William, along with his son, both felt that this was a relatively mild form of court-martial. The thought of losing his Silver Star for bravery and potentially a dishonorable discharge was something they both felt was on the table, but with Tommy's record in service as a Ranger and his drug use long ago curtailed, they felt relatively safe. The hearing was scheduled to be held at Fort Mason, and the commissioned officer assigned to the case was an officer named Colonel Robert Quatrone. He would cite the charges, allow the subject to respond without an attorney to make a judgment on the punishment, if any. In essence, he would serve as judge, jury, prosecutor and defense counsel. It wasn't long before Tommy's comrades and friends learned the news of his Summary Court-Martial. Sergeant Dan Salerno and Sheer were especially incensed, having just completed the dangerous mission as Ranger comrades in Korea, but they, too, felt that Tommy would be judged lightly and maintain his Silver Star.

CHAPTER 30

COURT-MARTIAL

On the day of the hearing, the only people allowed in the military courtroom other than Tommy were his mother and father, William and Rita Doyle. Tommy attended the hearing on crutches and was scheduled to be transferred to the therapy center at Fort Mason. The residing Officer, Colonel Quatrone, entered the courtroom, and before he even opened his mouth, Tommy had a sinking feeling that this was not going to go well. The Colonel read the charge of lying about his drug use when he enlisted in 1951. He then asked if Corporal Thomas Doyle had anything to say. Tommy responded and apologized for his error in judgment, but went on to cite his record, the fact that he was a member of the Rangers and had served valiantly in the Korean War.

After what seemed an interminable pause, Colonel Quatrone responded… he knew all about Tom's performance in the military and he lauded him for his service, but that did not justify lying, especially about use on the entrance to the U.S. Army. The Colonel was severe and menacing in his remarks, and it was clear that he had absolutely no sympathy for anyone who would lie on their enlistment form. Without any pause, he went on to say that it was his judgment that Tommy would not be recommended for his Medal and be subject to 30 days confinement, which would begin in two weeks. Quatrone said that would be enough time to appeal his judgment and get his affairs in order. With that, he banged his gavel and left the courtroom.

The shock on the faces of the three Doyles was palpable. They were anticipating a slap on the wrist, but not a sucker punch! Word of Tommy's punishment spread rapidly throughout the Bay Area military communities. For the people who knew him, there was just plain shock, and for the communities at large who were aware of Tommy's bravery and subsequent honesty, they, too, were having a hard time understanding the military's judgment. The following day, an editorial in the San Mateo Times was scathing and suggested that Tommy should definitely appeal his conviction, which they labeled "an unconscionable military Kangaroo Court" and should be overturned. In fact, the paper pointed out that the Summary Court-Martial was designed to "dispose of minor offenses."

Thankfully, there was one saving grace. Tommy found he could appeal his judgment within five days to the next higher level of command. The commander at the higher court can decide whether to leave the punishment in place, reduce the punishment or eliminate it altogether. The five days seemed interminable. Tommy was allowed to have one defense witness, but beyond that, a relatively minor change, the second Court-Martial would be the same as the first. The officer this time was a Brigadier General, who was a significantly higher rank than Colonel Quatrone. There was one other change in the venue. Family members would be allowed in the Court. Another encouraging sign that was purely subjective; Brigadier General Robert Cheskin was much older, highly decorated and had an air about him that was anything but menacing. Once everyone was seated, he asked Tommy to rise as he read the charges and the recommendation of the lower court. He stated that he would hear from Tommy later, but for now, he wanted to hear from William, the only witness allowed. William stood and respectfully submitted to the judge his defense of his son. He went on to say that he feels he bears some of the responsibility for Tommy's behavior. He emotionally explained that as a father, he had always taught his sons "The value of a buck." Even though they were a family with means, William talked about his methods when it came to Tommy's desire to play a musical instrument or, for that matter, purchase his own bike to deliver the San Mateo Times. William expounded how his son did have musical talent, and in very short order, he was not only playing the saxophone in the school dance band, but he also earned money playing with various professional bands, which proved to be devastating when he was offered 'reefers,' leading to more addictive drugs such as cocaine.

With pride, William told the General that Tommy realized that he had a severe habit that he had to deal with if he wanted to achieve ambitions consistent with his family's values. He knew he had to get clean. He went on to say that when Tommy entered the Army and ultimately qualified as a Ranger, he had been off the drugs for several weeks. For closing comments, William spoke of the competition between the two brothers, which probably had a dramatic effect on Tommy's overzealous need to achieve. His brother Mark had served bravely during World War 2 and was the recipient of the Medal of Honor. As William was set to go on, the General interrupted and asked… 'Was Mark Doyle the same Petty Officer who saved all those lives in the USS Indianapolis tragedy?' William responded that it was, and that Mark had recently passed away. The General seemed dumbfounded, and when he finally spoke, he looked directly at Tommy and said, "Your brother was one of the great heroes of the Second World War, and as I look at your record with this minor hiccup, I can honestly say that your brother would have been proud of you." General Cheskin went on to say that he was going to consider dismissal before he heard from William, and now there was no question about his final judgement… all charges would be dismissed. He closed with a remark directed at William: "Mister Doyle, you have every reason to be proud of your sons… and don't let anyone tell you that you are anything but a great dad." The courtroom breathed a sigh of finality. Judge Shelton, Coralyn, Rita and Sara were rightfully jubilant. They entered the court with high hopes, but this resolution was far beyond their wildest anticipation. With one closing bang of the gavel, the Doyles hugged, and some wiped away tears.

With the one serious roadblock behind him, Tommy Doyle was determined to set his life in order, starting with his education. Tommy knew that applying to a university was only part of what he needed to do. He had not finished high school, and for now, that was his priority… The GI Bill, which had been initiated directly after World War II, would literally pay almost all his expenses, including tuition, housing, meals, and books. Tommy was now free to take a series of tests that would provide him with an accelerated high school diploma. After two months of marathon studying, Tommy took the examination and achieved step one in his planning that would hopefully qualify him for college entrance. In the meantime, he was evaluating the universities in the Bay Area. His one criterion was a school that provided a course of studies in Communications. Tommy had determined that a job in television was what he was setting his sights on. There were five television stations in the Bay Area, including KGO, KRON, and KPIX, all affiliated with the three networks. KTVU in Oakland and KNTV in San Jose were independents.

Thankfully, there were some high-quality universities and colleges, including USF, a nearby Jesuit school, the University of California in Berkeley, San Jose State College, and Stanford University in Palo Alto, to consider. To determine which school would be right for him with a course of study that would be compatible with his stated goals, he consulted the members of his family who had degrees. Sara had just completed medical school and was in the throes of applying for her internship. Sara and Judge Shelton were both well qualified to provide him with the input and guidance he needed. Tommy proceeded to engage both Sara and the Judge and was more than satisfied with their input. For now, Tommy settled on the University of San Francisco just blocks from Sara's apartment. If he were accepted at USF, it would not only be convenient, but it also would have the curriculum of study he was looking for, i.e., Radio and Television. The school had a major in Communication that included a broad range of subject matter in television, radio, magazines, and human resources.

It was now early April 1954, and if he applied himself now, he fully anticipated that his entrance exam would be required early this Summer, and he could enroll for the Fall Semester. Tommy was attempting to plan the next few weeks when he got a phone call from Jimmie Walsh, his dad's employer and probably his best friend. He was calling to congratulate Tom on the results of the Summary Court-Martial and, at the same time, invite him to come to Southern California to go on a fishing cruise around Catalina. Jimmie had just bought a 40-foot yacht with all of the amenities, including two state rooms with baths, an elaborate living area and a fully stocked galley. Initially, Tommy thought no, but as he listened, the thought of some recreation before he hit the books was probably exactly what he needed. Korea, Mark's passing and the Court-Martial had drained all of his energy, and the idea of a relaxing fishing trip with Jimmie Walsh sounded better and better as he talked. On the positive side, he had just received an honorable discharge from the Army and thankfully, with his Silver Star intact. When he agreed, Jimmie could not have been more pleased and considered the possibility that he might have convinced Tommy to join the Company. William had already asked his son to consider Walsh Inc., but perhaps this might be the right moment with the trial over.

Tommy decided that it was time to buy his first car. In 1954, he was just 20 and had never owned a car! He went shopping with Sara as his guide, and they visited several showrooms, but he had made up his mind almost instantly when he saw the new Ford Thunderbird. When he took it for a test drive, he asked Sara's opinion, and she responded with a telling eye roll. The car was fully loaded with a black and white exterior. Tommy had saved judiciously with his earnings from the bands he played with almost 4 years ago, and his military mustering-out paycheck. With hands trembling a little, he purchased the T-Bird, and that evening, Sara invited Tommy over for a well-earned celebratory dinner. It proved to be a delightful evening that started with Tommy taking the twins for a ride in his T-Bird, followed by a dinner of freshly caught sea bass. A week later, Tommy was on his way to Palos Verdes behind the wheel of his new T-Bird.

When he arrived at the Walsh estate in PV, he never failed to be impressed. It was a spectacular Spanish modern mansion that sprawled over a cliff overlooking an uninterrupted view of the ocean. Jimmie and his wife, Karen, greeted Tommy. The Doyles had always said the Walshs were 'just like family,' and with the reception of warmth that he received, there was no truer statement. He had not seen Jimmie or Karen since his brother's memorial three years earlier. They adjourned to the den for drinks, and to see Walter, the family patriarch, who had just turned eighty. Barbara had passed away five years earlier.

When they entered the room, Walter was being served a drink by a young lady with her back to him. When she turned, Tommy felt a rush. The girl was the daughter of the Walsh's maid, Anna Alvarez, who also served the family. Years ago, he had seen a cute little girl playing in the back garden. Could this stunning vision be her? At 20, he felt ancient, but truth be told, he was a mere three years her senior. Walter exuberantly welcomed Tommy and introduced him to Lisa Alvarez. Their eyes instantly met and held, and they were both tongue-tied. Tommy could not get any words out, and neither could Lisa. Walter, Jimmie and Karen all looked at each other and smiled broadly as if they knew what was going on. Anna walked into the room with perfect timing to say hello to Tommy Doyle, the little boy who had visited many times with his brother years ago. She thankfully broke the silence with an introduction to her daughter, Lisa Marie.

Tommy regained his composure and warmly greeted Anna, whom he had not seen in over 10 years. The rest of the visit before they fished was all a haze to Tommy. All he could think of was the vision of Lisa Marie Alvarez. The conversation over dinner was revisiting the 'remember when' script, which was always enjoyable, but on this occasion, Tommy had nothing to add. Walter, in his wisdom, knew exactly what was going on, and he reveled in seeing these young people try to orchestrate what could be 'the start of something big.' He knew that Lisa had a boyfriend, but he was just a kid, and Tommy Doyle… well, Tom was a man. Soon after dinner, Anna answered the door, and a very young man was introduced as Lisa Marie's boyfriend. They had a date to see the new movie "The High and the Mighty" with John Wayne. As they were leaving, Lisa faced Tommy, put out her hand and said, 'It was nice seeing you again.' Tommy did not want to let go of her hand, and she didn't pull away.

The conversation on the ride to the movie must have been interesting. The next morning, Jimmie and Tommy got up early, had coffee and headed for the Long Beach marina. When they arrived at the dock, Jimmie was anxious to show off his new boat, and he wasn't exaggerating. The one thing he left out was the name of the boat… 'MARK TWO.' Tommy didn't know whether to laugh or cry. The boat was spectacular and just short of being pretentious. The exterior of the Mark Two did not do justice to the interior with its galley and living area. Before they left the marina, another worker from the company had come on board with fresh live bait. There was a crew of two who, in addition to the fishing guide, were there to fix meals, clean the fresh caught fish, provide tackle and serve drinks. Tommy was impressed, but he maintained a poker face just to make Jimmie concerned. Finally seeing his friend's discomfort, Tommy broke into laughter while he told Jim how spectacular the boat was. That's what Jimmie needed, and once he got it, he joined Tommy in a good 'gotcha' laugh.

The cruise to Catalina took almost an hour, and once they were at a spot that was proven for Corvina, they dropped anchor and baited their hooks with live bait. The fishing that day was almost too easy, but so enjoyable. They caught their limit, and that evening the staff prepared the day's catch and joined Tommy and Jimmie Walsh for dinner on the fantail or rear deck of the Mark Two. The next day, they weighed anchor and headed north toward the Charter Islands, where they anchored again, only this time the fishing was for Halibut. Tom had to admit that the fishing, sun, drinks, food and friendship were just what he needed. For the first time in many months, he could feel the anxiety and stress he experienced in the past three years evaporate. He shared that with Jimmie as they headed back to Long Beach after three days of pure pleasure.

As they approached the marina, Jimmie opened a new conversation that literally floored Tom. Evidently, he had some concerns about keeping his boat in Long Beach and was planning on moving the Mark Two to San Francisco, not only because it was more secure, but also, he had never cruised or fished outside the Golden Gate. There was a good reason why so many fishermen chose to work at Fisherman's Wharf. Jimmie went on to say that he had already rented a slip at Pier 39, almost adjacent to the Wharf. He then asked Tom what his plans were. He outlined his progress with USF and shared his near-term goal of working in local television and eventually entering politics. It was time for Jimmie to drop his bomb. He wanted Tom to live on the boat in exchange for maintaining it and providing security. Tom did not hesitate, and again it was all about timing. He was planning to go apartment hunting when he returned to the Bay Area. The crew would move the Mark Two the following week, and hopefully, could Tom be ready to move in soon? Tom was convinced that his life was now on a positive path with the Court dismissal, meeting the girl of his dreams, and now living on a luxury yacht.

The following morning, Tom was ready to drive back to San Francisco, but before he did, he wanted to talk to Lisa to see if the attraction was real. Truly, all he could think about was this beautiful Mexican girl. They met in the covered patio where Tom knew she was working. Haltingly, he asked if they could talk for a moment as he was leaving later that morning. They faced each other, and it was then that he knew that whatever was happening was real. They shared their feelings and, with great hesitation, admitted to each other that there was a profound connection that needed resolution. As they stood to part, they found each other and for a moment embraced. Tom was facing a real dilemma. He knew his future depended on education, and just today, he had received a letter from USF granting him entrance to the University that Fall. Also, he had met the woman whom he would want to spend the rest of his life with.

In the meantime, the Mark Two had been delivered to its new mooring at Pier 39, and power and water had been serviced. Tom asked the two Mexican employees if they wanted to have dinner at Fisherman's Wharf before they returned to LA late that night. They agreed, and that evening they met at Scoma's, which was Tom's favorite restaurant on the Wharf. Nothing fussy, just great seafood and service. Over cocktails, they talked about the boat, their jobs and the kindness of the Walshs. Jose Aguilar had been employed by Jimmie for almost 20 years, and he spoke glowingly of his wife, Soledad, and his two children. Dominic Gomez was hesitant to talk about his life and history with the Walshes. It was clear by his dress and manner of speaking that he was in some way a more senior employee of the family. While the Mark Two was being moored, Dominic had taken care of all the details with the Port Authority, and while he was friendly enough, he seemed less open to sharing his life and experiences. He knew of the Doyle family and was well aware of their close relationship with the Walsh family.

Tommy was curious and unwilling to settle for the cryptic response from Dominic. He had too many cocktails, and now the mysterious Walsh staff member presented a challenge, and Tom began to prod. With a nod, two martinis, and a hesitant laugh, Gomez finally opened up. He was Lisa's uncle, and, in addition to her mother Anna, he had made her upbringing a priority. To that end, Walter, Barbara, and Jimmie Walsh had all contributed to Lisa's education and guidance. Tom went on to ask about her father… Manuel Alvarez. During the War, he was a member of the First Marines and had his initial taste of combat at Guadalcanal, and from there, fought his way to Okinawa, which was the last bastion of the Japanese during the War, and they fought with a protective fury. After the two drinks, he added, "Did I tell you he was a medic?" Manuel had received a Bronze Star and the Purple Heart, which he earned bravely while saving a comrade. He died on the plains of Okinawa in the last major battle of the Second World War. Before the War, Manuel was in charge of Quality Control for Walsh Inc., and he and his family had been embraced by the Walshs and honored his memory by committing themselves to help in the future upbringing of Lisa, a little girl who was loved by many. He had to admit he was reticent about telling Tommy all this history. Dominic was indeed hesitant due to the fact that they could see in one visit that he and Lisa had connected. They were all protective of young Alvarez, and at some point, if Tommy continued to show interest, they would all, in unison, ask what his intentions were. At 17, she wasn't what you might call sheltered, but a man like Tom Doyle could sweep her off her feet if she wasn't ready for it.

Dominic went on to say that he knew all about Tommy, including his military history, his wild teens and his drug use. With that, Tommy filled in the gaps and pledged that he was on track to attend the University of San Francisco this Fall and, regardless of what they may have heard, he had been clean for over two years. As the two martinis turned to three, Lisa's uncle was proud of the fact that she was an A student and was on the honor roll of her high school every year. *(Here it comes)* But even more important, he went on, was the fact that she would be attending the University of California at Berkeley this Fall. Tom's jaw dropped. The one thing that was standing in the way of any potential romance was distance! Berkeley was just across the Bay, and this proximity opened the door to his potential relationship with Lisa. Tom drove the two men to the airport for their short trip back to LA. The three were now alcoholic best friends, and the evening had been thoroughly enjoyable. Dominic's last words as he was boarding were, "Don't get me in trouble. Anna can be a terror!"

Tom spent the summer preparing for class, which was something he had not done since he was a sophomore in high school, and he wondered if he could effectively make the transition. In addition, he had written to Lisa every day, and she had responded. They were both hesitant about committing, but the fact that they were both entering universities in the Fall backstopped the conversation. They were on the verge of romance, and they were both more than a little anxious and even frightened. For that reason, they talked "cabbages and kings"… small talk. Family members, by now, were aware of the burgeoning long-distance romance, and to a person, they were pleased. Rita and William had known Lisa and her family since she was a child, and who didn't love her? They were willing to share this new family turn of events with the Judge, Coralyn, and most importantly, with Sara, who already knew of Lisa and listened intently as he recounted his feelings. Tommy was such a favorite of hers and the twins that she literally could not wait to meet her. That wish was sooner than they thought. It so happened that Lisa was coming to Berkeley for orientation the following week, and she insisted on flying to San Francisco alone! She was not fragile.

CHAPTER 31

SAUSALITO

After more than a month on board the Mark Two, Tom had reintroduced himself to his Alto Sax and was able to earn money sitting in with the bands that were playing in the City. San Francisco in the late Fifties was already delving into the world of countercultures, and Tom, with his adventurous spirit, loved what was happening to his City. Admittedly, drugs remained part of the musical culture, but while tempted, Tom swore he would never indulge, and he meant it. Sitting for extended periods resurfaced what he thought was a manageable problem. The wound to his left leg had become a problem that he had thought was a non-issue, but he knew he might require additional therapy.

One evening in the middle of summer, he was sitting in with the Turk Murphy band at the Italian Village, and when he stood for intermission, he had to rub his eyes… Sara was sitting at a table with Lisa. In a daze, he literally fell into Lisa's arms, and all Sara could do was giggle. After Tom said goodbye to the band, he was paid two hundred dollars by Turk, who said, "Any time, Tommy." Sara consciously left the couple alone at the Buena Vista, where they were closing out the evening with Irish coffee. Tom and Lisa picked up where they had left off in LA, only now they had shaken the jittering, dazed feeling of their first meeting. They spent an hour lost in each other until the bar closed, and without hesitation, they took a cab the short distance to Pier 39. Nothing could have been more romantic than a yacht at 2 am, sitting in San Francisco Bay.

To say that this beautiful couple had fallen madly in love would be an understatement. They stayed up the rest of the evening, ate baguettes, drank champagne, and necked until their lips were sore. Lovemaking would have to wait. After two hours of sleep, they woke, drank more champagne, painfully kissed and walked across The Embarcadero for breakfast at the Fog City Cafe. Finally, a real conversation ensued, and Lisa said she absolutely had to be on campus at Cal for orientation by 2. With that, Tom volunteered his T-Bird, and one hour later, they were in Berkeley. Tom said he would wait, and Lisa merely nodded with a smile. The ensuing conversation was all about class at the two schools in the Fall and how sensational the weekends would be!

That evening, they picked up two fat Dungeness crabs at the Wharf and a round loaf of San Francisco sourdough bread. The only thing needed was a bottle of good Sauvignon Blanc, which was part of the well-stocked wine cabinet on the Mark Two. The sun was going down over the Golden Gate, and Thomas Doyle and Lisa Alvarez drank it all in and reveled in the reality of being in love. That night, they breathlessly undressed each other and followed up on the initial lovemaking with more than any man could only hope for. The picture of a sweet, innocent, protective little girl was out the porthole. Lisa Alvarez took charge of the sensuous lovemaking. Tom was shocked but at the same time pleased with the animal instincts of his newfound love partner. The surprise was easily absorbed by a man who had just been to Nirvana. They stayed in bed until the next morning and woke with a smile on their faces and a painful, good morning kiss.

The word had spread, and Tom got a call from Lauralie demanding that he come to Sausalito with Lisa, who at this early stage was shaping up as the family mystery woman. The truth is, Sara had called her full of elation over Tom's sensational Latin choice. Lauralie had to see them! After raiding the cabinets in the boat's galley, they settled on Biscotti's and coffee for breakfast, straightened out last night's disarray, hopped in the T-Bird and headed for Sausalito, where Lauralie was there to greet them, dressed in a Kimono and wearing almost no makeup, something that very few could get away with. Now in her late forties, Tom's definition of what a sex goddess should look like was still defying gravity. Her lifestyle remained avant-garde, and she continued to thumb her nose at anyone who had the guts to challenge her unique way of living. Lauralie's home was a chalet perched on the hills overlooking the art community of Sausalito. Her taste was impeccable, and she dressed with some genuinely impressive original artwork, including Monet, Erté and Kush. It was almost like being in a museum. Upon meeting, Lisa and Lauralie instantly connected and recognized in each other the pursuit of honesty with no bullshit. Pleased with the obvious direction of a new friendship, Tom poured gin and tonics, and they adjourned to Lauralie's glorious deck overlooking Sausalito, Tiburon and the entire San Francisco Bay. Life was good.

That evening, they had dinner at the Spinnaker, ate oysters, drank wine, and luxuriated in the second sunset without fog. The reputation of fog in San Francisco in August was true, and the fact that Lisa's first two days were sun-drenched was probably an omen. With school still out, Lisa spent the remaining month on the boat with Tom. On weekends, Tom continued to sit in with familiar bands in North Beach, including the Blackhawk, The Jazz Workshop, and Birdland, which seated 500 people and featured such bands as the Count Basie

Orchestra, which was a regular booking. Tom's embouchure had returned, as well as his skill as a musician. Lisa attended the clubs where Tom was playing and was still in awe of his skill playing an Alto Sax. Every day was a round of tea at the Japanese Gardens, Dim Sum at Sun Hung in Chinatown, a drive to the beach where Tom parked his car as they strolled through Playland, where they played Skeeball, ate crab cocktails, and ventured up the hill to the Cliff House and next door Sutro Baths. The Cliff House offered an extraordinary view of the famous Seal Rocks, where, on any day, you could observe seals lounging.

Tom took immense pleasure in showing off the San Francisco he dearly loved. On weekends, they would drive down the Peninsula with stops in Burlingame and San Mateo. This gave Tom an opportunity for Lisa to meet his family and friends. In one visit to Burlingame, they met the Shelton family, who, as anticipated, showed the affability and warmth that were their signature. Judge Shelton embarrassed Tom when he brought up the many girls who were vying for Tom's attention. He did so with a wink to Lisa. In addition to the Sheltons, Sara and her twins were visiting, which was an added bonus. Lisa found that after the initial greetings, the entire family infused her with a genuine, sincere welcoming. Lisa met the twins, who represented all that was good about their deceased and revered father. Visually, they were a study in contrast.

Olivia bore an extraordinary resemblance to Mark, which, as she turned eight, was even more complementary to her father's looks. The one fundamental resemblance was her coloring. Olivia's hair remained somewhat blonde, but her skin was light brown, which served as a palette for the most exotic blue eyes she had ever seen, with a unique hazel coloring inside the overall blue in one eye.

Olivia's racial ambiguity almost guaranteed her unusual beauty as the years went by. She was verbally precocious and talked with a confidence that initially could be off-putting to an adult. She was challenging and enticing at the same time. There was one final note that Judge Shelton had observed about Olivia. At the tender age of eight, she continually pestered her grandfather about the law, and she was unrelenting about fairness and equality. Put a pin in that.

Mark, on the other hand, was the polar opposite of his sister. Physically, he was much larger than Olivia, and, like her, had the gift of gab, which almost seemed like the twins' signature. That's where they parted. Mark was dark with hazel eyes and totally complemented his mother's African heritage. His features, however, resembled his late father. At eight, he showed a propensity for music and, like his father, seemed to gravitate towards the piano. He was already astute enough to play with basic skills, which would be nurtured in the near future.

Lisa was totally impressed with Sara's absolutely beautiful twins and understood why the family totally doted on them. There was no question that Olivia and Mark would be a formidable duo who could conceivably influence the future of their generation. It wasn't often that a family with so many disparate members could find the right spot to usher in a surprising compatibility. This spoke to the initial meeting between Lisa and Sara at the Italian village. They got along famously, and there was no doubt that they would become fast friends. Tommy could not predict how these family introductions would evolve, but so far, she was hitting a home run.

On a subsequent weekend, they drove to San Mateo to meet Tommy's father and mother, William and Rita Doyle. Over the years, the couple had solidified the extended family with William and the Judge's weekly gabfest, regular family get-togethers with Sara and the twins, and even Coralyn and Rita's sturdy friendship. Lisa's first impression of the Doyles was their home was tastefully decorated with a stamp that clearly supported Rita's artistic skill. Every room had a sense of being lived in, which made visitors feel comfortable and at ease, even though their home was resplendent with expensive furnishings and decor. On the wall in the den, Rita's skill as a talented artist was displayed. Lisa had heard about Rita Doyle for years, but this was the first time that she would see her exceptional art. The wall displayed some of her early artwork, which consisted of pencil sketches exclusively before she transitioned to multi-media. Lisa was in awe of the precise art, which portrayed every feature and component of the subject with nothing more than a #2 pencil. As she moved into watercolor and ink, her art became much more all-encompassing, with subject matter that ran the gamut from detailed personal sketches to couples and family members. Her work was art with a female sensitivity that Lisa believed could rival the genius of Norman Rockwell. She was by no means an expert, but she had always shown an appreciation for talented artists.

Rita and William were as comfortable to be with as the Sheltons. For openers, Rita took pleasure in Lisa's unpretentious knowledge of art. Visitors had come and gone through the years with nothing other than words like 'remarkable,' 'splendid,' and 'talented.' Lisa, on the other hand, recognized fine art when she saw it and almost professionally critiqued Rita's artwork with praise. Summers on the peninsula in August were unlike the typical fog-shrouded day in San Francisco.

Sunny days were the rule and not the exception. Redwood City, a few small communities past San Mateo, had a sign over El Camino Real, the main peninsula thoroughfare, that proudly stated 'Climate Best By Government Test.' The fog invasion in the City by the Bay would stop at Brisbane, which provided the county line between San Francisco and San Mateo counties. Both William and Rita were a pleasure to be around, and the couple was invited to stay for dinner. In this large, luxurious home in Baywood, you would think a resident in this elite neighborhood would employ at least a part-time chef, but that wasn't the way Rita ran her home. She enjoyed entertaining and took great pleasure in the art of cuisine. That evening, she prepared a rack of lamb with mashed potatoes and asparagus spears with mint jelly. Lisa, once again, in the few hours they had spent with Tom's parents, thoroughly enjoyed Rita's artistic flair, whether on her drawing table or in her gourmet kitchen. Rita Doyle was definitely a force.

The following morning, when Tom and Lisa were chatting about the successful weekend in San Mateo, Tom received a phone call from Doris Doyle informing him that Patrick, his beloved grandfather, had passed away. The patriarch had been ill with pneumonia for several weeks, but there was never any indication that it was potentially fatal. Patrick had been close to both Mark and Tommy. His passing was the end of an era. Patrick and Doris had been married for ten years, and after losing their mates, had come together for what was anything but simply adequate or a compromise. They genuinely loved each other as if it was the first time for them both. Tommy had so many warm memories of his grandpa, and for Rita, it was the loss of the one person she could lean on when her own father had disowned her. William, in his grief and with a heavy heart, notified all of the Doyle family, both on the West Coast and in Boston. Patrick was indeed a favorite in the Doyle clan, and he would be sorely missed and remembered. He was the last of a generation who left Ireland for a new life in America, and by all measures, he had influenced the building of a foundation for the entire family in Boston.

William took charge of the Irish funeral planning. He had to determine just how much of the extensive traditions should be incorporated into Patrick's funeral. The first thing he did was alert the East Coast relatives and let them decide if they planned to travel West to Patrick and Doris Doyle's home in El Segundo. Four years ago, they determined that apartment living was not for them, and they purchased a lovely little cottage near the water. El Segundo was a quiet little town that the couple dearly loved, and Doris was planning the wake at the cottage and the funeral at St. Anthony's Catholic Church. William did have a dilemma over how much tradition should be included in Patrick's funeral. In truth, Patrick was not a regular churchgoer, and frankly, he leaned towards a less traditional form of religion. He would prefer that his passing be celebrated, and to that end, the one thing that appealed to him was the wake. Family and friends would spend up to three days celebrating and telling stories about the deceased. There were so many ritualistic traditions, and William knew that his father was one who was not much for all of the Irish trappings, but the funeral was in his mind more for the living. William and Doris settled on inviting friends and family from both coasts to participate in the celebratory wake with Patrick's body at their home for no more than one day. Then they moved to St. Anthony's for any additional days of celebrations. A traditional Irish funeral would follow the wake.

The date of the wake was distributed, and it should not come to anyone's surprise that the East Coast family showed up en masse. The Donovans were there as well as the Boston Doyles, but what surprised William was how many friends showed up for the wake. These people would be required to make travel arrangements that would include hotel accommodations as well as air travel. Most of these friends could still afford the expense of traveling West, but this was for Patrick Doyle, who was genuinely loved by many. William and Doris settled on some unique traditions to be incorporated, while Patrick's remains and the open casket were displayed at the cottage. They would cover all mirrors and encourage the mourners to bring food and alcoholic beverages, along with flowers. They were asked to dress in black to show their respect.

As it turned out, there was enough food and drinks at the wake for several funerals! The crowds in attendance were close to unmanageable. Attendees at the peak of the day stretched as far as the street. William, Tommy, Rita, Sara and her parents, along with the twins, were there with old friends from William's Hollywood days, including the Grossmans, Johnny Walker, Tony Fernandez and, of course, Lauralie and Jimmie Walsh. There was nothing somber about Patrick Doyle's wake. The family told stories, sang traditional Irish songs, drank beer and booze, and in general, sent Patrick off in style. There is no good way of saying it, but this was a party that Patrick would definitely embrace. Six male family members and friends carried the casket from St. Anthony's after the formal service to the cemetery where he would be entombed. If there is such a thing as a successful funeral, this was it.

Lisa was invited to the wake, but she decided to defer based on the fact that she did not really know Patrick and that she would be uncomfortable. However, she agreed to attend the funeral services with Tommy at the church. After the ceremony at the burial site, Lisa was surprised at how many people walked up to her and welcomed her to the family. It was, to say the least, premature, but Lisa was pleased that so many of Tom's friends considered her, even at this early stage of their relationship, a member of the family. After the graveside ceremony, William had invited some close family and friends to his home in San Mateo for a champagne brunch. This part of the three-day event turned out to be the most enjoyable and welcoming for Lisa, who continued to be amazed at how many people gave her the clear impression that she and Tommy were definitely 'a couple' and that was all there was to it. The get-together at William and Rita's home further enforced the impression that Lisa and Tommy were a fait accompli. Lauralie and Rita gave her comfort, but at the same time included her as 'family.' Tommy did absolutely nothing to discourage this warm embrace of Lisa. Although she had met many of the direct family members in recent weeks, seeing everyone together was somewhat jarring but definitely pleasant. The brunch seemed to solidify her feeling that Rita, Sara, and Lauralie would provide the nucleus of her future confidants. She had absolutely no idea that Rita and Lauralie specifically were at one point rivals in vying for the attention of William. The fact that the hatchet, if it ever existed, was buried because it was clear that these two stunning, talented women were close friends, and someday in the future, Lisa would be included in that circle.

CHAPTER 32

KRON

In the next four years, with Tom attending USF and Lisa at Cal, seeing each other regularly was sometimes problematic. There were no issues dealing with the health of the relationship; it was more a matter of the couple finding it difficult to make it through the school year with limited time together. When they were together, it seemed almost like their first date. Being together merely two or three times each month and then having to say goodbye was painful, but they both realized that education was a priority and the key to their future together. Additionally, it gave them both the time to confirm through their course of study what they would do after graduation.

Tommy was more convinced than ever that television investigative reporting was the avenue that was professionally appealing. He loved to write and follow through on storytelling that could make a difference and contribute to what people needed to know. Currently, in 1960, there was no reporting or investigative subject matter, and Tom became convinced that locally or at the Network level, this form of reporting was sorely lacking. In truth, Tom was well aware of the fact that, with one exception, his life was generally gratifying. He was living on a luxurious yacht, more convinced than ever that television was his future, and found that academia and the learning process were far more appealing than he ever dreamed. Lisa's limited presence was the one component that was missing. He was miserable without her, and a couple of days a month was just not enough.

For Lisa, across the Bay in Berkeley, there was some of the same enthusiasm for her major. Hotel management was in the throes of change, with the Marriotts and Hiltons of the world finding that the services that they offered were limited and that smaller hotel management like Four Seasons and Ritz-Carlton were introducing comprehensive luxuries that their customer base demanded. That included expansive spa facilities and points that rewarded customer occupancy frequency. Like Tom, she was enthusiastic about her chosen major and could not wait until she could become a part of this aggressive new approach to hotel management and services. Also, like Tommy, she found it difficult, in her limited free time, not to let her mind drift to the joy of their passionate weekends.

While Tom and Lisa were investing in college, other members of their families were also not letting time stand still. Sara Doyle had graduated from Stanford Medical School and completed her residency at Peninsula Hospital in San Mateo. Because of her superior performance at Peninsula, it wasn't long before her reputation was instrumental in generating offers from Bay Area medical facilities. Sara was flattered, but it didn't take her long to accept a full-time position in the Orthopedic group at UC San Francisco Medical Center. Her good fortune would also have a positive effect on convenience, with the hospital being near her Telegraph Hill home. The big bonus was that she could spend more time with the twins, who were now 12 and even more of a handful.

For this reason, childcare was even more of a problem. Olivia and Mark were doing well scholastically, but Olivia had a social conscience, which, on occasion, would cause conflicts with the school. One of those moments was currently problematic. Olivia saw fit to challenge her teacher over the school's policy on racial balance.

The teacher had no control over who would be seated in her classroom. Even at 12, Olivia signaled her activism as an adult, but she was motivated to speak up without any real foundations for her arguments. She knew that white students in her private school had the means to attend St. Francis. The school had no policies that showed racial preferences. If a student could afford a private school education, it was, along with scholastic performance, part of the school's entrance policy. This knowledge did not deter Olivia. She knew that St. Francis had a fair and even form of entrance, but that was not enough for Olivia. She wanted to change the system, and to that end, she saw fit to shake up the policy, whether fair or not. While she sometimes frustrated her instructors, the teachers secretly lauded Olivia for her willingness to stick her neck out and stand up for anything that she felt was an injustice. Interestingly, Sara did not reprimand her daughter because she was proud of Olivia's harmless spirit. She was indeed signaling the force that she would represent as an adult.

Mark, on the other hand, took an entirely different view of the role of an educator. He enjoyed seeing his sister challenge the system, but that was not his approach, and unless it was a blatant infringement, he remained neutral. The contrast between the twins was apparent even at this early stage of their development. Ever the doting uncle, Tom was absolutely in awe of Olivia and felt that if she did not choose law as her vocation, he would be surprised. The twins, at this early stage of their education, were Tom's pride. He always encouraged their willingness to dissent. He had just graduated from USF, where in his last two years, he changed his major from the broad scope of Communication to Journalism. Olivia and her attitude towards social injustice actually influenced Tom's direction to be more focused on his education. He finished near the top of his class and showed a clear propensity for what he described as "investigative journalism."

At 26, Tom was anxious to move his career into high gear, which meant refining his programming idea and setting up introductions with members of the local television market. To him, the graduation ceremony with the lead-up was time-consuming and of little consequence. William and Rita were disappointed in Tom's decision primarily because, like Lisa, he was the first Doyle to graduate from a university, but to him, the diploma was merely a ticket that could open the door to opportunity.

Now that he had his diploma from a prestigious university, he considered his next move. He knew that most students chose to lean on letter writing to introduce themselves to their potential employers, which was not Tom's style. He believed in an introductory letter, which clearly stated that he planned to make in-person calls as a follow-up. He was convinced that the meek do not inherit anything, and being aggressive about his employment was essential. Since investigative journalism was not a commonly used practice at the traditional television station, Tom felt that his mission was to clearly articulate his rationale and enthusiastically explain the approach he intended to initiate. He started the interview practice at KNTV in San Jose, and while they did not turn Tom's ideas down on hand, their status as an independent could not monetarily support his ideas. The next step, after his initial foray, was to line up interviews at the San Francisco network outlets. Crying for funding was not a legitimate argument at these television stations. Tom knew that his mission was not to talk economics but rather an approach that spoke to the value of his reporting format and why investigative journalism would enhance the profile of their station and put them in line for industry recognition. Tom continued to seek support from KTVU, the San Francisco independent offered the same response the San Jose station had come up with, i.e., "We could not fund such a concept." Undaunted, he continued on his mission to convince just one San Francisco TV outlet to embrace his approach to reporting. The fact that no one had responded to his entrance letter was somewhat discouraging, but Tommy put his head down as he visited his most likely stations. Both KGO and KPIX listened intently, but by now, Tom knew the difference between real interest and being placated.

That was four down, and only KRON remained. If he struck out there, he intended to move his pitch to the Sacramento stations. KRON was located right on Van Ness, just blocks away from the apartment house that was the 1940 home of his family's first stop in the Bay Area. Tom was ushered into the General Manager's office. In addition to the GM, the leader had assembled her News Director and Program Manager. This was the first time that this level of interest was offered with the station's top-level management in attendance. The GM, Fran Gitler, opened the conversation by acknowledging the achievements of his resume, including both military and educational accomplishments. Tom was convinced that this was the first GM to have actually read his resume and the rudiments of his project. In addition, this was not only the first encouraging meeting, but also the first woman General Manager whom he had met. The conversation swiftly moved to staffing, subject matter and finally budgetary considerations. Gitler was not patronizing Tom. She was genuinely enthused about the prospect of adding this hard-hitting form of journalism that could differentiate KRON from the other television outlets. She added, she was recently hired to take the station to rating leadership. KRON had dwelled in the rating cellar for years, and Tom's concept was probably the best idea she had considered since she took over two months ago.

The discussion heated up as the three managers felt even more enthusiastic as they began to organize the investigative format. The news director, Jim Bosley, began to flesh out the staffing requirements. Jim outlined the kind of investigative experience that the format would need. He volunteered as a unit lead by his current assignment editor, who had years of extensive knowledge in the field and was well-versed on the most significant controversial issues that were front and center in the Bay Area. Tom knew that his lack of experience would be an issue if the concept were to move forward. Thankfully, Tom was a pragmatist and offered that "pride of authorship" need not be a concern. The managers in the room almost perceptibly breathed a sigh of relief. To Fran Gitler, Tom Doyle would initially be like an intern learning the basics of reporting. She had no intention of squeezing Tom out of an idea that he was passionate about. The fact that he had majored in Journalism at USF was of minimal value. A month in the field would be worth all four years he spent at the University. Gitler was an instinctual leader, and while she didn't bring it up, Tom's medal for heroism, his combat wound and his knowledge of the San Francisco music scene added up to a very attractive profile that would be valuable once Tom took a leadership role. Finally, a series of meetings was set up with Tom and the station management team, and her closing remark was like a shot of adrenaline: "Mister Doyle, your idea is a go!" That night, Tommy drove home to Pier 39 and couldn't wait to share his exciting news with Lisa.

CHAPTER 33

THE "I TEAM"

Lisa was indeed thrilled that Tom was able to sell his idea of investigative reporting to a local television station. His tenacity and unwillingness to back down on his concept were a lesson for Lisa. She admired Tommy and encouraged him to achieve his goal to succeed. Tommy's dedication to his goal was one of his intense qualities that Lisa felt she could embrace as she entered the workforce. Other members of his family, including William, Rita, Sara, and, to no one's surprise, Olivia, were offering their congratulations on Tommy's success. Olivia, even at 12, was probably the most enthusiastic. The idea of dealing with Civil Rights, corruption in government, and Gay rights was on her list, and Tom would be addressing these social issues on his television reporting. In early July 1960, the initial organizational meeting was held at KRON and in addition to the General Manager, Fran Gitler and the News Director, Jim Bosley, were representatives of production personnel, including writers, researchers, editors, field reporters, producers, and photographers. The staff would be augmented with interns and production assistants. As Bosley reeled off the extent of the production personnel required to bring the reporting to life, Tom was visibly in awe of the extent of staff requirements. During the meeting, Tom had nothing substantial to contribute other than the name of the unit he suggested. The moment he offered the "I Team," there was an instant series of head nods and smiles. Gitler chimed in with, "I cannot recall a time when choosing a title for a television show was so positively declarative. Congratulations, rookie."

Once the staffing requirements were resolved, the hard part of the 'point of view' or subject matter and budgetary needs were discussed. Here again, almost apologetically, when investigative stories were being explored, Tommy came up with the issue of "Building the Embarcadero Freeway, corruption in Rapid Transit, Civil Rights, and the Gay Communities' growth in North Beach." Bosley glanced at Tom and reinforced the feeling that, although Doyle had no hands-on experience in television production, you could have fooled him! After the round of appreciative applause, Fran Gitler adjourned the meeting and set July 20th as the next meeting to address finalizing staffing and the most controversial hair-pulling when the I Team budget was addressed. Before the meeting broke up, Bosley announced that he anticipated that the I Team would not premiere in the Fall. Seeing the confusion in Tom's eyes, Bosley went on to say that it would take more than a couple of months to gear up the new unit. In addition to transferring and hiring new personnel, determining and producing the first piece, and promotion, The I Team would not premiere until January 1961. He added that viewing was at its highest level in the first quarter of the year.

The more Tommy thought about what the News Director had said at the closing, it made sense. The investigation of the initial stories would require an abundance of research and promotion if they wanted to ensure the success of the new I Team. One more thing… Jim said he anticipated that because of the intensity of the format and the potential for lawsuits, the I Team reports, at most, would air once a month. Tom realized just how much he had to learn after only two meetings. It also convinced him more than ever that working in television was exactly what the world had in store for him. He would do everything in his power to cooperate and make sure that the introduction of the investigative I Team would ensure a resounding success.

Lisa's graduation from Cal was everything she had hoped for. Unlike Tom, who didn't formally show up for his graduation ceremony, Lisa was thrilled at the prospect of being a member of the 1960 University of California graduating class being held at the Berkeley Coliseum in the last week of June. Lisa was rightfully proud of being the first college graduate in her family. Tom's unwillingness to attend his graduation ceremony rightfully confused her, but that was his choice, and she respected his decision. The family and friends arrived in numbers that included the Walsh's Jimmie, Lauralie and the man himself, Walter. Also in force were her parents, her brother and sister, and friends. With a graduating class of eight hundred, the alphabet and "Alvarez" being her last name was propitious. And when 'Lisa Alvarez' was called, the volume of applause and whistles from her supporters almost made Lisa blush. That evening, William hosted a graduation party for both Tom and Lisa. The party was catered, which gave Rita the time to join in on the festivities.

In the four years that the couple had spent at the two universities, much had changed. Sara was now Doctor Sara Doyle. Tommy had not only graduated with a degree in journalism, but in a very short time, he had landed a full job at KRON, the local NBC affiliate. Lisa, on the other hand, had decided to attend graduate school at Cal. The one thing that had not changed was their love for each other. Unresolved was the marriage date. Olivia and her twin brother Mark were now 13 and living up to their great expectations. Olivia had undoubtedly determined that the law profession was her future. To that end, she had not only pestered her grandfather, Judge Shelton, but whenever she could find the time, she visited the San Mateo courthouse and the domain of the Judge. Mark was directing his attention towards medical school after graduating from high school.

Judge Shelton, not to be outdone, announced that Earl Warren, the governor of California, had named him Chief Justice of the State of California Supreme Court! Not wanting to take any of the limelight from the exciting things happening to so many close family members, the Judge had not yet told anyone except Olivia, who was so proud of her grandpa that she just blurted the news out at the party. Yes, it did steal some of the thunder from the twins, but when Judge Shelton confirmed his appointment, everyone was genuinely pleased and congratulatory. Chief Justice of California was an honor no one could have anticipated.

Coralyn went on to say, with some hesitance, that they would be moving to Sacramento. She made it clear that their beautiful home in Burlingame would not be sold. Coralyn suggested that Sara and her family move from their apartment in San Francisco to the charming Burlingame address. The timing could not have been better. Olivia and Mark were sharing the same room, and at 13, it was clear that they both needed some privacy. While leaving San Francisco would be painful, the roomy Burlingame home offering them the privacy of their own bedroom was greeted with enthusiasm. Everything they had heard about San Mateo High was positive, which added to the ease of moving from the City.

On July 20, Tom attended the final planning meeting for the I Team. He continued to be impressed with the commitment KRON was making and the foresight of Fran Gitler, the new General Manager of the station. For this meeting, the full staff of the new I Team was introduced. The Producer of the format would be the current Assignment Editor of the six o'clock news, Pat Pallilo. He had asked the General Manager to move him to a producing role, but because of his good judgment, she needed him at the Assignment desk until they could find a strong replacement. The two camera operators were long-time professionals of TV news: Dick Carr and Abe Espinoza. The field reporters, Victoria Domke and Prudence Peterson, were much younger and had recently graduated from San Jose State with degrees in Journalism. The support team included three researchers and two production assistants. New personnel would be added as the format of the I Team evolved.

The final discussion involved subject matter, the proposed building of the Embarcadero Freeway, which would be constructed directly in front of the Ferry Building, a San Francisco landmark. The growing evidence of corruption was highly controversial and the perfect subject matter to lead off the new investigative reporting. It wasn't until the meeting was ready to wrap up that the News Director, Jim Bosley, announced who the face of the I Team, or the on-camera talent, would be. They had settled on a young graduate of Stanford, Cynthia Dobbs, who was widely perceived as one of KRON's rising reporters at just 23. There were some nods of approval, but just as many grimaces. The addition of another female in a top position at the station, Cynthia's age, and limited experience were among the complaints. Dick Carr added that Cynthia's age and appearance conceivably would not be well received by the viewers. Fran Gitler responded that she was precisely the right person to be the face of the I Team. Television news audiences were, by and large, older, and youthful viewers were highly prized. Bosley added that the choice of Cynthia would hopefully attract young viewers, specifically because of her attractiveness and obvious intelligence. With that, Bosley asked Cynthia, who was waiting in the next room, to join the meeting.

Tom was the only one who had not met Cynthia Dobbs. She was short, red-headed with searching blue eyes and a near-beautiful face that exuded confidence. The staff asked a series of difficult questions to set their minds at ease, and Dobbs responded with all the right personal and journalistic answers. Finally, Tom spoke up and, with an amusing look, asked what his role would be. Bosley responded instantly with the final announcement of the afternoon. Tom Doyle would serve as Executive Producer of the series, which meant nothing specific other than entering the learning process. His good instincts on content would continue to be a resource. The next step was to give the staff an opportunity to coalesce and get to know each other. Bosley ordered pizza, and for the rest of the day, the newly minted I Team staff had an opportunity to begin the jelling of a brand new, challenging Investigative unit. The initial subject dealing with the new controversial freeway was the kind of content that the team could sink their teeth into. The two-person research staff went right to work along with the field producers to begin the investigation of the Embarcadero Freeway.

Tom had been given access to all avenues of news reporting, and he took distinct advantage of every opportunity to learn. He was earnest and anxious to learn, and his intelligence was apparent to everyone. He stayed out of the way and asked questions that were precise and reasonable. Tom's winning personality once again served him well. He became a welcome contributor to the I Team. The first day of shooting was to set up the controversy and eventually follow up with a series of interviews, which would shed light on why the freeway extension was unfortunate and riddled with corruption. For the next six weeks, the reporters and production team were totally engaged in ferreting out the shameful corruption and poor planning on the freeway.

Prudence Peterson, who was known for her veracity and instincts, was able to interview two City Commissioners who initially refused to appear on camera, but through Prudence's tenacity, agreed to be interviewed with limits. In a back doorway, it turned out she was able to elicit some burning accusations. The Commissioners were not aware of each other's comments, and they were at odds. The difficult work of verifying information and accusations was a touchy part of editing, and only with precise collaboration could a storyline be included in the final report. After weeks of digging and verifying what had been gleaned by reporters, the five-part series was ready to be aired and promoted. With fairness in mind, KRON invited the leadership of the planning commission to a private screening before the documentary was aired. On the day of the screening, ten members of the City government, including the mayor, were in attendance. Before the viewing, GM Fran Gitler made some remarks outlining how the reporting process worked and when the station intended to begin airing the reports. The response at the conclusion of the field pieces was shock and anger from many members of the city government. The mayor was unfortunately not aware of what had transpired in the planning and budget of the new freeway extension.

The next day, Fran Gitler and Jim Bosley received what can only be described as a cease-and-desist letter from the City of San Francisco. In internal response, KRON checked and rechecked their sources and consulted with their attorneys. The consensus was a bright green light to proceed. All through the holiday season, the station began to promote the I Team investigative report on the freeway debacle. When the actual date of the premiere airing was known, there were threats, including violence, from any number of sources. The owners of the KRON had obviously heard from some city leaders and asked Gitler not to run the documentary series. The GM did not budge and chose to keep her integrity intact by airing the report when it was scheduled to begin in three days.

What followed was a sea of ridicule from involved parties, but the public was totally behind the station's right to uncover corruption. While many staff members at the station were "hiding under their desks," in actuality, they were proud of the willingness of KRON to air this history-making series of reports over five days. It was Fran Gitler's intention to "shake up the status quo," and the shaking did not stop. The report card was a resounding success when it came to ratings, putting the station in first place in news. When the numbers were shared with the I Team and the KRON staff in general, there was a palpable sense of pride that rippled through the station. Throughout the five-day series, the station continued to be applauded by the public, resulting in the city canceling the Embarcadero Freeway until all of the issues raised by KRON were resolved. The station's ratings continued to increase, and both Fran Gitler and Jim Bosely, as well as the entire news staff, knew who was most responsible for the success of this form of investigative television news… Thomas Doyle.

CHAPTER 34

AUDITION

Once Fran and Jim had been interviewed by the three local dailies and Network TV reporters, the whole idea of Investigative news was being mulled in TV Stations across the country. During these conversations, they had mentioned Tom's name and the credit that he deserved. Not all that was happening in the field during the production phase of the hard-hitting investigative series was visible to the public. The Producer, Pat Pallilo, went to Fran Gitler with a complaint that could spell the death knell of the entire I Team. Here's what Pallilo was concerned about. The on-camera talent for the series, Cynthia Dobbs, had been flirting with Tom Doyle for the entire production. To Doyle's credit, he had taken Cynthia's overtures lightly and was under the impression that this kind of thing happened during shoots. When the documentary was "In the can," completed, she literally made a pass that Tom could not ignore. She had suggested that they celebrate the completion of the series at her apartment. This was the moment that Tom felt he had to speak to Pallilo. Pat and the crew had observed some of this banter on the part of Cynthia, but the thought that passed their minds was that she was just being playful with the "rookie."

To add to the crisis, Dobbs had recently been introduced to Lisa, Tom's girlfriend, who had on one occasion visited the shoot. One of the outlandish moments was that someone (evidently Cynthia) had called Lisa on the phone and warned her that Tom was having an affair with the show talent, Cynthia Dobbs. That day, Tom had returned to the boat at Pier 39, and when he greeted Lisa, she was almost instantly reduced to tears. Finally, when she regained her composure, she asked Tom if he was having an affair. Tom was dumbfounded and queried Lisa about where she had heard such a lie. Someone had called her and insinuated the affair after several hours of convincing Lisa that nothing had happened. He promised that he would get to the bottom of this bogus call.

The next day, Tommy reported this turn of events to Pat Pallilo. At this point, Pat asked for a meeting with Fran Gitler, Tom Doyle, and Jim Bosley. The meeting with the participants was held in Gitler's office. All that had transpired was outlined to the shocked General Manager. How in the world could this graduate of one of the finest universities in America have been reduced to this kind of troublemaking slurs? She obviously had severe emotional problems.

Regarding the phone call that Lisa had received, Fran volunteered to Tom that she would personally meet with Lisa and set her mind at ease. True to her word, Gitler met with Cynthia and asked about the accusations. Dobbs denied that any of this had taken place and defended her innocence. She threatened to take the story to the press and stated that she could destroy the I Team and smear the whole station. Gitler was anticipating this and had prepared to ask the nucleus of the I Team to join them in her office.

In this follow-up expanded meeting, the staff members recounted that what they had observed lowered the morale of the team. In spite of this internal volume of rumors and innuendo, the production went on to completion. With the key people present, Fran Gitler pointedly looked at Dobbs and stated that she was fired and that if any cheap, sordid events were reported to the outside press, she would see to it that Cynthia Dobbs would never work in television again. With that, she handed Dobbs a document outlining her actions and told her to sign it. Gitler went on to say that if she didn't sign, KRON would take the story to the press and eliminate any possibility of Dobbs ever working in Journalism again. A look of resignation came over her face, and a tearful Cynthia Dobbs signed the document.

The station did follow up with a phone call to Lisa Alvarez and set the record straight. That evening, Tom and Lisa were emotionally relieved, and the intensity of their lovemaking made it clear that they were a couple again after the first real challenge to their union. This sorry turn of events did open up some issues in the I Team that had to be addressed, not the least of which involved replacing Cynthia Dobbs as the voice of the unit. Pat Palillo did offer a suggestion that resonated with Jim Bosley. Pat said that one possible person who could have a positive impact on the format was Tom Doyle. He was handsome, likable, highly intelligent, with a solid speaking voice. The thought of editing the remaining episodes and inserting someone like Tom was considered, but the consensus recommended that they should wait until the next I Team investigation.

With that, Tom was called in to meet with Jim Bosley. He suggested that Tom literally audition for the role of talent on the series. Doyle was surprised and flattered at the same time. After the shock wore off, Tom asked if he could have a day to think about it. That evening, he shared the news with Lisa, who thought that he would make an excellent host. The next morning, Tom accepted the request for him to audition. Later that week, the audition was scheduled, and Tom found himself being made up and prepped for on-camera. He had never done anything like this, but if these television professionals felt he might be right to host the next I Team report, what did he have to lose? To no one's surprise, Tommy performed an excellent on-camera audition, and without any additional conversation, he was offered the job.

In the past six months, so much had transpired that Tom was almost shell-shocked, but with his healthy ego, he felt it would be a mistake to say no. Tom would continue in his role as Executive Producer and be involved in the editorial direction of future subject matter. In less than a year, he had sold the idea of an I Team to the station, seen the ratings on the first episodes spike, been caught in the middle of a sordid internal investigation ending in the show talent being fired and finally been offered the job as on-camera reporter for the series. Both Jim Bosley and Fran Gitler agreed that Tom should not say anything until a press release had been distributed. It was ok to share his new assignment with his immediate family. With that go-ahead, Tom and Lisa had conversations with Rita and William, Sara and the Twins, and Jimmie and Lauralie Walsh. The reaction was uniformly positive and stunning at the same time. Thomas Doyle's star continued to shine even brighter. Tom and Lisa had reason to celebrate. Tommy's salary as I Team on-camera host was upwards of $1,500 a week, including Executive Producer, a title he would retain. The staff had concluded that the next investigation would dig into the drug use in our schools. The research team on the subject was well underway.

For Lisa and Tom, it was past time that they announced their wedding plans. Many locations were discussed, and nothing seemed right until Rita suggested the "Mark Two." Realizing that the wedding party would be small, the yacht would be the perfect setting. It was large enough to handle 75 people, which would include family and close friends. It seemed almost too convenient, and the reason why Tom felt he needed to call Jimmie Walsh to see if it was okay to use his boat. Once Jimmie was on board, Tom's work was over. This was a labor of love for people like Rita, Lauralie, Sara, and Lisa's mom, Anna. Not having to pay for a facility and catering everything, food and drink, the reception was no longer a dilemma. The only thing the yacht didn't have was a dance floor, and Lisa and Tom agreed that it was not a deal breaker. Jimmie's yacht had everything for a beautiful wedding on San Francisco Bay.

The date was set early in July 1961. The invitation list was going to be just right, and if it grew by one or two couples, it would still be more than satisfactory. Tom wanted to include Charlie Benedict, Sergeant Salerno, John Sheer, Bruno Banducci, the I Team staff, and KRON management. Lisa would include her mother, Dominic Gomez, Jose Aguilar and his wife, Soledad. As far as the wedding itself is concerned, Judge James Shelton would conduct the ceremony. William and Rita could not have been more pleased with Tom's choice of Lisa Alvarez. She was not only physically beautiful on the outside, but inside, she had a sharp mind and a thirst for knowledge. The fact that she had completed her undergraduate studies at Cal and was moving on to graduate studies in Hotel Management was laudable. Tom and Lisa were a highly compatible, ambitious couple who would, by all standards, achieve their personal and professional goals. Tom had a clear idea of what he planned to achieve by aggressively selling his idea, seeing his concept brought to life, and finally, after less than a year, he would be the on-camera talent for the I Team.

 As William approached his mid-sixties, he would face the reality that retirement was not far off. Currently, he was as active as ever, and working for Walsh Inc. continued to challenge him as the face of the company continued to respond positively to a changing industry. The company had gone from the huge government contracts they realized during the War to a peacetime customer base. To that end, William had introduced the Luxury Cruise business to the service that Walsh Inc. offers, which was to provide fleets of cruise ships with mass interior design and execution. Walsh Inc. was also, with all the changes, able to maintain a factory of expert, loyal personnel.

With his office in Long Beach and his home in San Mateo, William and Rita agreed that the estate in San Mateo was no longer compatible with their lifestyle. Tom, Lisa and Sara were off on their own enterprise, and the large house should be sold, and at the same time they would shop for a home by the water, which was something that they had envisioned for a very long time. Karen Walsh, Jimmie's wife, was an outstanding, highly successful realtor specializing in nearby beach communities just south of Long Beach. Newport and Laguna Beach were among the most sought-after addresses in Southern California. After two weekends with some enticing tours of upscale homes, they found the right property that seemed to respond to all of their criteria. It was a two-year-old, three-bedroom, three-bath home on a Laguna Hills lot that featured an uninterrupted view of Laguna Beach and the sparkling Pacific Ocean. The couple who built the home and evidently sold the house when they entered into divorce proceedings had lived in the house for only a year. Rita and William were the first people to see the property, and they were almost instantly ready to make an offer.

One of the reasons that Rita found the Laguna address so appealing was Laguna Beach's reputation as the foremost art community in Southern California. The home had glass doors facing west with that extraordinary view, a living room with a stone floor-to-ceiling fireplace, a party room with adjacent sauna and exercise room, a high-end equipped kitchen/dining area with stainless steel appliances and a large deck for entertaining off the living room that featured a built-in bar and cabana. Karen let them know that they could make an offer that would take the home off the market for a short period of time. She added that it was the kind of property that would not stay on the market for an extended period. William responded that they wanted to make a firm offer, which was the asking price. Karen Walsh responded with the knowledge that the owner had told her that they would not entertain shopping the home if someone agreed to the asking price. Two days later, the dream house was in escrow. Rita and William were thrilled and thanked Karen with a huge commission. Parallel to showing the Laguna home, Karen Walsh had also conducted an open house for the San Mateo address. Less than a week after Laguna was closing, the Doyles had a serious offer on their home, which was also the asking price.

CHAPTER 35

THE WEDDING

The Doyles, Alvarezes and Walshes were enjoying life in Southern California with almost everything in their lives falling into order, which included the marriage of Thomas Doyle and Lisa Alvarez. On the day of the wedding on Jimmie Walsh's yacht, Tom and Lisa had to laugh about the fact that they were waking up at the site of their wedding. The boat was being transformed into a festival of white. Rita, Anna, Sara and Lauralie had spent many hours of their time to make sure that the event was memorable. The rear large deck would be the scene of the wedding vows with San Francisco Bay and all its beauty as a backdrop, and an arch of white carnations would fold over the couple, chairs were placed in two sections with an aisle down the center and additional seating on Pier 39, adjacent to the Mark Two. Since Tom would have many more friends and family in attendance, they consciously shared the opinion to use open seating.

Regarding Bridesmaids, it really wasn't all that difficult. Lisa had invited three of her very young cousins, aged 11, 9, and 14. Sara selected Olivia, who already had objected to wearing a dress, and three women from Medical School who were dear friends and graduated with Sara from Stanford. The "flower girls" format was jettisoned. Lisa shocked Sara when she asked her to be her Maid of Honor, and as far as the Best Man selection was concerned, Jimmie Walsh was the obvious choice.

The deliveries and the decorations were so tasteful and elaborate, they drew a small crowd on Pier 39. Other members of the wedding party included Lauralie Walsh, Sara Doyle, Olivia, Anna Gomez and Rita Doyle. On the men's side, among the crowd were Johnny Walker, Bruno Banducci, Robert Gibson, Ben Bernstein, and William Doyle. An hour before the ceremony, Tommy asked Dominic if he would mind taking his car and picking up a cane at Judge's house. It seemed that as the day wore on, Tom was feeling a lot of pain in his left leg, which was injured in Korea. Just before the wedding was to begin, guests were treated to some great jazz. A professional trio, people Tom knew from the Blackhawk, had been hired by Banducci for the evening. Piano, bass, and drums provided a special aura to the beautifully decorated yacht and glorious sunny day. In San Francisco, a day like this was so perfect that people labeled it "a natural high."

With all the special friends and family assembled and seated, the trio segued into "How High the Moon" as Lisa appeared, accompanied by her soon-to-be father-in-law, William Doyle. It was supposed to be Dominic Gomez, Lisa's uncle, who was nowhere to be found. Tom had asked him to take the T-Bird and pick up his cane. He should have returned hours ago. The wedding party adjourned to the forward decks of the yacht for the reception. Just as Tom was showing real concern about Dominic, two San Francisco Police cars arrived on the Pier. Tom walked up to meet them. The Police explained that a Mexican male, driving an expensive T-Bird, was questioned as he emerged from a liquor store. The man claimed that he was at the store to select a bottle of champagne for a wedding party on Pier 39. Police found his story fabricated, but just in case he might be telling the truth, they drove to Pier 39. Tom's car was impounded at the Police Station. A very angry Tom Doyle verified Dominic's claim as he emerged from the second police car. Dominic's face was badly bruised, and his left eye was black and nearly closed. Tom's degree of Irish anger rose to a level where he had to be held back from attacking the policeman. He told them they had not heard the end of this brutal behavior, to return his T-Bird and to "get the fuck off the pier!" Dominic was ushered on board and treated in a nearby bathroom. People at the reception were appalled, and Tom, still livid, asked the friends and family members to continue to enjoy the party.

In the meantime, Tom and the KRON leaders, including General Manager Fran Gitler, News Director Jim Bosley, convened and promised Tom that they would be the voice of the people of San Francisco and the police would not go unpunished. Dominic, now presentable, having changed his bloody clothes and received first aid, let everyone know he was okay and to please enjoy the festivities. Lisa and her mother, in tears, hugged Dominic Gomez, who assured them that his injuries were minor, which was not true. One of the party members, Charlie Benedict, had taken pictures of Dominic as he arrived. While the turn of events was troubling, the reception went on as the wedding party tried to put the disturbing distraction behind them. Unfortunately, it was impossible to ignore what had transpired, and while the party did continue, the revelry was, understandably, somewhat subdued. Surprisingly, most of the guests remained relatively sober and departed the yacht earlier than anticipated.

Tom and Lisa, along with Sara, William and Rita, Judge Shelton and Coralyn, and Anna and Dominic, stayed on board to provide support and discuss the evening's turn of events that disrupted the reception party. The twins were asleep in the port bedroom. Tom insisted that Dominic see his doctor and use the yacht as his address while in San Francisco. As they adjourned, the family raised their glasses for one more toast as a salute to Lisa and Tom. Because Tom and Lisa wanted to resolve the appalling issues with the San Francisco police, the newlyweds decided to, for now, curtail their planned honeymoon to Carmel.

The evening following the wedding, KRON aired the sequence of events and finished the telecast with a hard-hitting editorial that slammed the comportment of the San Francisco Police Department. The Chief of Police responded with a decision to suspend the police officers involved in the beating. In addition, the other Television Stations, i.e., KGO, KPIX, KTVU, and KNTV, regardless of their political persuasion, all chose to censor the SF Police. The brutality of the perpetrators was a shock to the liberal bent of the Bay Area. Because Tom was scheduled to be the host of the upcoming I Team reports in the Fall, Bosley made the conscientious decision to put him on the air now to continue to editorialize as a participant in the event. The station had just installed the first videotape machine and recorded Tom's message, allowing it to play with more frequency. Tom's appearance and messaging were well received by the Bay Area population. It also turned out to be exactly the right positioning as a preview of his I Team hosting. The Chief of Police did not wait to act. Three officers were relieved of duty and fired, and at the time, the Chief would go on television and in print media to apologize to Dominic Gomez and commit to a program of sensitivity training for the entire police force. Dominic did submit to X-rays, which showed that his jaw and two ribs were broken. Following the advice of Walsh's attorneys, Dominic sued the police department, which agreed to a settlement of $35,000.

With the satisfaction of a positive city-wide response, Tom and Lisa finally could go on their postponed Honeymoon and spend a week in Carmel, the charming community on the central coast of California.

They were able to reinstate their reservations at the Highland Inn. If there ever was a place to relax and temporarily put your troubles behind you, Carmel fits the bill. Lisa and Tom loved the European-style village and the fact that everything was within walking distance. From performing arts to boutique shops, restaurants and for Lisa, almost endless art galleries, the Doyles were in the kind of environment that embraced the love and romance that the newlyweds needed to nurture after all the time spent apart.

A week in Carmel was not enough time to fulfill their emotional needs, but returning home did promise an exciting time in their young lives. Lisa would be back in Berkeley for graduate school, and Tom would start his new role as on-camera talent for the investigative format that he had authored and KRON had executed. They were a couple on the go, and hopefully, they would find enough time to truly enjoy each other. After a joyous, rejuvenating romantic week in Carmel, they returned to their high-speed lives. Tom was dealing with a craft that, in many ways, he wasn't qualified for, but thankfully, he was the kind of young man who was able to absorb volumes of information. In other words, he was described as a "quick study." The I Team was already deep into the research phase of the next investigative five-episode series, which was scheduled to begin airing in early October.

In the 1960s, the era was marked by a massive Civil Rights movement, growing military commitment in Vietnam, anti-war protests, counter-cultural movements, and political assassinations. San Francisco was positioned as the leading edge of controversy. In the meantime, the State of California was rapidly becoming the largest state in the union. Aerospace, electronics, tourism, entertainment, and oil were dominant industries. The state led in everything from fashion to fads. The I Team in late 1960 had more than enough controversy. At the top of the list of inequality and discrimination in the Black and Hispanic communities was the practice of comprehensive zoning. Any attempt to build multi-family housing in white neighborhoods was stymied when the communities established zoning that allowed only single-family homes. Most black families could not afford single-family homes. When Willie Mays moved to San Francisco with the Giants, he attempted to buy a home in a white neighborhood, and the white community did everything they could to prevent him from buying.

It was only through City activists that blatant discrimination was overridden, but it was a solid example of just how rampant the policy of zoning was in the Bay Area. It was insidious, and zoning also impacted schooling for black students who were forced to deal with inferior facilities and curricula. It was no wonder that black test scores were significantly lower than their white counterparts. Neighborhoods like the Fillmore District, which was majority black, were eyed as a zoning target. Politicians labeled Fillmore as a "blighted" neighborhood, and it was bulldozed.

The investigative team at KRON had initially determined that the next subject to be addressed by the I Team would be Drug Addiction. While the expanding use of dependent drugs was controversial, especially marijuana, recent events in San Francisco had pointed even more emphatically to Civil Rights. The recent situation found the program's author and talent deeply engaged in a hateful example of failing racial rights. The African community, especially, had experienced decades of intolerance and discrimination. The city of San Francisco led the systematic and structural discrimination practiced in the Bay Area. When Dominic Gomez was abused with blatant racism by the city's Police, the I Team changed the current subject matter they would address in the Fall. The issues associated with zoning and its impact on housing and education in San Francisco, and the methods used to restrict blacks from settling in white neighborhoods, were fertile ground for investigation. Jim Bosley had real concerns about tackling a controversial subject that could backfire on the station. He contended that many white families in those neighborhoods would agree with the zoning rules and felt that multi-family units would have a negative impact on home values. Philosophically, they agreed that discrimination was a major issue, but not when it affected their pocketbook.

KRON became concerned that white advertisers and subscribers would blanch at the content of the investigation. Station General Manager Fran Gitler called a meeting with Tom, Jim Bosley, and Pat Palillo. She opened the meeting, stating that the owner of KRON had called her and expressed concern about the potential negative public reaction to the subject of Civil Rights. The initial subject dealing with drugs was much "safer" than opening a "can of worms." The owner closed with "of course, as General Manager, it is your decision." As long as he was on record, he felt he could avoid any explosive reaction from viewers. Tom remained silent and waited until Bosley and Palillo had their say. The News Director and Editorial Director did not disappoint. Bosley was the first to speak up, contending that the term "investigative reporting" was in jeopardy. Did they select subject matter that had a profound impact on what they decided to cover, or was it selected based on who or what we chose? Palillo chimed in and offered a compatible point of view. "If we decided not to cover the most hard-hitting public issues, were we kidding ourselves into believing that the 'I Team' was anything other than a sham?" Tom was intense as he said, "When I brought the idea of offering an investigative format, it was not my feeling that the only subject matter we would cover would be 'safe' subjects. Yes, by tackling Civil Rights, we have to anticipate that there will be a backlash, but I feel that the public that will support us will outweigh the naysayers. Furthermore, if we are true to our convictions and cover the issue comprehensively, we will be recognized nationally as true journalists. Awards will follow." Fran was pensive, and with the potential of losing her position, she said, "Okay, let's do it." The inspired male team erupted in applause.

Now the hard work began, and Tom and the I Team were in the field, and it wasn't always gratifying. Some of the subjects, including members of the City Planning Bureau, were either reticent or totally unwilling to be interviewed. Thankfully, however, there were enough caring politicians, City Planners, and real estate agents who were willing to go on camera and speak to power. Pru Peterson and Vickie Domke, as investigative field reporters, were adamant and unrelenting in their efforts to tell the story and not pull any punches in their zeal. The entire staff of KRON was openly proud to be a member of a station that showed that integrity meant something. To add to the positive convictions of the field unit, they were impressed with the sincere interviewing style and general on-camera presence of Tom Doyle. His peers were genuinely in awe of a host who, with very little training, could perform with the skill of a seasoned professional. The cameramen were just getting used to the new video camera technology that allowed them to play back what they had shot for reviewing. Tom was able to look at the day's video and make some editorial changes right on the spot. They didn't have to wait until the film was developed. As the team gathered an inventory of hard-hitting videos, the more convinced they were that what they were reporting mattered. The series on Civil Rights in the Bay Area was coming together and was very close to "a wrap." The title for the documentary was "Home Sweet Zone." The promotion of the soon-to-be-released investigative report "Home Sweet Zone" was almost instantly controversially received. Viewers were responding in ways that the station had not anticipated, including threats on Tom Doyle's life! Some sick individuals made hateful comments that included burning KRON to the ground. At the other end of the spectrum were congratulatory voices who were genuinely pleased with the station's willingness to tackle tough subject matters. It was a mixed bag of public reaction.

CHAPTER 36

THE DNC

The evening the series premiered, rather than being at the station, Tom decided to join Lisa at home and hopefully objectively view "Home Sweet Zone." Not prone to overreacting, Lisa was somewhat surprised to see Tom appear to be nervous. The Channel 4 logo came up on screen, and there was Thomas Doyle introducing the documentary series. The first part of the series traced the history of racism in the Bay Area and teased the content of upcoming episodes. The next showing of "Home Sweet Zone" would air in three weeks. The phone instantly rang. Holding his breath, Tom picked up. Jim Bosley was calling to say that the calls from the public were split, but the weight was on the positive side. He added that the station had overwhelming calls from young women who wanted to know if he was married and how "cute" he was. Jim laughed with appreciation and closed the conversation with "nice work, handsome." Obviously, Tom did not share the substance of the call with Lisa.

After the first episode of the series, the advertising community began pulling their ads from KRON and threatening to cancel even more ads if the station continued with the series. Fran Gitler and Jim Bosley were seeing intensified concern and threats from station ownership. The risk of revenue was very real, and only one of the five-part series had aired, presenting a dilemma. Gitler was aware of the risk of continuing with "Home Sweet Zone," and at the same time, she recognized that station leadership was in jeopardy of losing their jobs.

If station ownership is calling for a cease and desist, they will have no option. With that, Fran decided to call a meeting with the investigative unit to let them know that the series was going to be cancelled, and it had nothing to do with their work, but was a decision that she had no control over. Her authority had no bearing, and scheduling part 2 only to have it pulled would only be a Pyrrhic victory when the station brought in a new management team.

The staff was angry, dejected, and, to use the vernacular, they were just plain pissed. As a team, they looked to find a way to salvage the series, but in truth, they did not have power, and the idea that Fran Gitler and Jim Bosley would sacrifice their jobs was not worthy of any consideration. They exited the meeting with a sense of helplessness and frustration. Tom said nothing simply because he had no answers, but he did have one idea. Later that week, he asked the engineer on duty to schedule an I Team videotape promotion. Tom had checked the studio schedule for that day and chose the one open hour to record. Not telling anyone what he was doing beyond the techs who were recording, he sat on a stool with a blue background and asked the cameraman to shoot him from the waist up. When the tech asked where the producer for the "promo" was, Tom responded that the one-minute promo with no "B-roll" didn't require a producer, and furthermore, he was the Executive Producer of the I Team. Next, he checked with the Traffic Department, where the lineup for the day was initiated. It was the log which programmed all incidental material, including commercials, public service announcements, promotions and station IDs. Tom then asked a member of the Traffic Department to change a promo number, and once it was done, the log showed the new entry. The operating log was programmed for the control room, and the technician operating the videotape merely loaded the tape as directed.

What followed would make television history, not only in San Francisco but across the nation. The only one who knew what was on the tape beyond the technicians in the control and projection room was Tom. It was scheduled adjacent to the network evening news and exploded when it aired. The videotape featured Tom and no one else sitting on a stool and addressing why "Home Sweet Zone" was not going to continue to air for the remaining 4 episodes. He pulled no punches but made it clear that the First Amendment and Freedom of the Press were being challenged. As he closed the "Promo," he exonerated other members of the "Team" and stated that he had organized, scheduled and taped the announcement with no help from news management or the General Manager and that as Executive Producer of the series, he had total access and freedom.

The phones throughout KRON began ringing off the hook, and there just were not enough people to answer all the calls. When Jim and Fran saw the announcement from their homes, they were flabbergasted and joyous at the same time. The jubilation resonated throughout the station at 6:30 on February 10, 1961. Tom's home was bedlam. People on Pier 39 had seen the announcement, and waves of cheering rippled through the adjacent piers. His phone was ringing with no relief, so Tom and Lisa decided to go out for dinner to get away from "Tom Doyle's revenge." They were of the opinion that Scoma's on the wharf would be a safe resort. The minute they walked into the restaurant, it erupted. They knew Tom and Lisa as regulars, and most had seen or heard of the pirated tape. Tom had called for reservations, and he had never had a greeting like the one that befell him and Lisa. Most people would probably enjoy such a moment, but all Tom could feel was self-conscious embarrassment. People were standing, yelling congratulations and participating in endless applause.

Anticipating what he might experience at the station, Tom chose to stay home the next day, even with the phones relentlessly ringing. He finally just took the two phones off their hooks. The next morning, February 11, local media was all over the story. Both the Chronicle and the Examiner ran front-page stories with pictures of Tom and of all things in his Army uniform! Later that day, the story had spread East, and subsequently, media from all sources was airing the story. With their phones off the hook, the Doyles believed that a calm had set in, but such was not the case. As a matter of fact, people from the station, including Fran, Jim, Pat and the entire I Team staff, showed up at Pier 39. They absolutely needed to tell Tom what had transpired at KRON on a need-to-know mission. They all were invited to board the "Mark Two" by Lisa, while Tom had no idea what he should do except listen. Fran Gitler shared that they were intending to resign before Tom's "promo," and that they had waited all day for the boom to drop. To their surprise and amazement, there was no word from the owner of KRON, Ted Burchill. The station was being praised from every media corner of the City, and there was an embarrassing controversy. Dubs of the one-minute tape had been released and pirated by any number of sources, and it was playing on all California facilities and, conceivably, the nation. What Tom intended to use as his swan song and a way to take the blame off anyone else had turned into an all-hands-on-deck revolution!

What were the next steps, and would Tommy show up at KRON as a conquering hero? Jim Bosley had already sent a station-wide memo out stating that, in all likelihood, Tom would return to work, since there was no resolution, but he asked that people give him respect and space. Tom said okay, but he would like a couple of days to "allow things to settle down." On Thursday, February 12, with great trepidation, Tom did indeed show up at the station expecting the worst and was more than a little pleased that the staff was, by and large, congratulatory but reserved, and he began to relax. With the videotape distributed nationwide, the thought of firing personnel at the station was inconceivable. When Tom was settled, Fran Gitler called for a meeting with him, Jim Bosley, and Pat Palillo. It was clear that she had a narrow line to navigate. The turn of events was so startling, with Tom's mind-blowing message that defended the reporting to the station ownership, who found themselves in a no-win controversy. When the staff leaders joined Fran in her office, she had heard from Ted Burchill and board members. Their response was predictable, and it was up to her to share their decision-making with Tom, Jim and Pat.

Fran had no options and dreaded what she had to share with the editorial team. First, they had decided not to fire anyone… including Tom. Second, there would be no subsequent episodes of "Home Sweet Zone," and finally, the I Team would be disbanded. Fran went on to say that she understood the dynamics of the order that she had to implement. If they decided to resign, what would that accomplish? Their replacements would merely adhere to the demands of ownership. She went on to say that she had made up her mind to stay at KRON, and it was up to Jim, Pat and Tom to make their own independent decision. Pat and Jim took her advice to stay at the station even though they obviously had strong reservations. All eyes turned to Tom. He went on to say that he was pleased that his professional friends did not lose their jobs, but he was the one who was responsible for his actions and with the I Team disbanded, there really was no place for him. Fran responded that she anticipated his response, and to that end, she offered Tom the position of nightly editorial spokesperson. Without any hesitation, he thanked the General Manager for her support and understood her reasoning, but he had made up his mind to leave early on. Fran had one more issue to deal with, and that was the need to relay the decision-making to the entire staff.

Tom went to his office and thanked his staff for their dedication, and gathered his belongings. The News Department would absorb the I Team staff, and no one would lose their jobs. Tom's future was about to change in ways he had never anticipated. When he returned to Pier 39, Lisa was at school, and he decided to listen to the voice messages. Because his home phones were unlisted, the only callers would be from the station or friends and family. There was, however, one caller who aroused his curiosity. The Democratic National Committee wanted to speak with him and asked when the best time would be to call back. Tom thought, "Could it be that they are calling to see if I have any interest in politics?" There were other saved calls, including a message from the great director Elia Kazan asking for a time they could meet. Tom was flattered, but an acting career was not a consideration; however, the message from the Democratic Party did arouse genuine interest.

Later that evening, he shared his interest in politics with Lisa. She was so proud of her husband that nothing that he would do in life would be a surprise to her. She, too, was curious about the call from the DNC. All of a sudden, a light went on when she remembered a story in the Chronicle. The 11th District, which Barbara Firestone, a Democratic, held, announced she was retiring after thirty years in the House of Representatives. Lisa shared this with Tom, who instantly agreed that it was probably why the Democrats wanted to talk to him. He got up from his chair and began pacing the deck and talking in ways that Lisa had never seen. Tom didn't want to sound overanxious, but truth be told, this possibility was exactly the kind of political engagement that would allow him an opportunity to make a difference. If offered, it was a career change that he found especially appealing. Lisa had something to add. She had also read that a member of the City Planning Commission had already put her hat in the ring. The following day, Tom received a call from David Cullens, the Chairman of the Democratic National Committee, and their guess about what the call would deal with was indeed accurate. After the initial conversation, to test the waters in order to gauge Tom Doyle's interest, they set up a meeting at the Fairmont Hotel on Nob Hill. Tom and Lisa stayed up late that evening and went over and over what they believed would dramatically change their life. Their conversation finally ran its course when they realized that only the next day's meeting would answer.

David Cullens, the DNC Chairman, was younger than anticipated, around 45, with close-cropped hair atop a round, friendly face and a paunch that he should not have at his age. They had taken a suite at the Fairmont, and in addition to the Chair, there were several high-ranking members of the Democratic Party. The suite in one of San Francisco's most elegant hotels and the cadre of party officials gave Tom and Lisa a clear impression that they meant business. After the introductions, Cullen went right to the point. With the retirement of Barbara Firestone, they knew that to keep the seat, they needed to field the best possible candidate. The positive impact of Tom's reply on "Home Sweet Zone" was the final consideration in determining their search to represent San Francisco and the Democratic Party. In essence, he explained that they had been looking at Tom as a possible candidate long before the I Team debacle. His short but honorable career in the military as a member of the Rangers and the recipient of a Silver Star and Purple Heart for heroism, plus the fact that he had a solid reputation as someone who stood up for "the little guy," were all contributing factors in the search to succeed Firestone.

Even though Lisa and Tom were correct in surmising the reason for the meeting, it had a resounding impact when the words were spoken. He was flattered, but at the same time, he had many questions about the office of a United States Representative. How much autonomy would he have, how long Democrats had held the seat, what were the primary issues that they wanted to address and who would be his opponent? They checked everything off until they got to his Republican opponent. David Crump was an ultra-conservative who knew no ethical or moral boundaries. He was a "carpetbagger" who two years ago relocated to the Bay Area. Crump had lived in Nevada most of his life, where he served as a State Representative. The Dems were still looking for a reason why he moved. Tom didn't take long to respond with a commitment to do his very best to serve the people of the 11th District. Now it was time to get down to the basics. To that end, Cullen's assistant, a recent Harvard graduate, asked to meet with Tom the next day. Ned Younger arrived via a cab, which took them to the campaign offices at Third and Market Street in downtown San Francisco. With the election just four months away, activity at the office seemed frenetic to Tom.

In addition to the paid members of the DNC, there were several interns who represented colleges and universities in the Bay Area. Younger introduced Tom to the expanded staff, and many of the young people were aware of Tom Doyle's exploits and showed their appreciation with generous applause. Next, he was shown to his office and introduced to his secretary. Lily Morrison was a recent graduate of Lowell High School in the Richmond district; she had been accepted at Cal Berkeley, where she would attend starting in the Fall of '63. For now, it was her mission to do everything she could to see that a Democrat was elected in the mid-term elections. Lily was just 19 years old and already sported a zeal for anyone who committed to the liberal Democratic platform. She was thrilled to welcome Tom Doyle to the campaign, and her enthusiasm for Tom was a little obsessive, but he wrote it off as just the folly of youth. Lily was a dewy-eyed kid who showed an abundance of adoration for her new boss. She was very pretty in the so-called All-American way, and she did bear watching. The remainder of the staff was mostly women who, at first glance, represented a demographic cross-section of the City. In addition to Lily, his staff of 12 consisted of three patriotic older women, one Asian office and budget manager, two black males, one of whom was paid staff and the local campaign manager, and 6 interns from USF and Stanford.

 After being introduced, Tom went on to say how determined he was to take on his Republican opponent, David Crump, and how pleased he was to see the level of enthusiasm exhibited. Younger was leaving that evening for New York, but before he left, he issued a credit card to Tom, his official Democrat ID, a schedule of planned events and keys to the office. In just two short days, Tom had experienced a whirlwind that he was still trying to absorb. That evening, Tom, Lisa and Andrew Miller, the local campaign manager, spent the night going over his projected schedule and a profile of David Crump. Andrew Miller was a young, dedicated campaign manager who strongly believed in Democracy, even though, as a black man, he had experienced monumental levels of hate and intolerance that tested his allegiance to the American experiment. Andy, as he was called, had a wife and two children and lived in a mostly black area of Oakland. There was an ironic parallel with the subject matter of "Home Sweet Zone." Andrew and his family were living it. Miller had attended Stanford as a Political Science major and graduated Cum Laude in 1958… He was short in stature but obviously kept fit. He was the kind of intense personality who could be intimidating and, at the same time, endearing. Tom had no problem relating to Andy, as his sister-in-law was black. He did not share this with Andrew Miller, anticipating they would have more than enough time together over the next few months, and for now, he risked being perceived as patronizing.

CHAPTER 37

CONGRESS

The campaign to elect Thomas Doyle as the new House Representative for the 11th district, which encompassed the entire Bay Area, was underway. Already with just one day into his campaign, Crump had countered with his knowledge of the new Democratic entry with hateful rhetoric that pointed to Tom's inexperience and to his six months in the Army. Why had he been discharged? That was what a politician would call a "softball," meaning that Tommy could turn that accusation around, smiling the whole time. It was clear from the initial foray that Crump had not done his homework. Andy wanted Tom to stay away from personality rhetoric and concentrate on the issues that included the surging counterculture in North Beach and Haight-Ashbury, Civil Rights, the Black Panther Party and the free speech movement. The City had never seen this level of definitive issues surrounding the impact on Civil Rights. As a home for liberalism, it was no surprise that the voices of angry dissent would begin in San Francisco and move Eastward. As a matter of policy, Tom had a somewhat different position from the Democratic Party. He believed that the young people had the right to lift their voices in dealing with the Country's many inequities. As long as violence was not a cornerstone of their views, he supported their right to free speech.

In developing the Democratic point of view, Tom and Andy had significant departures from policy. In his heart, Miller was sympathetic to the candidate's liberal leanings, but the counterculture was spreading rapidly, and while the Democratic Party stood for freedom, they believed it should be tempered with a left-leaning middle-of-the-road campaign. They believed this would lead them to victory in a volatile environment. As a new politician and an intelligent candidate, Tom toned down his initial views, believing that his handlers knew best… with one caveat. If his opponent moved too far right in his messaging, Tom would have the latitude to move farther left. Andy agreed, and it didn't take long before Crump was leveraging everything from Tom's military service to his stance on Black Power. It was clear that the Republican nominee was going to sharpen his rhetoric with mere innuendo and full-frontal lies.

With the election just two months away, the Doyle campaign was feeling positive about the way the community was responding to his message. His opponent at this stage seemed to be teetering on the edge with his rhetoric. But not enough to modify the direction of his campaign. Tom appreciated his staff, and after two months in the political trenches, he had developed a campaign rhythm that included public appearances that no longer frightened him. The direction of his television, radio and print ads was comfortable, even if it was less hard-hitting than he preferred. The "comfort" wasn't going to last. David Crump had seen the same polls, and the tone of both campaigns was going to change to political hardball. Crump was still smarting from Tom's response to his accusations concerning his military career. The fact that Tom was underage when he volunteered for the Rangers and succeeded in rescuing two U.S. airmen in North Korea was a tough pill for Crump to swallow. The Purple Heart and Silver Star gave him indigestion, along with the fact that he received an honorable medical discharge. He just had not done his homework, and a simple bit of research could have saved him a lot of despair. Crump's next weapon was much more carefully calibrated. He found that Tom had been arrested for drug use in the '50s when he was a freelance musician. Andrew Miller saw his campaign immediately take a turn for the worse. The accusation was true, and anything dealing with marijuana was closely associated with the counterculture. Tom was not dismissive, but he knew that this point of attack by his opponent spelled real trouble. He huddled with his staff, and while Andrew was less than enthusiastic, Tom intended to go on television live and respond to the charge.

The following day, the Democratic National Committee had purchased time adjacent to the six o'clock news on all four TV stations. Tom was resolute and knew exactly what he wanted to say to his constituents. Because he considered this revelation a cheap stunt, he did not lose sight of the fact that it could be injurious to his chances. While his staff was anxious and deeply concerned, Tom was calm and ready to respond. That evening, with a huge Bay Area audience and nothing but a stool and a blue background, he started his comments with the admonition that the charge was hateful and at the same time accurate. He went back to his time as a Ranger and explained that after he was honorably discharged, his wound to his left leg, which he experienced on the rescue raid in North Korea, remained troublesome. As a civilian, he used his skill as a musician to find work. Marijuana was the one thing that he found that could relieve the pain in his leg while he was on the bandstands. He went on to say that the army cleared him of possession of a drug, which the local police agreed to with a commitment that he would desist from further use of marijuana. Tom closed his remarks with an apology and hoped that his explanation was suitable and that he would not be judged harshly by his constituency. Andy smiled as the initial response from the public was overwhelmingly positive. That evening and the following day, the people of San Francisco and the entire Bay

Area registered their approval, and Tom not only dodged a bullet, but by all judgment earned the voters' respect.

Election Day in November 1962 was by all standards a record for voter turnout, and while they would not know the results for several hours, the pundits were enthusiastically predicting that Thomas Doyle would be the 11th District's new Representative in Congress. It was difficult to remain neutral, and while the Doyle campaign was optimistic, they were somewhat reserved about the outcome of the election. Overconfidence was a reality, and they had to wait until the early hours of the morning or the next day. The entire team chose to wait at the DNC office for the results as the votes were released. At 4 o'clock, the initial votes amounting to 10 percent were in, and it was encouraging for the Doyle team. As the evening segued into the morning, there was even more reason to be enthusiastic, with 40 percent of the votes in, Tom was beginning, for the first time, to believe he could be the winner in his race. By 6 am, Tom received a concession call from the Crump headquarters! With 70 percent of the vote in, Tom Doyle had won the seat overwhelmingly and even though his team was exhausted, winning breathed new life into the Doyle for Congress campaign. Out came the champagne, along with the hugs and the warm glow that infects everyone when you are a winner. He knew his priority for now was an acceptance speech, which required a televised live announcement from the DNC headquarters.

Congressmen Doyle sat down and wrote a short acceptance speech and a thank you to everyone who had supported him. After it was televised, Tom couldn't wait to head home and share his good fortune with his wife. Before he left, he hoisted one more glass of champagne to salute his entire staff and to say thank you and the usual "I couldn't have done it without you!" Tom returned home, where Lisa had fixed breakfast, anticipating that he would be hungry and exhausted. She had taken a limited leave of absence from her classes in order to support her husband and to some degree participate in the election process. When Tom stepped onboard the "Mark Two," he embraced Lisa and said, "What do I do now?" He had run an effective campaign, and now he needed to know the next steps. He had just been on board for five minutes when his private line rang. It was Andrew Miller who responded to Tom's questions. He had called a meeting for the following day with the entire staff to outline the process for moving forward.

Tom ate breakfast and literally passed out on their bed. Twelve hours later, he awoke, and the realization of being elected to represent the people of the Bay Area was finally hitting him. He showered and headed for his headquarters to meet with his staff. Everyone had a night's sleep, and they were looking forward to Andy's comments. Tom had no sooner arrived when his phone rang. "This is the office of the President asking for Mr. Thomas Doyle." President Johnson came on the phone and immediately congratulated Tom and told him how important the 11th District was to the Democrat Party and how proud he was to see a wounded veteran achieve Congressional success. Tom responded by saying he would do his best to represent the people in his district. With that, President Johnson stated, "I know you will make our country proud," and a goodbye… at least he could say he heard from the President.

When the phone rang again, the conversation was substantially more important. It was the speaker of the House, John McCormick. His comments were congratulatory and welcoming, but that wasn't the reason for the call. On Thursday, October 6, 1963, the Speaker was inviting Tom to attend the new member orientation in Washington. Tom shared the substance of the two calls and went on to say the meetings in DC were, in his mind, ceremonial. Andy shook his head and said they were much more. In fact, the Speaker would use this opportunity to assign the new members to Committees. The more prepared Tom was, the better. Certain Committees were highly coveted and meaningful. Andy suggested the powerful Ways and Means Committee and the Rules Committee. At this point, Andrew Miller was worth his weight. Tom was due at the Capitol in just two days, and Andy was right, it could be consequential. That evening, Tommy shared the day's meaningful events. If he was going to Washington, why not take Lisa? It would not be a second Honeymoon, but it was an opportunity to do some serious sightseeing in our Capitol. Lisa, unfortunately, had taken too much time away from Berkeley, and adding to it would have a negative impact on completing her course.

Tom was starting to understand the complexities of being a member of the House of Representatives. The first thing he needed to do was hire a Chief of Staff and a Press Secretary. He would need a staff of five people and house them in the Blair Office Building adjacent to the Capitol. He had a lengthy conversation with Andy Miller, whom he asked to be his Chief of Staff. They agreed that he and the additional four staff members would be housed in Washington at the space in the Blair building. The office and how it would be organized, he would leave solely to Miller. Tom decided, unlike most House members, that he would maintain an office in San Francisco, where many of his constituents were. He determined that one of his five staffers would maintain this small office on Geary Street in the heart of San Francisco. He was also given a single-room office in the Capitol Building, where another one of the five staffers would reside.

Andy decided to hire Lily Morrison to take the post in San Francisco, and he also named Cynthia Fenneman as Press Secretary. She was a 35-year-old professional from San Jose and highly skilled in dealing with the Press. Tom knew that Andy was mounting a very thin staff, but he made up for it by hiring top-notch personnel. By early January of 1963, the space and organization under Andy Miller's leadership were completed, and the priorities of Committee assignments were next, and as stated, were significantly important. Still on the to-do list was to eventually find an apartment in the Bay Area, but for now, Jim Walsh encouraged the Doyles to continue to make their home on board the 'Mark Two.' Jimmie and Tom had gone out on the boat a few times on fishing excursions, but today that would not work for Tom and Lisa.

Regarding Lisa, she had just completed her graduate studies and her master's degree with honors. With her degree in Hotel Management, she sent resumes to all of the potential high-end hotels in the Bay Area. Lisa received four positive responses and had set up interviews. Initially, she thought the Palace Hotel would be her choice, but then she received a strong show of interest from the Mark Hopkins Hotel on top of Nob Hill. It had class and was a central location, allowing access to all the City had to offer, from Union Square to fitness centers. Ultimately, she found herself in an embarrassment of wealth. All of her interviews had gone well, including the Fairmont, which was across the street from the Mark on Nob Hill. The Mark Hopkins Hotel eventually made the "offer she couldn't refuse." She was hired as Assistant Manager and would be joining the Mark in two weeks, allowing her to clean up any loose ends in her life.

CHAPTER 38

CHIEF JUSTICE

Lisa and Tom, in a relatively short period of time, had totally turned their lives around. They were able to achieve their goals as a Manager and a Congressman! Once Lisa was settled in her new position, like Tom, she knew that their unique residence on Pier 39 would have to change. To that end, Lisa had hired a realtor to begin the search for what would be their permanent address in San Francisco. For now, it was time to celebrate Lisa's appointment with an expensive night out. Tom's trip to Washington, DC, was everything he hoped for. The city itself was a showcase of city planning, starting with the severe restrictions on building heights. There was so much to see, he did not know where to start. The buildings were inspiring, giving you a sense of power, strength and the grandeur of the U.S. government. The museums, government buildings, and monuments gave Tom a feeling of pride that made him grateful for being an American.

His office space in the Blair Building was small but adequate. Andy had preceded Tom to DC and had organized the space with recognizable trademark efficiency. He was introduced to the two remaining staff members, and it was clear that Andy favored women. To that end, he had hired two Georgetown graduates who were very young, enthusiastic, ambitious and more than anything, dedicated to serving the U.S. government and the decision makers who made it all happen. Susan Geller was a Nashville native who graduated cum laude and gave the clear impression that she was going to make a mark for herself in the world of politics. Diane Roberts, on the other hand, was for one thing very pretty and very organized, which is precisely why Andy put her in charge of the office. Tom could not have been more pleased with the work that Andy Miller had accomplished. He guided Tom to the Capitol, and the kid from San Francisco stood in the Rotunda and took an awe-inspired deep breath. He felt he had to pinch himself… it was that incredibly inspiring. The single-room office in the building was typical for a member of the House. Lily Morrison also had flown out with Andy, and again, even this space had been optimized. Lily had that sense of adoration that Tom chose to ignore because it was rivalled with intelligence and enthusiasm. Lily was being Lily… The same very young lady who was totally committed to Tom's election success in California. That evening, before he caught a red-eye back to San Francisco, he and Andy went to dinner to plot their strategy for committee assignments. Tom, for the first time, allowed his lieutenant to use his heroic deeds in the military, including the Silver Star, to grease the way for the right committees. Everyone loves a hero, and Tom must have wanted to be assigned the Ways and Means committee enough to sacrifice the privacy he held dear.

Of all the issues that needed attention in the early sixties, Civil Rights, the Black Panthers, and Freedom of Speech were the priorities. Two of the most prominent leaders of the Black Panther Party were Huey Newton and Bobby Seale. Both emphasized Black Nationalism, Socialism and the use of weapons to defend themselves in the face of police brutality. They were both influential and powerful speakers. Working in parallel with the Black Panthers were leaders who took a less aggressive stance on Black history. Martin L. King and Malcolm X were the most prominent. For his initial foray as an active

Representative, Tom recognized that San Francisco was front and center on the Bay Area emphasis on counterculture and specifically the Hippie Movement and the emerging "generation gap." With so many issues that needed to be addressed, Tom was pleased with his decision to open an office in the City. Lily Morrison had already researched the leaders of the free speech movements and recommended that he meet with Martin Luther King Jr., whom she considered the most conservative of the various counterculture movements. King was in the process of working with the NAACP and other Civil Rights groups to organize the March on Washington for jobs and freedom. Ultimately, in 1963, he attracted 250,000 on the March and delivered a historic, majestic address that stirred the imagination of Black Americans. Martin was also the driving force behind the Montgomery Bus Boycott. While Lily was providing the much-needed research, she also set up a meeting with King in San Francisco to ascertain how Tom could initially address the explosive Civil Rights movement. The two leaders met at the headquarters of the NAACP in the Mission District. Tom purposely asked to meet at the Movement headquarters in the City as opposed to the government office.

Martin Luther King Jr. was impressive to say the least, and Tom had the feeling that, as the meeting went on that he was in the presence of a genuine leader of men (and women!). King went on to say that his goal was to influence the signing of an all-encompassing Civil Rights Act, which would appreciably move the goal posts. The conversation opened up many avenues that Tom could address in his efforts to make a mark on providing a positive influence on Civil Rights in the Bay Area. They talked for several hours with Tom, primarily listening and literally being inspired by the most prominent leader in black nationalism. In the following weeks, Tom set meetings with black leadership that included Malcolm X and Huey Newton. While the Black Panthers took a more aggressive view on social justice, Tom again found that he could be an effective congressman if he spent his time listening. While he leaned toward the less aggressive views of Martin Luther King Jr., it was imperative that he found some ways to serve as a link between the white community and the Black Power movement. After his concerted initial efforts to provide this link, he found that he was included in some of the conversations that verged on a growing sense of trust.

Admittedly, it was difficult to make any real progress in communicating when the police were still relying on brutality and closing their minds to peaceful solutions. The March on Washington had been so successful that minds began to change, and this paved the way for Congress to finally pass legislation that was responsive and meaningful. In early 1964, Tom returned to Washington, and while he did not achieve all that he set out to do, the leadership of the Democratic Party was impressed with his progressive engagement. With this positive recognition, he was rewarded with a chair on the Ways and Means Committee and the Judicial Committee. Andy Miller was proud of his new boss and especially pleased that John McCormack, the Speaker of the House, had sought Tom out to get a feel for the activity of the Civil Rights movement on the West Coast.

As engaged as they were in demanding careers, Lisa and Tom were well aware of the fact that living on an expensive, luxury yacht on Pier 39 was not an address that would be appropriate for a member of the House of Representatives. They hired a realtor, Lynn Wahlberg, and gave her marching orders in terms of the kind of home they would envision. With the two incomes, they could afford a high-toned address, but neither of them wanted anything but a home that middle

America could relate to. To that end, Lynn placed the emphasis on the Marina district. There was a variety of options that spanned relatively small single couple efficiency homes to large quality four-bedroom addresses that could offer a home office. It was the latter that rang a bell with both Tom and Lisa. They also considered the fact that in the not-too-distant future, they would like to start a family. The home that truly responded to all the couple's requirements was a Spanish stucco, three-bedroom on Divisadero Street. This beautifully cared-for home offered exquisite scenery and an absolutely perfect location between the Bay and Fort Mason in the Presidio. It was a sufficient reason to sacrifice one bedroom. Lynn made a legitimate offer to the current owners, and they accepted! The home was within walking distance of Fisherman's Wharf.

Tom and Lisa were jubilant, and while they loved living on the Walsh's luxury yacht, it was time for the young Doyles to invest in a home of their own… and what a home. While the property did not scream expensive, it did have incredible features, including a flagstone patio in the front, beamed ceilings, two modern bathrooms and a kitchen that had been completely remodeled. There was even a separate garage for Tom's T-Bird. They could clearly envision it as a home that would be perfect to raise a family. Escrow closed in just two weeks, and on the third week, the Doyles moved into their new home. Tom made sure that Jim Walsh and their parents were alerted based on how quickly they could move to their new address in the Marina. Tom spoke at length with Jimmie Walsh, who was his dad's best friend, and shared the fact that the couple truly were appreciative of the Walsh's largess in allowing them to use the "Mark Two" as their luxury first address. Jim, in his inimitable way, told Tom not to say goodbye to the yacht so quickly: "There would be many fishing trips and weekend parties, so don't say a premature goodbye!"

On moving day, there really was not much to move beyond some kitchenware and personal belongings. In the next week or so, Jimmie and Walter Walsh made sure that the Doyles didn't even think about furniture. Lisa could come to their warehouse in Long Beach and select from their vast furniture inventory that could be delivered to the Northern California address in less than a week. This was a perfect opportunity to catch up with Anna Alvarez, Lisa's mom and Tom's parents in Laguna Beach. The road trip to Southern California provided Lisa and Tom an opportunity to reawaken their relationship and spend a few days in Carmel and Monterey as they wound their way South. They stopped at their favorite Highlands Inn, where they rented a superb cabin with a huge down-covered bed and a fireplace. They reveled in long walks on the beach, great bottles of wine, some spectacular meals served in their cabin, and the kind of lovemaking that was somewhat sacrificed in their high-octane two years together. It was intense, memorable sex that was exactly the kind of romance that reinforced the love that they had for each other.

After a week, they both got a break they deserved, which was unfortunately long overdue. They headed for Long Beach to select furniture and ultimately to Laguna to spend some time with loved ones. William and Rita looked like the picture of Southern California living. They may have gotten older, but overlooking a paunch that William had developed, they were still a handsome couple that could grace the front page of any retirement magazine. William was still going to the Long Beach office at least three days a week. Walsh Inc. continued to be a thriving business with some new, young and educated management blood that ensured the future of the company. Rita had established herself as one of the premier artists who made Laguna Beach one of the art world's destinations in California. Her refined multimedia style continued to be so well-received that she had recently opened her own showroom on Forest Street, the main avenue in Laguna. Manuel Gomez, Lisa's uncle, was what could only be referred to as a fixture at Walsh Inc. He was still Director of Quality Control, and in spite of some new, younger management, he held his own and continued to reside at his Long Beach office five days a week. Lisa's mother, Anna, had bought a small house in Seal Beach just up the road from Laguna, and after 30 years with the Walshes, she put her highly skilled food cuisine to good use and, the previous year, opened a small beachfront seafood restaurant. "Lisa's Place," in a few short months, was thriving. Anna's old friend and manager was Soledad Aguilar. Jose also continued at Walsh Inc., and their two children were attending San Jose State. Thomas Aguilar was two years ahead of his brother Arthur and was majoring in Mechanical Engineering. The younger brother, Arthur, was looking for a degree in Journalism.

The excursion to Southern California and time spent with Lisa's and Tom's families proved to be totally satisfying. They both had been on such a fast track that even close family relations suffered and ended up on the back burner. The furniture selection, which was the primary reason for the trip, proved secondary, but they did spend time selecting furnishings for every room. They could not wait to see it all put together at their new home in the Marina.

Another relationship that they had neglected was Sara and the twins. In 1964, Olivia and Mark Doyle would graduate from San Mateo High School, where they both, to no one's surprise, made their mark. Olivia was captain of the debate team, and Mark had excelled as an All-Peninsula League fullback, which earned him a scholarship at Stanford. No two siblings who were twins could be more uniquely different in almost every way, and yet they maintained the kind of close loyalty and affection that is, in most cases, consistent with twins. Olivia was deeply concerned and sensitive about the shortcomings of government and the rapid changes that were the hallmark of the social explosion in the country, led by the counterculture movement in San Francisco, and, for that matter, the Bay Area. Her Uncle Tommy, now a member of the House of Representatives, was engaged in trying to help guide the government in their attempt to negotiate a splintered modern society. Olivia had a limitless social conscience, and while the landmark Civil Rights Bill had been passed, the increasing involvement in the Vietnam War was a reason for concern and activism. While Mark was attending class at the relatively conservative Stanford University, Olivia, who could qualify for almost any school, chose the University of California in Berkeley, where she would major in Political Science.

In 1964, Cal Berkeley was turning into a hotbed of social activism and Olivia Doyle was totally engaged. In Vietnam, the incident at the Bay of Tonkin, in which supposedly North Korean boats attacked the U.S. Destroyer, Maddox, with torpedoes and machine guns, served to accelerate the U.S. involvement in Vietnam while opposition to the War mounted. Campuses across the country began to rapidly expand demonstrations against the War in Southeast Asia, and the loudest voice was coming from UC Berkeley. Mario Savio, a student leader, organized a march on the administration buildings to protest the recent University restrictions on Free Speech and over 500 students participated. Olivia joined the movement and was perceived as one of the leading student protesters. The Free Speech Movement had national implications, which constituted the true onset of the Counterculture. Olivia, as a recognized leader, traveled with a nucleus of high-profile protesters to various campuses on the West Coast to share their methods and organizing techniques with their campus counterparts at Oregon and Washington Universities. During one anti-war demonstration on the Berkeley campus, Olivia was arrested for spitting in the face of a campus policeman. While the charge was ridiculous, it did serve to not only put in jeopardy her attendance at Cal, but also caused red lights to begin blinking for Sara and genuine embarrassment for her grandfather, James Shelton, the Chief Justice of the State Supreme Court in Sacramento. Judge Shelton was sympathetic to the national campus demonstrations against the War, but his personal feelings had nothing to do with his primary responsibility of supporting the rule of law. The Judge had not seen the twins since they enrolled at Cal and Stanford. He admired and had limitless affection for them, but he felt their education should be their priority and anything that would jeopardize their future needed to be immediately addressed.

With the Holidays approaching, the Sheltons decided to ask Sara and her twins to join them for Thanksgiving. When Sara broached the subject with Mark, he instantly accepted an opportunity to visit his beloved grandparents. Olivia, on the other hand, was hesitant, surmising that Judge had an ulterior motive for the invite. Even if she was right, she decided to accept the invitation because her love for her grandparents superseded anything that might affect their relationship. Thanksgiving 1964 turned out to be close to a family reunion hosted by James and Coralyn Shelton. The Sheltons believed that Thanksgiving was the perfect holiday to bring a family together, especially during such days of social unrest and upheaval. The acceptance from the San Mateo Doyles served to make the holiday a true family get-together when Tom and Lisa enthusiastically accepted the Sheltons' invitation. But Judge Shelton had one more surprise. Without telling anyone, he was in contact with William and Rita and had told them what had transpired in planning a family Thanksgiving.

The senior Doyles had other commitments; however, nothing could compete with the get-together in Sacramento. James had received a go-ahead. Rita and William would fly in from the Los Angeles airport to Sacramento and arrive on Thursday morning. That was cutting it close, but they knew that they were the last cog in planning a true family Thanksgiving.

The Judge was like a little kid trying to hold back a surprise. For him, seeing the senior Doyles would be long overdue. When they moved to Sacramento, they sacrificed much of what was important to them, especially in terms of saying goodbye to friends. Sacramento was only 100 miles from San Francisco, but you might as well be halfway across the country. For James, the Tuesday morning breakfasts with William were dearly missed. To this day, he had not been as stimulated by meaningful and timely conversation since they had to give up the Tuesday morning breakfasts. It would be wonderful to see William and Rita. Lisa and Tom had just seen the Southern California Doyles, but to everyone else at the memorable Thanksgiving, it was a joyous reunion.

After the toast and the turkey, William and the Judge determined that the holiday was long overdue, but underneath was the concern about Olivia and her growing participation in the anti-war demonstrations. The strategy to address their concern about Olivia was orchestrated with the help of Rita, who used her art as a method to deliver Olivia to the den where William and James were having a brandy. She smelled a setup but chose to join her grandfathers, both of whom she held in great esteem. After the requisite "how are your grades and are you seeing anyone," to no one's surprise, Judge very directly stated that this triad was planned. Olivia was not a reactionary and chose to listen to what she knew would be well-meaning advice… but that is not what evolved. William drew a parallel with the ham-handed way he dealt with Herman Geller. Both men, held in high regard by Olivia, shared their experiences in confronting conflicts in their early years. Judge Shelton to this day related how he wished he had better handled the first time he was called an "uppity nigger." He used his fists and not an intellectual reaction, which would have been far more effective. William added that he admired and understood her social consciousness, and it was important to make your voice count, but it always comes down to not what you say but how you do it. Both men had one motivation, and that was to legitimately express ways to participate without putting her future in jeopardy. Olivia had a brilliant mind, and the Judge was proud of his granddaughter's choice to make the rule of law her priority, but the Judge went on to say that her voice could be heard in many ways, and it always should be compatible with her goals in life. William and James knew that Olivia had listened, and now it was up to her to think about modifying her activism… if they had accomplished that, the time was not misspent. Only time would tell. Perhaps they had placed their concerned emphasis on Olivia without seeing the signs of alarm that had nothing to do with her, but should have been a wake-up call that they didn't see coming.

CHAPTER 39

THE MARINE CORPS

- **The Gulf of Tonkin incident brings the U.S. into the Vietnam War.**
- **Anti-war demonstrations explode on college campuses.**
- **President Johnson chooses not to run for reelection.**
- **Vietnam launches the Tet Offensive.**
- **U.S. troops are bloodied in "the Battle of Hamburger Hill."**
- **The shameful My Lai Massacre**
- **The Pentagon Papers emerge as top-secret files.**
- **On April 29, 1975, South Vietnam surrenders.**

Mark Doyle, like his sister, had his personal mission, and for him it was the converse of Olivia's goals. He felt strongly that the war in Vietnam was essential as a barrier to stopping the spread of Communism. Mark's approach to dealing with those things in life that were important to him was internal. He was the silent type, but with an intellect that was screaming, "I need to be a part of America's goal of preempting Communism in Southeast Asia…" Mark Doyle enlisted in the U.S. Marine Corps, and he told no one of his actions, knowing that his family would be highly negative toward and displeased with his choice. When Mark finally shared his decision to join the military, it was a shock that spread alarm through the entire Doyle and Shelton families. No one could have predicted his strong feeling about the Nation's position in the world, let alone wartime policies in Vietnam. He knew that his mother would have done everything in her power to convince him, but he had made up his mind, and attempts to change his actions were senseless. The entire family was caught off guard with a genuine sense of helplessness. Mark had completed his sophomore year at Stanford and was heading to the Recruit Depot in San Diego for boot training and Officer Candidate School.

When Mark arrived for boot camp, he was fully aware of the fact that he did not qualify for Officer Training. He would require a four-year degree or be nominated by a superior officer. Admittedly, boot camp was far more demanding than he had anticipated. It was, to say the least, a formidable 13-week program that tested his strength, endurance and intellect. Mark graduated at the top of his class, and the commanding officer of the base was curious about why he did not apply for officers' training. Without hesitation, he replied that he was not interested in being an officer. After Mark completed the basic training program, he was given two weeks' leave before he would receive his assignment, which in most cases meant Vietnam. The training program had honed Mark's already muscular build, and his family saw a trained Marine who was proud of enlisting and serving his country. He never considered being drafted, and he knew that he could have qualified for a deferment if he had stayed in school. Sara had reconciled that Mark had made a conscious decision to join the Marine Corps, but she was having a difficult time understanding why the United States was getting so deeply involved in Vietnam. The French had lost Northern Vietnam, and now it had become a north/south Civil War. Olivia, on the other hand, was angry at her twin brother, believing that the war in Southeast Asia was unwarranted and, like so many of her schoolmates, was demonstrating to end the

War. For the first time in their lives, they were dealing with an issue that had no resolution to the impasse. Olivia broke down in tears when she saw her beloved brother in a United States Marine Corps uniform. They would never see eye to eye on why the U.S. was there. It was painful for all to see her identical twin in such a state of sorrow. There was nothing Mark could say or do to alleviate her pain and misgivings. Mark did have time to visit Tommy and Lisa in their new home in San Francisco, and while his aunt and uncle were supportive about his decision, the truth is they were just as opposed to the War as the rest of the family.

In 1966, the War in Vietnam had escalated rapidly after the Bay of Tonkin incident. By the end of the year, the United States forces numbered 385,000 men and another 60,000 sailors offshore. Approximately 6,000 soldiers had been killed, and 30,000 were wounded, and Private Mark Doyle was assigned to the First Marine Division already in the country. The South Vietnamese Army numbered 730,000. It wasn't long before Mark and his platoon faced a series of firefights with the Viet Cong, who infiltrated their soldiers from the North and were attacking Marine bases in the South. The constant U.S. air attacks on Hanoi did nothing to stop the Viet Cong advances.

Mark and his platoon had been assigned a forward position close to the North Vietnam border, and after a series of barrages from Viet Cong guerrillas, the platoon found themselves surrounded and asking for air support and reinforcements. Additional troops were on their way, but found stiff resistance, which seriously slowed their rescue progress north. Aid from the air was impossible due to the close quarters of the combat. Mark was wounded by a piece of shrapnel in his leg, but along with his comrades, they had temporarily held the enemy at bay. The intensity of the battle seemed to stiffen as it entered its second day, and the Marine rescue mission was not making the necessary progress to provide relief. The unit's commanding officer, Lieutenant Howard Gross of Pawtucket, RI, had been killed, and Mark found himself in a position of leadership as the two sergeants were badly wounded and were unable to take command. Mark attempted to rally the remaining Marines by digging trenches and preserving ammunition that was getting seriously low. Of the 43 men in the platoon, only 20 were alive, with some wounded. Finally, after three days, the reinforcement arrived, and Mark and the few remaining members of the platoon were relieved. During the battle, Mark had suffered another wound to his left shoulder as he and his comrades were evacuated by helicopter to Saigon's base hospital. The damage to his shoulder seemed relatively safe to treat until the surgeon found that it had developed into a serious condition that affected his heart. Mark would never get up from the operating table, and two hours after he arrived at the hospital, he was pronounced dead.

That moment in Berkeley, Olivia Doyle experienced a feeling that was indescribable. She sensed that her twin was in significant danger, and at the same time, she felt a deep foreboding. The Marine Corps, like other services, had a protocol for notifying the families of Marines who died in combat. Two Marines, one an officer, would be charged with delivering the painful news. On a rainy day in early December 1966, two soldiers knocked on Sara's front door and broke the news that no mother would ever want to hear. Mark had died heroically in service to his nation. Sara and Olivia were home, and the crushing news was almost more than they could absorb. Sara felt faint before the tears erupted. The Marine Corps officer presented Olivia with Mark's personal belongings and the American flag that Mark defended. Like his father, he had been awarded a Silver Star for his instinctual leadership when the platoon lost their lieutenant and two sergeants. Olivia knew that something very dark had happened before the Marines broke the news of Mark's passing. When she had regained some composure, mother and daughter supported each other as the truth of what had just transpired ultimately sank in.

As Christmas came and went, the two women knew they had to sorrowfully notify the rest of the Doyle family. The irony that almost all of the immediate family members had just spent Thanksgiving together was not lost on them. Sara was still so distraught that the idea of calling family with such devastating news was more than she could deal with. Olivia, still in shock, took on the role of notification. The phone call to Rita and William was terribly difficult, especially after they had dealt with the death of their son Mark. Disbelief, shock, and agony were the best ways to describe the response from Tommy and Lisa. Each phone call hammered home the morose feeling that her twin brother had died. Olivia also found herself in the position of having to navigate all the funeral arrangements. What kind of memorial would family members agree to, and where should Mark be set to rest? She shouldn't be asked to be the only one who would take on this agonizing responsibility. Who could be tagged to provide support to Olivia? The only person outside the Doyles was Lauralie Walsh. She was a favorite of every family member, and she was conveniently nearby in Sausalito. This involved still one more phone call, but at least Olivia knew she could rely on Lauralie Walsh. Predictably, she agreed to do anything that was requested of her. One thing that was clear and that is the fact that Mark had a very negative view of traditional religion, which was consistent with almost every family member, with the exception of Lisa Doyle.

Lauralie recalled the memorial for the senior Mark. It had no religious ceremony but rather an invite to all friends who were encouraged to recount their positive stories about Mark and how he had an impact on their lives. This was all Olivia needed to feel that the process was underway. Lauralie agreed to research Mark's friends and find an appropriate venue for the memorial. Olivia was pleased to find that San Francisco had a serene military burial site high up in the hills of Skyline Boulevard. It overlooked the entire Bay Area. The family started to arrive a few days before the funeral, which would be held at the Legion of Honor Museum in Golden Gate Park. Tommy and Lisa invited the immediate family members (and the Walshs) to their new home in the Marina prior to the memorial, which was relatively close to the Park. In the meantime, Lauralie had invited a constituency of friends from high school and college, as well as Marines that he served with in Vietnam.

On the second Saturday in February, a crowd of mourners arrived at the Museum. The decision was made to hold the memorial outside, and if the weather didn't cooperate, they would merely move indoors. As the day broke in San Francisco, the sun was shining as it does regularly in this City known for fog. Judge Shelton agreed to serve as the master of ceremonies for the day and called on the sequence of friends and family to share their moments with Mark. One by one, they spoke, and the whole day was unerringly similar to the ceremony for Mark the Second at Sigmund Stern Grove years earlier. Allen Sims, who was Mark's roommate at Berkeley for the two years he spent at Cal, relayed how, despite the cultural upheaval at the University, Mark was his own man, and in the face of ridicule, he was emphatic about being an American. He was genuinely patriotic and felt that the demonstrations on campus went too far. This is why he joined the Marine Corps and was willing, in the face of disparaging antagonism, to fight for what he believed was right. Sergeant Lawrence, one of the two wounded noncoms in the combat, spoke of how unassuming Mark was and how everyone in the platoon respected him, and that is why when the leaders were killed or wounded, they responded to Mark's orders even after he had been wounded. There was a vacuum, and Private Doyle filled it and, in so doing, saved a lot of Marine lives. Barbara Lutton was a roommate of a girl named Geraldine (Jerry) Fay, who was dating Mark. She shared that he was so different from the typical campus males. Jerry couldn't help but be impressed with a young man who actually treated a woman with respect. Barbara said that she was jealous of Jerry because boys like Mark were few and far between. She had the impression that he had a sound upbringing where people were respectful of other people's opinions, and he did not try to force his beliefs on others. Tom Doyle shared the fact that the friends they had heard from were accurately describing the Mark that he knew as his uncle. He didn't have a phony bone in his body, and while you may fervently disagree with Mark, he accepted your point of view. True, he smoked and probably drank a little too much, but in the grand scheme of things, they were minor vices.

As the memorial proceeded to relive so many memorable moments of true endearment for Mark Doyle, many of the attendees found it difficult to hold back the tears. The burial site at the San Francisco National Cemetery was highly emotional for the invited family and close friends, and as they adjourned to Lisa's and Tom's home, there was a feeling that what they had witnessed from early in the day through the burial was a fitting memorial. This was the first time since they moved in that Lisa and Tom had company in their newly decorated home. The moment was not passed over, and the family agreed that if anything, Mark's passing brought splintered relationships together. Olivia was especially curious about Barbara Lutton's comments about Geraldine Fay. Olivia knew of Jerry, who was also a Political Science major at Cal. Their mutual awareness was because Mark had been dating Jerry, and she wondered how much that relationship had to do with the fact that Fay was African American. Was there a perceived connection because of the common gene? Olivia believed that Jerry had a chip on her shoulder. Despite the passage of the Civil Rights Act and Voting Rights Act the following year, the Montgomery, Alabama, marches, and the brutal police response were enough to make anyone angry with a sense of hopelessness. Jerry was not a part of the campus demonstrations and surprised many of her friends when she did not return to Berkeley after leaving in the middle of her sophomore year.

Olivia's sources provided her with Fay's phone number in Oakland. When they talked, Jerry seemed distant and tentative throughout the short conversation, and even more surprised when Olivia suggested that they have dinner together to share her memories of her brother. Geraldine Fay was more than a little curious about what Olivia's ulterior motives might be. In truth, she did think it was past time that she made some contact with Mark's family. The two women met at the Fog City Cafe, a casual favorite of Olivia's. They greeted each other with some hesitation, probably due to the fact that they had hardly spoken in school. The discomfort was real as Olivia waited for Jerry Fay to talk. When she finally opened the conversation, it was direct, painful and wrenching. In tears, she shared that she had a relationship with Mark through much of their sophomore year and had begged him not to enlist. She confessed that she loved Mark and admittedly was heartbroken and only had one reason to live… she was carrying Mark's child. Olivia was shaken to the core, and after what seemed to be an interminable pause, she asked what had happened to the pregnancy and did Mark know that she was having his child? Again, in tears, Jerry answered that she didn't know she was pregnant until Mark had completed basic training and was on his way to Vietnam.

She had a healthy boy whom she named Mark, and as the conversation continued, Olivia suggested that Fay should have second thoughts about the name. Olivia shared the history in her family of men named "Mark." The Doyles lost the first Mark during the First World War when he was taken in the 1918 Spanish Flu epidemic. Mark number two died facing a gunman in a robbery attempt, and now she had lost her brother, who was also named Mark. Olivia did not doubt Jerry Fay's story and tried to comfort her highly emotional account of what had transpired over the past year. The two young women were beginning to have an emotional understanding, and after a meal that went untouched, they agreed that Jerry and her son needed to come out from under the cloud and be introduced to the Doyles. Jerry's family was aware of the child and insisted that she contact Mark's family, saying it would be a tragedy if they kept the news to themselves. Most of her family lived in Mobile, Alabama, but her mother was in San Francisco working as a housekeeper for a family in the Pacific Heights neighborhood. Her father had died in Okinawa toward the end of the War. Jerry had received a generous scholarship from the University and was now living with her mother in the Fillmore. The Doyles had been awarded a $100,000 death benefit from the Marine Corps, and Olivia knew that if the rest of her family was convinced the child was indeed Mark's, the money would rightfully revert to Jerry.

The two women agreed that Olivia would break the news to the family and determine a time when the newest 'Mark' could be introduced.

On her way back to Burlingame, Olivia had a chance to regain a semblance of composure after the momentous news she carried. Breaking what had just transpired to her mom would be one of those "you need to sit down" conversations. That evening, without mincing words, Olivia told Sara that Mark had fathered a child, she had met with the baby's mother, and she had no reason to doubt Jerry's story, which was consistent with everything she knew. Doctor Doyle did indeed need to sit. After the initial high intensity shock, she shook her head to make sure this was not a dream, and did something that was for her uncommon, mother and daughter shared a shot of whiskey. Their conversation went on for hours. As the sun was coming up, they needed to sort out how Jerry and Mark would be introduced to the Doyle Family. Olivia added that Jerry's mother, Clair, should be included and ultimately their extended family in Alabama. Olivia had never seen her mother this shaken, and late in the conversation, she concluded that she was a grandmother at 41 and waited until the conversation with Rita and William and the Sheltons, when they found that they were great grandparents!

In the moments and days that followed, the excitement was palpable. The day to meet was set for a weekend in March 1967, and all involved would convene at Doctor Shelton's home in Burlingame. The senior Doyles arrived in the middle of the week and checked in at the Benjamin Franklin Hotel in San Mateo. They needed to spend alone time with Sara and Olivia, and more than anything, ask Olivia if she was sure that the boy was Mark's. They, too, were concerned about what may seem ridiculous to some, the grim fates of three generations of boys named 'Mark'. William and Rita were the first to arrive for their conversation on the authenticity of the child and how they would address the name. Tom and Lisa followed, and soon after

Judge Shelton and Coralyn. Geraldine and her mother with baby Mark were scheduled to arrive at 1 pm.

As the hour approached, the relatives in the room were surprisingly quiet and pensive. When Jerry and her mother, Clair Fay, arrived with baby Mark, the room erupted. It wasn't just seeing a six-month-old baby, but it also cleared up any concern about whether Mark was indeed the father. The baby was a ringer for his father. There was no confusion when a child so closely resembled his paternal parent. Rita even brought a picture of Mark at six months, offering further truth, which really was not needed. Baby Mark reminded everyone of Olivia's coloring, although he was darker in skin tone, but there were the blue eyes and the anticipation of straight brown hair. The boy had absolutely taken on the best features of both of his parents, and he was a big 6-month-old. Turning to Jerry and her mother, there was a lot to digest, starting with the fact that they both were surprisingly tall. Geraldine was a little over six feet, and her mother, Clair Fay, was at least the same height. If you knew anything about the Watusi tribe in Africa, individuals could reach more than seven feet tall! In addition to their height, the two women were incredibly attractive. Jerry and her mother were medium brown with dark, wavy hair and features that were as European as they were African. They were a stunning pair!

As the afternoon proceeded into the evening, the Doyle family and the Fays were bonding, and little Mark was at the center of it all. The conversation finally came around to the concern over the name. No one was really superstitious, but they still wrestled with the irony. The Judge suggested that the Mark handle be moved as a middle name, and what was the middle name? It was 'James.' Could James Mark Doyle work? The Fays were hesitant, but the shared knowledge of what the name Mark had meant in the dark history of three generations was reason to consider. Rita finally said that they were twisting in knots, and it would make more sense to put the name conversation on a back burner. The important thing was that Mark Fay or Doyle, or whatever his name turned out to be, the child was responsible for bringing much joy to both families, and had brought them together to share in the wonder of it all.

Mark was loved and, after that day, cherished and adored by two families. The day could have been disastrous if, for example, custody was an issue, but clearly the Fays were doing a wonderful job in raising Mark, who seemed to be emotionally well-adjusted and cared for. Admittedly, when it was time for the two women to return to the City, there was a sense all around of not wanting to separate from the mutually loved child. During the latter part of the evening, Jerry had put Mark down in the front bedroom, and just seeing him engaged in sleep brought on 'ooohs' and 'ahhhs' from the Doyles. It was terribly painful to bid goodnight with the realization that the little boy would be going 'home.'

All in all, the reunion had gone well and served as an opportunity to reinstate and expand their union and togetherness. For Olivia, the introduction of baby Mark seemed to change and modify her feelings about her participation in the counterculture demonstrations that were swirling all around the Berkeley campus. With the war in Vietnam expanding and the attendant casualties rising, a sense of hopelessness permeated all sectors of the University. Olivia did continue to demonstrate and let her voice be heard, but without the fervor and intensity of the early days of awakening. Also, she admitted that the passing of her brother and the conversations she had with her grandfathers did begin to reshape her attitude toward her future. She knew that a career in law was without question her goal, and now, as she was entering her junior year, the prospect of applying for Law School became high on the priority ladder. Her first two years at Cal were not even close to recognizing her potential, and certainly did not help her once she began applying to the upper-tier Law Schools. Her Uncle Tom, more than anyone, was a good sounding board. Without his degree, he felt that it would be questionable whether he could succeed in the brutal give and take of politics.

CHAPTER 40

SEPARATION

Tom was proving to be a standout representing the Bay Area as a member of Congress. Whether it was legislation that helped lower property taxes or fighting for benefits for the elderly, he was highly visible and considered a young man to watch by members of the Senate. Tom was the kind of Representative who relished the give and take of being a member of Congress, unlike so many of his compatriots who were merely treading water and picking up their paychecks. Seeing the results of your efforts and meeting the constituents who benefited were what Thomas Doyle lived for. He was devoting so much time to his responsibilities that it was beginning to have a negative impact on his marriage. Lisa was beginning to spend more and more time at the Mark Hopkins, and like Tom, her job as assistant manager of the hotel could be time-consuming, but the truth is, both Lisa and Tom were drifting away from their marriage.

There was a temporary coming together when they moved into their new home, and they both took pleasure in selecting furniture and enjoying all aspects of interior design. They felt that their good taste preempted the need to hire a professional, and they were right. Their home was tastefully put together. This was probably the last time that the couple truly enjoyed each other, but that was over a year ago. They didn't argue or take issue with anything that might require a conversation. In other words, their relationship was deteriorating, and they didn't talk about it. It was no wonder that Lisa was having a torrid affair with the maître d' at the "Top of the Mark" restaurant and lounge. The fact that her late evenings could be chalked up to a growing responsibility did not arouse any curiosity on Tommy's part, even though it was a sure sign of unraveling. When they did periodically entertain friends, it was clear that their marriage at one time was considered to be enviable… not anymore. The fact that Lisa was having an affair and Tom was not even curious was a formula for marriage disaster. The disaster happened when Tom stopped by the hotel to talk to Lisa about unionizing hotel workers. He went to her office on the second floor. When she wasn't there, he asked her assistant where he could find her, and she reluctantly mentioned the restaurant. When he got off the elevator, there was Lisa tucking her blouse into her skirt and the maître d' looking foolish. There was nothing subtle about that picture, and Lisa's attempt at an excuse fell flat. Tom didn't even get off the elevator and just took it back to the lobby. For the first time in months, he at least felt something. Was it his pride, or was there some residue from their three-year marriage? The next day, Tom joined the men and women who felt that their mate had done them wrong and moved out.

It took a week or so before members of the family became aware of the separation. Olivia had called her uncle to ask his ideas on the name issue. Lisa perked up when Olivia asked to speak to Tommy. She was silent, and finally, after a long pause, she said they were separated and burst into tears. Olivia was shocked and asked Lisa if she could come over and talk. To her surprise, Lisa welcomed someone who could potentially be sympathetic. Olivia's honesty and intelligence were what Lisa needed. The two women talked for hours, their conversation repeatedly interrupted by understandably uncontrollable tears. Ultimately, Olivia recognized that Tommy and Lisa had taken each other for granted and drifted to a point in their marriage in which there may not be any room for reconciliation. Olivia took issue with Lisa's defeatist attitude and then asked if she still loved Tom? After no discernible hesitation, she almost screamed YES. What followed was a recognition that they had ignored their partner and, in essence, were victims of their own lack of commitment. Olivia countered with the fact that she was certainly not in a position to offer advice. She felt she could see the gaping holes in the relationship, but it was clear that they needed professional help if they both wanted to salvage their marriage. Only time would tell…

Tom, on the other hand, was not showing the extent of his pain, and to him it was not "Manly" to show his feelings. The first evening of the separation, he slept in his California Street office, and when Lily Morrison arrived to open the office at eight, she was taken aback when she saw her unshaven, rumpled boss asleep in his chair. Tom woke, and seeing the surprise in Lily's face, he came up with a nonsensical excuse about working late. It crossed his mind that this might be an opportunity to take 'revenge sex' with Lily. He knew that she would respond based on the adoration she had shown for her boss. Tom just could not take advantage of this dewy-eyed 20-year-old. It was his morality and nothing more. Lily was a beautiful woman who any man would probably want to take advantage of, but… he could see that Lily was concerned, nervous and sympathetic, and with that awareness, he could also see that Lily was understanding what had transpired. She asked Tom if she could book a hotel for him. He considered his options and said yes to Lily, but if this separation was real, he would call Jimmie Walsh and ask if the "Mark Two" was available. Lily did book a questionable room for Tom. Down the street from the Mark was the Stanford Court, a new, smaller luxury hotel. He questioned her judgment, but he was just too exhausted to challenge her. No sooner had he checked into the hotel than he got a call from Jimmie. While he gave the green light to Tommy, he expressed concern about the marriage. Tom begged off having that conversation with a promise that they would have lunch together and he would provide the latest on the separation. The next day, he checked out of the Stanford Court and called Lisa to tell her he was coming over to pick up some clothes. She was silent, issuing a whispered 'ok.' Returning to their home after just one day seemed strange with the anticipation of seeing Lisa, but she was nowhere in sight. It was better that way. With clothing and some personal belongings, he headed for Pier 39. When family members heard about the separation, they were in disbelief. Tommy and Lisa were considered to be the one couple you would never consider having marital problems. They had purchased a new home in the Marina, and both were doing well in their professions.

The combination of the emotional surprise of the newest 'Mark' being added to the family, the shock of the separation of Tom and Lisa, and Mark's death in Vietnam was one giant blow after another to the family. Olivia found herself in the center of each mind-numbing event, and it was more than she wanted to deal with as she entered her final year at Cal. She was distracted, and just when she was hitting her stride and placing far more attention to her grades, she knew that she had to set her priorities. Realistically, the one family issue that she wanted to continue to shepherd was the introduction of 'Mark number three.' Throughout the emotional roller coaster, she had connected with Jerry, who was trying to balance her care of baby Mark with her desire to return to Berkeley and finish her education. After a conversation with her mother, Sara came up with a solution that would require sacrifices on the part of many family members.

Doctor Doyle committed to taking leave from Peninsula Hospital and going into private practice at home, where she could take on the responsibility of caring for her grandson for at least two years while Geraldine was completing her senior year at Cal. Jerry would be in close physical proximity, and there were weekends. Sara, Olivia, and Jerry and her mom met, and while Clair raised some objections, ultimately, she came around to the plan. The four women were sympathetic and heartbroken at the same time, but they all realized that the move was the best of all options. To add to the planning process, the elderly Walter Walsh committed to subsidizing Jerry's remaining two years at Berkeley. Finally, though painful, the parts were falling into place. Jerry could complete her education, Doctor Sara Doyle could bond with her grandson, and Olivia could apply herself to finishing her critical final year at school.

Olivia began applying to elite law schools, with Stanford and Harvard at the top of the list, and from there, Michigan and California schools, which were also highly rated and regarded. Olivia knew that with all the distractions during her junior year, her grade point average had suffered. However, after the conversation with her grandfathers, she had put her nose to the grindstone and increased her grade point to an average of A+, and Olivia was making sure that her senior year would eclipse all of her scholarly skills. While she was heartsick over Tom and Lisa's marriage problems, there was nothing she could do other than to say that she loved them both and would do almost anything to bring their marriage back together. She had just learned that Lisa had an affair, and rather than fault her, she was abundantly aware that Lisa would not have strayed from her marriage vows if there were no overriding reasons.

While Tom was emotionally broken, the time he spent alone brought to the surface the true and lasting feelings he had for Lisa. Being alone gave Tom the necessary time he needed to ask, 'Why had their marriage failed so abruptly?' He was honest with his thoughts, and because he genuinely loved Lisa, a certain reality began to surface. They had taken their loving relationship for granted and were 'too busy' to continue to invest in their marriage. Living at Pier 39 was exactly the right place to be alone with his thoughts, and hopefully, he would be open enough to attempt to put the pieces back together. Tom was experiencing a level of emotional pain that was foreign and yet allowed him the perspective of looking at their life together, and the reality was not what even a week ago he would have ever imagined. Lisa was so emotionally depressed that she couldn't sleep and even considered ending her life! No, she was not happy in their life together, and she knew there were horrible fractures, but the last thing she ever desired would be an end to their marriage. She loved Tommy Doyle, and her feelings of guilt were overwhelming. No matter how unraveled their relationship was, how could she have had reason to stray that far? Could the words 'I'm sorry' ever be enough to salve the unrelenting sense of guilt that continued to overwhelm her?

She knew that Tom was living at Pier 39, and this only gave her the longing for the way things used to be. Lisa attempted to pick up the phone and say those two words at least ten times a day, but she could not bring herself to do it simply because of what he might say. Finally throwing off the weighty victim label, Tom did indeed pick up the phone after five days of constricting pain and called home. Lisa was so shocked and thankful that after saying hello, she dropped the phone. Retrieving it, she simply said, "…Tommy." Lisa was in tears, not believing that her husband had called when she knew that she was the guilty party. With five minutes of uncomfortable pauses, there were enough salvageable words to bode well for some potential. They said enough to agree to meet at the "Mark Two," which seemed to be neutral territory even if it was Tom's current address. It rained the day they had chosen to meet, and as she stepped out of the cab on Pier 39 at 7 pm on a Friday evening, the sun replaced the dark clouds. As she stepped on board the "Mark Two," she was unable to control her emotions, and as Tom came toward her, she burst into a well of 'forgive me' tears. They did not embrace, although they wanted to, but both were sensing unsure, tentative pride. Lisa, in her all-consuming way, wanted to find the words that would make the last week nothing more than a bad dream. Tom, on the other hand, wanted to take the woman he loved into his arms and say, "It is all better."

Not knowing the depth of the other's feelings, they both continued to stay somewhat aloof when, in all actuality, they wanted to be hugged. Ultimately, with moments of unwieldy hesitation, they agreed that they wanted to find out if their life together was salvageable. To that end, Tom volunteered to seek out a qualified marriage counselor on whom they both could agree. As Lisa was leaving, she had a sense of having just experienced an out-of-body moment. They were in the same place, but they weren't together. That night, maybe out of sheer exhaustion or more likely a semblance of relief, Lisa slept for 12 hours. Tommy called Lauralie Walsh, who would be the best person he knew to help him select a marriage counselor who would be acceptable to both Tommy and Lisa. Lauralie continued to stay connected to the Doyle family and was especially close to Tommy and Lisa. She was flattered when she received the call from Tommy, primarily because she had heard about their surprising separation and was hoping she would be called on to help.

Lauralie, now in her late forties, had experienced almost every kind of marriage and interpersonal relationship imaginable. Knowing this and how she had survived in the face of physical and emotional moments in her life made her the family's go-to person for help. Rather than provide a list of highly qualified therapists in a phone conversation, she felt that the only way she could make a sound, caring recommendation would be to meet with Lisa and Tommy independently before making a decision on who would provide the most effective fit. The timing for this role was not the best. Lauralie had just opened her third "Omelets Etc." in Tiburon, a short distance from Sausalito, and she was being urged to run for mayor of her hometown. Yes, she wanted to run for mayor of Sausalito, but to Lauralie, her priority would always be her close friends. In the following days, she met in person with Lisa and later Tom. She was encouraged by what they shared with her. Lisa was open about having an affair and was quick to show her feelings of guilt and sorrow without accusing Tom of his responsibility. Tom, on the other hand, pointed to the fact that he had taken Lisa for granted and, in so doing, had spent an overwhelming amount of time dealing with his constituents and not enough time with his wife. It wasn't often that a separated couple was so unwilling to point the finger of blame at their partner. This marital situation was not going to be as difficult as Lauralie had anticipated. In fact, after having heard all she needed to know, she knew exactly who would be best to provide the counseling that the Doyles required. She got in touch with Charla Simpson, one of the Bay Area's most successful high-profile therapists. Without hesitation, she agreed to meet with Tom and Lisa. Initially, setting up one-on-one meetings and ultimately, if she was encouraged, she would schedule sessions with them together.

Charla Simpson's home and office were on Powell, three blocks north of Market. With its Art Deco exterior and lobby, the Amber House was home to 20 well-heeled San Francisco professionals, including two bestselling authors and a major restaurateur. Charla lived alone and had been married twice, which seemed ironic for someone who helped others solve their relationship problems. Her apartment was tastefully cluttered and reminded you of a movie actress's home in the early twenties. She was tall, almost painfully thin, and used very little makeup, which for some reason made her look younger than her 62 years. When Tom arrived at her apartment on a foggy August morning, he was nervous and at the same time curious about what was to transpire. From what he had heard about Charla Simpson, she was highly professional and yet warm and, in her way, sympathetic. Tom had no idea what to expect, but if a third party could help bring his marriage back from the depths, then he was more than willing to be emotionally honest and open. After an hour of concentrated conversation, Tom felt that while painful, the release of pent-up emotions was therapeutic. He found that Charla had the skill to challenge the 'why' of their marriage, and Tom had no choice but to open up. He left her apartment and felt relieved after an emotional therapeutic experience. Charla liked Tom and felt that his honesty served as a foundational component for future visits. In truth, it was not common for a first-visit subject to unburden themselves emotionally without feeling a need to accuse their partner of blame. She found herself literally looking forward to her meeting with Lisa, which was unusual in her thirty years of counseling.

When Lisa arrived, she had grave reservations about sharing the intimacy of her marriage to Tom, but at the same time, she would do and say almost anything to save her marriage. Charla was not what Lisa anticipated, either in appearance or style. The therapist was welcoming, and her unique, cluttered apartment, for some reason, gave her an initial feeling of confusion. There was no 'couch' and nothing of what she had envisioned. Charla Simpson had an instant impression after meeting Lisa that this subject would not be as open as her husband's. She was nervous and unable to look Charla in the eye and yet did not seem uncomfortable. This was a beautiful, complex woman who had issues in her life that she really could not independently deal with and indeed needed help. Like Tom Doyle, Lisa was also someone who engendered a fundamental aura of likeability. After Lisa's first visit, Charla had a relatively clear understanding that while she did refrain from admitting that she felt that she was the guilty partner, there was more to her story that Lisa was unable to come to grips with. In the second session, they talked about Lisa's upbringing and her relationship with her mother and other members of her family as she was growing up. She addressed her first contact with Tom and how they had fallen in love almost instantly. When the conversation segued into her family members, Lisa spoke lovingly of her Uncle Dominic, who essentially had taken the place of her father, who she lost in the War.

Dominic Gomez was a gentle man who took his family responsibilities and his religion very seriously. Alarm bells started to ring for Charla. She asked Lisa how Dominic approached his Catholic religion and what part it played in Lisa's upbringing. Lisa was candid and said that being Catholic was an important part of her early years. She went to an orthodox Catholic school where the teachers were all nuns and very strict, but she considered this merely a typical element of child rearing. Charla went on to ask what the extent of her sexual experiences was. Lisa said that she had one teenage relationship prior to meeting Tom, and while she enjoyed sex, this early encounter made her feel guilty in the eyes of the Church.

At the third session with Lisa, Charla began to form a picture of why she had an overwhelming sense of guilt that even conjured suicide. With clearly articulated reasoning, Charla explained to Lisa that her firm Catholic religion was the reason why she felt this unbending sense of wrongdoing. She understood that Lisa would feel guilty, but the degree of this misstep in her marriage was magnified by her Catholic belief, which took umbrage with sex outside of marriage. Charla was not criticizing Catholicism but merely pointed out that in her case, the orthodoxy of her religion was out of proportion with mainstream thinking. Charla felt she was now ready to have Tom and Lisa return for a meeting together, and in the final analysis, this couple was sincere and totally dedicated to wanting to retrieve and restore their marriage.

They did not arrive together, and that had nothing to do with how they felt about each other. Again, they wanted to, but each was waiting for the other to initiate togetherness. The therapy went on for over an hour, primarily because Charla felt that this might be the final session for the Doyles, and she wanted to allocate the time necessary. She addressed Tom's overemphasis on his work for the State and Lisa's sexual impropriety. After almost two hours, Charla closed by saying it was very seldom that she had an opportunity to counsel two people who, without qualification, were genuinely in love with each other. She hoped that she had opened their eyes to what can only be termed 'a frightening pause' in their flawed but totally salvageable marriage. It was also unusual for her clients to hug her and say thank you. Unlike the separate ways they arrived for their therapy, Tom and Lisa left Charla's office together. They hugged for an extended minute and went home.

One of the first things they did was to call Lauralie and invite her for dinner the following Friday. The problem-struck Doyles of yesterday vowed to be together for the rest of their lives. The sessions with Charla were not the Holy Grail, but darn close. Initially tentative, Tom and Lisa went to bed together that night and had an extraordinary evening of much-needed sexual contact. It was a spectacular night of lovemaking. A week later, Lauralie was the Doyles' guest for dinner, and it felt like a celebration even after the third toast. The couple had nothing but praise for Lauralie's friendship and thanked her over and over again for introducing them to the all-seeing Dr. Charla Simpson. A second bottle of champagne arrived, and the three friends spent the night together toasting whatever came to mind. It was one of those truly wonderful evenings of abandon and recognition of what was most important in life, and it wasn't all booze talk!

In subsequent days, Tom and Lisa were true to themselves and their professional involvement and, in Lisa's case, disengagement. Evidently, after that joyous lovemaking three weeks earlier, Lisa found herself pregnant. When she broke the news to Tom, he was understandably jubilant and thankful. Tom and Lisa were experiencing a new beginning. A week later, Lisa unceremoniously left her job at the Mark Hopkins. While all this was unfolding with Tom and Lisa, Jimmie and Karen Walsh remained content to go on their professional ways. Jimmie was essentially the CEO of Walsh Inc., and Karen was selling homes at a breakneck pace. They were not interested in having a family and seemed happy. Sylvia Geller divorced Herman after 40 years of living with someone she was learning to despise. She loved her grandchildren and had genuinely become a part of their lives. David Grossman had also divorced his wife of almost 35 years and opened a second men's store in Thousand Oaks. He saw the elder Doyles during the Holidays and was dating a

35-year-old. Johnny Walker had finally made his showbiz dreams come true. He was one of the featured lawmen in the Zorro serials. He moved in with his no longer estranged daughters. Sergeant Dan Salerno had recuperated from his wounds and ended up helping train qualified men for the Rangers' Army program. He got married and was the proud father of a boy and a girl.

CHAPTER 41

ATTRACTION

Olivia heard that Tom and Lisa had gone to a marriage counselor, and she learned that after just two months, they had a positive result and were back together. She was thrilled to know that the couple in the family that she gravitated towards was on their way to solving their marital issues. The last two months had been monumental with the knowledge that her brother had fathered a son, and now Tom and Lisa had been through reconciliation. After spending so much time with Jerry during the process of placing little Mark with her mother while Jerry returned to Berkeley, Olivia and Jerry had an awakening. Jerry was well aware of her sexual preferences, and while a heterosexual relationship gave her some pleasure, she preferred the company of a woman. She had just met Olivia, and from the start, she felt a strong attraction to her that included a positive vibe. Olivia did experience a unique attraction to Jerry, but was confused about her feelings. She was one of those women who intimidated men primarily because her beauty deterred their ability to ask her out. This attraction to Jerry was a different kind of desirability. During one of their moments together, Jerry did something that put all of Olivia's confusion to rest. Jerry merely leaned over and kissed Olivia. Both women felt the same emotion. For Jerry, it was verification, but for Olivia, it was an awakening, which she initially resented, but it took a mere second to recognize that she was finding the contact highly pleasurable, and that was the start of an explosive and meaningful relationship with Jerry. Sexual attraction was one thing, but with Jerry, it was far more and now Olivia was responding.

One more complication was not welcomed, but it was time for Olivia to restart her life, and the connection left no doubt about what she required in a relationship. Like Jerry, she had experienced heterosexual encounters, and while it did introduce her sexuality, the satisfaction was limited. Olivia chalked it off to the reality of what sex was all about until she kissed Jerry. Olivia had no intention of 'coming out.' In 1967, there was no real approval of a lesbian union.

On the other hand, Jerry had shared her sexual leanings with her family a full year ago, resulting for the most part in acceptance. In the following months, Jerry and Olivia shared classes in their mutual Political Science major. The relationship became so intense that it was occasionally difficult for either of the women to concentrate on their studies. Jerry was not as committed to her major as Olivia, who was bound and determined to go to law school. Both of her initial choice responses had been disappointing, but she had received acceptance at both Cal and Michigan. Her mother had encouraged her to study at Berkeley, but Olivia knew that she needed to get out of the San Francisco 'bubble,' and she would have accepted the offer from Michigan until Jerry entered her life. Both universities were equally well-received, and Michigan was offering a full-ride scholarship. And while Olivia did consider Michigan, Jerry was the absolute tie breaker. Sara was under the impression that her daughter had made up her mind to attend law school at the University of California. Both her uncle Tommy and grandfather William had offered full funding through the three years of law school; how could she say no? She would have preferred attending Michigan just to, for once, spend some time away from the Bay Area, but circumstances dictated her decision.

CHAPTER 42

JERRY

1968

- **Nixon wins the White House.**
- **Anti-Vietnam demonstrations explode on college campuses.**
- **Assassination of Martin Luther King.**
- **Assassination of Robert F. Kennedy.**
- **Apollo 8 orbits the moon.**
- **LBJ steps down, and Hubert Humphrey is nominated.**
- **The Democrats hold their convention in Chicago.**
- **In 1973, the US and North Korea signed the Paris Peace Accords, leading to the withdrawal of American troops.**

While Jerry was deeply attracted to Olivia, she continued to express anger over the Vietnam War. With LBJ announcing that he would not run again, and Hubert Humphrey accepting the Democratic nomination for President, Jerry could not stay home. The anti-war demonstrations in Chicago were exploding, and the assassinations of both King and Kennedy further complicated the Convention. Jerry was disappointed when Olivia decided not to accompany her to Chicago, but she just had to participate. Along with several Berkeley students, they made their way to Chicago. When they arrived at the Convention Center, there was bedlam. Literally thousands of primarily college students were letting their voices be heard. They were carrying placards that spelled out their anger, and students engaged in real conflict with Chicago police, using everything from empty bottles to bricks to fight back.

In one of those melees, Geraldine Fay found herself right in the middle of the mayhem of students facing off with the Chicago police. No one could say for sure how it happened, but a missile hit Jerry in the head, and she fell to the ground, unconscious. With all of the combat going on around her, very few stopped to offer help. Ultimately, after almost half an hour, she was rushed to the hospital with a bleeding head wound. Her mother was notified, and Clair Fay knew that she needed to contact Olivia. A shaken Olivia Doyle got on the first plane to Chicago and rushed to Northwestern Memorial Hospital. When she arrived, she asked the nurse to show her to Jerry's room. The hospital responded that only Jerry's immediate family was allowed to visit. Olivia was livid, and it wasn't until Jerry's mother arrived that she could be accompanied to Intensive Care, where Jerry remained unconscious. Eventually, the doctor in attendance joined them with news that Jerry was in very serious condition, and it was touch-and-go whether or not she would survive. She had lost a lot of blood and had received several transfusions. There was no good news, and the only thing the two women could do was to wait for any change in Jerry's condition. The picture was dire.

After six hours, a physician came towards them with a sad look on his face. Olivia and Clair knew the worst had happened. Geraldine Fay had passed away. The words from the doctor were redundant, and they just washed over them with disbelief. The death of her love ushered in overwhelming sorrow and grief. Lover and mother leaned on each other for support, and while they returned to LA sitting side by side, hardly a word was spoken. For weeks, Olivia felt like she was sleepwalking through her daily routine. She had just found her emotional and intellectual partner, and in an instant, she was taken away. She began to look pragmatically over the decisions she made based on her love for Jerry. The first thing that came to mind was her intention to attend Law School at Cal Berkeley. Thankfully, Olivia had not accepted the offer from Cal. Her initial pre-Jerry decision to attend Michigan Law was now in play. Making any life choices without Jerry was heartbreaking. She went ahead and accepted the Michigan offer that included a full scholarship. At least she would not have to rely on Tommy and her grandfather William for assistance. Tom had always been supportive of his niece's choices, and her sorrow was palpable.

The family patiently waited for the Olivia they knew to reemerge. That moment did not rise up to meet her until a momentous opportunity surfaced. Tom had been an exemplary House Representative, and the Democratic National Committee became abundantly aware of his political acumen and success in working across the aisle. In just two years, he had authored many pieces of legislation, including sponsorship of the Child Tax Credit and a bill to initiate gun control with his Universal Background Check proposal. There was no question that Thomas Doyle was far and away the darling of the left, and they were about to show him that his work in the House was being acknowledged. He was in the San Francisco office, attending to his next piece of legislation on health care, when Lily received a call, covered the mouthpiece, and told Tom it was James Lynch, President of the DNC. He absolutely had no idea what a call from Washington could bring, but he was about to find out. Lynch repeated the fact that the Democratic Party was extremely pleased with his performance, and with that in mind, he went on to say that they would like him to run for the Senate in 1970.

The incumbent Republican Senator Robert Favor was ripe for a challenge, and everyone internally was highly supportive of Tom's potential candidacy. This call was the last thing he expected, but it was not only flattering but also something that he had coveted in the relatively distant future. An opportunity to run in 1970 was a dream come true, and Tom instantly green-lighted the offer to run. That evening, he broke the news to his very pregnant wife, and Lisa was almost as excited as her husband. A lot would change if he was successful, but tonight that seemed almost incidental. Lisa looked at the possibility as the last cog in reinstating their marriage. They were back together, and their relationship was at the mending stage, but if Tommy was elected Senator, it would be a genuine fresh start. Their baby was due in December, and to no one's surprise, they were still expecting another boy in the family. They were thrilled and were already thinking about names. One thing was evident. After all the sadness associated with the name Mark, that was not a consideration. But coming up with the right name was relatively easy. Their son would be named Patrick after his great-grandfather.

Sara was also trying to deal with the care of Jerry's son, Mark. He was now three, and with every fading year, he looked more and more like his departed father. She adored him, and their bond became more intense with each passing day. When she received the news of Jerry's death, she realized that any question about custody would now be in the hands of Clair Fay or herself. Sara knew that her priority had to be a conversation with Jerry's mother to determine whether or not there would be a custody fight. After three years, Mark referred to her as "Noni" and stopped asking questions about his mother for almost a year. He was far too young to understand that his birth mother had died. In truth, Sara had filled the vacuum in her heart with her son's child. Her private practice was thriving, and she was able to spend the time and energy needed to raise her grandchild. It may sound a little over the top, but Dr. Sara Doyle asked Clair Fay if they could meet at the serene Japanese Tea Garden in Golden Gate Park. There, they could have a serious conversation without worrying about interruptions. Sara had absolutely no idea what Clair was thinking in terms of custody.

Over the past three years, Clair had visited her grandson twice, and while she loved little Mark, he continuously reminded her of her departed daughter, Jerry. When they met in the Garden, Clair looked much older than Sara remembered. Her height made her seem very imposing, but as Sara would soon find out, her demeanor was warm and receptive. Also, to her surprise, Clair had a foregone conclusion that Sara would raise Mark, and she felt that putting the child in a different environment after three years would not be in Mark's best interest. If a more formal declaration of custody was required, Clair made it clear that she would sign it. Internally, Sara felt a deep sense of relief. The two grandmothers continued to talk, and the conversation ranged from the pain that Clair experienced with the passing of her daughter to questions about her future visits with her grandson. Sara found herself sympathetically engaged with Clair to a point where she made it clear that she encouraged as many visits as possible. As they parted, Clair embraced Sara, kissed her on the cheek and expressed gratitude for the wonderful, loving care that Mark was receiving.

When Sara returned home, Olivia was anxious to hear the results of the emotional conversation she had with Jerry's mother. When Sara shared the positive news about their meeting, it was even more than what Olivia had hoped for. She could leave for law school in Michigan, knowing that Jerry and Mark's son would continue to be a part of her life. Tom and Lisa received the news of the agreement between Sara and Clair, and they were understandably pleased. Their son Patrick would have a close family member to grow up with. For now, however, Tom's priority was to run a successful campaign for Senator. He was nominated by consent, which left him in a position where he could direct all his attention to dealing with the current Republican Senator, whom he was challenging. His team of Andy Miller as Chief of Staff, Cindy Fenneman as Press Secretary, Diana Roberts as Office Manager, Suzy Geller at the Capitol, and Lily Morrison holding down the San Francisco office served as the veteran members of what would be a much larger staff.

Predictably, Senator Robert Favor wasted little time in trashing Tom once he was the Democratic candidate. He had traced Tom's history to find that he had been arrested for marijuana use and was excused because of his connections. He made no note of the fact that Tom had been honorably discharged. Tom felt he had to respond and pointed out that General Cheskin had pardoned him because of his extraordinary service as a member of the U.S. Rangers and his subsequent Silver Star. After this initial volley from Favor and his successful response, Tom decided to concentrate on the issues with no intention of getting into a mean-spirited campaign, but it seemed that his competition wanted nothing to do with a campaign addressing very real, substantial issues. Obviously wounded by Tom's first round response, Favor decided to dig even deeper into the mud. While he didn't claim authorship, a truly nasty, disgusting thread was released pointing out that Tom's wife, Lisa, was black and a member of the female Black Panthers. The fact that the accusation was false did not seem to matter. Senator Favor and his campaign continued to spread the lie while claiming that he absolutely had no knowledge of this 'rumor.' Racism was still rampant in many parts of the country, but

San Francisco was by all standards relatively free. That isn't to say that racism didn't still have a significant effect in certain quarters of the voting public. Doyle's campaign did respond and point the finger directly at Senator Favor, who continued to claim innocence. Tom and Andy Miller huddled to discuss the best ways to counter the continuous mudslinging from the Republican side. The idea of challenging Favor to a debate on television was a brilliant idea.

The Presidential debate in 1962 between Kennedy and Nixon was clearly seen as a turning point in that election. Tom and his team set the idea in motion by publicly challenging the incumbent to a debate, which would be carried live by all of the Bay Area television outlets. The Favor campaign was caught off balance and initially determined that debating Doyle wouldn't serve a really good and useful purpose. They soon found that any thought of not participating was not an option. Pressure from many important constituencies was making it impossible to say no. Tom's campaign was jubilant but not overconfident. They knew that Senator Robert Favor was an experienced debater who would be formidable, but the only way to shut down the dirty campaign lies was to face it head-on during a debate. The first Senatorial debate in America was scheduled for Monday, October 12, 1969, at 7 pm for 90 minutes and would air live on KGO, KPIX, KRON, and KTVU, the Oakland Independent. Jim Blue, a well-known San Francisco journalist, would announce and referee the debate. The viewers would be able to get a visual impression not only of what the candidates were saying but also how they looked as they expressed their views.

On the day of the debate, Tom and his opponent, along with members of staff, arrived at KGO, the ABC affiliate in the City. The station would be the host network for the other primary regional outlets.

Because of the tone of the campaign, neither man shook hands as they were seated facing each other in the studio, separated only by the moderator, Jim Blue, who would ask the questions previously entered by a cadre of local journalists. The first question dealt with San Francisco's counterculture movement. Senator Favor responded that he thought that the 'hippies' were trying to take over the City and that law and order should be more active in controlling the movement. Tom took an entirely different view, stating that free speech was a cornerstone of our nation, and as long as the various organizations adhered to peaceful demonstrations, the police should not interfere. The audience was a balance of liberal and conservative citizens. The next question: How would you deal with the aggressive behavior of the Black Panthers? Tom was the first to respond, and he asked the moderator if he could answer one question on the subject. "Is there or has there ever been a female branch of the Black Panthers?" After the laughter, Jim Blue responded, "Not that I know of." Tom had made his point to Favor's chagrin and went on to say that he would offer the same response that he cited in the first question, i.e., if they are peaceful, the law has no role. As the historic debate concluded, each side claimed a win; however, even with the 'balanced audience,' Tom seemed to have won the day. The coverage in the Bay Area print media the next morning could be definitive. The area papers did indeed weigh in, and it was no contest. All the daily publications, without exception, concluded that the Democratic candidate, Thomas Doyle, won the debate. Senator Favor responded that all the local papers were liberal. He attacked with a level of anger that could not possibly help his floundering campaign. When election day arrived, most of the polls showed a 5-point advantage for Tom, and as election night progressed, it became clear that the challenger had toppled the incumbent. With 75% of the vote in, KGO and the San Francisco

Chronicle called the election for Doyle. In the next half hour, the remaining media lined up behind Thomas Doyle, and at 1 am on November 6, he had been elected Senator for the State of California.

There was bedlam at election headquarters, and while the campaign staff had been relatively confident, there was always the fact that, in most cases, the incumbent won reelection. Not this time. Without missing a beat, Andy Miller called a staff meeting to discuss next steps. There was a significant difference between the prestige of a Senator and a member of the House. The size of the staff would grow exponentially. Tom decided to maintain the San Francisco office with Lily Morrison in place. The Washington personnel structure would change from a Representative's closet to a real, prestigious office in the Capitol, where three aides could be assigned, and the remainder of the staff would be ensconced in the Blair office building next to the Capitol. Tom and Lisa were thrilled with the results, and the new Senator and his wife decided to celebrate Tom's success. In her heart, Lisa was convinced that the election was over and their soon-to-be-delivered baby boy, Patrick, would finally put their marriage on a solid path.

The Doyle family at large was delighted that a member of their family had been elected to the United States Senate. Some, like Olivia, were inspired to consider politics as an arena that she might consider when she graduated from law school. As she entered her third year, she had a highly successful apprenticeship at one of Washington's largest and most prestigious law firms, which already had offered her placement when she graduated. Lampson Inc. had also committed to providing Olivia with all the tools she would require to take the Bar examination.

DENOUEMENT

Olivia

As the years advanced, exciting progress and events were favoring the Doyle family. Olivia was assigned to work out of the San Francisco office of Lampson, where she took responsibility for Criminal Law cases and political engagement. To that end, she received accolades when she added Senator Thomas Doyle to their representation. It was a huge feather in Olivia's cap and would serve to guide her as she considered running for office herself in the not-too-distant future. She became deeply engaged in California politics with her Uncle Tommy serving as her mentor. With several successful years under her belt, in 1978, she decided to run for Attorney General for the state of California. Lampson Inc. was pleased that one of its lawyers was running for political office and proved to be highly supportive by using their wealth and prestige to help finance her run for Attorney General. With her huge salary compounded every year, Olivia purchased a beautiful home in Pacific Heights with her partner, Louise Gates, whom she met and ultimately fell in love with during law school in Michigan. Louise was also an attorney, and everything seemed to fall into place. Obviously, in the 1970s, while the Gay community was just getting the recognition they had fought for with leaders like Harvey Milk, a San Francisco City councilman, their relationship would have to remain neutral. With funding led by Lampson, Olivia easily won the State Attorney General race in 1978.

Mark

Like his grandmother, the third Mark quite naturally seemed to gravitate towards a career in medicine. His mother, who died during the 1968 Chicago Democratic Convention, never had an opportunity to realize what she might have been. Her social conscience seemed to dominate all of her thought processes. She had a big heart… and so did Mark. For Sara, Mark filled many gaps left by her husband's passing. Now, 25 years later, her grandson was a physician whose black heritage did not interfere with his practice of general medicine. He could have moved his career in any direction, and Sara was convinced that he chose the healing art not because of her, but because he seemed to have a natural talent that surely was influenced by his grandmother's medical skill. She was convinced he had an internal force that dictated a future in medicine. As a child, Mark showed a special compassion for any creature that required help—a wounded bird who needed a wing repaired, a cat who got his head stuck in a bottle or the skill at treating dogs when they showed any sign of pain or illness. He attended Stanford for his undergraduate training and then moved on to Medical School, where his desire to heal was abundantly in evidence. He could not be defined as the most skilled in Medical School, but being a great specialist was not what drove him. Helping creatures of all origins was what he lived for. That is precisely why his first instinct was to join Doctors Without Borders. This was an organization of skilled medical volunteers who would go anywhere there was a need to help, whether it was the brutal war in South Sudan or the children who got in the way of the Sandinistas in Nicaragua. ***Doctors Without Borders*** were there. They survived on donations and contributions from a variety of sources, but it was never enough. Mark Doyle had found the place he needed to be.

Patrick

Patrick Doyle and his cousin Mark were raised together and extremely close, but that was where the relationship ended. They were completely opposites when it came to what they wanted from life. Mark's North Star was to give of himself and spend his life helping others. Patrick, on the other hand, was all about himself. It isn't that he didn't have the capacity to care for others, but it was buried deep into his 'me first' mentality. He was a C student at best and found school to be a waste of time. If he could, his major in college would be booze and women. Like Mark, he was black, and while there were mixed racial issues that he had to deal with, Patrick was incredibly handsome, and women did adore him. His devil-may-care mentality limited the universities he could qualify for, given his low grades. This upset his parents, Tom and Lisa, but his innate charm was always the equalizer. Patrick ended up attending San Mateo Community College, and while he attended classes, he spent his time doodling on his papers. The 'doodles' were appreciated by his friends. Patrick, like his grandmother Rita, had artistic skill. Could the artistic genes have skipped a generation? The encouragement from his friends motivated Patrick to take a course in art appreciation, and that one course turned out to be a turning point in his life. The instructor, Janice Polasky, saw through his off-putting personality and clearly stated that he had genuine talent. Janice guided him from pencil sketching to other art media, including watercolor, acrylics, and oil. Patrick began to respond, and a serendipity moment began to surface. He was absolutely enthralled with oil as an extension of his talent. Janice Polasky had opened a sleeping artistic talent! Patrick was in art class early every morning, waiting for Janice to arrive and ignored all his other studies. He became manic, spending every waking moment in class experimenting with oil painting.

Eventually, he quit school, bought his own art supplies and set up an art studio at his home in the Marina. Lisa encouraged him and enthusiastically supported his newfound hibernating talent. For six months, Patrick spent from morning to night in his studio. Lisa could not get him to the table for meals, so she ended up delivering plates of food to her dedicated son. Patrick ultimately completed several pieces that were so unique that Lisa called Rita in Laguna and requested her presence. When she arrived, she was startled by what she observed. Patrick Doyle was an extraordinary talent, and while his technique was somewhat primitive, it was without question beyond what Rita anticipated. She shared some of her professional skills with her grandson, and after another six months, decided to feature his art in a special showing in Laguna Beach. Rita was thrilled that her talent was being inherited by her grandson, and if truth be told, Patrick's skill was far beyond her capability, and she needed to nurture it. Rita was highly respected in the Laguna Beach art community, and when she announced that her grandson was having a showing, they made it a point to attend. When the opening weekend arrived, Patrick nervously paced Forest Street in Laguna and left the display to his grandmother and her cadre of professionals. To say that the showing was a success would be an understatement. All 15 of Patrick's paintings were sold for top dollar! The community was asking for more, wanting to be among the first to discover the newest American talent since Jackson Pollock. Like his cousin Mark, Patrick Doyle had found his place in life.

Senator Thomas Doyle

In early 2001, the highly respected 4-time incumbent Senator from California was asked to consider running for President of the United States in 2004. Tom was flattered, and while he initially thought of not accepting the nomination, the Democratic National Committee was determined to convince him to run and to that end set up a dinner meeting in New York. Tom and the top members of his staff joined the Party leaders at "Windows on the World," the chic restaurant was on the 107th floor of Tower number one of the World Trade Center. It was September 10th, 2001.

ACKNOWLEDGMENT

At 90 years old, I've found myself navigating many of the challenges that come with being a first-time author—technology among the most daunting. In that regard, I consider myself truly fortunate to have a neighbor like Tom Ciesielski. Tom not only helped organize Sunset into its soon-to-be-finished form, but he also played a pivotal role in guiding many of the editorial decisions that followed once the manuscript was complete. To this day, I still feel a pang of guilt for pulling him away from his family during the holiday season.

I was also incredibly lucky to have the insight and expertise of George Merlis, the retired Executive Producer of Good Morning America. George's editorial eye was invaluable—he smoothed out many of my more tangled sentences and corrected my grammar and phrasing with the precision of a true professional.

Finally, I owe a heartfelt thank you to my family members, who offered both objective feedback and unwavering encouragement. Prudence and Sam Gingold and Victoria Behnke gave me the motivational push I needed, cheering me on with sincere enthusiasm about seeing Sunset published. Hardcover copies will be making their way to them in gratitude and love.